THE LADY OF STONEWYCKE

Michael Phillips
Judith Pella

BETHANY HOUSE PUBLISHERS
MINNEAPOLIS, MINNESOTA 55438
A Division of Bethany Fellowship, Inc.

Copyright © 1986
Michael R. Phillips and Judith Pella
All Rights Reserved

Published by Bethany House Publishers
A Division of Bethany Fellowship, Inc.
6820 Auto Club Road, Minneapolis, Minnesota 55438

Printed in the United States of America

Library of Congress Cataloging-in-Publication Data

Phillips, Michael R., 1946-
  Lady of Stonewycke.

  (The Stonewycke trilogy ; 3)
  Sequel to: Flight from Stonewycke
  I. Pella, Judith. II. Title.
III. Series: Phillips, Michael R., 1946-   Stonewycke trilogy ; 3.
PS3566.H492L3   1986   813'.54   85-30748
ISBN 0-87123-856-X (pbk.)

THE LADY OF STONEWYCKE

Dedication

To Judy Phillips, from whose ideas *The Stonewycke Trilogy* was born.

The Authors

MICHAEL PHILLIPS, editor of the George MacDonald reprint series, has also authored ten books of his own. A magna cum laude graduate of Humboldt State University in Arcata, California, he owns and operates a chain of bookstores on the West Coast as well as carrying on a heavy writing schedule. He and his wife live in Eureka, California, with their three sons.

JUDITH PELLA, an avid reader and history buff, makes a home for her two children in Eureka, California. She received her nursing degree in 1971 and later a B.A. in Social Sciences from Humboldt State University.

The Stonewycke Trilogy

Scottish Romances by George MacDonald retold for today's reader by Michael Phillips:

Contents

Introduction

Life is not lived without heartbreak, loss and tragedy; such is the human condition. As Job said, "Man is born to trouble."

But a person's moments on earth are merely a flicker. The joys and miseries of circumstances ultimately fade into nothingness, and all that remains is the character one carries from this life into the next. The physical world provides the training ground for the deeper life as we learn to respond to the God who made us. Temporal loss can be the price of timeless gain.

How could Maggie know that an eternal destiny called her to America, there to discover the forgiveness which would allow His healing to wash over her? How could she have seen that in the agony of her loss, the hand of God was drawing her to himself? God's way is often beyond man's understanding.

How could Ian, in his bitterness, perceive the loving Hound of Heaven stalking his spirit as it tried to hide from its sorrow?

Temporal suffering clouds our sight and limits the scope of our heavenly vision. But the story for Maggie and Ian does not end with their farewells. Their history is not one of earthly happiness, but of eternal gain. It is a saga of God's unrelenting pursuit after the heart of man, a chronicle of healing. It is a trilogy of three intertwining lives who experience the threefold nature of God's forgiveness.

The drama does not end with Maggie's parting from Ian on the docks of Aberdeen. In the infinite provision of God's wisdom, the story of their love comes full circle to its victorious conclusion through His work in the generations who come after them.

God's plan for reconciliation is never exhausted. The prayer of a broken young woman on the prairie of the American West resounds through the heavens, awaiting the arrival of the moment when its fulfillment is at hand.

Prologue

The sun had begun its ascent in the east. In the harbor the large schooner readied itself to sail with the tide. As the morning's pale light rose on the Aberdeen skyline and farewells were said, passengers slowly separated themselves from family, friends, and well-wishers.

The bustle of activity on the teeming dock seemed incongruent with the early hour. Only a short distance away in the heart of the city, the town was barely beginning to stir. One by one storekeepers opened their doors to display their wares to the day's customers. A wagon laden with sweet-scented hay meandered into the dirt street from a side alley and made its way toward the waterfront, heralded by the tired groan of its iron-rimmed wooden wheels.

Without warning, the clatter of horse and rider shattered the tranquillity of the morning. The horses reared. The farmer jumped to his feet, grasping the reins firmly in a desperate attempt to keep his frightened team from overturning the load.

"Hey, ye curs'd bla'guard!" he shouted. "Keep yer de'il o' a beast oot o' my way!"

But the horseman was oblivious to all obstacles in his path. He slashed the leather straps mercilessly across the chestnut mare's neck and galloped on down the street.

Reaching the dock the rider yanked back viciously on the reins; the mare flailed savagely in an attempt to bring her huge frame to a halt.

Amidst trailing dust from the thundering hooves, the horseman dismounted and hastened toward the schooner. Frantically his eyes searched the deck of the ship, but too many bodies blurred together. He turned to scan the faces of those scrambling up the wooden-planked gangwalk but could not find the one he had ridden so hard to see. In desperation he rushed toward the ship, his face drenched with perspiration and splotched with dirt from the dusty road, his eyes recklessly probing the crowd before him.

The young auburn-haired woman did not see him at first.

She had been occupied briefly as he stampeded up. Turning toward the dock, she first spied the chestnut mare, flanks heaving from the exhausting gallop.

He had come!

13

She had nearly given up hope . . . but the mare could be none but his!

All at once she heard her name above the clamor, and at last their eyes met.

For a moment the girl forgot the voyage before her and ran, pushing her way through the crowd. As she reached the gangway a grizzled sailor called for her to stop.

"We'll be castin' off, lady. Ye better stay aboard!"

She heard nothing—neither sailor nor crowd nor the deafening clang of the ship's bell tolling its scheduled warnings. She shoved her way down the narrow ramp, heedless of all else, and ran into the arms she had feared would not hold her again.

"I thought you weren't coming," she said, as she took the packet from his hand.

He clasped her tightly as if to prove that her fears were unfounded. "I would have hated myself if I had been too late." He gently kissed the soft tresses of her hair. "It's bad enough that you must go—"

"Then, please, let me stay and stand beside you."

"No. We already agreed this is the best way . . . the danger is just too great."

"I know," she replied. The tension in her voice hinted at previous conflicts. "But what good is honor if it forces us to part?"

"A man's honor is all he has."

She swallowed hard and fought back the gathering tears. A sick feeling stirred in the pit of her stomach, but she would not let the evil premonition take shape. Yet she knew only too well what she feared— that she would never see him again.

"We could talk to my father again, maybe—" she began, her eyes pleading at him helplessly.

"Your father! Don't you realize that he hates me?" He stopped short, and when he began again, though his words were soft, they seemed but a thin veil over the passions surging within him. "Oh, my love . . ."

He cupped her face in his large gentle hands and looked down tenderly at her slight girlish frame. "Let's not spoil these brief moments. Let's only think about when we shall be together again. The weeks will pass before we know it. Then we will begin anew. It will be a good life we will share in America."

"If you could but come with me now . . . they would never find you."

The innocent hope of her naive words stung at his resolve.

"I'll not provide a life like that for you," he replied. "We will be free . . . able to hold our heads high, not cowering in fear of the past."

"But—"

"I know this sacrifice is hard. I know how you love this land."

For a brief moment the girl reflected that her mother had said those very words before she left. The heartbroken woman had placed the envelope in the girl's hands and spoken emphatically, almost desperately: "In this, find the hope of your return. But more than that, the safety of this land we love. No matter what happens, my dear child, *it is yours!*"

The girl's hand unconsciously sought the pocket where she had tucked the envelope. She had not yet even had a chance to look at it. But whatever it contained, she knew it would always serve as a bitter reminder of the tragedy that had torn her life apart.

"All aboard . . . last call!" shouted one of the ship's mates.

He drew her close and kissed her. "I love you, Maggie," he said through trembling lips.

Then she knew she must go. It was his will, after all, that she go. She loved him, and she would obey.

She turned and walked slowly toward the ship. As her foot touched the gangwalk a chill gripped her. With each step up its incline the agony of misgiving increased. Reaching the deck she looked away out toward the sea she would soon cross. Tears rose quietly to her eyes. Before her loomed . . . she knew not what. The great unknown.

She turned and looked back toward the man she must leave. If only it could have been different!

"I love you!" she shouted from the deck. "Ian . . . do hurry!"

He waved, but could find no words. She saw him lower his arm to sweep a sleeve across his tear-filled eyes.

On the deck the riggings had been loosened and the signal to cast off given. Beneath her she felt the first signs of motion. She opened her mouth to speak his name one last time, but could not. Her lips were unable to form that beloved name again.

Soon his form faded to a speck in the distance. She turned toward the far side of the ship where she tried to divert her attention to the sails, the outriggings, the movement of the sailors. She wiped her eyes with the back of her hand, then sucked in a deep draught of the clean salt air. The wind whistled through the masts and sent her long hair flying. She could not hear the beat of the mare's hooves retreating into the distance.

The schooner eased its way out of Aberdeen harbor, and the girl did not turn and look again toward her homeland until only the white-capped open sea met her gaze.

1 / From Out of the Past_____

Joanna was glad when they finally cast off.

The tranquillity she now felt, however, had not come upon her immediately. As the excited throng of passengers boarded, most had pressed against the ship's rail, shoving and straining for a better view of the crowd on shore. A stout little man in a checked, double-breasted suit had turned on her with sharp words.

"No need to push!" he snapped.

"I . . . I'm sorry," came her timorous response as she eased away.

Where she stood mattered little. There was no one waving to her from the dock. Her future and her hopes lay in the opposite direction, out to sea. A moment later the great horn of the *Atlantic Queen* blasted, shattering both her ears and thoughts. The tremendous girth of the modern liner, the pride of the new century's shipbuilding excellence, cleared its moorings and powerfully eased its way eastward.

As their speed mounted and the last view of New York's harbor and receding skyline thinned to the horizon, the passengers slowly dispersed to the many corners of the vast ship, leaving Joanna alone at the railing.

There she still stood an hour later, gazing out upon the watery expanse before her. The *Queen's* prow plowed through the swelling waves, sending churning whitewater spraying before it, mesmerizing her in the infinite dance of salt and foam, spray and wind.

A gradual sense of calm surged through Joanna's spirit as the sea quieted her soul. For the first time in weeks she found herself thinking in a realistic way about the adventure events had launched her into. She—reserved and cautious Joanna Matheson, who had never set foot out of the Midwest in all her twenty-one years—was sailing on a luxury ocean liner for Scotland, the land of her ancestors!

What would she find?

All she had to guide her were her grandmother's imploring deathbed words and the enigmatic puzzles she had discovered in her great oak secretary.

I wonder what kind of ship brought Grandmother to the States? she thought. *What it must have been like forty-five years ago! Times were so different then. And she was so young!*

Unconsciously Joanna clutched the pendant hanging from her neck—

17

one of her few remaining links with the heritage which had brought her into the world. Lost in retrospection, she thumbed the golden locket.

Grandmother, she mused. *Grandma . . . if only I had taken the time to know you better*.

Joanna's thoughts trailed back . . .

Only a few weeks earlier she had returned from Chicago after her grandmother's accident. Nearing the house on Claymor Avenue where she had lived as a teenager, Joanna found a flood of memories rushing through her. As she walked up the broken sidewalk, she gazed with new awareness at the dilapidated two-story structure. She'd never realized how run-down it was—the paint peeling and chipping away, the shutters hanging sideways, the screen door torn, the rotting picket fence missing nearly every third board. The memory of that drab Denver house contrasted starkly with the glamor of her present circumstances aboard the magnificent vessel, sailing with what was doubtless a wealthy crowd.

A tear rose in Joanna's eye as she remembered those last days with her grandmother.

She shuddered at the recollection of the cold chill and the antiseptic bleakness of the hospital where her grandmother lay.

"Grandma, I'm here now," Joanna recalled saying as she pulled a chair next to the bed.

"I'm glad you've come . . ." returned a thin, strained voice. Joanna's grandmother had always been slight, but extremely energetic and youthful for her age. Yet now she lay almost motionless. A week earlier she had been walking to the market, as was her custom. But on this particular day as she crossed the dusty intersection, a child had darted into the street, ignorant of the dangers of the horseless carriage. As the driver swerved to miss the youngster, the car had careened toward the cross street, hitting Joanna's grandmother. The woman lay unconscious on the hard-packed dirt, her leg broken. At the hospital, the doctors found serious internal hemorrhaging. They fought the bleeding and managed to keep her alive, but their prognosis for her recovery was grim; the damage was too widespread. She awoke for a feeble moment, insisted they send for Joanna, then immediately lapsed back into unconsciousness.

"They won't tell me . . . but I know I'm dying," she said weakly.

"Don't be silly, Grandma," Joanna returned, trying to sound more confident than she felt inside.

"Think what you will, child," continued her grandmother. "But I have to make my preparations. I've very little time left, and there's something you have to do for me." Her voice trailed off and her eyes closed.

"Anything, Grandma," responded Joanna. "You always took care of me; now it's my turn." Even as she said the words, Joanna could not tell whether her grandmother heard her.

Almost as the words were out of her mouth the door of the room opened.

"The doctor would like to see you, Miss Matheson," the charge nurse informed her. "He's just down the hall."

Joanna turned to follow the nurse from the room.

Suddenly the ailing woman's eyes jerked open. Even in the dim light of the hospital room, they flamed with intensity. "You mustn't let them take it, Joanna," she cried out. *"It's yours. . . !"*

"It's okay, Grandma," said Joanna, turning again and leaning toward her. She reached out an uncertain hand toward the bed and gently let her fingers rest on the trembling arm, now limp on top of the bedcovers. "Everything will be fine."

Once again the older woman's eyes closed and she lay still as Joanna left the room. Outside the doctor approached and introduced himself.

"I have to be candid with you, Miss Matheson," he said. "Your grandmother is dying. We've been very fortunate to keep her alive this long. She's lapsed in and out of consciousness many times already, and every time we think we've lost her. But she has a resilient body, and her faith seems to be sustaining her beyond reason."

"And there's nothing more you can do?"

"It's up to the Almighty now, my dear. And of course your prayers would avail much."

Joanna's gaze dropped suddenly and awkwardly to the floor. When was the last time she had prayed? If her grandmother's survival depended on her prayers alone, then it was indeed hopeless.

The doctor caught the shifting of her eyes and sensed the meaning of it. He laid his hand on her shoulder. "We will both pray and hope," he said. "I've known your grandmother for many years, and she is a fighter."

"How long do you think it will be?" asked Joanna with a faltering voice.

"As I said, it is in God's hands. It could be any day. Medically speaking, there has been extensive internal damage, not to mention the broken leg and three fractured ribs. The surgeon did as much as he could, but she's lost so much blood, and I'm especially concerned with these lapses in consciousness. Every time she fades out, I fear for a coma. But she keeps fighting back."

"What would happen then?"

"Once a patient is comatose, then it's just a matter of waiting.

There's nothing medically we can do at that point to bring them out of it."

That evening Joanna returned to the old house. How different it seemed, how empty of life! Perhaps for the first time she realized just how much her grandmother meant to her. She crept upstairs to what had once been her room, intending to arrange the few things she had brought with her, but instead she sat down on the bed and glanced about. A lump rose in her throat, and she found herself choking back tears for the woman who had practically raised her.

She wept, not for her grandmother alone, but for herself, because not until now did she find her love for the woman surfacing. She had gone to live with her grandmother at the difficult age of thirteen. Whatever was troubling the girl the grandmother could never quite tell, and Joanna was careful to keep her young emotions tucked deep inside. How could she ever tell the older woman that her own now-departed daughter Eleanor was at the root of Joanna's troubled spirit?

Joanna's mother Eleanor died in childbirth, just three hours after Joanna had been born. Eleanor was one of those exquisite creatures found so rarely in life—not only because of her fine-featured, flaxen-haired beauty, but also in her gentle, godly spirit. She loved and gave freely of herself without even knowing she did so. Stephen, her husband, loved her completely and was devastated by his wife's sudden and unexpected death.

In life she would have been a strong guiding light and example to her daughter. But in death, the child's thoughts and the husband's memory of the gentle woman became a source of pain and enmity between the two she left behind. For some time Stephen could not even function rationally, and his dead wife's mother cared for the baby for several months until her son-in-law could take the responsibility on his own. But he never could fully accept the child whose life he felt had been traded for his beloved Eleanor's.

Perhaps things would have been different if Joanna had been allowed to remain in the care of her grandmother. But shortly before she was a year old Stephen Matheson moved from Denver, ostensibly because of his job. If he could have admitted it, the truth was simply that he could no longer bear the memories in their Denver home. First Wichita, then St. Louis, and finally Minneapolis—Stephen could settle nowhere, because in one form or another the memories always followed him. In Minneapolis his sorely neglected health failed him at last, and he died one snowy morning in his own bed. Thirteen-year-old Joanna could never shake the awful conviction that somehow she had caused his death, just as she had her mother's.

Because Stephen Matheson had no family of his own, Joanna's grandmother gladly welcomed Joanna into her home. But it was impossible for the older woman's love to penetrate the shell that had by that time hardened around the young girl's heart. The cool distance separating them simply could not be overcome. The grandmother did not know how; Joanna, on her part, was unable to let down the walls of her defenses to see that all her grandmother wanted to do was love her. The inner child within Joanna's heart was still too tender. The guilt and unworthiness she felt blocked her ability to receive the love which might have been shown her.

Had her thoughts been formulated more distinctly, Joanna would have asked how anyone could love her—especially her grandmother, the mother of the woman whose death she had caused when she came into the world. She knew what a saintly woman her mother had been—had she not heard it constantly from her father? Whenever she was naughty, did not Stephen rebuke her by reminding her she would never grow up to be like her sweet and beautiful mother?

"I hate my mother!" the child had exploded once, in the bitter confusion of mingled guilt and longing for the mother she had never known. How could she possibly cope with the conflicting emotions of love for her mother on the one hand and self-blame on the other? She, after all, was responsible for the death of the one person her inner child so desperately needed.

At those words Stephen slapped her face in anger. Never again did Joanna speak ill of her dead mother; she could control her voice, but she could not control her thoughts. Her yearning for her mother was mixed with equal portions of resentment—a paradox her immature mind could not sort out. She resented her goodness and grew to despise the angelic picture that her father kept on the piano. Yet at the same time she hated herself for feeling as she did. What kind of an awful person must she be? Thus if her father did not love her, his disdain was no more than she deserved. And as Joanna's childhood years progressed, the twisted, confusing emotions, rooted in self-condemnation, drove her more and more deeply into the shell of her aloneness. She could find no place of belonging and began to feel as an alien, even under her father's and grandmother's roof.

The kindhearted lady tried to do what she could for her granddaughter. She taught her to bake and sew. But nothing could spark the girl's interest. She read the Bible with her each morning at breakfast and prayed with her as often as possible. But while Joanna showed courtesy to her grandmother's faith, she was never able to embrace it fully. For its foundation was the single element Joanna could neither understand nor accept—love. She was unable to forgive herself for the grief she felt she had caused. How, then, could she accept God's love and forgiveness when she herself stood condemned?

One Saturday morning when she was sixteen, Joanna entered the kitchen to find her grandmother sitting with her sewing basket beside her. Joanna ambled toward the stove in an aimless manner and held her hands over the wood fire to warm them.

"Joanna dear, would you like to embroider a sampler?"

"Oh . . . I don't know, Grandma," replied the girl with indifference.

"Come on—sit down here with me. I'll show you how."

With lukewarm interest Joanna shuffled to the table and sat down. Her grandmother handed her a fresh piece of cloth and proceeded to instruct her on the rudiments of embroidering her name.

After fifteen minutes Joanna threw down the needle and cloth in frustration.

"It's no use! I can't do it!"

"You're doing fine," said her grandmother, encouraging her to continue. "You should have seen the first time I tried it. I was much younger than you. I'm afraid I bit off more than I could chew—"

"Oh, Grandma," interrupted Joanna, rising to her feet. "I'm just not interested."

"It takes practice, dear. I'm sure if you—"

"Not now . . . I'm sorry. I just don't want to do it anymore."

Joanna hurried out of the kitchen, leaving her grandmother alone at the table.

If only I could find something to interest her, the older woman thought, reflecting on her own first efforts to stitch her name on a piece of linen. "That was so many years ago," she whispered to herself. "It seems like another lifetime."

She rose slowly, walked toward the large kitchen window, and stood staring out. Her thin shoulders and graying head cast a shadow into the small sunlit room. Yet in spite of her years, her eyes revealed the inner strength and fortitude passed on to her from her own Scottish mother. The image of Joanna's dejected young face rose in her mind. Gradually her thoughts drifted back to her own teen years. *I suppose her life has been no less turbulent than my own,* she thought. *But at least I had someone who loved me to share it with—if only briefly.*

As if unconsciously drawn by the memory, her hand sought an antique golden medallion which hung around her neck underneath the faded pink sweater. She had worn the locket almost constantly since that sweet day in her youth when it had been given to her. Now, gently stroking it with her thumb, the memory of the miniature pictures inside brought a lonely tear to her eyes.

Sunk in a reverie of faces long past and places far away, she stood motionless—for how long, she did not know. At length, Joanna's footsteps on the stairs brought her back to the present, and she turned from the window with a sigh and returned to the kitchen to begin supper.

Joanna never knew how many hours her grandmother agonized over her. As she grew older and things did not seem to improve, the older woman became troubled about the girl's future. Perhaps, the grandmother thought, there might be one step she could take to improve the girl's feelings about herself. Joanna had always been a good student; perhaps she might excel in some career. As a last hope, the woman scraped together her meager savings and sent Joanna off to college in Chicago. Women were beginning to make their place in the world. In the city, perhaps, Joanna could discard the shackles of her past and develop a sense of her true worth and abilities.

Joanna complied with her grandmother's suggestion, not because she cared about women's achievements or even her own, but simply because she ached to get away—from the house, from Denver, from the painful memories of years she would like to forget. She had few other opportunities from which to choose.

The time away had indeed matured Joanna in many ways, though the walls still remained closed around her deepest self. Not until she returned home after her grandmother's accident did some small inroads begin to penetrate her pent-up heart. In the time she had been gone, not a single repair had been made in the house, which had always before been well maintained. The cupboards contained but the barest of necessities, even for a woman living alone. The icebox was empty except for a bottle of sour milk.

What had happened?

At the hospital, the nurse explained that her grandmother was on public assistance. Joanna was appalled. Certainly they had not by any means been wealthy, but money had never been scarce. But when she sought out the family lawyer, Joanna learned of the self-sacrifice which had been made on her behalf.

Her grandmother had poured every available dollar into her granddaughter's education. Had Joanna known, things might have been different. But she hadn't known. For her, college merely represented an escape from the one-dimensional world of her upbringing. Completely oblivious to the cost required in sending a young woman into the predominantly male world of higher education, she had never given the expense a second thought.

Now jolted into reality by her grandmother's sudden accident and by the lawyer's revelation, Joanna found her attitude immediately altered toward the woman who lay dying in her white hospital bed. Perhaps by attending to her grandmother faithfully in these days of her greatest need she could, if not equalize the scales, at least perform a portion of the duty she should have acknowledged much sooner.

2 / Memories

In the days that followed Joanna gave herself completely to the care of her grandmother. She went daily to the hospital and relieved the nurses of many of their duties to the lady in bed number six.

Each day the woman grew weaker, her mind floating in a dream world of semi-consciousness. Yet as incoherent as they often were, her spasmodic ramblings offered Joanna her first glimpse into her grandmother's early years, previously shrouded in silence. Her grandmother's girlhood in Scotland had ended abruptly in a youthful flight to America, and there the past seemingly vanished from memory—until now. During these moments at her grandmother's bedside Joanna realized that, with her own parents gone and with neither brothers nor sisters, her only tie with her heritage hung by the slenderest thread to her grandmother's ebbing life.

If only I had been more interested in these things before! she thought to herself. Half of what her grandmother said made little sense and now Joanna painfully admitted that her curiosity had likely come too late.

On the third morning after her arrival, Joanna came to the bedside. She was suddenly struck with how different her grandmother looked. This woman who had seemed to laugh at the advancing years, to exhibit an energy which could keep pace with women twenty years younger, now lay injured and helpless. The accident had changed everything.

The moment the tired face saw Joanna a gleam lit her eye and she stretched out her hand. Joanna vacillated a moment then took it, smiled, and felt a weak squeeze on her fingers. The older woman was attempting to say something but couldn't get the words out.

"That's all right, Grandma . . . I'll be right here. Take your time."

She continued struggling to make herself heard. Her ethereal voice was barely audible and her breathing labored.

". . . you here . . . I've waited . . . must tell you . . ."

"Just rest, Grandma."

"The house . . . I gave it up . . . had to leave . . . my family . . ."

The words were so soft and indistinct Joanna could barely make them out. She leaned closer and turned her ear toward the feeble voice. As if grasping a lifeline, the woman clutched Joanna's hand.

Just then her voice rose with passion and her head lifted off the pillow. *"It's yours!"* she cried. "Don't let them take it. . . ." She fell back, exhausted by the sudden exertion.

A nurse approached with a breakfast tray. "She's been going on like that all night," she said. "I don't know what's gotten into her." She set the tray on the bedtable. "Don't bother waking her to feed her. She probably wouldn't eat anyway."

Her grandmother slept until the cold breakfast was replaced with a lunch tray. Joanna was debating within herself whether to wake her when the frail woman's eyes shot open.

"It's there. . . !" she cried, hoarsely pulling herself nearer her granddaughter. ". . . the treasure . . ." Now her voice came out in labored gasps. ". . . in the nursery . . . find it . . . hidden away all these years."

Once the words were out she seemed to relax. Joanna tried to get her to eat some of the bland food the nurse had brought, but she pushed it away. Then her hands went to her neck; she fumbled a few moments until her efforts were at last rewarded, and she lifted up the gold locket. Her mouth moved silently as she tried to put her thoughts into coherent words.

"I'm going to die . . . you must take this . . . I never . . . never forgot him . . ."

Joanna hesitated a moment. "No, Grandma," she said through her tears. "You're not . . . you can't . . ."

But before she could finish her grandmother took her hand and dropped the locket into it with the words, ". . . yours now . . ."

With tears in her eyes Joanna took it, then with trembling fingers placed it around her own neck.

"Joanna," her grandmother went on, struggling desperately to make herself understood, "the treasure's in the nursery . . . the house . . . yours . . . I always loved it . . . but now it's time for me to pass it on to you . . ." But her mumblings grew incoherent, and at last she fell asleep.

That night when she returned to the lonely house on Claymor, Joanna felt emptier than she had ever felt in her life. Her grandmother's words seemed little more than delirious ramblings, but they caused Joanna to realize that there was much more to the woman who had given birth to her own mother than she had ever allowed anyone to see. A sickening fear gripped Joanna, the realization that she might never have the opportunity to know her grandmother as she suddenly longed to.

She stared silently out of the dirty window toward the railyards, now shrouded in the pallor of a wet, smoky dusk. Tiny raindrops clung trickling to the windowpane, adding to the gloom her spirit felt.

What would become of her once her grandmother passed away?

She had certainly never been a compassionate granddaughter. Now she chided herself for thinking of her own future while the last vestiges of life seemed to be slipping from her grandmother's weakening grasp.

Still . . . she had to face the fact that she would be left completely alone—probably penniless as well. Of course, there must be work she could do. She wondered if there was anything of value in the estate. But even as she framed the question, she chastised herself for thinking of money at a time like this.

Was what her father always said about her right after all—that she was callous and unfeeling? Yet as she thought about it she realized he had never actually *said* such things to her. But somehow she had always *felt* that he thought it—words or not.

Stephen Matheson never purposely hurt his daughter. Beyond losing his temper that one time, he had never so much as spanked her. Nor were his words ever harsh. It probably would have pained him to know how deep were the hurts in his daughter's heart as the result of his unintentional actions, and worse, his lack of action toward her. His attitude revealed itself in offhanded comments of which he undoubtedly remained completely unaware. He probably would have scarcely even remembered the piano recital, but the memory still stung painfully at Joanna's heart.

Her mother had been an accomplished pianist, which undoubtedly contributed to Stephen's encouraging the lessons for their daughter. If anything remained symbolic of the woman Stephen loved, it was her piano.

Joanna had practiced hard, wanting to surprise her father with her progress. For the recital Joanna chose "Three Waltzes" by Franz Schubert, a somewhat complicated piece for a nine-year-old, but she mastered it well. On that day she donned her prettiest dress of pink organdy and lace, tied a pink ribbon in her auburn hair, and went to get her father. He was sitting in his chair reading the newspaper, still dressed in his work clothes.

He had forgotten. She prodded him to his bedroom where he changed his clothes and together they went to the auditorium. Joanna was too excited to sense his reluctance. This was the first time in her life she had ever felt proud of herself.

She played the cheerful waltzes flawlessly. But her father's only comment was, "You should have heard your mother play Schubert. She could make his pieces sound like the very music of heaven!"

He had wept during the performance, but whether from sorrow for his wife or pride in his daughter no one—especially Joanna—would ever know. All she knew was that she had done her best and it hadn't been good enough. Still she fell short. The phantom of her mother had caused her to be rejected again.

Soon thereafter Joanna gave up the piano. But from that day onward she gave up more than music. She retreated ever deeper into her protective shell, building resentments she could not voice, insecurities she thought she deserved, guilt she could not understand.

3 / A Captivating Stranger

The blaring of the *Queen's* horn jolted Joanna from her reverie.

She heaved a deep sigh and looked about. All remained the same as before her lapse into reminiscence, except for a small fishing vessel off the port side. That must have been the object of the great horn's signal.

How much time has passed? she wondered.

She ought to get back to the cabin to check on Mrs. Cupples. Her matronly employer and companion had mentioned taking a nap after coming on board. But she should peek in to see if she might be needed for anything.

Joanna turned and walked along the railing toward the stern of the ship. All about were excited travelers—many, she assumed, like herself, voyaging on the Atlantic for the first time. Some already occupied themselves with the classic shipboard activity of shuffleboard. Others lounged in folding wooden deckchairs, soaking up the warm sunshine and gentle May breezes, reading their favorite books and magazines.

Taking the long way back to the cabin in order to have a quick look at her new surroundings, Joanna continued toward the rear of the ship. She stopped and looked out behind her toward the land she was leaving. A great white wake widened into the distance, stretching as far as the eye could see.

"There's nothing more thrilling than setting out on a journey," said a masculine voice behind her. Joanna turned slightly, uncertain whether the comment was directed at her, nodded doubtfully, and returned her gaze to the sea.

"Don't you agree?" he persisted.

"Oh . . . oh yes, I suppose," Joanna halted, glancing toward him briefly, then diverting her skittish eyes toward the ocean.

"I've been on many cruises," the man continued, "and the thrill is always there. Is this your first?"

Joanna nodded again.

Her mood was far from conversational, but the handsome stranger could hardly help but draw her attention away from solitary reflections. Not particularly tall, his square, broad shoulders nevertheless gave the imposing appearance of towering above her own 5'6" build. The impeccable gray, pin-striped suit covered a physique any girl would definitely look twice at. An elegant derby, angled perfectly atop his head, outlined the well-sculptured features. Below the brim showed neatly clipped black hair, distinguished with streaks of gray. But most conspicuous were the piercing jet-black eyes, striking in their intensity.

He flashed a disarming smile.

"I'm sorry to have intruded. I can see you have other things on your mind." He turned to go.

"Wait," faltered Joanna, "it's okay. I'm just . . . not very talkative."

"And you do have something on your mind?" he queried, with another good-natured grin.

"I suppose you're right. My life's rather . . . well, everything's uncertain right now and I can't help thinking about it."

"Anything you'd like to share with a stranger?"

Joanna said nothing but shifted her gaze once more to the open sea.

"No," she replied at length, with a sigh. "It will fit together in time—once I get there."

"Where's that?"

"Scotland."

"Is that so. . . ?"

"Yes—Aberdeen first."

"What a coincidence," he said with a calculated gleam in his eye. "Traveling alone?"

"Yes . . . well no, actually," she added. "I mean, I'm traveling with an older lady, as her maid and companion. But I scarcely know her."

Joanna squirmed under the investigating stranger's eyes. But she could hardly escape the charm of his apparent interest, and something inside her tingled with excitement. Her shyness, however, could never allow such a feeling to show. After all, she hardly knew this man. Yet she found herself wishing she had followed Mrs. Cupples's advice and worn her fashionable navy and white chemise and the dark blue felt hat adorned with its daring red feather. In this severe brown tweed suit she felt like an old schoolmarm!

Joanna's soft-spoken reserve, however, only added to her mystique. Though hardly a showy dance-floor beauty, she was certainly no schoolmarm. Her abundant auburn hair, now pulled back into a bun, could be positively alluring when allowed to drape over her shoulders. She gave her thick-lashed brown eyes and creamy soft skin little credit. And she would have considered her shapely figure far from perfect. Yet they were sufficient in themselves to draw most any man's interest, and would have done more than that had she given encouragement—which she never did.

Notwithstanding her restraint, Joanna's new shipboard acquaintance was not accustomed to waiting for opportunities to unfold; instead he created his own.

"I hope you don't think me too forward," the man said, "but I would like to introduce myself."

Somehow Joanna knew her consent was a mere formality which wouldn't alter his plans one way or the other.

Weakened under the discomfiture of his gaze, Joanna replied, "I . . . I don't know—I really should be getting back."

"I sense you are a young lady not given to talking with strangers. But I assure you I am respectable enough. The Captain will vouch for me. And I am hoping you will make an exception in my case."

He paused, removed his hat, and with a slight bow and smile, proceeded.

"I am Jason Channing. And I do hope I'll have the good fortune to see more of you on this voyage."

"Thank you, Mr. Channing," returned Joanna, summoning the courage to put aside her reticence for a moment and respond in the demure manner she knew was called for. "I am flattered."

She could feel the color rising in her cheeks.

"But I really must get to my cabin," she went on. "I left Mrs. Cupples there immediately after we boarded and haven't looked in on her since. Good day."

Joanna turned and walked briskly away, hoping to maintain her confident composure at least until she was around a corner and could relax. The probing eyes of Jason Channing followed her every move till she was out of sight.

Once in the cabin Joanna sat down on her bunk and exhaled a long sigh. Mrs. Cupples stirred from her nap, and Joanna spent the following hour attending to her needs as the two women acquainted themselves with their stateroom and made themselves as comfortable as possible in their limited surroundings.

About four o'clock in the afternoon a knock came on the cabin door. Joanna had dozed off momentarily. She started up, rose, and answered it. There stood the ship's steward.

"Are you Miss Matheson?"

"Yes." Joanna, still groggy from her brief nap, frowned in confusion.

"I've been asked to give you this," the steward said, handing a personalized card to Joanna.

She took it, reflecting that she hadn't given her name to anyone on the ship, and closed the door.

The card she held simply bore the name *Mr. Jason Channing*, printed in fine script. Turning it over she read the handwritten words: "I pray you will do me the honor of dining with me this evening at 7 p.m. I will be at the Captain's table."

It was unsigned.

4 / Advances

"Please," said Joanna, "you're embarrassing me."

"Miss Matheson, surely I'm not the first to tell you how lovely you are?"

The pink that rose still higher in Joanna's cheeks was undoubtedly all the answer Jason Channing needed. But she felt compelled to make some response.

"Not quite like that." She smiled nervously.

"I didn't think the men in Chicago were so blind."

"I didn't often mingle. I'm not much of a social butterfly."

"Let me change all that."

Joanna looked down toward her plate and made a pretense of stabbing another chunk of the tender beef with her fork. But she was not hungry. For three successive nights she had accepted his dinner invitations. But tonight his compliments had progressed a bit further than she had anticipated, and certainly further, if they continued, than she knew how to handle comfortably.

He was not a man easily disregarded, nor were his blandishments easy to sidestep. His was, admittedly, a dashing personality. She liked him; indeed, it would have been extremely difficult not to be enchanted with his magnetic charm. No man had paid such attention to her before. Who was she to refuse the admirations of such a distinguished and handsome gentleman of the world?

Yet, why was such a man interested in her?

Jason Channing, for his part, had made a point of isolating Joanna the moment the voyage had begun. What had been calculated to come across as a chance meeting was in reality nothing of the kind. He had consulted with the Captain, as he always did prior to sailing, for a look at the passenger manifest. It was his custom to know what eligible, unattached young ladies would be aboard for his enjoyment. On this particular occasion Joanna fit the bill. He found her to his liking, invited her to dinner, and had been slowly moving in on her affections ever since. And at forty-one, Jason Channing—self-made millionaire, real estate developer, and entrepreneur—was a man whose plans eventually were fulfilled to his satisfaction. He was not in the habit of failing in anything he undertook.

"Miss Matheson," he said, "you've been drifting off again."

"I'm sorry."

"I was saying that I'd like to change that timid image you have of yourself. Come to London with me when we dock."

Joanna did her best to conceal her astonishment. Was this dubious proposal what it appeared?

"I . . . I really couldn't," she said in a wavering voice.

"Why not? This is the time to cast aside your sheltered past," Channing urged. "This is 1911; times are changing."

"I have plans . . . I must get there."

"Change your plans. What difference will a few days make?"

"But . . . aren't you going to Scotland too? Didn't you say that?" she asked.

"Only for a few days. I have some dreary business in a godforsaken little village. The people there are such bores, speaking a ridiculous dialect no one can understand. You'll never fit in there, Miss Matheson. London is where the life is. Piccadilly Circus, Buckingham Palace . . . perhaps I could even get you an audience with the King."

"The King of England!" exclaimed Joanna. "You don't really know him?"

"Well, actually," Channing laughed, "I've only met him once. But I have several contacts in high places. I think I could arrange some sort of an invitation from the royal family for my special lady-friend from the United States."

"I . . . I don't know, Mr. Channing." Joanna's head was spinning. "I suppose—"

"You must come, Miss Math—"

He stopped, reached across the table, and placed his hand gently on her arm.

"—Joanna."

She looked away momentarily, then back toward him. Her uneasiness was clear to Channing's trained eye. It was not his first venture into such a situation. He derived a certain masculine pride in confronting inexperienced young women with daring overtures, even if he did cause them to squirm. "It's good for them," he rationalized. "They need to grow up and face the world eventually."

But even if Joanna were contemplating his offer, a decision was forestalled temporarily. She breathed a sigh of relief as a man approached, whispered briefly in Channing's ear, and then retreated as abruptly as he had come.

Channing rose, excused himself, and hastened away.

From her table near the edge of the outdoor dining area, Joanna looked out over the railing of the ship's deck. The rising moon cast a golden reflection on the surface of the calm sea. Hardly a breeze stirred, and Joanna felt as if she were on a South Sea island rather than a moving ship. Her midwestern origins had offered little exposure to the sea, and she had been apprehensive about the trip. But now she found she loved it.

Her thoughts strayed across the sea to the Scottish village that was her destination. She knew nothing about the place except that it was situated on the northern coast and that she made a vow to her grandmother that she would go there.

She glanced toward the interior of the dining room and saw Jason Channing returning. She had to refuse his invitation; even if Scotland were not tugging at her, how could she do such a thing? But she feared it would not be easy to turn him down. Had he not told her he always got what he wanted?

And now, it seemed, he wanted her!

Part of her wanted to shed the schoolgirl image, cast caution to the wind, and accept his offer.

Dare she?

He approached, conversing with another of his business associates, a short, balding man Joanna had seen before. Judging from Channing's gestures the discussion had grown heated. About ten feet away they stopped. Channing turned abruptly on his companion.

"Look, Ed. I don't care about all that!" he said sharply.

The short man retreated a step or two, his face twitching under the tongue-lashing of his superior.

Then in a measured tone, controlled, but stern with intensity, Channing went on: "You just get it done. Whatever you have to do—just get it done! If you're going to work for me, that's the only thing I care about. Do you understand?"

He turned and made his way toward the table, broadly grinning. Behind him she saw the man he called Ed hesitate a moment, and then walk away slowly in the opposite direction.

As Channing sat down, the conversation resumed, but she could detect a smoldering glint of anger flickering in his eyes. "I should know better than to mix business with pleasure," he said.

"Is something wrong?" Joanna asked.

"No, not really. One in my position just has to be firm, that's all. But enough of that—let's get back to the pleasure."

Rising from his chair he walked around the table and took Joanna's hand. "Come with me, will you?"

She complied.

He led her to the ship's deck, then moved close beside her and slid his arm around her waist.

"Do you see that moon?"

Nervously Joanna nodded.

"Do you know what moonlight shimmering on the water represents?"

She remained silent.

"Romance, Joanna, romance! Come to London with me. Let me show you the city. It's time you free yourself to experience what life has to offer. It can be wonderful!"

Joanna could feel the heat rising in her neck and cheeks; even in the cool breeze she was perspiring.

He grasped her shoulders firmly, turned Joanna toward him, and gazed intently into her eyes.

"But . . . but what if I—"

"Refuse?" he said, completing the sentence for her.

"That's not what I was going to say . . . exactly."

"But it's what you meant, is it not?"

Joanna said nothing.

"I wouldn't like that, Joanna." He paused. "It would mean I'd have to work that much harder to convince you."

He drew her to him and kissed her full on the lips, once, then again, this time more fervently. His kisses were warm and intense, leaving her little room to respond.

Overwhelmed, she tensed and raised her hands to separate their bodies.

"Mr. Channing . . . please! Not here."

"Then come to my cabin."

"I couldn't. I'm not—"

She stopped and turned away, breathless. She couldn't bring herself to say she wasn't "that kind of girl." It seemed such an unsophisticated thing to say in the presence of someone so . . . so worldly and experienced. Would she ever meet another his equal?

He took her hands. "I'm sorry to appear forward, and to make you uncomfortable. But when I see something I like, I see no sense pretending otherwise. And, Joanna . . . you are so beautiful—"

"Please," she interrupted. "I just . . . don't know . . ."

Thoughts of her grandmother and the unclear mission before her tried to crowd into her mind, but they were dimmed in the immediacy of Jason Channing's powerful presence.

Then Joanna became again aware of his soft words whispering into her ear. She was once more in his arms, though she scarcely remembered him embracing her.

"I could make you so happy, Joanna, if only you'd let me."

He kissed her again, this time gently and tenderly.

Again she stiffened. "I . . . I can't think right now . . . we have plenty of time . . . I should go . . ."

"The present is all the time anyone has, Joanna. There is no tomorrow."

His arms encircled her waist firmly. She felt her body crushed against his powerful torso as his lips moved against hers. Her head swam. But by degrees she relaxed and yielded to his passion. Even as she did her own desire mounted. She found herself returning his kisses with more emotion than she would have thought possible.

For a moment Joanna felt not at all like herself. Could she indeed be the sophisticated woman Jason deserved? But the thought lasted only a moment. When she heard voices in the distance, she stiffened and pulled away.

She managed a smile before retreating several steps, then turned and hastened down the deck toward her cabin.

When she arrived, to her great relief, Mrs. Cupples was sound asleep.

5 / Clues from the Past _____

Joanna threw herself on the bed and fell to dreamy dozing. Someone cared for her! She had experienced little caring in her life. Asked if she was in love with Jason Channing, she would have hesitated in finding a response. But that couldn't change the fluttering in her heart.

Amid these thoughts, Joanna fell asleep, and in the dim phantoms that accompany light slumber, dreamed about Jason Channing throughout the night.

Dawn woke her.

She had all but decided to accompany Jason to London. What could a few days matter one way or the other?

Yet as she lay reflecting in the early morning hours, her mind continued to focus on her destination. A gray morning fog had settled in during the night, and as she peered through the tiny porthole Joanna found herself wondering if last night's interlude with Jason had been but the wild fancy of an active girlish imagination.

No! she corrected herself. *I am not about to lose this moment of happiness. Scotland or no Scotland, I will go to London!*

Why shouldn't she have a good time? She wanted to be shown the city. She wanted a man beside her—a man with experience, style, and gallantry. A man like Jason Channing!

Then her thoughts turned again toward that unknown northern coast of Scotland. How curious that a place she had hardly even heard of could suddenly loom so important. She simply could not rid herself of the deep gnawing urgency to press on immediately. Try as she might, Joanna could not get her grandmother's imploring words out of her mind. Whatever she was supposed to learn of her grandmother's family apparently had to be discovered before her death, if that was possible. Time was crucial!

Time. The word triggered such a deep response in her brain.

There was never enough when you needed it; too much when you didn't.

Time . . . time . . . time, she mused.

As her grandmother lay dying, Joanna had become so aware of time's pull. Constantly she was haunted by her careless squandering of the years she had had with her grandmother. And now it was too late. There was no time left. No time to build the relationship which had been so one-sided. She could not redeem the minutes and hours in the bond she had earlier neglected. As Joanna sat by the fading woman's bedside, she began to find within herself a capacity to love she had never known existed. Her grandmother's need drew her and made her forget all else. If only there was something she could *do* to demonstrate her love!

By the eighth day, her grandmother actually seemed a little improved. The rain had temporarily stopped and a thin beam of sunlight slanted across the room, brightening the woman's face. She gave Joanna a smile of recognition as her granddaughter sat down in the familiar chair. She reached toward the bedside table and awkwardly fumbled about. The exertion was clearly fatiguing, and Joanna stepped forward quickly to help.

"What do you need, Grandma?"

"My book," she answered.

The only book on the table was a black cloth-covered Bible. It was the hospital's, for when Joanna had brought a few of her grandmother's personal items from home she had not thought to bring the woman's old worn leather-bound Bible.

Once the book was in her hands, the grandmother opened it immediately. Her fingers turned the pages with difficulty but at last she appeared satisfied and handed the open book back to Joanna.

"Read . . ." the words formed soundlessly on her lips, but Joanna understood clearly enough.

She knew immediately the passage her grandmother had been seeking. There were four psalms on the page, but Joanna knew without question that she wanted to hear the 23rd. It had always been her favorite, and many times she had read it to Joanna, though the girl had usually listened with polite detachment.

"The Lord is my shepherd," Joanna began, "I shall not want. He maketh me to lie down in green pastures: he leadeth me beside still waters: He restoreth my soul: he leadeth me in the paths of righteousness for his name's sake. Yea, though I walk through the valley of the shadow of death—"

Suddenly Joanna's voice caught on the lump forming in her throat. Unexpected tears rose to her eyes; her lip quivered as she tried to continue.

But it was her grandmother's faltering voice that took up the words:

"—I will . . . fear . . . no evil. For thou . . . art with me . . ." Her voice trailed away. She seemed too tired to go on.

"Thy rod and thy staff they comfort me," Joanna went on, forcing out the remaining words past her emotion.

Did her grandmother genuinely not fear death? Did she truly believe God was with her?

How Joanna longed to ask her those questions! But she knew the woman had not strength to form the answers. How many opportunities she had once had to ask them. But no more. The realization heaped still more regrets upon her burdened shoulders.

By the time Joanna finished the psalm her grandmother was asleep. The rays of sunshine waned and deepened into evening shadows. Joanna knew she must leave before the streets were dark, but still she lingered.

After a while her grandmother's eyes opened once more. Immediately Joanna could tell something had changed in her countenance.

"Joanna," she said, ". . . mind clear . . . want to tell you the story."

Joanna leaned forward in her chair.

". . . it's there, do you understand? . . . yours now . . . in the house somewhere . . . the paper . . . I have to give you . . . just help me get up . . . important . . . my mother . . . the day I left . . . gave me . . ."

She struggled to rise, then winced in pain and fell back again.

"No, Grandma," Joanna protested, "you mustn't. We'll find it another time, maybe tomorrow."

". . . find it . . . it's in the nursery . . . you must go there and find it . . . you must go *now*!"

"Go where, Grandma? What do you mean?"

"Strathy, child. You have to go . . . before it's too late, before they find out I'm gone . . . always caused so much grief . . . if only the land had belonged to the people instead of our corrupt family . . . I couldn't have it . . . didn't want . . . but you . . ."

"Grandma," urged Joanna, "calm yourself. We can talk about it again tomorrow."

". . . might not be a tomorrow. I'm dying, Joanna. It was mine, but I'm now passing it on to you . . . have to promise me you'll go— *now*. It's the only thing I ask of you . . . mustn't wait for my funeral. I've neglected it too long . . . I love—"

She stopped, choking back the tears.

"—haven't even said the name in years . . . Oh, Lord, have I neglected what you gave me? . . . how I loved Stonewycke! Now you must take my place . . . must go back and find it. *It's yours now* . . . want you to have it. I'm not rambling. My mind is clear. Promise me, Joanna. You must *promise* me you'll go!"

"All right, Grandma, I promise."

"Promise me you'll go. Before I die I need to know you'll have what is yours . . . who knows what my brother has done? . . . should be yours . . . *you must go now!* Don't wait for me to die. You are my only hope, Joanna. Remember your promise. You must go *now*!"

Further words failed her and she fell back against the pillow, exhausted.

When she spoke again after several minutes of silence, the lucid quality had departed from her voice. Instead she sounded weak, worn, as if now that she had spoken her last urgent message she could relax and let death take her.

". . . wind the music box, Mommy . . ." she murmured in a childish voice. "Such a pretty melody . . ."

"Yes, it is," replied Joanna softly, not knowing whether to speak or keep silent.

". . . doesn't matter anymore . . ." said her grandmother, again with her normal voice. "Won't be much longer . . . the paper . . . Strathy . . . my mother . . ."

"Oh, Grandma," Joanna sighed painfully.

"The nursery, Joanna . . . *it's all there* . . . won't be long before I'll see *his* face again!"

She closed her eyes with a radiant smile on her lips, and fell back into silence.

Joanna took her hand, held it tenderly, and stroked the soft, white skin. The hand felt so lifeless, thought Joanna. Yet it too had once been young and supple like hers. Soon her grandmother was sleeping soundly. Joanna sat by the bedside another thirty minutes, gazing on the tranquil face that lay barely breathing, cradling the warm, thin hand in hers. At length she laid the bony hand across her grandmother's body. She rose quietly and left the hospital.

The following morning Joanna arrived at the hospital to find that her grandmother had slipped into a coma.

"I'm afraid there's nothing we can do," the doctor told her, "other than wait . . . and pray."

"Wait for what?" asked Joanna.

"As I explained," the doctor began, then hesitated. "You must understand, Miss Matheson . . . her injuries were just too severe. It's only a matter of time . . ."

"Before she dies," said Joanna, completing the doctor's unspoken words. Tears welled up in her eyes.

"Yes, I'm afraid that's it."

"And there's no chance of recovery."

"None whatever that I can see. Of course there are isolated cases on record . . . and who can say what the Lord might choose to do? But medically, no. I see no possibility of recovery." As he spoke he led Joanna to some chairs in a small waiting room.

"You spoke to the nurse of her urgent plea for you to go to her homeland?" he went on.

Joanna nodded.

"I see no reason why you shouldn't fulfill that wish. Who knows what might come of it—for her sake and for yours. This thing may draw out interminably, and you have your own life. I will keep you informed of her condition. And if the inevitable happens . . . well, at least you can know you were fulfilling her final wish."

Joanna was silent. Her grandmother's words of the day before came back to her. She had hardly understood anything she had said. There could be no doubt that her voice had stressed the urgency of Joanna acting quickly. Yet how could she leave her grandmother, knowing she might die any day? On the other hand, if she was in fact dying, her one last wish was that Joanna go to the place called Strathy immediately, not even waiting for the release of death.

". . . no chance of recovery." The words rang in Joanna's ears. What good would it do for her to wait at her grandmother's bedside if by doing so she neglected the woman's last appeal to the only living relative she had left?

And what if, despite all the doctor had said, she did somehow miraculously recover? Would it still not then have been best for her to go, for her grandmother's sake?

"I promise, Grandma." Joanna's words came back into her mind. She had spoken them with no inkling of what they truly meant, merely to satisfy her grandmother's imploring entreaties. Yet now all at once the words took on solemn implications. She had committed herself to fulfill her grandmother's final desire, perhaps her deathbed wish. How could she not honor it? And if she waited until her grandmother was actually gone, then it might be too late. The nature of the urgency she could not imagine. But there must have been something her grandmother had left undone that she was now depending on Joanna to set right— something which she might not be able to rectify if she waited too long.

That evening, still full of conflicting thoughts about what to do, Joanna entered her grandmother's room. She had not done so since her arrival from Chicago, and now a shiver ran through her body. How cold and lifeless it seemed! There was no spirit left; only possessions. She opened the closet door. There hung clothes which had once held meaning. Now they seemed ghostlike. With a sigh Joanna closed it. She walked to the window. The rain had stopped and the sun was making an effort to shine. But the room remained dreary.

Against the far wall, opposite the window, stood an ancient oak secretary. Joanna could never recall a time it wasn't there, a mute reminder of the past. There it had been, for years.

She walked toward it. The fine oak surface was engraved with intertwining carvings of leaves and primroses. Never as a young girl in her grandmother's home would she have dreamed of opening it. In fact, she could never recall seeing anyone open it.

Now, alone in the chamber where its owner had lived for so many years, Joanna approached, then reached out to run her hand along the smooth texture of its polished oak finish. What a beautiful piece of furniture! What secrets it could tell!

With reverence she rolled up the top and peered inside. A dozen or more small drawers and compartments met her gaze. Opening several at random she found the usual hodge-podge of bills, receipts, stationery, pencils, pens, article clippings, rubber bands, thread, needles, paper, envelopes—years of accumulated miscellany.

To the right beneath the roll-top were four larger drawers. Joanna worked her way from top to bottom, opening drawer after drawer and sifting through a similar assortment of an old lady's collection. Reaching the bottom drawer, she gave it a tug. Locked! The only locked drawer in the entire secretary!

Hadn't she run across a key somewhere already?

Her curiosity piqued, she retraced her steps through the drawers once again till she came to a tiny compartment, one of several of the same size, in the upper-left section of the desk area.

Now she remembered.

The drawer had been empty, and she had inadvertently pulled it all the way out of its frame. And there, attached to the back of the drawer, where it never would have been visible, was a very old-fashioned key.

Hastily she loosened it and inserted it into the keyhole of the locked bottom drawer.

It opened.

Joanna trembled with excitement and awe.

She knelt on the floor and gazed with wonder at the contents. Here was an altogether different collection of possessions. Unlike the other compartments in the secretary, in this drawer every item was packed carefully. Catching her eye first was a very old, hand-carved music box, small enough to fit in the palm of her hand. How lovely it was! With great care Joanna lifted it out, wound it, and set it down on the wooden floor beside her. In ancient, crisp metallic tones it played Brahms' lullaby, perhaps for the first time in countless years. The nostalgic strains sent Joanna into a reverie lasting several moments; the simple melody repeated itself over and over in an ever-diminishing tempo.

Was this the music box her grandmother had been mumbling about the day before she lapsed into a coma? It must have been a childhood heirloom of her own.

As its resonant sounds wound down, Joanna came to herself. She next lifted out two oval-shaped pictures from the drawer. They were considerably faded, but the likeness of a man and woman remained clearly discernible. The man was adorned in full Scottish dress: tartan kilt with small leather sporran in front, broadsword gleaming to one side, a great brass shoulder-brooch, high stockings, leather brogues, and round bonnet to match the kilt. The woman's dress was exquisitely old-fashioned, high-necked, reaching to the floor, and fully laced all around. If she could but see the colors!

Were these her grandmother's parents? Her own great-grandparents? Joanna's pulse quickened as a thrill surged through her spine.

Hastily she removed from her neck the locket her grandmother had given her. She had scarcely found time to examine the faces in it. But now as she looked—no, they could not be the same persons as the two miniatures she had just discovered in the drawer. But there could hardly be a doubt that the one face in the locket was her grandmother, though it was small and faded. Who was the young man in the other picture? Joanna had not a clue.

Returning to her task, Joanna came upon an aged packet of heavy brown paper. Slowly she opened it. Several official-looking documents were inside. Though well preserved for their age, she could nevertheless decipher nothing of their meaning; the old script appeared to be in another language. On one of the documents, however, she could clearly make out the name of a certain town—a "Port Strathy" in the county of Banff, Scotland. As her eyes strayed further, a single date leapt off the page—1784. Her mind reeled momentarily. This paper was almost a hundred and thirty years old! Examining it further she could just make out what appeared to be the single surname—Ramsey.

Immediately Joanna's thoughts turned to her grandmother, about whose past she knew so little. Why had she always kept her background so veiled? Were these the papers she had been talking about yesterday?

Eyes straining from the effort, Joanna refolded the papers, carefully laid them back into their pouch, and reached down to the last of her grandmother's personal treasures that she had hidden in this most private and cherished vault. There lay a folded piece of fine linen, no larger than fourteen by ten inches. Joanna opened it and gazed in amazement on a finely embroidered sampler displaying four generations of a family tree. Though obviously stitched by a young girl, it had been sewn with care and tolerable precision. Along the top the name *Ramsey* had been stitched in flowery old English script. A colorful band of primroses and forget-me-nots bordered the linen, and all the names for four generations were carefully worked into a pyramid design.

Names . . . they seemed to shout out at her. But what stood out most blatantly was a blank spot where a name had been torn out. The fabric had faded slightly around where the letters had been, but she could still make out the vague outline of the single name—*Margaret Isabel Duncan*.

With a knot rising in her throat Joanna recalled that day not so many years earlier when her grandmother had tried to interest her in embroidering a sampler and she had thrown it down in frustration. This was no doubt the very cloth she had mentioned that day.

A tear fell from Joanna's eye as she sat gazing upon her own genealogy preserved by her own grandmother as a young girl—a heritage she never knew existed until this very moment. She stroked the fabric gently, still exquisite after all these years. Then absently she rewound the music box.

As it repeated the haunting melody, Joanna sat fondling the linen, rocking back and forth, a child at heart once again. She had already forgotten the other items in the drawer. For this discovery transcended all else. Just seeing those names pierced her heart with a sense of belonging such as she'd never known, more permanent, more secure. Even if they were all dead, even though her own parents were dead, even though her only remaining relative—her grandmother—was now on the verge of death, somehow, she still belonged to a family. Though she knew nothing about them, she had roots.

She sat as one entranced, caught up in the dying tones of the lullaby. Her mind drifted back to those faraway days she had never known, to that Scotland she had never seen, to those people to whom she might belong.

From that moment of discovery in the secretary everything changed for Joanna. A purpose began growing deep inside, but its progress was so gradual that at first she did not realize it or understand it.

That night she slept fitfully, waking frequently, always with the impression of having left something undone. Once she arose to check all the doors to make sure they were locked. Another time she climbed out of bed and surveyed the kitchen to assure herself all was in order there.

Later, in one of her dozing dreams, a fragmentary vision of waves crashing against a rocky coastline came over her. Set back from the water's edge she could make out a small village with crude buildings of stone and brick sparkling in the sun.

When she awoke the following morning, without quite realizing it, Joanna had crossed an important threshold.

A decision had been made.

She could not even say she had actually made a decision. Rather, she sensed that one had been forced upon her by some power greater than herself. She knew she had to follow her past, wherever it led her.

She had to find Port Strathy. She had to be faithful to the promise she had made. She had to honor her grandmother's wish.

She had to go to Scotland!

Telling her plans to one of her grandmother's friends, though it felt good to vocalize the decision, was far from encouraging.

"Do you have any idea how much it costs to sail to Europe?" the neighbor had asked.

"No," Joanna had replied. "But I'll get there. I'll find a way."

As it turned out, this same acquaintance opened the door. The aunt of a friend was traveling to Europe; because of poor health she had been in search of a companion—a maid, attendant, and friend all rolled into one. For a suitable person, she was prepared to pay the expenses of passage. Joanna could hardly believe her good fortune when Mrs. Cupples engaged her for the voyage.

And now, less than a month later, here she was, aboard the *Atlantic Queen*, on her way to Scotland, perilously close to falling in love with a millionaire. It all seemed like a fairy tale. Her grandmother still lay in a coma in the hospital, unchanged. Joanna only hoped whatever she was to find at the end of her journey would not come too late.

Joanna lay dreamily in her bunk and sighed. Two months ago she had no purpose in life, no goals other than to float along with whatever came her way, hardly caring what it was. Now, all that had changed— perhaps she had changed, too. Whatever happened, this trip was an adventure she would never forget.

6 / The Storm

How quickly the sea could change!

The following morning the sky, once clear and blue, cast a gray pall over turbulent whitecaps. A heavy dampness hung in the air stirred only slightly by the warm breeze.

By midafternoon the temperature had dropped fifteen degrees and the wind had intensified as it swung around from the north. Great waves slapped against the huge white hulls of the ship. Toward evening the wind had grown to a full gale accompanied by a heavy downpour. The *Atlantic Queen* was more than up to the assault, but nonetheless the liner's great bulk found itself tossed by the wind and great swelling waves.

Joanna's stamina during the voyage surprised her. Not once during the trip had she felt even a twinge of seasickness. Mrs. Cupples, on the other hand, was not so fortunate. From the first moment of the storm she had grown ill and by evening had taken to bed.

For the next three days of the tempest, Joanna's hands were full running errands for her bedridden mistress—a bit of broth from the galley, some seltzer from the dining room, a concoction of ginger tea or a hot-water bottle from the dispensary.

Joanna did not see Jason Channing for a day and a half—although he had been in her thoughts. His invitation had been constantly on her mind. While attending to Mrs. Cupples's needs she had fantasized herself on his arm, in the midst of London's gayest society. She had almost convinced herself she was ready to lay aside her timid personality in favor of confidence, self-assurance, and charm. She would lure him and bedazzle him with her wit, her coy glances, her disarming smile. Yes, the time had come to step out of the backwoods. She was ready to become a woman—his London lady. She would find him, seek him out. She would tell him. Yes, she would go.

Scotland could wait a few days; her grandmother would understand.

On the afternoon of the storm's second day, Joanna found herself walking to the galley. Her slicker was dripping from traversing the port deck where the fierce wind blew in unhindered. Leaving the deck she entered a short corridor, shook off as much of the rain as possible, and headed through a set of double swinging doors into the dining room.

Quickly she scanned the sparsely populated room for Jason Channing's face. Unsuccessful, she turned her steps again toward the galley. All at once he stood right before her, in front of the door through which she had to pass, arms folded nonchalantly on his chest, head tilted to one side, eyes gleaming.

Starting, Joanna looked at him casually in a manner intended to communicate the self-confidence she was determined to muster.

"Why, Mr. Channing," she said in a measured tone, "what a surprise!"

"Mr. Channing, is it?" he answered with mock alarm. "I thought we had gone beyond that, Joanna." He flashed a knowing smile intended to convey what his words had left unsaid.

"I . . . I don't know what you mean," her voice faltered.

"Come now, Joanna." He stepped toward her and took her arm firmly in his own. Without a word he led her to an alcove just off the dining room.

He drew her toward him, slipped his arms around her waist, and kissed her several times, each kiss hungrier than the last. Finally he held her at arm's length.

"That's what I mean."

Joanna found herself too dazed to speak. For the past two days she had secretly looked for him with every errand. She had even worked herself into feeling bold and sophisticated. She had carefully orchestrated in her mind exactly how this meeting would take place. She would lead him on, force him to beg her to come to London. At the last moment she would accept. Then together they would disembark the ship.

But now her words caught helpless in her mouth. Her clammy hands trembled. She was nothing but a simple country girl after all. She had fooled no one but herself.

"I thought perhaps you had been avoiding me," Channing broke into the silence of her thoughts.

"N—no. I . . . I was," Joanna attempted awkwardly. "I mean, Mrs. Cupples has been sick. I've been nearly cabin bound. But I have . . . well, I've thought a lot about what you said."

"So, Joanna, have you decided to throw aside those old-fashioned values of yours and come with me? I believe, Joanna, that it's what you really want."

She looked away.

"Your first step," Channing continued, "will be London. I won't take no for an answer."

"Oh, Mr. Ch—, Jason," she said. "I would love to go to London with you."

She hesitated again, searching frantically in her mind for a reason, after all, to abandon logic and say yes. But at the last moment, uncertainty and fear overpowered her indecision.

"But, Jason," she said finally, "I . . . I just don't think I'm ready for that right now. Please understand. I would love . . . to be with you. But I can't—not now. My ticket is for Aberdeen. And something tells me I must go on without delay."

Joanna's voice trembled. She knew she sounded uncertain and hesitant.

". . . perhaps after I've been in Scotland a while I could arrange to come—"

"I may not be in London that long."

"You said you were coming north also," suggested Joanna.

"I don't know," replied Channing, whose voice suddenly seemed to grow cool.

"If we met later," said Joanna, "I . . . I—"

She struggled for words.

"I might be ready . . . then."

"As I said, I don't know. It may not be convenient then." Cool distance supplanted Channing's previous passion. "Now, Miss Matheson," he added, stepping back and offering a slight bow, "I must bid you good day. I have several people I must see this afternoon."

He turned and walked briskly down the corridor.

Joanna's eyes followed him.

Oh, Jason, she thought with a sigh, *I might be in love with you. But, I just don't know.*

She turned, walking toward the sheltered starboard side of the ship, went out to the railing, took a long breath of salt air, and looked out on the gray, stormy sea.

"Next stop, Aberdeen," she murmured as a gust of wind blew through her hair.

After several more moments, she turned and continued her errand to the galley.

The last pothole nearly jarred Joanna's teeth loose.

Unfortunately, the road wasn't getting better. The empty haywagon gave every evidence of searching out the largest, deepest, and muddiest holes before determining which direction to go. Then its steel-rimmed wheels bisected each with uncanny precision, sending its two occupants into the air and down again. The unyielding, straight-backed wooden seats offered no cushion, and muddy water from the puddles splashed up freely.

"I'm thinkin' ye might ha' doon better waitin' fer Monday's schooner, mem," said the driver—a tall, gangly Scotsman about fifty years old. "Makin' the drive over wi' me two horses there an' a sweet-smellin' load o' cut hay ahin' me in the ol' wagon, 'tis a right comfy ride. The hay keeps the wagon settled doon a mite, ye know."

Joanna nodded as best she could between bumps.

"But," he went on, "the return's always tolerable tougher on me sore bottom an' bones, the wagon jostlin' up an' doon the way she do." His reddish-blonde hair revealed hardly a trace of gray, but life in the severe northern climate had weathered and wrinkled his pale, freckled face like a dried apple doll. His pale blue eyes seemed always to give the impression of looking through rather than at you, but his hands and muscular arms revealed a certain time-worn strength as they gently fingered the compliant leather reins and maneuvered the wagon down the rain-soaked road.

"I don't mind," said Joanna through clenched teeth, bracing herself for the next jolting bounce into the air. "I was fortunate to find you, Mr. MacDuff."

Joanna had arrived in Aberdeen on Tuesday. From there a coach bore her to Fenwick Harbor on Thursday, where her intention had been to catch the schooner sailing north around the coast to Inverness. It would have taken her to her destination just beyond Troup Head. However, once she learned of the schooner's scheduled two-day layover at Peterhead, not putting out again until Monday, and another stop at Fraserburgh, she considered her chance meeting with MacDuff fortuitous. He had assured her the overland drive would take only two days and that he could put her in the village a full three days ahead of the schooner.

At the time it seemed the sensible thing to do. Of course, she hadn't foreseen the condition of the road.

"Ye jist missed the storm," MacDuff was saying. " 'Twas a bad'n fer this time o' year. But we sometimes get a late spring outburst tryin' t' sneak all the way t' June or July."

"Well, it's lovely now," said Joanna.

"Aye, 'tis that," beamed MacDuff, proud to hear the weather of his native land extolled by a foreigner.

The bright blue sky peered down upon them as a testimony to their praise. Great white puffs of clouds dotted the blue, but as decoration, with no threat in mind. The rain had washed the landscape clean, bringing every blade of grass and tree leaf into crisp, brilliant focus. Joanna thought she had never been so close to such beauty. She could not distinguish ash from oak, birch from pine, or larch from fir—her world had always been too closed for an appreciation of nature's splendor. But the woods and pasturelands, even the desolate moors through which they had to pass, all combined in her heart to give her the sensation: "This is what I came to Scotland to discover!"

She recognized the dainty faces of white, purple, red, yellow and blue primroses breaking through their rough shells among the country grasses. The sight of their delicate faces kindled the memory of her grandmother.

She was actually in Scotland! It still took awhile to sink in.

Then she pondered her purpose in coming here. *Grandma,* she thought, *this is as much for you as it is for me. If I can find your people, whoever and wherever they are, I will have fulfilled—*

Her thoughts came to an abrupt halt. She didn't know what she would have fulfilled exactly. Maybe that, too, was part of what she had to discover here in her grandmother's native land.

Another bump jarred her thoughts back to the present and to the sound of MacDuff's craggy voice.

"Ye'll no doobt find oor wee village a bit backward after all the big cities ye've traveled through. But 'tis a bonny place, all in all. Though maybe ye'll be thinkin' I'm a mite prejudiced, havin' lived there most o' my life. Ye must ha' thought I were from the wee toon up the coast bearin' my name. An' maybe my people had some association wi' the toon o' MacDuff way back, but 'tis beyon' my recollectin'."

He attempted to edge the horses around a small pond in the middle of the road, hitting two rough-edged potholes in the process.

But soon he resumed his irrepressible talk. "Canna see what would be in oor village t' bring a lass like yersel' clean from America. 'Course I dinna mean t' pry . . ."

"That's all right, Mr. MacDuff. My grandmother was from Scotland. I don't know much about her past. But she left to come to the United States when she was a young girl, and I have reason to believe she may have been from Port Strathy."

"Why don't ye ask her, mem?"

"Oh, I should have explained. She's had an accident and is now in a coma," said Joanna. "She's not expected to live."

"I'm sorry, mem."

"I never had the chance to find out more before . . . She didn't talk much about her early life."

"Hmm," muttered the driver. "So ye're comin' here t' find relatives," he went on, "t' settle her affairs . . . the will . . . an' so on—is that it?"

"No," Joanna laughed. "No . . . I'm here, I suppose, as a last favor to her. I promised her I would come. She seemed to think there was something for me to find or do here. But I don't really know. I guess I'm here for myself too, to discover what I can about my own heritage."

Joanna paused.

"Takes a heap o' money t' travel so far jist t' gaze at the countryside," said MacDuff in some astonishment. "Yer parents must ha' some bank account t' sen' ye all this way, mem."

"I'm sorry to disappoint you, Mr. MacDuff," Joanna said with a tender smile at the talkative man. "I really have nothing. I worked my way here on a ship and I've only got enough money with me for a few weeks' lodging. After that, I have nothing. You see . . . my parents are both dead."

Rebuked by her response, MacDuff fell silent, staring at the road that wound ahead of them as far as the eye could see.

"And who knows?" resumed Joanna, "I may still have some relatives living in the area. I suppose down deep, that's what I'd like to discover, Mr. MacDuff. That would make the trip worthwhile. Be it a twelfth cousin or what," Joanna sighed at the thought that she had for the first time put into words. "And perhaps if it's not too late, it might still help her."

"Weel," the old man said, falling back into his talkative mood. "Ye're comin' at a gran' time. Big doin's up oor way these days. 'Tis lookin' as if some real prosperity is comin' t' oor toon."

"What's the cause of it all, Mr. MacDuff?"

"Weel, the laird died na too lang ago, an' since there be no heirs, the estate's t' be sold. Talk has it that some o' the proceeds from the sale will be put right back int' the toon an' the surroundin' crofts. Maybe even some outright cash fer the tenants. Mind ye, the laird weren't so ill a man, as lairds go. But this weren't his regular home, an' well, it seems he let things go a bit o'er much."

MacDuff paused while he coaxed his horses over a particularly tricky stretch of road. After a time he resumed.

"Ye'll be seein' yer first Scottish gloamin' no doobt, Miss Matheson," said MacDuff as the sun lowered toward the horizon.

"Gloamin'?" asked Joanna.

"This far up north, mem, late in the summer, the sunset lasts all the night long. Jist goes right over t' sunrise it does."

"It must be beautiful!"

"Aye, it is, mem. Pink sky all the night long. An' we call oor long summer sunsets the gloamin'."

"Will I see it tonight?" Joanna asked.

"We'll have the gloamin' all right. But it'll be gettin' prettier later in the summer."

MacDuff explained they would spend the night at an inn in a little hamlet called Northhaven. He judged they would complete their trip by midday tomorrow.

At that point the wagon collided with another pothole, sending MacDuff's hat flying into the wagonbed behind him.

"These roads aren't nothin' t' brag aboot, as ye can see, mem," MacDuff said. "That's why most folks, travelin' folks like yersel', mem, prefer the sea roads."

"Perhaps some of the funds from the laird's estate should go for road improvements," said Joanna.

"Aye," said MacDuff. "They should put ye in charge o' the estate, mem!" He laughed good-naturedly.

8 / Port Strathy

The following morning dawned fresh and crisp with a lingering chill of the spring just past. The wagon proved even more uncomfortable as Joanna climbed aboard, rubbing her sore hindquarters, hoping somehow the road would be smoother today. But her spirits remained undaunted; her destination now lay close at hand. As she looked around, the frost clinging to the grass reminded her that she should have been cold. But instead she tingled with the warmth of anticipation.

"A tip top mornin', 'tisn't it, mem?" said MacDuff as he hitched up the horses.

"It couldn't be lovelier!"

"Aye, 'tis a gran' day t' climb Strathy summit t' look oot on the sea."

As they settled into the ride the sun gradually thawed the frozen earth and by midmorning had blanketed the surrounding countryside in sunny brilliance.

The terrain grew increasingly rocky and woodsy, with trees coming up to the road on both sides as the pastureland ceased. Hardly noticing the difference—it had come about so slowly—Joanna was surprised when her guide pointed out to her:

"If ye'll look behin' ye a bit, mem," he said, "ye'll see we've climbed a considerable height."

Turning around, Joanna was startled.

"Why, Mr. MacDuff, I had hardly noticed! But you're right, the road is definitely dropping off behind us, for as far as I can see it."

Joanna took everything in with a flush of excitement.

"She said she loved it," Joanna murmured aloud, "and now I see why . . ."

"Mem?"

Embarrassed that she had been caught voicing her thoughts aloud, Joanna blushed, then stammered out a quick explanation. "I—I was thinking of my grandmother."

"There is somethin' mighty special aboot yer own kinfolk," he replied. "Ye say she was from aroun' here?"

"I'm reasonably certain she may have been."

"How long's it been since she left?"

"I'm not sure," Joanna replied.

"Hmm," he mused, ". . . ye say yer name was Matheson?"

Joanna nodded.

"Can't say as I recall any Mathesons from these parts," he said after he had brooded on the name for a moment, " 'cept it be the dry-goods Mathesons down in Aberchider . . ."

"Matheson was my father's name, not hers."

"An' what was her name, then?" asked MacDuff.

"Margaret Duncan."

"Duncan!" exclaimed MacDuff, making an attempt at a whistle. He paused, then—in a noticeably subdued voice—said, *The* Duncans?"

"You've heard of them?" asked Joanna, momentarily oblivious to the bumps in the road.

"Who hasn't, bein' the laird o' the land an' all? But who am I t' be tellin' ye aboot that?" he replied, in which seemed to be a cooler tone.

"I know nothing about my grandmother's family, if these Duncans you're talking about should be the same Duncans at all."

"Then ye were na comin' fer the funeral?"

"Funeral? I . . . I don't understand?"

"The laird's, like I were tellin' ye aboot, mem. Guess it matters little noo, since ye missed it. The buryin's lang since come an' gone. An' meanin' no disrespec', mem, an' everyone's sore distressed aboot it. But 'twill no doobt turn oot best fer the toon."

"Because of the sale of the estate?"

"Jist like I said, yesterday, mem. Jist how are ye related, mem?"

"I don't even know that I am," replied Joanna. "I'm sure it's just a coincidence of names."

"Could be . . ." MacDuff ruminated softly. "Could be . . ." He said not another word for some time.

Joanna also grew pensive and silent. What had caused the silence of the loquacious man, Joanna could not tell, and she was reticent to ask. For the first time, she began to wonder if this whole thing had been a mistake.

Joanna turned her attention once more to the countryside and at length commented, "We're still climbing, aren't we, Mr. MacDuff?"

"Aye, fer jist a couple furlongs more, mem," he replied, seeming his old self again. "We're almost t' Strathy Summit. An altogether peculiar name fer a mountain."

"Why do you say that?"

"Why, 'tis a complete contradiction o' terms. *Strathy* means valley, mem. Hoo can ye ha' a valley summit?" He chuckled at his wit.

"How did it come to get such a name, Mr. MacDuff?"

"I suppose the toon got its name first. Since this here's the way int' it, more than's likely the first folks must o' climbed this mountain, come doon the other side int' the valley—that's where the toon is noo, mem—an' called the place Strathy. Then someone later must o' named this mountain after the toon. 'Tis all I can figure.''

"I'm sure you're right. That makes all the sense in the world.''

After a few minutes more, the wagon rounded a curve, cresting the summit, and Joanna suddenly caught sight of the sea in the distance, far below them. It lay spread out like a radiant sapphire, at the end of a vast green carpet of trees descending from the peak of the hill, down to a hundred feet above the water's surface. There the sea lay spread out at the foot of a sheer rocky cliff.

Joanna jumped up in the wagon, excitedly straining for a better look.

"Oh, Mr. MacDuff . . . it's absolutely beautiful!'' she exclaimed.

"Aye, mem, an' so are ye yersel', an' I dinna want t' lose ye jist yet. So take it easy an' hold yersel' in the wagon. 'Tis a steeper climb doon the fellside, an' then a narrow road doon the edge o' it t' toon. Ye'll ha' time t' see it all.''

Joanna resumed her seat but kept her eyes riveted on the coastline, though the trees continued dense and frustrated her view.

As they wound down the hill the trees began to thin until the wagon emerged at the top of the great cliff.

"What's that?'' Joanna asked, pointing toward a huge protruding rock that came into sight. "Is it an island?''

" 'Tis Ramsey Head. An' no, mem, 'tis no island.''

"It looks like a small mountain. You mean it's connected to the shore?''

"Aye. But too rocky an' steep t' do folks much good, though some take the path up it noo an' then. From the top ye can see Strathy Harbor clear as a bell. I'm guessin' the Head's mainly there jist t' let the sea-fearin' folk know Port Strathy's aroun' the next bend.''

Joanna wished she were one of the graceful gulls so abundant about the Head—she wanted to fly from the wagon, off the cliff's edge, to the huge rock bearing the Ramsey name. The moment MacDuff had said the word a thrill had surged through her; she instantly remembered it from the embroidered sampler she had discovered among her grandmother's things. She kept her thoughts silent, however. At the first mention of her grandmother's name she had detected a curious change in MacDuff's bearing. She did not want to bring up anything more just yet.

Keeping her seat, Joanna was disappointed to find the road veering away from the cliff, leaving the sea momentarily, as they began the descent down into the village.

Her disappointment was short-lived, however, for almost immediately she spied on their left the first sign of habitation since leaving Northhaven that morning. A small hut with thatched roof was nestled snugly in a grove of tall firs. So thoroughly did the tiny cottage blend into its surroundings that Joanna would have missed it altogether had it not been for the bright red flannels hanging from a tree branch in front.

As the wagon rumbled past, a stone skittered across the road behind them, striking a tree to their right.

" 'Tis Mackinaw's place," explained MacDuff, reigning the team to a stop. "Likes his privacy . . . an' his red underwear."

"Why would he build his house so near the road then?" asked Joanna turning to get a better look at the ancient hut.

" 'Tweren't no road here when that hoose were built, mem." Then over his shoulder MacDuff's voice rose to a shout: "Look here, Stevie, dinna ye go bein' so unsociable!"

"I meant nae harm," yelled back a voice as ancient as the house. No face appeared. "Jist wantin' t' see wha b' trouncin' 'pon my yard!"

"Got a visitor all the way from America!" returned MacDuff. Then when no response was forthcoming, he turned to Joanna. "Dinna be mindin' him," he said. " 'Tis really a friendly place, Strathy is. Ye'll soon see fer yersel'."

It was hardly the sort of reception Joanna had anticipated. But every place must have its eccentrics, she told herself.

As the wagon moved on past the hut, Joanna was unable to see the cavernous eyes peering out from a crack in the shutters at MacDuff's retreating wagon. Nor did she hear the faint whistle emitting from the wrinkled lips. She had no way of knowing that Stevie Mackinaw, for all his advanced years, remained sharp as ever and never missed his mark unless it was his intention.

At increased intervals cottages and houses came into view along the roadside. Not all were as old as Mackinaw's, but most were small and impoverished. In some yards chickens scratched about; others displayed a pig, a goat or two, with here and there a family cow. The seeming poverty of the place, however, was offset by lovely attempts at gardens. Bright nasturtiums and daisies, along with climbing vines of morning glories, bedecked many a porch. Bushes of rhododendron and azaleas, alive with springtime, appeared around nearly every corner. And each house, it seemed, had its own private little crop of primroses.

A woman dressed in a simple flowered house-frock stepped onto her porch, shaded her eyes from the sun with a hard-working hand, and waved. Her wide, unassuming smile eased Joanna's heart, and she returned the greeting.

"Mornin' t' ye, MacDuff," the buxom young woman called out, but her friendly eyes rested instead on Joanna.

"Mornin', Mistress Creary," shouted MacDuff in return. "I've brought a visitor t' oor fair village all the way from America!" he went on, giving every indication that he had personally conveyed Joanna the full five thousand miles.

"Welcome t' ye!" Mrs. Creary called out to Joanna as the wagon passed.

"Thank you," replied Joanna, noticing two smudge-faced little children peeking out from behind the woman's full-length working dress. Joanna could not help laughing.

As the wagon continued down the widening lane, other curious folk—mostly good-natured women—peered out from their houses, while a few stepped boldly out to offer their friendly welcomes and exchange a greeting or two with MacDuff and his passenger.

Before long the houses bunched together and the badly pitted country road grew into a tolerably smooth lane winding its way through the small town toward the water sparkling two hundred yards away. The smells of salt, sea, and fish mingled together to tell Joanna she had finally arrived.

"Does the road take us right to the water's edge?" Joanna asked in delight.

"The Bluster 'N Blow is next t' the wharf," MacDuff replied. "Ye'll ha' yer fill o' the water soon enough, I'll warrant!"

"The Bluster 'N Blow?" inquired Joanna, ignoring for now the rest of MacDuff's words—she could never have enough of the sea.

Visions of waking to the crashing of the waves and the shrill squeals of gulls filled her heart with anticipation.

"The inn. 'Tis where ye said ye'd be stayin', 'tis it not?"

"Oh yes," Joanna nodded. "I didn't know the name."

" 'Tis the only one in toon, regardless. 'Tis where all the visitors t' Strathy stay—when we ha' 'em."

9 / Local Speculations

"Weel, MacDuff, are ye goin' t' stay tight-lipped ferever, man?"

"Can't a man ha' a bit o' drink in peace?" MacDuff put his hand to his mug of ale and proceeded to lift it to his mouth, but Rob Peters' large hand reached across the thick oak table and restrained him.

"Not every day this town o' oors sees someone all the way from America," Rob persisted.

"Come, MacDuff," put in another of the men at the table, who had emptied his first two tumblers of the strong local brew rather too quickly and whose head was growing hotter by the minute. "No more o' yer cat-an'-mouse games wi' us! Oot wi't or we'll drag't oot o' ye!"

"I ain't a man given t' gossip."

A ripple of laughter through the group indicated they knew MacDuff only too well.

" 'Tis only gossip when womenfolk do it," returned Peters. "What we're doin' here's discussin' the welfare o' oor town." Rob could not keep back the hint of a mischievous grin around the corners of his mouth even as he said the words.

"My wife says she's some awful bonnie—though a mite on the scrawny side," offered Douglas Creary.

"Weel, MacDuff," put in several in unison. "Oot wi' it!"

MacDuff freed his hand from Peter's grasp and slowly lifted the frothy mug to his lips, leaving a foamy remnant on his overgrown moustache. He well knew he would reveal all he knew to the small gathering of friends in the Bluster 'N Blow's common room. But he rather enjoyed being the center of attention and desired to stretch the moment out as long as possible. Thus his delays and shadowy allusions to knowing more than the others achieved their maximum design. He took two long swallows of the strong Scottish beer.

" 'Tis a top-notch ale ye ha' oot today, Sandy." MacDuff savored another slow draught.

"Ay . . . top-notch!" MacDuff continued. "Fittin' fer such an important day. 'Course, I expec' such a highborn lass would be goin' fer nothin' so ordinary as what we commonfolk be drinkin'."

"What d'ye mean, highborn?" came a chorus of voices at once.

MacDuff had his friends exactly where he wanted them.

" 'Tis only speculation, o' course," he said solemnly, leaning forward in his stiff-backed chair and lowering his voice perceptibly; "—not likely t' be true," he added. "But it do make a body think."

"What are ye talkin' aboot?" snapped Peters, beginning to think the news might not be worth the frustration of drawing it out of one so coy as his friend.

"The lass says she's a Duncan." MacDuff at last dropped the full weight of his revelation into the midst of his companions, then folded his arms and rocked back on his chair as if to say, "Noo . . . wasn't that tidbit o' news worth the wait!"

The various reactions around the small gathering ranged from astonishment to disbelief. This same group of men drank ale, played cards, regaled one another with stories (the truth or falsehood of which was rarely important to their full enjoyment), and shared the latest town gossip (which they steadfastly insisted was *news*) every Saturday evening in Port Strathy's only establishment of its kind. But rarely had there been much of note to report until the laird's death had stirred up the nest of speculation about the town's future. Coming on its heels, this latest piece of information was fraught with possibilities for discussion.

"Her name's Matheson," said Sandy Cobden, the innkeeper, firmly. "Got it written in my register clear as day."

"What says ye t' that, MacDuff!" laughed Creary.

The conversation would undoubtedly have continued on in this vein for some time, growing ever further afield in its range of individual conjectures, had not the object of their discussion at that moment made an appearance. MacDuff opened his mouth to speak once more, but stopped the moment he heard a creaking on the stairs above him.

All heads turned to see Joanna walking slowly down, seeming to test each one of the rickety steps with her toe before easing her weight fully onto it.

Sandy jumped from his place at the table and hastened over to her as she descended.

"Evenin', mem," he said. "Trust ye had a pleasant rest in yer room. Bed weren't too hard?"

Joanna shook her head. "No," she said. "The room is fine."

"I hope it'll be warm enough fer ye."

"I'm sure everything will be perfect."

As she spoke, Joanna tried to conceal the awkwardness she felt from the hush that had come over the room. Leaving her room she had heard sounds of friendly conversation from below. Now, however, the common room had grown still as a tomb. Without looking up she instinctively knew all eyes were turned upon her.

"Ye'll be wantin' some supper," Sandy continued. "Come o'er here an' set yersel' doon."

"Just something simple will be fine," said Joanna with a smile. "I'm still rather tired and would like to retire again to my room early tonight."

The innkeeper led her to a table on the opposite side of the room. She sat down while he bustled off toward the kitchen. Joanna fidgeted uneasily on the hard wooden seat while the conversation between the men across the room resumed by degrees into other channels of talk. When the eyes of one would glance Joanna's way, she would offer a smile and her greeting would be returned with a slight tip of the hat. The awkwardness gradually subsided, and the ale, stories, and "news" once again flowed freely.

After Cobden returned with a hearty loaf of brown bread, butter, a slab of sharp cheese, and a pot of steaming tea, Joanna began eating with the uncomfortable notion that each bite was being scrutinized by an anxious cook. At length she finished and, excusing herself, returned to her room.

The men removed their hats and said, "A good evenin' t' ye, mem."

Their conversation, however, never turned in her direction again.

The following morning Joanna once more descended the broad staircase. The previous evening's bright and cheerful fire had grown still, replaced by gay morning sunlight streaming through the windows. Already two of the tables were occupied with village folk come to the inn for breakfast. Sandy and his wife were both busily engaged in the kitchen and with their guests.

Joanna sat down. As she waited for her meal her eyes scanned the room, taking in more details than she had been aware of the day before. Coarse wooden furniture stood on bare wood floors in plain but homey surroundings. She noted with surprise that the only windows in the room were high on the wall, and none faced the sea.

"I'll have a fire goin' afore ye know it," said Sandy, entering with an armload of fresh wood. " 'Tis the only warmth we get in here, an' I keep a few embers most days from the night before. But this time she went oot on me."

After a sound night's sleep, Joanna could hardly sit still long enough for breakfast. She was anxious to see the town, the sea, the shoreline, to explore her new surroundings. The Scotland of her ancestors beckoned her!

When she had arrived at the inn the previous afternoon, Sandy Cobden's plump, good-natured wife had led her to her room to settle in. Joanna planned to have a look around Port Strathy that very day. She had lain down on the bed, just for a moment. But the weeks of traveling had taken their toll. When she awoke, hours had passed, and a glance outside told her the "gloamin' " had come. There would be no walking about her new environs today. After arranging her few belongings, she had gone downstairs for her bread and cheese and then back to her room for the night.

Now as she sat watching the struggling fire take hold, Sandy Cobden appeared with a tray laden with two fresh biscuits, a pat of butter, a bowl of steaming oatmeal, and a small pitcher of fresh, local cream.

"I hope all is t' yer likin', mem," he said. "I'll bring ye some tea too, if ye like."

"It looks delicious, Mr. Cobden," said Joanna.

With that word of approval, the innkeeper made the rounds to his few other morning guests and then to the counter-bar where he began cleaning the tabletop, wiping glasses with the bottom of his apron, and straightening up. He was a large man, both in height and girth. One hardly expected such quick movements from such an oversized frame. But he worked quickly and gave the appearance of constant motion.

Joanna listened to the clinking of glasses and bottles, continuing to take in the scenes about her, until she had made a hearty inroad into her meal. Sitting near the counter, she looked toward Sandy still busily engaged in his work.

"Do you know any Duncans around Port Strathy?"

"Mem?"

"The Duncans—I'd like to go visit them, if there are any still around. Do you know where anyone by that name lives?"

Sandy set down the mug he had been wiping. "Weel, mem," he said, "the ol' laird died a month ago. 'Twould be him ye'd be asking aboot?"

"I heard about the laird," Joanna said. "But no, I'm just looking for anyone by that name, possibly not even in this laird's family at all. Surely there must be other Duncans about?"

"He were the last. The auld hoose be empty noo, 'cept fer the factor an' the hoosekeeper—an' o' course, auld Dorey. All the other servants been sent away."

"Perhaps I could go to the house and speak to one of them."

"The Duncan affairs'll soon be a closed book aroun' here, mem."

Were Cobden's words a mere statement, or was there a subtle warning in his cool tone? Whatever it was, Joanna recognized the same distance she had noticed when she mentioned her grandmother's name to MacDuff.

"I'm sure it is no concern of mine," Joanna assured him.

"Hmm," muttered Cobden, more to himself than to her, but with still a trace of hidden suspicion in his tone, as he returned to the glass he had been wiping.

"Could you direct me to their house?"

"*The* Hoose," the innkeeper corrected. " 'Tis up on the hill . . . *the* Hoose on the hill," he added.

"And which direction is—"

But just at that moment Mrs. Cobden appeared and called her husband to the kitchen.

With the words, "Best see what the missus wants," Cobden made a hasty retreat. But before he disappeared behind the kitchen door, he paused and said to Joanna, "Ye might enjoy yer day more if ye spent it lookin' at the fishin' boats, mem." Then he was gone.

Giving little thought to his parting words, Joanna rose and walked outside. In a town this size, it shouldn't be difficult finding "*the* House on the hill."

10 / Olive Sinclair

Exiting the Bluster 'N Blow for her first thorough walk about Port Strathy, Joanna thought she had never seen a bluer sky. And the sea, only a hundred yards away, reflected a perfect match. Of course from the inn's name and the limited knowledge she possessed of the winter storms on Scotland's north shore, she knew today's calm must be the exception rather than the rule.

She walked slowly toward the harbor, practically outside her front door. Maybe she should follow Sandy's advice. All the boats were securely docked. But as picturesque as were the many varieties of large and small fishing vessels bobbing gently in the clear salt water, Joanna's mind remained occupied with other things.

She turned, crossed the street, and proceeded back the way she had come on the other side of the street. She had ridden this very way on MacDuff's wagon yesterday, but somehow she had missed so much. Today she was more immediately conscious of the shops and houses crammed tightly together, bordering the street on both sides.

This was clearly Port Strathy's chief region for commerce and activity. Joanna noticed a number of shops, old and a bit run-down, but nonetheless pleasant: a dry goods dealer, a chandlery, a cobbler's shop, and several others jumbled together in uneven profusion. Interspersed were houses, large and small. Not until she saw the shops were closed did Joanna realize that today was Sunday. That accounted for the relative sparseness of any crowd, although a number of people were about.

Reaching the end of the straight thoroughfare, a quarter mile inland from the water's edge, the street ended at a broad thoroughfare running at right angles in both directions. Arriving the previous day from the east, or left, today Joanna chose to follow the road—obviously intended as a highway through the small town for travelers moving along the coast—to the right.

Quickly she realized, however, that the town—whose nucleus clustered tightly around the precincts of the short street between the harbor and the intersection—soon came to an end. The houses became less numerous, shops disappeared, and in the distance Joanna saw farms and fields coming down to the road on her left. To the right of the road stretched sandy beach grasses down to the water's edge. A narrow beach, no wider than twenty or thirty yards, glistened with smooth, white sand. Some five or six hundred yards away the sand turned rocky, and gently waving grasses quickly gave way to a cliff shooting high in the air, bordering the small natural harbor to the west.

Taking in this scene at a glance, Joanna vowed to return to this magnificent stretch of coastline another time. Turning, she made her way back into the town, angled left at the intersection, crossed to the right of the street, and walked leisurely back toward the inn.

Church—which was situated about a half mile south of town—had by this time dispersed, and more and more of the townspeople were about. A barefoot boy ambled by carrying a crude handmade fishing pole and burlap bag, obviously heading for an afternoon's fishing from the pier. Two men clad in overalls sat chatting in front of one of the houses; they stopped as Joanna approached, tipped their hats as she passed, and then went on with their conversation in subdued tones.

Down the wooden sidewalk in front of her Joanna saw a stooped old woman, carrying a rather large basket, enter the market. Deciding that to be a logical place to obtain the information she sought, she increased her pace and followed the woman inside.

In the cluttered little room Joanna was inundated with a score of smells; the first two she was able to identify were dried fish and mint. On the counter stood a row of tempting glass jars full of peppermint sticks, gum drops, and several varieties of fish and beef jerky. All about the walls, stacked twelve feet high, stood shelf upon shelf of merchandise of every imaginable type—salt and flour, corn and wheat, seed, chemical fertilizers, kitchen utensils, bacon, and miscellaneous household adornments. A marvelous variety!

As Joanna stood staring about taking it all in, a voice interrupted her thoughts:

"Be with you in a moment, dear!" it boomed.

Glancing up, Joanna spied a grayish-black head looming over the clutter on the counter. The shop's proprietor, a middle-aged woman of above average height, her face dominated by protruding eyes and a large roman nose, stood helping the elderly woman who had preceded Joanna into the shop.

"Thank you," replied Joanna. "I'm in no hurry."

When the other customer in the small establishment had completed her business and gone, Joanna stepped forward.

"Actually," said Joanna timidly, "I'm rather surprised to find you open today."

"I always open for a couple hours on Sunday afternoon," the lady said in an intimidating voice, loud enough to match her imposing stature.

"The folks sometimes needs things and can't wait till the morrow, you know."

"Well, I'm glad you are," replied Joanna. "I'm new here and—"

"You'll be the lass from America, no doubt!" echoed the voice. "I'm Olive Sinclair."

She thrust out a large hand across the peppermint sticks and grasped Joanna's firmly. "Pleased to make your acquaintance at last. I knew I would sooner or later. Everyone ends up in here. Especially am I glad because seems like you're all a body's heard about these last two days. Like I say, everyone ends up here—and more so when there's news to spread."

A flush rose to Joanna's cheeks.

"I don't see why I've caused such a stir," she said.

"We don't get many visitors up our way, you see, miss. Was a Frenchman visiting the laird a few years back. 'Course, we common folk didn't see much of him. But you didn't come in my shop to listen to me ramble on, now did you? What can I do for you this bright day?"

"I don't mind listening," said Joanna. "But I was wondering if you could direct me to the Duncan's house?"

"You mean *the* House?"

"That's just what Mr. Cobden the innkeeper said. You both make it sound as if it's the only house in town."

"In a certain manner of speaking . . . sorry, Miss—Matheson, isn't it?" Olive Sinclair asked, casting Joanna an interrogative glance.

"Yes . . . Joanna. Joanna Matheson."

"Well, like I said, in a certain manner of speaking, Miss Matheson, Stonewycke Castle *is* the only house in town. Leastways, the most important. Been that way for over three hundred years."

Joanna's eyes widened in surprise. A small smile stole onto Miss Sinclair's thin lips as she realized how old that must seem to an American, especially as wide-eyed a young girl as now stood before her.

" 'Tis a fine sight for travelers to see," Miss Sinclair offered. "The rare foreigner that came to our town was often given a tour of the place. But things'll no doubt be changing with the laird gone . . ." A hint of regret was obvious in her final words.

"Well, I hardly expected a tour," said Joanna, "only possibly to talk with some of the servants."

"Is it true what folks have been saying about you?"

Joanna tensed, wondering if she should keep her reasons for coming to herself. Yet she did not sense the same discordant tone in Miss Sinclair's voice as she had in others with whom she'd talked. Instead, there was a sincere friendliness. A certain warmth emanated from the loud and imposing woman.

"I don't really know. My grandmother is a Duncan. She wanted me to find her home. She's very ill. That's practically all I know."

Suddenly Miss Sinclair leaned over the counter, drew her alarming features close to Joanna's, and said, "If she was born here . . ."

She stopped abruptly, glanced around to make sure the shop was still empty, then went on in little more than a whisper, ". . . there could be no doubt she'd be related to the laird. The Duncans *is* Port Strathy, if you know what I mean. I never heard mention of any other family by that name in these parts. No, if you be a Duncan, dearie . . ." and here the animated shopkeeper simply let a long, low whistle complete her thought. Then she nodded her head with lips squeezed tightly together as if to add still more force to her unspoken conclusion.

"Well, dear, you go on to the house," she went on. "Who knows what may come of it. I'd take you there myself, but I can't leave the store. I left for a bit yesterday while Tom was cleaning up the back room for me and the place was a mess when I got back. I don't know how his wife puts up with him. I only thank the Lord He saw fit to endow me with brains instead of beauty. Leastways I don't have to worry about keeping a no account like that in tow."

"Where exactly is this . . . Stonewycke Castle?" Joanna asked, the name feeling awkward on her tongue.

"About a mile northeast of here. The road crosses the one you came in on—you can't miss it."

"Thank you so much for the directions," Joanna said, turning to leave.

"If I might just leave you with a bit of advice, before you go, dearie," the woman said, following her to the doorway. Then she motioned Joanna closer and lowered her voice again. "I suggest you keep all this about your grandmother, well . . . to yourself for a spell—at least till you know something for certain."

"But . . . why?"

"Folks are a mite touchy these days. Since the laird's death, you know. The old town's changing. New people coming in. Important folks from London, even the States. You're not the first. No. I'd just not stir anything up unnecessarily."

"That's not my intention. But how will I find anything out unless I ask questions?"

Joanna stopped. Suddenly her grandmother's words raced through her mind.

She turned and looked at Miss Sinclair standing at the door, then smiled. "Thank you, Miss Sinclair, for your advice. I'll try to do what you say. I know you mean well for me."

"Folks has to do what they have to do," she replied. "But take it from me. 'Tis best you walk warily for a while. And if you do make it up to the House on the hill, you'll be seeing old Walter Innes. He's the factor. Bit of a grouch at first. But he means no harm. He'll help you out."

11 / The House_____

After leaving the main road into town, the approach to the estate wound its way through a moderately wooded, hilly country for perhaps three-quarters of a mile. Joanna crossed a stream on a rickety little wooden bridge, then came among some small hills covered with larches. Other hills displayed cultivated crops, and still others bore only bright yellow broom and the wiry heather shrubs which now held in secret their purple flame, waiting for the outburst of autumn. The avenue had been well-maintained and lacked the deep swampy ruts and broken stones of the road she had traveled with MacDuff.

Joanna strode down the middle of the road, sucking in the warm pure air and taking in the lovely sights. Dwarfed oak or mountain ash or silver birch occasionally extended down to the edge of the road. Then the trees gave way to green fields, fenced with walls of earth or stones overgrown with moss, stretching away on both sides, dotted with grazing black and white cattle.

With no sign of human life, the solitude at length began to grow eerie; Joanna began to wonder if she had mistaken Miss Sinclair's directions and taken a wrong turn. But just as she was about to reverse her course, the road turned sharply and a towering gray castle suddenly loomed in front of her. Caught off guard, Joanna realized that the imposing structure had been shielded from view by the particular approach taken by the road winding its way through a tight grove of trees. The still, sullen place was surrounded by woods, young and ancient firs interspersed with beeches.

A great iron gate stretched across the road before her, from which extended a thick, ten-foot-high hedge in both directions. Through the iron bars she saw a cobblestone courtyard immediately in front of the house. In the center stood a fountain with a rearing horse at the center, whose open mouth—presumably intended to greet guests with an impressive spray of water into the air—now stood empty and dry as a silent reminder that death had taken the head of the Duncan clan.

Joanna wavered a few moments before summoning the courage to lift the heavy iron latch of the gate, which appeared to be unlocked. She could not shake the feeling that she was an unwelcome interloper.

The latch creaked as she moved it upward in its unoiled slot. With a slight shove the gate swung open and Joanna stepped inside. Her steps were timorous as she walked toward the great carved door of the house. The place seemed possessed of another time, another world in which she had no part. She tried to conjure up visions in her mind of automobiles and factories to remind herself that this was indeed the twentieth century. But she felt like Alice entering some ethereal, fairy-tale realm.

A brass bell hung on one side of the door with a rope dangling from its center. Joanna reached up, hesitated momentarily, then pulled the rope.

The clanging of the bell echoed in her ears. She waited, scarcely breathing, wondering if perhaps some spectre from out of the past was going to open the door.

No one answered the bell.

She tugged at the rope again, but the sound so shattered the solitude that she stepped away from the door. Slowly she backed away, glanced around again, descended the three stone steps, and began walking timidly around the right side of the house in order to circumvent the ivy-covered stone walls.

After rounding a projection in one of the walls she came upon a grassy area extending from the house toward the hedge. It was so pleasant, like a miniature well-tended meadow, that for a moment she almost forgot the awesome castle on her other side. Neatly pruned azalea and rhododendron bushes bloomed with bright splashes of lavender and orange and vermilion. Rose bushes clung to the bleak stone of the house, and their red and pink buds heartened Joanna with a spirit of newness and hope.

In the distance beyond the lawn she spied a structure detached from the house, constructed of stone and wood. She continued walking toward it, wondering if she might find someone there. However, before she was halfway toward it, some movement among the roses caught her attention out of the corner of her eye. She turned sharply to see a man standing less than twenty feet from her. She had not noticed him because he had been kneeling down among the bushes. He was an elderly man, by appearances well into his sixties.

"Hello," she called. "Are you Mr. Innes?"

For a moment he did not reply, just stared toward her with a strange intensity in his eyes, as if he were trying to bring her into focus.

At length his voice uttered a single word. "No." The sound was toneless, as if it had come from far away.

After an awkward silence Joanna was about to walk closer, when from behind she heard the loud rumbling sound of an approaching vehicle, the first such sound she had heard since her arrival. The gardner's eyes rested on her with that same disconcerting hard gaze one instant more, then he turned and bounded away with more speed than she thought could be possible for a man of his years. But she had little time to ponder the brief encounter, for a new voice was already shouting out behind her.

"Ye dinna *look* like a common trespasser!"

Joanna spun around to see a tall, gaunt man, perhaps in his late forties, glaring at her as he climbed down from a plain, serviceable-looking automobile. Though her heart was pounding from his sharp words, her first thought was of Abraham Lincoln without a beard. The image was heightened by his dusty black frock coat and pin-stripe trousers. The man's small, close-set eyes were not altogether welcoming.

"Weel?" he said, coming fully out of the auto and stalking toward her. "Who give ye leave t' come aroun' here scarin' auld Dorey?"

"No one . . . I mean, I had no intention of trespassing," Joanna stammered, trying her best to conceal her uneasiness. "There didn't appear to be anyone about and . . . I came to visit, and—"

"Visit, ye say! Who would ye be comin' t' visit? I ken o' no invitations bein' sent out!"

"I wasn't invited. I only—"

"Then ye're trespassin'!"

"No—I mean . . . I didn't know I had to be invited. I only wanted to speak with the servants or the factor."

"What for?"

"I—I thought they might be able to tell me about the Duncans that used to live here. The laird's family. Or any other Duncans in the area."

"There are no others. An' the laird is dead," he returned, with more gruffness than sadness in his voice.

"I just thought—" Joanna began, then hesitated. She reflected on Olive Sinclair's parting words to her.

"I'd like to know more about him," she continued at length. "It's important."

"I'll be the judge o' that, mem. Jist what is yer business here, if I may ask?"

Joanna's only answer was silence. What did she dare say that would keep her from alienating everyone?

"Look here, mem," said the man, softening his tone almost imperceptibly, though not relaxing the force of his words. "I'm the factor here, an' anythin' that concerns Stonewycke concerns me. The place is mine t' take charge o'er, fer the time bein' at least."

"I understand," said Joanna, attempting a smile. Then she held out her hand. "I'm Joanna Matheson. I'm new here and I don't know the rules and customs yet."

"Name's Innes," replied the man, apparently touched by Joanna's admission yet unwilling to relax his tough stance and chilling gaze.

"If you're Mr. Innes, then perhaps you can help me. Miss Sinclair at the store recommended you."

"She did, did she?"

"You see, if you know the Duncan family, then . . ." Joanna hesitated, choosing her words carefully, "I'm trying to find out if there might be some common blood between these Duncans and myself. You see, my grandmother—"

"So that's it!" Innes' eyes narrowed as he bristled once more. "Come t' see if ye can grab a piece o' the pie, no doobt! Weel, it won't work, young lady!"

"No . . . that's not it at all, Mr. Innes," insisted Joanna. "I don't know anything about the estate . . . or the laird . . . or any of that." A lump rose in her throat.

"It's entirely personal," she added, her lower lip quivering.

"Noo, dinna cry, lass," said the factor. The tears that had begun to gleam in Joanna's eyes seemed to support the truth of her claim to the surly Scotsman, and his former gruffness dissolved by degrees into an apologetic tenderness.

"It's jist that I heard o' some lass come from America makin' all kind o' claims. So naturally I thought ye be jist another o' the vultures come t' lay yer hands on the spoils o' death."

Through her tears, Joanna said in a soft voice, "I haven't made any claims at all. I came here never having heard of the laird."

"I dinna mean t' cause ye grief. I jist knowed what I been hearin' an' when I seen ye, an' seen poor Dorey runnin' off like that, weel, I was naturally on my guard."

"But I mean no harm."

"Weel, I have a job t' do here. This muckle hoose 'tis kind o' like my responsibility noo. I already failed him once. An' failin' him at the end o' his life, I'm not goin' t' fail him in death. So ye see how I canna be lettin' jist anybody in. Maybe ye mean no harm, but even wi' the laird dead, I do have my orders, ye ken."

Joanna dried her tears, sniffed, and said, "Can you tell me about the laird's family? I only want to know—"

"Maybe I can, maybe I canna. 'Tis best ye go t' Mr. Sercombe first. If he gives ye leave . . ."

"Mr. Sercombe? Who is that?"

"Palmer Sercombe. He's the executor o' the Duncan estate. Been the family's solicitor for years. He'd be able t' tell ye more'n anyone. His office is in toon, only two doors from the store."

Indicating her appreciation Joanna began to walk away. Before she had gone three or four paces, Innes called to her:

"Would ye like a ride back into toon?" he offered. "I'm a wee bit unhandy wi' the motor car. The laird brought the contraption from Glasgow. But I reckon I'll get ye there."

"Thank you, Mr. Innes," returned Joanna. "But the walk will be nice. I enjoyed myself on the way out and have nothing else to do this afternoon."

She turned and gave one more parting look upon the great house. Suddenly her eyes were diverted to a small tower, high on the north side. At the window a lean figure stood gazing out. But the moment Joanna's eyes turned toward him, the form vanished inside. She continued to stare in the same direction, but no one reappeared. Finally she turned and continued on. She did not look back again.

Walter Innes raised a bony hand to his chin as he watched her until she was out of sight. "An interesting pass this'll be," he muttered to himself; then he strode back to the automobile, climbed in, ground it into gear, and drove in the direction of the stone outbuilding which was, in fact, the stable. Still mumbling, he parked the car in front of the building, a symbol of the modern industrial age strangely out of place so near an ancient castle.

The stalls needed mucking out, but he couldn't do that in his Sunday best. Instead, he dug a pail of oats from a burlap sack and carried it to the stall which held the only horse in the stables.

"Here ye go, lad."

He dumped the oats into the trough.

"The laird said ye was always t' have the best—nothin' but the best for his Flame Dance." The factor's voice caught momentarily.

"Weel, 'tis the least I can do now," he went on, "takin' good care o' ye—so ye'll hae all the oats ye can eat."

The great roan stallion snorted and stamped his hoof in anticipation. Innes wiped a hand across a damp eye.

"Yer in sore need o' exercise, lad, but I canna help ye there, stubborn beast that ye are."

Innes patted the horse's nose and for a moment the animal's savage eyes seemed to soften.

By the time Joanna reached the main road, her feet were throbbing. Beautiful though the countryside was, if she continued such traipsing about, she was going to need either different shoes or tougher feet!

She was relieved to find the streets of Port Strathy empty. She had had enough of the place for one day. All she wanted to do was go to her room and rest, and perhaps read one of the books she had brought along with her.

But just as her foot touched the threshold, Mrs. Cobden's cheerful voice rang out.

"Back at last," she said. "Ye missed tea, but I'd be glad t' fix ye somethin'. The biscuits are warm an' there's still some broth on the stove."

"I think I'd rather just go upstairs and rest awhile, Mrs. Cobden. But thank you."

"My Sandy said ye were goin' oot t' the Hoose."

"Yes, I did."

"Did ye talk wi' anyone?"

"I saw Mr. Innes, who was nice enough, and there was an old man named Dorey, who didn't talk much at all."

"Ah," the innkeeper's wife intoned, nodding her head knowingly. "Too bad ye ran int' him—noo, there's a strange one."

"Who is he?"

"The gardener—leastways he's done up the grounds real bonny since he's been there. Even come in t' the toon once or twice an' got most o' the folks plantin' flower gardens. But, weel . . . he sort o' gives a body the shivers t' talk personal like wi' him."

"What's wrong with him?"

"Who can say? Jist leanin' a bit t' port, as the fishers say."

She chuckled at her wit.

"Been like that ever since I can remember, an' we been here near twenty-five years. He's been oot t' the castle since then an' weel before, from what I hear. But I can see ye're tired an' so I dinna want t' bother ye no further. Would ye be wantin' me t' call ye fer dinner?"

"Yes, thank you. I'd like that."

Joanna continued up the stairs to her room. She headed right for the bed, took off her shoes, and lay back on the soft feather mattress. Why had she even bothered to come? She was never going to find out anything. If this had all been for naught she might as well find out quickly and set about to find some means to get back to the States.

She sighed heavily and all at once the face of Jason Channing filled her mind.

Maybe she should have gone to London after all. This trip to Scotland wasn't working out. There was no family here. Only people with something they didn't want spoiled, whispering words behind her back.

At least Jason would have been able to get her back home. But now here she was stuck in the far north of Scotland!

Unconsciously Joanna's hand sought her purse, and her fingers felt for the documents she had kept carefully with her since discovering them in her grandmother's secretary. Along with the music box, the locket, the linen embroidery, and a few photos, she had brought these momentos with her, as her only solid reminder of the past she was seeking to uncover.

Perhaps in these papers lay the place to start. Instead of asking questions and making a nuisance of herself it would be best simply to show someone the documents and ask what they meant.

This Palmer Sercombe, a lawyer of some sort, she gathered, would be a likely place to begin. She had seen his office on her way back from Stonewycke, just as Walter Innes had described it. The words *Mr. Palmer Sercombe, esq., Solicitor* were painted on the window in precise black script. Venetian blinds on the window had been closed so she had been able to see nothing inside. The Duncan family attorney would surely be able to tell her about the documents and perhaps even about her grandmother. It would be good to get everything settled once and for all.

She would visit him first thing the following morning.

12 / Palmer Sercombe

Palmer Sercombe shuffled briskly through the aged papers. One bushy black eyebrow was cocked slightly.

"These are your grandmother's, you say?"

Joanna nodded.

"I found them among her things after her accident."

"Yes . . . I see." He drew the words out thoughtfully. "They do appear to be genuine."

He continued perusing the documents. "What did you say your grandmother's name is?"

"Margaret . . . Margaret Duncan."

"Hmm," he responded, more to himself than to Joanna. He was clearly deep in thought.

The office in which Joanna found herself—surrounded with rich, dark walnut, plush red velvets and china lamps, with a fine Persian rug covering the floor—stood in stark contrast to the rough fishing village she had thus far seen. But no less a contrast was the eloquent, impeccably dressed lawyer himself. His thin, pale lips articulated almost perfect English with scarcely a trace of the Scottish brogue her ears had already grown accustomed to. The eyebrows and lips were perhaps the only notable features on his rather unexpressive clean-shaven face. His countenance conveyed no warmth or friendliness, neither antagonism nor villany. It remained utterly devoid of feeling. Either Palmer Sercombe was a totally impassive man or he was exercising great restraint in Joanna's presence to conceal his emotions. But for whatever reason, Joanna was growing more convinced by the moment that she could learn little from his expressionless countenance.

"You say your grandmother went to America when she was a girl?" he asked at last.

"Yes."

"But you have no proof—er—documents indicating her parentage?"

"No. She spoke very little of her past. I was hoping maybe you'd be able to tell me something . . . from these papers."

"Well, Miss Matheson, these documents—if they indeed are genuine—"

"What are you saying, that they may not be?"

"Not at all, I am merely posing the question in its broadest terms. As I said, these documents really tell us very little. Now you are certain your grandmother's name is Duncan?"

"I . . . I never actually saw her birth certificate if that's what you mean, but I—"

"I see," interrupted the lawyer, "and you say you are not absolutely certain her birthplace was Port Strathy?"

"Again," said Joanna, growing uncomfortable with the challenging direction of Sercombe's questions, "I know nothing for *certain*. I have nothing to go on but my grandmother's last words . . . and these papers. She spoke of the family and about Strathy and the house."

"What exactly did she say about the family and the house?" asked Sercombe leaning closer and revealing a deep furrow in his brow.

"Well, nothing, actually. She just used those words—the *family* . . . the *house*."

"She didn't specifically identify either?"

"Not exactly . . . no."

"Ah . . . I see," he said, leaning back once more in his chair and appearing to relax somewhat. "So we don't actually know if she—as a Duncan—came from the laird's branch of the family, or from Port Strathy, or what. For all we *know*, these documents—"

"But, Mr. Sercombe," insisted Joanna, "surely you can see that all the signs indicate that—"

"I admit, Miss Matheson, that on the surface things look rather, shall we say, intriguing as to the possible connection between your grandmother and the laird's family, the Port Strathy Duncans that is. But when we—I'm speaking of lawyers, of course—when we settle the affairs of an estate, we have to have proof of these things, solid, documented proof."

"But it's not the estate I'm so much concerned with," said Joanna. "I simply want to know who my grandmother is, where she came from, if there are any living relatives still here."

"Of course, of course," he replied with the hint of a grin.

"Have you never heard of my grandmother . . . of a Margaret Duncan?"

"It was so long ago, my dear."

"But if you've been the family lawyer for some time, surely someone would have referred to her, at some time."

"I've been with the family only some fifteen years, Miss Matheson. How old did you say she is?"

"In her early sixties. Surely there must be someone still in the area who might have known her, or known of her."

"I am well acquainted with all the families around here and I doubt—"

"There must be any number of townspeople sixty-five or seventy or older who would remember what happened, especially if it involved a family so important as—"

"My dear," interrupted the lawyer in soothing tones, and rising from his seat, "I'm afraid this may be little more than a wild goose chase for you. I'm sorry you have gone to so much trouble and expense, but these papers really say very little—and then, too, we have no way of knowing how your grandmother came by them."

"You're not implying—" began Joanna, growing uncomfortable with Sercombe's insinuations.

"No, my dear, I'm not implying anything. I wouldn't think of casting suspicions on your grandmother. It may have been someone else. The point remains that the documents, knowing no more than we do about their origins, raise more questions than they answer."

"Well, they must say something," said Joanna, biting a quivering lip. She wasn't about to lose control of herself in front of this man. "As a lawyer, could you at least interpret them for me? I want to know if there's anything for me to pursue, if I'm heading in the right direction. All I want to know is if I have family here—is that asking too much?"

Sercombe had made his way slowly around his huge desk and approached Joanna in a manner indicating his gracious attempt to show her to the door, responding to her last question even as he did so: "As I have said, Miss Matheson, these papers would offer little help in that direction."

"Surely there must be someone—"

"Alastair Duncan was the last of his line. Of course, Duncan is a very common name here in Scotland. There would be literally thousands with that surname."

"But I heard her say the word Strathy."

Sercombe nodded his head sympathetically.

"It would be impossible to contact everyone with that name in other localities!" Joanna said, her voice nearly breaking with emotion.

"I'm sorry I can't offer more encouragement."

At length Joanna rose from her chair. "These are all I have to go on then," she said, reaching for the papers the lawyer still clutched in his hands. He made no move to yield them, appearing instead to withdraw almost imperceptibly from her.

An awkward pause followed momentarily, until he answered, "Perhaps I should hold on to them awhile . . . for safekeeping."

"I assumed they were essentially worthless," said Joanna, eyeing him questioningly.

"Of course they represent no monetary value," he said, "as historical or antique documents, but I recognize the sentimental value they possess . . . for you, that is, and I wouldn't want anything to happen to them."

"Is thievery a serious problem around here?" asked Joanna with the slightest hint of sarcasm in her voice.

"No, of course not," Sercombe assured, "but there is the poverty which cannot be ignored. And well, we must face it—poverty can drive men to do anything."

"And greed?" suggested Joanna.

"Yes . . . of course, that too. All the more reason it might be best for me—"

"Still, I don't like to part with them," insisted Joanna, stepping forward once more and reaching her hand toward the papers.

Again Sercombe retreated a half step. "Then, too . . . it may give me a chance to have a closer look at them."

"From what you said I assumed you were certain—"

"You never know," he interjected. "I may have the opportunity to speak with someone who is more familiar with this sort of thing." His impassive exterior could not hide his reluctance to yield them.

"Nevertheless," she found herself saying, "I do want to keep them myself for a while longer."

She held out her hand, this time with more certainty, and at length the lawyer relinquished them. "Of course, of course . . . if you insist so strongly on it I have no objection." He shifted uncomfortably and glanced from Joanna's face to her hand holding the ancient documents.

Replacing the papers in her bag, Joanna left the office and turned toward the inn. Just now she did not feel like returning to her room, or enduring the silent, staring faces of the townspeople. She simply wanted to be alone . . . to think . . . to decide what to do. Without consciously framing a decision, she found her path leading toward the sea.

Her mind was filled with only one thought—her grandmother. *Is it my destiny to fail everyone who loves me?* she wondered.

Her own life had been traded for her mother's; how many times had the pangs of guilt caused her to wish she could have reversed that process! How gladly she would have died twenty-one years ago in order that her mother could have lived. Then everyone would have been happy.

But instead she had come into the world. She had lived . . . her mother had died . . . and grief had been the result. She had killed her mother, she had failed her father, and now it seemed she could not even honor the last request of her grandmother. Was she destined to fail her too?

Oh, Grandma, I wanted so badly to do this—for you; for once in my life to do something for someone else! But everyone is determined to block me and I'm just not strong enough to know what to do.

I ought to just demand that those people tell me something!

But, she realized with a sigh, *I won't. I'll probably give in under the pressure rather than push it.*

She thought of Jason Channing. His presence had overpowered her, too. Whatever her resolve had been when alone, once his eyes fell upon her she became her fainthearted self again. And in many ways Palmer Sercombe had the same effect on her. Would she be able to stand her ground against him?

Joanna made her way slowly toward the sea and then westward along the beach. She avoided the harbor where a group of fishermen were tending their boats. For the present she had nearly had enough of this town and its people.

She found she had to negotiate some distance of rather rocky terrain before gaining the wide expanse of flat sand which she sought. Once her foot slipped, twisting her ankle. She let out a little cry, but the pain only increased her frustration. She would be glad to leave this place! It had been a mistake to come.

When at last she was rewarded with the feel of soft sand beneath her feet, Joanna removed her shoes and wiggled her toes in the warmth of it. Standing for a moment, she stood staring about her. Then she took a few tentative steps. The sand was warm in the sunlight, comforting, inviting. Throwing down her shoes, Joanna ran toward the water's edge where six-inch-high waves lapped gently against the sand. Cool, salty water splashed against her feet and soaked the fringes of her dress. She stopped, walked a few feet farther, then turned and ran back onto the beach, water splashing about her feet in all directions. The sea could be a great healer. Her cares receded in the joyous ebb and flow of the foamy tide.

Joanna reached down, scooped up a handful of water, and sent it flying into the sunlight. The water receded and she ran toward the beach, then turned and followed the water's edge, farther away from the town, making a straight row of footprints in the wet sand. She stopped and turned, watching the incoming water fill the impressions and gradually erase them. Unconsciously her toe spelled the name D-U-N-C-A-N in the sand. Then another silent wave rippled in, washing the letters away. Did the motion of the seas represent her efforts to discover her heritage? Were her grandmother's past and her desperate request destined to disappear into the silent vaults of history even as these waves obliterated any memory of the footprints she had made but a few moments earlier?

She ran farther down the sand, then stopped and looked toward the vastness of the ocean to the north. On the right, Port Strathy's harbor and buildings faded into the distance. An urge overcame her to throw caution to the wind and rush headlong into the oncoming waves. Summoning her courage she held the bottom of her dress above her knees and ran a few steps. But when the water reached her knees, the boldness disappeared and she bolted for the safety of the shore.

Suddenly the unwelcome sound of a man's laughter interrupted her childlike play.

"If ye be intendin' t' have a swim in oor icy water, mem, I'm afraid ye'll spoil such a bonnie dress as ye be wearin'." His words were followed by another chuckle, this time more subdued.

Standing some fifty feet up the beach, on the gradual rise of a small dune, was a man dressed in worn overalls and faded blue cotton workshirt. That he was broad-shouldered she could see immediately, but Joanna could not judge his height because of his vantage point on the dune above her. He appeared to be tall. Straw-colored hair was blown by the wind, though he did not appear to be the type who would worry about keeping it combed under calmer circumstances. His face, for all its roughness, bore a youthful look, beaming in good-natured laughter. He looked no more than twenty or twenty-two, but was in reality twenty-seven.

Crimson crept into Joanna's cheeks.

Her first thought was to ignore him. She was in no mood today to pass the time of day with a stranger who seemed intent on making sport of her.

"Please," he went on, seeing her silently standing still at the water's edge, "don't stop yer fun on my account. I dinna mean t' interrupt ye, mem."

His tone and her downcast spirits filled her with indignation.

"I think I've entertained you enough!" she snapped, angry and embarrassed.

"I'm sorry. 'Twas rude o' me not t' let ye know I was there. But truthfully, mem, I only jist this second came over the rise o' the dune here an' saw ye. An' ye was havin' such a wonderful time in the water."

His laughter faded but there remained a twinkle in his azure eyes. That he appeared to be enjoying this made it all the more exasperating.

"How dare you!" said Joanna with growing perturbation. "Why aren't you out fishing or mending your nets with the others?"

"Deed, I am sorry, mem," he said, chuckling again but trying to conceal it, "but ye don't understand—"

"What makes you think you have the right?"

"I'm no fisherman, mem. I was only makin' my way back t' the town. I beg yer pardon again," he said, but his tone conveyed that her pardon meant little to him. He clearly did not take the encounter with the seriousness it carried to Joanna. He then turned and disappeared on the other side of the dune as quickly as he had come.

Joanna stood stock-still, staring after him a full minute after he was gone from her view.

Then, the earlier spell of the morning gone, she gathered up her shoes and bag and walked back to Port Strathy in somber uncertainty over her future.

13 / Foul Play

Joanna stared in disbelief.

The whole room had been torn apart—ransacked!

She blinked back the tears. The mess she could clean up, but why would someone do this to *her*? Why was she so unwelcome?

"How can we make this up t' ye?" exclaimed Mrs. Cobden, wringing her hands together.

"We've never had anythin' like this happen before," said her husband. " 'Tis a disgrace! Ye can be certain the magistrate'll hear o' it!"

Joanna climbed over the upturned mattress and picked up a few of the belongings which had been scattered from her suitcases. Clothes were strewn about the floor, her bags had been recklessly emptied, the drawers in the dresser were pulled out, the bed was in disarray, and the clothes she'd hung in the closet lay scattered about the room.

"Can ye tell if anythin' has been taken?" asked Sandy.

"I had nothing of value," Joanna replied.

Nothing of value, she thought, grasping her purse which still hung from her shoulder. Fortunately she had her only possessions of value with her. Apparently the burglars hadn't considered her grandmother's music box valuable enough to take, for it sat undisturbed on the dressing table. She reached out and picked it up, winding the silver key, then replacing it, relieved in mind once again just to hear the delicate strains of the lullaby.

"Let me fix ye a nice hot cup o' tea," said Mrs. Cobden, placing a tender arm about Joanna. "I'll help ye clean all this up later."

Reluctant to face the ominous task of putting the room back in order, Joanna accepted the offer and descended the stairs to the common room. She found a seat while Mr. and Mrs. Cobden went into the kitchen to prepare the tea. There were no other guests.

Joanna sank deep into thought, lamenting this latest turn of events.

After some moments her consciousness woke to words drifting out from the kitchen, whisperings clearly not intended for her ears but which had grown loud enough for her to make out.

". . . not her fault . . . she doesn't know . . ."

". . . more'n she's lettin' on . . ."

"She's just an innocent lass."

"Serves her right, that's all I'm sayin'." It was Sandy Cobden's deep bass voice.

"What a thing to say!" came Mrs. Cobden's voice, now raised above a whisper.

"I'm not sayin' I think it's right t' go tearin' her room apart. I can understan' the poor lass's plight. I'm jist sayin' that's what comes o' comin' into a place an' stirrin' up trouble."

"She's caused no trouble, an' ye know it, Sandy. She's oor guest!"

"I know, woman. An' I like the child," returned Sandy. "But I venture even ye yerself'll be singin' a different tune if she takes the laird's money an' the sale o' the land falls through."

"She wouldn't do such a thing!"

"And why not, I ask ye? This town means nothin' t' her. She can jist turn around an' sail back home t' the States. An' I don't have t' tell ye what the new harbor would mean t' us. If that sale falls through, it's not goin' t' do oor inn any good, an' that's God's truth."

"Keep yer voice down, Sandy!"

But the innkeeper's wife need hardly have worried. Long before their conversation had reached this stage they had been left alone in their inn. When they reentered the Common Room with preparations for Joanna's tea, their guest was nowhere to be seen.

Joanna left the inn to continue what she had done for most of the day—wandering about the town, thinking, pondering, weighing what to do. She had had very little to eat all day, and had considered walking again out to the Duncan House but decided against it. That she had stirred up speculation in this little fishing village could hardly be doubted. She hadn't intended it when she came. But it seemed her grandmother's very name was a goad to the people who had for so long lived under the Duncan hand.

Maybe all this was what came of poking in where you weren't invited. More and more she felt she didn't belong in Port Strathy. But she didn't belong in London with Jason either, or in Chicago, or even in Denver if her grandmother died.

Somehow she had hoped here it might be different, that . . . but no, it was no use. Tomorrow she would spend what little money she had left to book passage back to London. She still had Jason's card. She would look him up and ask him to help her get back to the States. Even if she had to borrow the money at interest, he would help her. She just hoped he didn't expect too much in return.

Immediately Joanna felt a sense of relief.

Having decided what to do removed the burden of uncertainty. She would put her things in order tonight. Then in the morning she would make arrangements to leave at the soonest possible moment.

Joanna wandered westward from the town. The road ran parallel with the shore but lay removed from it by some hundred or two hundred yards, separated from the water by a huge dune. Though she could not see them, Joanna could hear the crashing of waves, growing louder now with the incoming tide. They beat against the large rocky base of a cliff-like precipice which rose at the westerly end of the broad sandy beach about a mile from the town's sheltered harbor. Likewise, the road along which Joanna walked rose gradually until it, too, bordered the edge of a great cliff which overlooked the beach, the harbor, and tiny Port Strathy in the distance.

Breathing hard from the climb, Joanna stopped and looked behind her. The pink and yellow glow of the early summer's "gloamin' " took her breath away.

"It's beautiful!" she said softly to herself.

Away below her the sea stretched out in a dull evening blue-gray. Gulls squawked as they flew swiftly along the surface of the water hoping for an easy catch. Silent-sailed fishing boats drifted leisurely out of the harbor for the night at sea.

Joanna then began the walk back down the road to town for what she hoped might be her last night in Port Strathy. If only she could be lucky enough to find some means of transport tomorrow—either overland as she had come, or on a vessel bound around the northeastern head of the country toward Fenwick, Peterhead, or at best Aberdeen. By the time Joanna reached the first cottages at the town's edge, it was past nine o'clock and the sky had grown as dark as it intended to get, a deep bluish gray with fringes of the endless pink sunset in the west. As the night progressed, the light would imperceptibly shift around to the east and eventually give way to a brilliant sunrise.

Port Strathy was closed tight.

Its fisher families were either in their homes or beds by this hour, or their men toiling out on the water. Joanna saw no living soul as she walked through the streets toward the intersection which would lead her back to the Cobden's inn. A quarter moon had risen from the horizon in the direction of Stonewycke and added to the silent, eerie enchantment of the solitary evening. Again Jason Channing came to her mind. It would be a lovely night for a walk through these quaint streets with him.

She wondered if he took moonlight strolls. Perhaps, if things fell right, within a week she might find out for herself.

Well, regardless . . . she had no one to walk with tonight—and no where to go but back to the inn where her room, still in shambles, awaited her corrective hand. She passed Miss Sinclair's store, now darkened and still. She had liked Olive Sinclair. Out of all the people she had met, she would be one Joanna would miss. She would liked to have gotten to know her better. And MacDuff, whom she would probably not see again.

Joanna stepped down off the wooden walkway to cross an alley. The inn lay only about fifty yards in front of her, yet already appeared darkened for the evening. The only sign of life lay in the thin wisp of smoke reaching from the chimney straight into the windless night.

Suddenly a hand shot into her midsection!

She felt another rough hand close over her mouth as she struggled to free herself.

In the confusion she could not make out the features of the man who had been waiting in the shadows of the alley, hidden behind the corner of the building. The moment she stepped down onto the dirt of the street, he pounced.

"Ye won't git hurt if ye jist gi' me yer purse," hissed the assailant, holding her fast.

She felt the man tug at the strap of her purse. Unable to scream for help, she kicked at him. Finally, fighting frantically, she partially freed her mouth.

"Help!" Even as she shrieked, a strong, fleshy hand clamped down once more over her mouth. Clinging desperately to her purse, she worked her teeth into position, then bit down into the hand with as much force as her jaw could summon.

"Ow!" hollered the attacker. "Ye bloody shrew! Take that, ye good fer nothin'!" he cursed at Joanna, and he allowed his grasp on her to slacken just enough to punish her with a fierce slap across the face.

The blow sent her reeling backwards, temporarily free.

Just then a voice from behind called out: "Hey! what's goin' on there?"

The attacker swore in frustration, then darted down the alley and disappeared as quickly as he had come.

Joanna tried to turn toward the voice that had frightened him away, but everything seemed to whirl around her and she felt herself becoming faint. She struggled to retain consciousness, but the blow had been a hard one.

Her knees buckled, her head spun, and the hurriedly approaching footsteps faded into hazy nothingness.

She felt she was falling forever in a slow motion as the night around her grew steadily blacker.

Then she knew no more.

14 / Friends

A flickering amber glow first touched Joanna's senses.

Where was she . . . what had happened? If only she could remember!

She struggled to rise but found the effort too taxing and lay down again. Her bewildered mind remained in a foggy blur as she sank back into the bed.

Why did her head hurt so?

Wakefulness crept gradually back into her confused brain. The pain in her right cheek grew more severe. She reached toward her head, and the moment her hand touched her face she realized the throbbing came from her hot swollen jaw. Then first the memory of the attack on the street returned.

Joanna twisted her head slightly to the left.

Even her neck muscles were sore. Her whole head felt ready to explode. From her vantage point in a corner of a dimly lit room, she saw the hearth opposite her, from which the glow and warmth radiated. The fire was a small one but had been burning for some time, and its fiery coals emitted a pleasing heat. She was lying on the soft cushions of a drab brown couch.

As the haze began to lift, Joanna took in the rest of the room in which she lay. Faded chintz curtains hung from the windows. A worn Persian rug lay before the hearth. The furnishings were Victorian, several polished oak pieces no less beautiful in that they had clearly been chosen for their practical and functional value. She immediately thought of Palmer Sercombe's office and an involuntary chill ran through her. Momentarily she wondered if that was where she now lay. Yet she quickly realized that here the trappings of refinement had seen better days. Unlike the lawyer's office, this room possessed an air of charm and simplicity if it lacked elegance, if its beauty were perhaps more humble.

To take all this in took scarcely a moment before Joanna's attention was drawn away by soft, yet heated, conversation in the background.

"Jist let me get me hands on the filthy bla'gard!" came a masculine voice. "They may be auld, but they're hard-workin' hands, an' strong!" Though its owner kept his tone subdued, the voice seethed with passion.

"The lass'll be fine, Nathaniel," came another, a voice Joanna recognized but couldn't place.

"But the rascal must be punished, Olive. Ye must see it!"

"You know what the Lord says . . . vengeance is mine." Now she remembered; the voice belonged to Olive Sinclair.

"But sometimes the Lord's wantin' jist a wee bit o' help from His people doon here, ye ken."

"You've already helped Him plenty by drivin' him off and bringin' the poor lass here," said Miss Sinclair. "Don't be making it worse by runnin' off and doing somethin' foolish."

"Ah, but it makes the blood in my auld Highland veins boil!"

"The Lord'll not let the scoundrel go unrewarded, that you can count on, Nathaniel," said Miss Sinclair, gently moderating his anger by degrees.

Just then Joanna's stirring attracted the attention of her hostess.

"Well, dearie, are you awake? You just lie still a while longer. How's the head? You took quite a blow, from the looks of it."

Joanna looked toward the shopkeeper and attempted a smile. "I . . . I'm fine—I think. My head does hurt awfully . . ." She glanced in the direction of the other face, now gazing silently on her. He appeared friendly enough. "Have I been here long?" Joanna asked.

"Nathaniel brought you in only a few minutes ago."

The man with Olive Sinclair was large framed, in his fifties Joanna guessed from his sparse graying hair. His deep-set, small brown eyes were framed with crow's feet, the inevitable reward of long years of hard work outdoors. The denim trousers showed signs of heavy wear and appeared a little large. The plaid work shirt was a faded red.

"Then it was you," Joanna said, "who came to my aid?"

"Weel, mem, I dinna do much," he replied. "That no good, cowardly brute jist ran off as soon as he heard an honest voice."

"And it's a good thing for you, Nathaniel Cuttahay, that he did," put in Miss Sinclair with a touch of irony.

"Hoot, mem!" exclaimed the man with animation, "I only wish I could ha' caught 'em. But at the time I was tryin' to keep this young lassie's head from fallin' against the street."

"I'm indebted to you," Joanna said. "I don't know what I would have done—"

Her hand suddenly jerked to her side as her face blanched. "My purse!" she cried. "He didn't get my purse—?"

"Don't fret, lass. It's right here." Miss Sinclair picked up the bag from the table where it lay and handed it to her. Joanna grabbed it hastily and plunged her hand inside. Everything was where she had left it. She breathed a sigh of relief.

"He was after my purse," Joanna explained.

"The thievin' scroundrel!" exclaimed Mr. Cuttahay in a fresh outburst of Scottish anger. "The idea o' tryin' t' rob a visitor t' oor toon!"

"I doubt they were after my money," said Joanna. "I have precious little left."

"You must have a low opinion of our town," said Miss Sinclair, bringing Joanna a hot cup of tea as she sat up on the couch. "Why don't you just sit there a spell and relax and sip this good strong tea. It'll bring the life back into you."

"I'm afraid there's nothing wrong with your town," said Joanna at length. "I've brought it all on myself. I've caused offense from the very moment I arrived."

Joanna closed her eyes and took a swallow of tea. It felt good warming her deep within.

"But . . . excuse me," said Miss Sinclair as if suddenly waking from a reverie. "I've been amiss in my introductions. Joanna, this is Nathaniel Cuttahay . . . Nathaniel, meet Joanna Matheson from the United States."

Joanna smiled.

"Pleased t' make yer acquaintance," said Mr. Cuttahay, "although a formal how-do-ye-do hardly seems necessary after what we went through t'gether, eh?"

Miss Sinclair laughed. "Right you are there, Nathaniel!"

"But I dinna understand how ye could be thinkin' ye brought yer troubles on yersel'—a harmless an' honest-lookin' lass ye seem t' me," Nathaniel added.

"I just meant maybe I had no right to come here, asking questions, trying to find out about the past."

"Joanna has come here hoping to find some of her grandmother's long-ago kinfolk," Miss Sinclair explained, directing herself to Nathaniel. "If indeed this was her grandmother's original home."

"I don't know what to think," said Joanna. "Earlier today my room at the inn was broken into and searched . . ."

She stopped and turned her head away, unable to continue while she composed herself.

" . . . I really think coming to Scotland was a mistake," she went on in a tremulous voice. "I was going to try to find passage to London tomorrow—"

"My dear," interrupted Miss Sinclair, "you must just try to rest for a few days. You're not up to traveling now. We'll have to find you someplace safer to stay though, and that's the truth."

" 'Tis jist a sore disgrace!" exclaimed Mr. Cuttahay. "Makes me ashamed t' call this toon my home . . . e'en though 'tis usually not such a bad place. But why should a body aroun' here care that ye be seekin' yer kin?''

"Joanna's grandmother was a Duncan," put in Miss Sinclair.

"Ye don't say? A Port Strathy Duncan."

"So I thought," said Joanna. Then she briefly told them of her grandmother's condition and last words. "But Mr. Sercombe thinks I'm on a wild goose chase," she finished with a sigh.

"What was her name?" asked Nathaniel.

"Margaret Duncan," Joanna answered.

"Lord preserve us!" exclaimed Nathaniel, and the color drained from his face.

"What is it, man?" asked Miss Sinclair in alarm. "You look like you just saw a ghost returning from the grave!"

"Maybe I have, Olive," he said, sinking deeply into the chair and shaking his head in disbelief. Then he shot a penetrating glance at Joanna and eyed her intently. "I jist canna believe it," he finally said at length. "I jist canna believe it!"

"Well, don't keep us in suspense, man!" demanded Miss Sinclair. "What's given you such a start from hearing the name? Come on, out with it!"

He hesitated, then drew a deep breath.

"Ye're new around here, Olive—what is't, twenty years since ye came here from Leeds? So ye wouldn't hae had cause t' hae heard o' Margaret Duncan. But time was, that was a name what caused quite a stir in these parts. 'Course I was but a wee lad myself so I dinna really ken much o' what happened."

"What do you mean, Mr. Cuttahay?" asked Joanna impatiently. "What about my grandmother . . . you didn't know her?"

"No, no. I was only eight or ten at the time."

"But you knew of her, is that it?"

"Everyone knew o' her . . . an' ye dinna ken hoo she came t' leave Scotland?"

"I know nothing about her past. She only made a few delirious references to Port Strathy before the coma. Please . . . tell me about it."

" 'Tis not a pretty tale, lass," he began. "An' as I said, I know but fragments o' the story. 'Twas so lang ago. Maybe she left for America because her heart was broken. Suddenly she was jist gone. No one in the toon knew why. 'Course, it was no secret that her father, the laird, an' her had a great falling oot o'er an ill-fated romance; her father was determined t' put a stop t' the affair. The scandal was kept quiet an' the next thing anyone knows Margaret is on her way t' America. Nothin' more were e'er heard o' her. What e'er it was atween Marg'ret an' her family, it must've been somethin' great for her t' walk away from her inheritance like she did an' turn her back on all that would hae been her's someday—she was the eldest o' the laird's children. The auld laird, that is."

"The laird that just died?" asked Joanna. "Who was he?"

"The auld laird's son; Marg'ret's younger brother Alastair."

Joanna sat stunned.

"So that's what everyone's so suspicious about," said Miss Sinclair. "Don't you see? They think Joanna's come to claim the estate."

"I never knew a thing about any of this," said Joanna with a numbed sigh. "I can't even get into the place."

"You had no luck at the big house up on the hill?" Miss Sinclair queried.

"None," Joanna replied. "I spoke briefly with the factor, but he said nothing of consequence; said he couldn't speak without permission from Mr. Sercombe. And when I went to him, he told me my papers were worthless."

"Papers?" asked Cuttahay with interest.

"Some documents I found among my grandmother's things after the accident."

"Do ye hae them with ye?"

"They're in my handbag," said Joanna. "I showed them to Mr. Sercombe early this morning. He said they didn't mean anything, but he did offer to have someone else examine them."

"Hmm . . ." drawled Nathaniel.

Joanna set her cup on the table and took up her purse and removed the brown envelope containing the documents. She then spread them out before her two new friends.

"They 'pear mighty important," said Nathaniel.

Olive Sinclair looked closely at them without saying a word, studying the details carefully. After a few moments she said, "Perhaps my own ignorance is deceiving me," she said, rubbing her chin thoughtfully. "But it doesn't look as though it would take much to interpret them— once you get past the archaic language and all. And that would be no obstacle for a lawyer."

"What do you make of them?" Joanna asked.

"This one looks like a surveyor's report . . . wouldn't you say so, Nathaniel?"

The man drew closer, looking over Miss Sinclair's shoulder, and at length nodded and mumbled an uncertain assent.

"You see there," went on Miss Sinclair with her finger pointing the way, "all these property lines and various distances, so many furlongs from such-and-such a line. And here's the starting point of it all—the

Firth of Lindow. That's the border of the laird's lands—where the River Lindow opens into the sea, some ways down the coast west of here. What this—this, Rossachs Kyle means, I don't know that one.''

" 'Tis gone now,'' put in Nathaniel. " 'Tis all covered wi' the sea. 'Twas a strait o' land some three miles east o' the harbor up the coast. In ancient days it was a harbor o' sorts, but its ownership was always in dispute wi' the laird o' the adjoinin' land east o' here. Finally the laird—''

"Which laird?'' Joanna asked. "I'm confused.''

"Talmud Ramsey, lass. He would o' been Marg'ret's grandfather, her mother's daddy. Anyway, he took legal possession o' it when he was laird. I suppose 'twas so important back then because it provided a natural line o' defense fer the toon.''

"And what happened to it?'' asked Miss Sinclair.

" 'Twas a muckle storm at sea, back in '60. Near destroyed the whole toon. The fierce tides that whole winter jist pulled doon that narrow spit right back int' the sea. Brought the inn doon that year too, if I remember aright. I wasna e'en five at the time, but old-timers talked aboot it fer years.''

"Well, maybe this surveyor's report was made to settle some dispute after that.''

"No, it couldn't have been,'' Joanna pointed out with growing interest. "Look at the date—1845.''

"That would be jist aroun' the time Atlanta Ramsey married James Duncan—that would be yer grandmother's parents, lass,'' said Nathaniel.

"James Duncan must have had the report made to confirm the extent of the property,'' said Miss Sinclair. "Marrying into the family like he did, and property lines being kind of uncertain, he probably wanted to be sure how much land he held.''

"Or how much his wife held,'' suggested Nathaniel. "Remember, James Duncan only married int' the Ramsey estate. Some said he was a sly ol' fox who only wanted t' get his hands on the land. An' o' coorse Atlanta was the only survivor o' the Ramsey name at the time.''

"Nevertheless,'' went on Miss Sinclair, "this other paper might even be of greater interest. Look here, Nathaniel. Can you make out any of this Old English?''

" 'Tis written in such a fancy script t' make it all the more illegible. I don't see why they dinna—''

"Never mind,'' interrupted Miss Sinclair, anxious to proceed with her investigation. "It seems to be a deed of some sort. Just look—'The lands heretofore known as Port Strathy . . .'—the ink is smeared there but that could be a reference to a survey report or some indication of boundaries. And then it says, ' . . . Ramsey and all legal heirs, by royal decree shall govern and possess . . . by the grace of King George III and his Almighty God . . . this 17th day of April, 1784 . . .' "

She stopped and exhaled a long sigh.

"What does it mean?" asked Joanna.

"Who can say for certain?" replied Miss Sinclair. "But if it was up to me to decide, I'd say this was the deed to the Ramsey estate—the Duncan estate now, that is."

"I should probably explain what you've told me to Mr. Sercombe," Joanna said. "Maybe if he took a closer look and I told him about—"

"Joanna," began Miss Sinclair, " 'tis not my habit to be speaking ill of another, especially as he's practically my neighbor. But if I were you, I'd say nothing more to him for a while. If he had anything to tell you, he'd have done it this morning."

"In any case," said Nathaniel, " 'tis far too late t' settle anythin' tonight. Letty will be worryin' hersel' o'er me by now."

"I'm sorry to have kept you so long," apologized Joanna, but before the words were scarcely out of her mouth both her newfound friends silenced anything further in that direction. "In any case," she added, "I must be getting back to the inn. I have to put my room in order and get some sleep. Then tomorrow I'll try to decide what to do about leaving."

"We'll have no more talk of you leaving town," insisted Miss Sinclair as she gave Joanna a friendly hug, almost smothering in its gentleness. "And your going back to the inn alone is not a good idea. Whoever went through your room—"

"Lass," broke in Nathaniel, "my Letty an' I hae a wee croft only aboot two miles south o' town. 'Tis far from fancy, but we've a spare room an' we'd consider it a great honor if ye'd bide a wee wi' us, leastways till yer rested or until some course o' action presents itsel'."

"I . . . I don't know," stammered Joanna as Miss Sinclair readily nodded her approval, "you hardly know me, and I don't want you to get into trouble from befriending me."

"Hoots, lass! It'll be best fer all concerned, gettin' ye oot o' town and away from the glare o' gawking eyes watchin' ye. Ye'd do the same fer me if I was a stranger, wouldn't ye now? An' ye know what the Lord says about bein' a stranger and takin' him in? No, lass, ye must come, I couldn't sleep myself fearin' tonight's incident might be repeated, an' me not nearby t' help."

The fire had burned low and the light in the room was now dim. The night was silent around them. Joanna gazed at her two companions across from her—Nathaniel's homely simple, brave face, and Miss Sinclair's stout, honest, true countenance.

"You don't know how much this means to me . . ." she said through tear-filled eyes. "Thank you both . . . so much."

Was their gentle compassion and goodness part of what she had come to Scotland seeking?

15 / A New Home

The meadow spread out before her like a blanket of rich green dotted with countless white and yellow daisies. In spots the grass reached as high as her knees as she made her way purposefully through it, plucking a bouquet of flowers as she went. Looking back, the Cuttahays' cottage had already faded into the distance and was just barely visible.

Joanna had awakened early. Lying on the straw mattress, she attempted to place where she was. But the sunlight streaming through the window, the homely sounds of Mrs. Cuttahay singing hymn after hymn in the kitchen, and the hazy memory of her ride home the night before in Nathaniel's wagon soon restored order to her brain. As did the pain in her jaw!

She lay quietly a few moments, listening to the rustic alto voice singing "Blessed assurance, Jesus is mine. . . ," and gradually a great peace stole over her.

Later that morning, after Nathaniel had returned to town for some of her things, Joanna remained at the farmhouse, trying to help Mrs. Cuttahay.

"Oh, I've only a wee bit left t' do, lass," the cheerful woman had said. "Ye jist rest an' dinna trouble yersel'." Letty Cuttahay was several inches shorter than Joanna and, as Nathaniel was apt to say, "nicely filled oot." Her brown hair, amply peppered with gray, was always braided and the braids neatly wrapped over the top of her head. Her small brown eyes seemed to twinkle constantly with merriment. This morning she was wearing a blue flowered cotton dress covered with a crisp white apron.

The house appeared immaculate, yet the energetic woman never stopped with her chores. "Ye've been through plenty, lass," she said. "Ye jist take yersel' easy." So Joanna sat on a small wooden stool while Mrs. Cuttahay peeled and cut up a pile of potatoes. She tossed them into the three-footed iron pot suspended by a heavy chain within the chimney of the fireplace, where they boiled and frothed in anticipation of midday dinner. It was not long before the older lady's unpretentious cheerfulness put Joanna completely at her ease.

They had only chatted briefly the previous night, but the reception could hardly have been more gracious. Letty Cuttahay's first reaction to her unexpected houseguest was a warm, welcoming hug; she blinked not an eye at having to ready a bed in their spare room at midnight.

Shortly before noon Letty said, "Why don't ye have a look aroun' the place? We'll be havin' some dinner as soon as Nathaniel gets back, an' ye'll be gettin' bored stayin' inside on such a bonny day."

Therefore Joanna had set out on a walk from the little cottage. Her destination was a small knoll she had spotted that morning from the kitchen window. It was hardly high enough even to be called a hill, but from it Joanna gained a wide view of the surrounding countryside. She could not see the town, but away eastward—where the terrain rose steadily—she thought she caught occasional glimpses of the sun reflecting off the towers of Stonewycke. Beyond to the north lay the glistening expanse of the sea. To the west, but out of sight, she knew from Nathaniel's description of the surrounding terrain, lay the River Lindow. A thin line of lush green trees lay off in the distance and Joanna wondered if they bordered the river as it wound to the sea. An afternoon's hike in that direction would be an adventure to undertake one day, she thought . . . if she was here that long.

I was going to make plans to return to London today, she thought suddenly. She had nearly forgotten.

Joanna looked again toward the outline of the great house. It could only be a couple of miles away, but it may as well have been in another world. Did the secrets of her grandmother's past lay hidden there? Should those secrets be left alone?

Joanna lay back in the grass, closed her eyes, and allowed the sun to bathe her in its fragrant summer warmth. How long she lay thus, half dozing, half daydreaming, she could not tell.

All at once she heard a great bounding, and something wet and scratchy brushed against her face. She opened her eyes in terror to find herself face to face with the largest, shaggiest sheepdog she had ever seen. He stared at her, tongue hanging out, eyes alive with the joy of being, when a sharp whistle sent him flying back down the hillside.

Joanna stood up and saw Nathaniel crossing the pasture toward her.

"Hello, lass," he called. "I'm afraid auld Reiver must hae disturbed ye. Hope he didna give ye too much a fricht—he's harmless enough, though."

"He is rather big!" laughed Joanna.

"The missus sent me oot after ye. She was wonderin' if ye'd be ready fer some dinner wi' us?"

"That sounds nice," Joanna answered, ". . . that is, if you don't mind?"

"Mind!" rejoined Nathaniel in something like disbelief. "Why, lass, ye're oor guest, practically family by now. Ye jist put all such thoughts oot o' yer head!''

Joanna smiled. As she descended the hill, Reiver ran toward her once again. She stooped down and ran her fingers through his shaggy mane, encircling his neck with a hug.

"I think he's already taken a special likin' t' ye," said Nathaniel.

Watching the dog dart off after a butterfly, then return to walk a few steps with her and Nathaniel, Joanna realized she felt more secure and at peace than she had in days.

"I stopped by the inn," said Nathaniel at length.

"Will everyone know where I am?"

"Won't matter much, I think," he replied. "I let it be known that ye were plannin' t' leave Port Strathy soon, t' see some o' the rest o' the country before returnin' t' the States. I didn't know yer plans fer certain, but maybe that'll take some o' the pressure off ye fer a while, if folks dinna think yer tryin' t' stir up trouble."

Dinner proved a pleasant occasion at the Cuttahay home. They sat down and Mr. Cuttahay offered thanks. "Oor Lord, we thank ye fer yer special care, an' especially fer bringin' young Joanna safely t' us. Lord, protect her an' give her guidance in these troubled times an' may she feel welcome in oor humble home as long as she like. And now, Lord, we thank ye fer the provision o' this food an' fer the roof over oor heads. We thank ye fer the life ye hae given us. Amen."

Touched by the man's words, Joanna looked up. Both husband and wife were smiling at her. She knew the words were no mere tokens but sprang from genuine love. Was there something in that prayer to explain what made these two people so special, what set them apart from so many others Joanna had known in her life? She recalled similar words and prayers from her childhood and youth. Her grandmother had spoken such things from the heart. Why hadn't she listened then as she was now?

The hearty oatcakes, which Mrs. Cuttahay referred to as bannocks, broth, boiled potatoes, and dried herring were served with pride and enjoyed with gusto. That life's simple pleasures of nourishing food, good company, and warm conversation could be surpassed by anything seemed impossible to Joanna at that moment. The Cuttahays spoke openly of everyday life in Port Strathy and plied Joanna with questions about America. When the meal ended, Nathaniel stood, stretched his long legs, then ambled toward his favorite chair. Sitting down, he lifted his legs to a three-legged wooden footstool and lit his favorite pipe.

"Jist time fer a wee smoke before I hae t' git t' work," he said.

The room fell silent for a few moments as the two women cleared away the dishes and Nathaniel puffed contentedly on his pipe.

"There was one thing I dinna tell ye aboot my trip t' town this mornin'," said Nathaniel after a moment. Joanna and Letty stopped their work and looked toward him expectantly. "Dinna ye say, lass," he continued, "that ye bit the hand o' that man last night?"

Joanna nodded.

"Weel, I saw Tom Forbes at the inn an' he was sportin' a fresh bandage on his hand."

"Oh, poor Tom," said Letty with dismay.

"I hate t' think o' it bein' him," Nathaniel went on. "But I'm afraid I couldna put it past him, either."

"An' after all that sweet Olive has tried t' do fer him too," Letty sighed.

"Sometimes the likes o' him are beyond help, Letty."

"Beyond oor help, maybe," answered his wife. "But not beyond His help who made him—so we mustn't give up on 'im, either. An' all this time I thought he was doin' so good, gettin' over his accident."

"He's been spendin' an uncommon amount o' time at the Bluster 'N Blow lately—I hear none o' the boats will hae him on."

"His poor family!" said Letty. "First thing tomorrow, I'm goin' t' call on Annie . . . maybe take her some preserves."

"That'd be nice o' ye, Letty. Ye're always tryin' t' find what the Lord'd do, aren't ye, my bonny lady?"

Watching the man gaze on his wife, Joanna thought she had never seen a man look at a woman with quite that same look in his eyes before—a look of admiration, not a little awe, and certainly a deep and reverent love. Here was simplicity itself. For the first time Joanna found herself wistfully desirous of something like this from a man, a love she wondered if someone like Jason Channing could ever give, or would even recognize or care about if he saw it.

"But all the trouble he's been through," Nathaniel went on at length, "still canna account fer such a deed."

"I still don't understand it," Joanna said. "What reason would he, or anyone, have for doing it?"

"I'll warrant it has somethin' t' do wi' them papers, or at least wi' ye bein' a Duncan," Nathaniel said.

"But Mr. Sercombe said they were worthless."

"Lawyers!" Nathaniel scoffed. "They're sly rascals, an' Palmer Sercombe's no different."

"Why, Nathaniel," Letty chided gently, "you forget about dear Mr. Ogilvie doon in Culden. He's a real nice man."

"I ken, Letty, but they're few an' far between. I'll na be surprised if Sercombe doesna stand t' make a tidy sum fer himsel' oot o' the sale."

"How can ye be sayin' such aboot the man?" Letty said. "Wi' all the things he's arrangin' fer the town?"

"Calm doon, Letty," Nathaniel returned in a tender tone. "Holdin' folks up t' Christian virtues may be one thing. But sometimes ye trust people too far, even gowks like Tom an' Sercombe. I'm goin' to give every man the benefit o' the doobt. But the Lord warned us t' be wise as serpents, ye know, an' we be boun' t' keep oor heads clear an' no be gowks oorsel's."

"What is Sercombe doing for Port Strathy?" asked Joanna.

"Weel, since there is no legal heir," Nathaniel said, "Sercombe's arrangin' fer the estate t' be sold. An' supposedly the man's agreed t' improve the harbor. An' there's been talk that a share o' the proceeds will be passed on t' each o' us tenants t' improve oor houses an' invest in oor crops an' fishin' boats an' the like."

"Nothin' like it's happened since I can recall," Letty added. " 'Tis all folks hae been talking aboot. These last two winters were rough ones. An' this is jist the sort o' thing t' give this auld village a boost."

The small household fell silent for a few moments.

Soon Nathaniel stood, knocked his pipe clean in the hearth, put on his red wool cap and, bidding the ladies a pleasant afternoon, went outside to tend to his chores.

Letty took a kettle of hot water from the hearth and filled the dishpan in the small adjoining kitchen, humming softly. As she watched, Joanna could not help wondering what life was like in Port Strathy fifty years earlier. Could this very house have been standing then? What were times like for her grandmother? And what had happened to drive her away? She tried to imagine Port Strathy two generations earlier and wondered if the look of the town had changed.

"How I wish I could have been there then . . ." Joanna mused out loud.

"Child?"

"I was just wondering what it was like when my grandmother was here," Joanna replied.

"Ah . . . the Lady Margaret was a bonny lass."

"Did you know her?" came Joanna's startled reply.

Letty smiled as warm memories filled her head. She dried her soapy hands and sat down at the table with Joanna. "I only ken what my mama would tell me aboot her o' an evenin'. She was the one who knew Lady Margaret. I guess they were as much friends as their different stations in life would allow. That was one thing that was sure different in those days t' be sure. Folk had their place, an' the lady o' the estate had her place an' a poor crofter had hers. But my mama said Lady Margaret was different. 'Twas like she *wanted* t' be like the crofters.''

Letty sighed and fell silent for a few moments; the far-away look in her eyes told Joanna that the older woman had been transported to that time so long ago. At length Letty began again. "When I was born, the Lady came t' see me. Ye see I wasna expected t' live through the night. But she came jist t' look in on my mama an' me—that's hoo much she cared . . .''

"Did your mother ever say why Lady Margaret left Scotland?''

"She only liked t' tell me o' the good times,'' Letty replied with a note of sadness in her voice. "When the Lady left, weel, I think my mama felt like a piece o' the heart had been cut oot o' Stonewycke. No one really knew what happened. Some said it were the romance. But the laird forbid anyone t' speak o' his daughter in his hearin'. An' soon folk jist found other things t' interest them. An' though I hate t' say it, through the years most jist forgot aboot her. Not my mama though, an' there were perhaps a few others o' the folk that loved her. But they werena given t' gossip.''

"Could it—'' Joanna began, but then paused as if she was afraid to frame the question that so dominated her mind. Finally she blurted out: "Is it truly possible that this . . . this *same* Margaret is my grand-mother?''

In answer, Letty clicked her tongue thoughtfully, then said, "It appears t' me, child, that there's jist too many coincidences if she's not. Aye, I'd say 'tis more than likely.''

Joanna knew, however, that one way or another she would have to find out—on the basis of more than mere coincidence. Wasn't that why she had come to Scotland?

The remainder of the day passed leisurely. Though her first day at the Cuttahays' had been a wonderful change and relief, when evening came Joanna found herself nearly exhausted. The emotional drain of her few days here had finally taken its toll.

That night she retired early. Drifting slowly into sleep, her final thoughts were of her grandmother and the gray stone walls of the "muc-kle hoose'' on the hill. She dreamed during the night, and that was a vision of a tall thin man in gardener's clothes running through a broad field of yellow daisies, chased by a shaggy sheepdog.

16 / An Unexpected Meeting

Joanna awoke early.

It was full daylight, but a quick glance at the clock in her room revealed that it was only 5:30. Knowing further sleep to be impossible, she crawled out of bed, dressed, then crept from her room. She found Nathaniel sprawled out in his chair, fully dressed but sound asleep. She couldn't tell if he had never been to bed or had slept, risen some time before her, and fallen asleep once again. She stole past him and outside into the sharp morning chill.

Reiver lay next to the chicken coop as sound asleep as his master. The frosty air was quiet and Joanna felt as though she should walk on tiptoes so as not to disturb its tranquillity. How strange it seemed for the sun to rise so early in that northern land!

All at once the silence was torn by an inhuman blood-curdling cry. Joanna froze!

She told herself it was nothing but one of the many usual animal sounds one grows accustomed to on a farm. But her assurances couldn't quell the thumping in her chest. Looking toward the barn, from whence the awful sound had come, Joanna crept slowly in that direction.

She approached the open door and peeked inside.

All she could make out were dark shadows. She stepped tentatively in and looked hurriedly to her right, then to her left. Nothing appeared amiss. Her eyes slowly adjusted to the dimness, but she saw the stack of empty milk pails a moment too late.

Toppling to the ground they crashed and clanged against one another until each rolled to a stop.

"Yow!" answered a loud yell from the opposite end of the barn. "Nathaniel, what are ye aboot? Keep quiet, man!"

"I'm sorry . . . it's not Nathaniel," Joanna's answering voice sounded so small.

"Weel, keep quiet will ye, whoever ye are! The noise frightened the bo an' she nearly crushed my arm."

Knowing she was unwelcome, yet driven by curiosity, Joanna inched forward toward the last of a group of stalls in which Nathaniel's cows spent the night. A dim light from that direction drew her, and she slowly made her way across the dirt floor strewn with dry straw. Reaching the end of the row of stalls, she saw a man kneeling on the ground next to a great prostrate form. The man's back was toward her as he tended an unmoving beast; his muscular frame was stripped to the waist and dripping with sweat despite the morning's cold. Steam rose from his shoulders, accented by occasional silent puffs from the animal's wet nose.

"I'm sorry," said Joanna again, "I thought I heard a strange sound, and—"

"And what do ye expect from the poor beast!" he interrupted, spinning around. Catching full sight of Joanna for the first time, his frustrated face flashed recognition. "You!" he exclaimed.

Joanna started in dismay.

It was the man she had seen on the beach. Only this time the tables were turned and she had disturbed him, an occurrence which had clearly upset him.

Before she had a chance to say a word the cow let forth another heart-wrenching low wail. He patted her flank and whispered some soothing Gaelic words Joanna could not understand.

"Is she sick?" she asked, glad to have the attention diverted away from the disturbance she had obviously caused in the proceedings.

"Jist tryin' t' give birth," he said. "And no doubt all this racket has set her back hours!"

He stood and walked over to a bucket of soapy water. His right arm was caked with dried blood and Joanna's stomach lurched uncertainly for a moment. He dipped both arms into the water and attempted to scrub the blood away, but most of it still clung to his skin.

"An' what might ye be doin' roamin' aboot the Cuttahays' byre at such a time o' day?" he asked with a tone of authority. The fact that he had been awake most of the night had shortened his usual degree of tolerance.

"I told you," she answered defensively, "I heard a noise."

"That ye did . . . ye'll be the girl from America?"

She nodded.

"Stayin' wi' the Cuttahays, are ye?"

"Well, I have for a couple days. That is, I don't know what—"

Her words were cut off by the whines of the cow.

"Back t' work," he said, hastening to the cow's side. "Ye run an' fetch Nathaniel . . . quickly!"

"He's asleep."

"Must've dropped off—the man's been oot here wi' me most o' the night," he said, then hesitated as he thought for a moment.

"Weel," he went on, " 'tis no time noo. Ye'll have t' help me yersel'."

"Me!" exclaimed Joanna, "I don't know anything about—"

"Don't argue! There's no time!" In his exhaustion he was in no mood to debate with a fainthearted female.

"But I—"

"I'll tell ye what to do," he said, and without waiting for her consent, he took a rope from where it lay next to his bag of instruments and quickly tied a slipknot in one end. Kneeling down he slipped his arm into the straining animal.

Joanna gasped as his hand and arm, still clutching the rope, disappeared inside the hindquarters of the cow.

This was no time to be sick, but she felt her stomach giving way!

For the first time she noticed the pungent stench of manure and stale urine in which the cow was lying.

"Stand ready when I call!"

Joanna's hand unconsciously sought her mouth. She had to keep her queasy stomach in check. She couldn't lose control of herself now!

"If only I can get that head around . . . " the man was saying. "I think the calf is still alive."

He paused, concentrating on his task. "Aye . . . it is!"

Long moments passed.

Joanna found herself—in spite of the nausea which threatened to erupt at any moment—awed not only by what she was witnessing, but also by the man kneeling on the hard, dirt-packed floor. For all his homespun appearance, his features managed to retain a certain boyish gaiety. She recalled his unassuming laughter on the beach—which annoyed her so. And though he certainly wasn't smiling now, his eyes were alive with excitement—as though he were a boy on a wonderful adventure.

But it wasn't his taut muscles or craggy features that captured her attention, but the gentle intensity with which he devoted himself to his task—his comforting murmurs to the cow and his determination to deliver a healthy calf no matter what . . . no matter whose help he had to enlist. He appeared totally consumed by the event.

"I've got it!" he exclaimed at last. The strain in his voice masked the triumph he felt.

"Noo, lass . . . grab the end o' this rope!"

Joanna hesitated.

"Noo!" he barked. "Kneel doon here . . . take the rope."

Joanna stepped forward and reluctantly knelt down. Her knees oozed into the soft layer of muck coating the floor of the stall. He forced the rope into her hands and her fingers slowly closed around it. She was grateful that in the dim light she could not tell if the slime she knelt in was brown or red.

"Don't yank it, jist pull slowly . . . a nice even tension on the rope."
Joanna obeyed.

"That's it . . . nice an' easy."

Joanna could feel the calf struggling on the other end. A surge of wonder shot through her frame. She was holding a new life! An unborn being was attached to this rope she held, and she was pulling it into the world.

In that instant she forgot her dress, buried from the knees down in a smelling black mess. She forgot the putrifying reek which would have sent her into a deathly faint only a week earlier. She forgot her dainty pride and feminine dignity. She forgot about her grandmother and Jason Channing and deeds and papers and plans and problems.

She only knew she was helping to give life!

"Ah, lassie . . . ye're doin' great!"

Joanna smiled and still held on, arms and shoulders beginning to ache from the pressure.

"Thank you," she said.

"I was meanin' the cow," he said. "But ye're doin' jist fine too!"

The cow's movements and the vet's words of encouragement increased in intensity. Joanna's heart pounded and her throat had gone dry. Then she saw the tiny pink muzzle emerge into the open air. The man eased back to Joanna and grasped the rope with her.

"Now she's right where we want her. Together . . . let's pull her on oot!"

Before Joanna knew it, the bloody, wet newborn calf lay on the floor.

But the vet's job had not ended. He grabbed up a handful of clean straw and began rubbing it over the brown and white spotted calf, lying there limp and lifeless. Still it made no move. Hurriedly he pried open its tiny mouth, scooped out mucus with his fingers, and blew several forceful breaths into it. He continued to massage the little animal's chest until its eyelids flickered. Suddenly the calf jerked wildly and struggled to gain footing. He was still too weak for that, however, and slumped back to the ground.

"I've never seen anything so beautiful!" said Joanna, through tears streaming down her cheeks.

He continued to rub the newborn calf down with straw, then dragged him to his mother's head. The listless cow lay exhausted, but as he drew her new baby near, her nostrils distended, she sniffed, then began to lick the tiny young face vigorously.

"Aye . . . it never fails to stir me!" he said. As Joanna turned toward him she thought she detected the faint glistening of moisture in his eyes too. And such deep blue eyes they were!

They each stood in silence for a few moments, observing the tender spectacle being played out before them. They hardly noticed the rising sun's attempts to penetrate the cracks in the walls of the ancient barn as it now poured in through every available slit. A sound of clomping boots behind them hurrying through the barn interrupted the peaceful morning silence.

"Hullo . . . Alec . . . how's she doin'?" called out Nathaniel, fearful he had overslept the time when he was needed the most.

"Relax, Nathaniel," the vet called out. Just then the old man burst through into the crowded stall.

"Ye have a fine new bull, Nathaniel," beamed Joanna's unknown companion. "Jist what ye were wantin'!"

"Weel, the Lord be praised! An' it certainly is alive, too. What would I do wi' oot ye, Alec? An' me off asleep whilst ye did all the work! How'd ye manage it?"

"This new guest o' yers, Nathaniel. She did the work o' a stout woman!"

"Why, lass!" exclaimed Nathaniel, seeming to notice Joanna's presence almost for the first time. "Jist look at ye, all dirty an' wi' the sweat standing on yer brow . . . ye been workin' hard!"

Nathaniel's pride could not have beamed more brightly had Joanna been his own daughter. He threw a strong arm around her and gave her a tight squeeze. Joanna blushed, then laughed outright.

"I never had the chance to thank ye fer all yer help," said the vet, the earlier edge to his voice softening as he turned toward Joanna standing at Nathaniel's side.

"Certainly," she replied. "I wouldn't have missed it . . . even if I did stumble in here by accident and upset all the milk cans."

Now it was the young man's turn to laugh. "No harm done," he said good-naturedly.

"Weel," said Nathaniel, "I'm glad t' see that the two o' ye hae made such fine acquaintance."

"Actually, there was hardly time fer a fit introduction. Yer lass walked in on me and I put her t' work."

"Weel then, Joanna, I'd like ye t' meet, official-like, oor young vet'narian in these parts, Alec MacNeil. Alec, this here's Joanna Matheson, oor visitor from America."

Alec extended his hand, but then remembering its appearance and where it had recently been, quickly withdrew it. Joanna laughed. "My dress isn't in much better condition, Mr. MacNeil," she said.

"Noo, come," said Nathaniel. "Wash yersel's up. Letty's fixin' up a hearty breakfast fer us all. I'll fetch ye some fresh water from the well."

Holding up the edges of her ruined dress as they walked out of the barn together, Joanna felt happier than she had ever been in her life.

17 / A Peaceful Afternoon

Joanna slipped a jar of Letty's bread-and-butter pickles into the basket. Only one or two more items and all would be ready.

This was wonderful! A real picnic in the country!

She had been awake almost since dawn waiting impatiently until she heard Letty stirring in the kitchen.

The morning had progressed at an interminably slow pace while Nathaniel hurried through his day's chores to free himself for the afternoon. But at long last Letty asked Joanna to fetch the basket and begin the preparations.

She had fairly skipped to the pantry!

"This jar o' marmalade an' those four plates there, an' that should do 't," said Letty, handing the jar to Joanna.

At that moment Nathaniel walked into the kitchen. He plucked off his cap and ran a sleeve across his brow. "Weel, the stock's all fed—we can go when Alec gets here." He reached into the basket for a biscuit but Letty gave his hand a gentle swat.

"Those are fer later," she scolded.

"Jist thought I might lighten the load a wee bit," he said with a laugh. Letty looked at the twinkle in his eye, weakened under his smile and handed him his prize.

" 'Tis a grand day fer an afternoon in the meadows," he said as he munched on the fresh-baked oatbiscuit.

"We're ready," said Letty.

"Oh, where is Mr. MacNeil?" said Joanna, trying to conceal her impatience but not wanting to lose a single moment of the day.

It had been two days since Alec MacNeil had been to the Cuttahay farm to deliver Nathaniel's new young bull. Since that morning—which had proved nearly as momentous for Joanna as for the calf—she had scarcely thought once about leaving Port Strathy. Something had changed for her that morning. Seeing the sights, smelling the smells, and getting on her hands and knees and participating in such a fundamental experience of Scottish country life had established a bond deep in her soul with this lifestyle which earlier had been so foreign to her. Suddenly London seemed distant, far removed from these earthy values and priorities of simple existence.

The Cuttahays accepted her so totally and shared their humble life and provision with her so entirely that after just two brief days, Joanna felt as if she had belonged there all her life.

It was another half hour before Alec MacNeil finally arrived, out of breath as he galloped up the dirt road and hastily dismounted, sweaty and disheveled.

"Sorry I'm late," he said. "I've spent the mornin' wi' the Kerrs' bull, an' he wasn't the most cooperative o' patients."

"We're jist glad ye could come, Alec," enjoined Letty heartily.

"Nathaniel, could I put my horse up in yer byre? He's in sore need o' a rest after the way I ran him."

"O' course," Nathaniel replied. "I'll go oot wi' ye. I have t' bring the wagon 'round."

At last the little party assembled, loaded into the wagon, and was soon rambling along behind Nathaniel's two trustworthy horses. The dirt trail they followed led from the Cuttahays' cottage south and west, across mostly flat terrain, toward the neighboring county across the Lindow. It would take them most of the way toward their destination, a secluded little meadow of soft green grass abundant with wildflowers and surrounded by a dense growth of pine trees. Nathaniel and Letty had discovered the spot quite by accident when they were courting, and it had remained a special place ever since. Jostling along the bumpy road Alec held the reins, with Nathaniel perched on the seat at his side. Letty and Joanna half-reclined on blankets in the wagon bed behind them, chatting away, enjoying the wonders of early summer.

The morning was in full flower and gave promise of continued clear skies and warm sunshine. "If only ye could see the heather in bloom," said Letty to Joanna with a sigh. "Right here," she said, sweeping out her hand toward the low-lying hills to their left, " 'tis absolutely stunning, a thin mat o' purple as far as ye can see."

"When will it bloom?" asked Joanna.

"Later . . . not till September or so, depending on the weather."

"It's beautiful now," said Joanna with a satisfied smile, drawing in a huge breath of the sweet fragrance born on the southerly breeze. "I can't think of any place I'd rather be."

Letty returned her smile and placed a motherly hand on Joanna's arm. "An' I'm glad ye're here wi' us, child," she said.

Alec directed the two bay mares along the barely passable road, first in a southerly direction, then veering gradually toward the west. They had been riding nearly an hour when Nathaniel said, "Weel, here's oor stop. Pull the horses up over yonder, Alec. There's plenty o' fine grass here t' keep 'em occupied."

Tying the horses and gathering the blankets and basket, the small group began to traipse through high grass, over a rocky, rugged hill and finally through a tiny wood. At last their efforts were rewarded.

"It's . . . it's lovely!" exclaimed Joanna in mingled delight and wonder. "Such a magnificent tiny meadow, hidden away from the world like this!"

"It's oor own private little hideaway," said Nathaniel with pride.

"Aye," said Letty, "we been comin' here fer years and never saw another soul."

"An' do my ears mistake me, or do I hear the river?" asked Alec, equally taken with their scenic discovery.

"Aye, ye do, Alec," said Nathaniel, "trees on three sides an' the river on the fourth. 'Tis a perfectly protected little spot."

The older couple proudly showed the youths all about, at last making their way to the far side. The river was still swollen with winter runoff and rumbled along mightily on its way to the sea. In late summer the banks would drop away nearly ten feet to the water. But now the water reached the top of the rocky edge.

"In my younger days," said Nathaniel, "I tried t' impress my leddy by comin' here, rippin' off my shirt in one motion, an' divin' into the water t' swim across."

"First time he did," laughed Letty, "I nearly died wi' fright!"

"Water's mighty icy this time o' year," said Nathaniel, "but when I was yoong an' foolish I dinna seem t' mind."

"Are ye goin' t' give us a demonstration today?" asked Alec with a grin.

Nathaniel laughed heartily. "No, no. I hae na jumped into the Lindow fer years. How 'bout yerself, Alec?"

"Not today! But, Nathaniel, isn't that a part o' the Dormin on the other side, there?"

"Aye. A side o' it few people see—another part o' the charm o' this little meadow o' oor's."

The Dormin to which Alec referred was the thick and verdant Dormin Forest, a small but unusually dense little wood measuring approximately a mile across and no more than two miles in length. Since its discovery centuries earlier the Dormin had been under special royal protection, though it remained unfenced and rather loosely enforced. It was teeming with dozens of species of trees and shrubs, moss and grasses, ferns and wildlife. No hunting, cutting, collecting, or gathering of any kind was allowed; during the warm months of late autumn a stream of biologists and botanists from Scotland's universities made their way to the Dormin to study its spectacular array of flora and fauna.

But today the picnickers only gazed at the Dormin from across its bordering river, content with the splendor of their own grassy meadow.

Letty and Joanna spread out the blanket beneath a large elm and set out the lunch from the basket.

"Ah, ye've seen t' everything, Letty," said Nathaniel.

"Joanna did most o' it," said his wife.

"So ye think we ought t' keep her, then?" asked Nathaniel, flashing a grin toward Joanna. "Mighty fine yoong woman she be t' have aroun'."

Joanna blushed at Nathaniel's tease, then laughed.

"I thought she already was oor own," said Letty. "I'd already forgotten she was but oor guest."

"Weel, the Lord be thanked fer sendin' her to us, that's fer sure," said Nathaniel.

A leisurely meal followed, to the drone of inquisitive bumble bees overhead and the sound of gently flowing water.

Joanna felt light with a joy she had never known.

Thoughts of Alec stole into the edges of Joanna's consciousness quite by accident and wholly unnoticed by her. There remained an unspoken nervousness within her stemming from their first quarrelsome encounter on the beach. He had never mentioned it. But she felt she should apologize for her rudeness, though she was too embarrassed to bring it up.

Alec, for his part, however, showed not the slightest hint of a corresponding tenseness. He talked and laughed easily. But was there more to this rugged young Scotsman than could quickly be discerned by the superficial gaze of a near-stranger like Joanna? Casting him a sidelong glance, she found him silent and thoughtful, gazing into the Dormin, seemingly mesmerized by the slow flow of the Lindow, as if his gaze might be able to penetrate the rich, tangled forest.

How Joanna would liked to have screwed up her courage to ask him about his thoughts! But she could never have intruded so. Besides, that was the one area where she had already discovered that his tongue did not flow freely—when talking of himself.

Lunch completed and the conversation dying to a peaceful silence, Alec stood and stretched his long limbs.

"I'm fer a bit o' exercise," he said. "Nathaniel, why don't we take oor guest t' the top o' the Marbrae?"

"Alec, ye forget my age! I hae na climbed the Marbrae fer five years an' dinna think my auld bones are up t' that hike today. Not that I dinna intend t' do it again one day. But today . . . I think I'll jist leave that t' the two o' ye youngsters."

Alec turned toward Joanna with a questioning look.

"I'm agreeable," she said. "But what's the Marbrae?"

"A great hill on the other side o' the road from where we left the wagon," said Nathaniel. "A great hill, but not quite a mountain. Rises steeply from the valley here an' ye can climb t' the very top in only an hour—an easy enough walk . . . that is, when ye're yoong."

"We'll meet ye back at the wagon in two hours, Nathaniel," said Alec.

He then led the way, and for the next hour Joanna found herself desperately trying to keep pace with her long-legged companion. The trail was narrow, necessitating walking in single file. Conversation was therefore infrequent as Alec seemed intent on their destination. By the time they gained the summit, she was out of breath, perspiring, and ready to drop.

Turning around and first perceiving her state, he said, "I'm sorry I've gone too fast fer ye."

"Oh no," said Joanna, a bit breathlessly. "I'm tired, but . . . well, I made it."

"Whenever I come here I can't seem t' keep from walkin' fast. I always get caught up in the adventure o' it. I guess I forget I've been here before an' am a bit used t' it."

It took a few moments sitting on a rock regaining her wind for Joanna to begin to take in the view that spread out before her. Then she saw why Alec had wanted to make the climb, and why—even though he had apparently been here many times—he termed the hike an adventure.

Below them, on the side opposite the more gradual eastern slope up which they had ascended, the Marbrae dropped off abruptly. Joanna gasped as she peered carefully over the precipitous edge and quickly retreated a step or two to the safety of Alec's side.

"Oh my!" she exclaimed. "That's quite a cliff!"

"But jist look at the view, Miss Matheson. Doesn't it jist make ye forget every care ye ever had?"

The Lindow River, winding its way through forests and fields on its slow trek toward the sea, floated on noiselessly below them on the west, widening considerably at its mouth, or firth.

"Yes," she answered, "I suppose you're right. I wonder where Nathaniel and Letty are right now?"

"That's easy," said Alec. "I'll show ye."

He walked confidently toward the cliff, reached it, then looked back. Joanna stood stock-still, not moving a step.

"Don't be afraid," he said. "No harm'll come t' ye. Here, take my hand."

He turned toward her with outstretched arm and offered his right hand.

Gingerly Joanna approached a few steps and reached toward him. His large, rough hand closed firmly around hers, tiny and weak inside his powerful grasp. But she sensed that it was a good hand which now held her tight, a hand of strength and safety. She continued toward the edge until she stood close by his side, clasping his hand like a vise, terrified yet feeling secure at the same time.

"If ye look down there," said Alec pointing with his left hand, "where the river seems t' disappear fer a moment, ye'll see that the forest an' trees appear a bit darker. That's the Dormin. Few o' the folks that come visitin' it know about this place an' what a view o' things ye can get from here. Weel, that's where they are, jist on the other side o' the river from the Dormin. Ye can almost make out the lush green o' the meadow, but I canna tell if it might jist be my eyes playin' tricks on me."

"I think I see it!" said Joanna excitedly.

Further north, the sea spread out in all directions in a vast expanse of deep blue, splotched with green and occasional patches of gray. Under the day's clear skies the thin line of the horizon was sharp and clearly defined. Toward their right some six or seven miles distant lay the small buildings of Port Strathy, brown brick and white-washed walls discernible against the backdrop of the green fields and blue sea. Further beyond, Ramsey Head rose mightily out of the sea, huge even from this great distance. To the east was Strathy Summit, with the low-lying fields, pastures, and wooded areas of Strathy valley between it and the place where they stood.

"It's . . . it's breathtaking!" said Joanna, retreating a step or two.

Alec released her hand and sat down on a large rock several steps away from the cliff.

"Why," Joanna went on, unable to contain her expressions of delight at the scene, "you can see everything from here."

"Aye, 'tis a gran' place," he said. "Nathaniel an' Letty have their meadow. But this has always been my special spot."

"You come here often?"

"When I need t' think, or get away from my cares. I sit an' look oot t' sea an' sometimes imagine I can see oor Viking ancestors sailin' their great ships across the sea."

"You're a descendant of the Vikings?"

"Aye, but that was hundreds o' years ago."

"I suppose I've never made the connection in my mind," said Joanna. "The Vikings were so fierce and barbaric, and after meeting Nathaniel, I've grown to think of Scotland as a gentle land."

"Ah, but yer typical Scotsman's a rough-hewn character. We're a tough breed. Remember the man who attacked ye? Scotland's history is a violent an' bloody one. Surely ye've heard o' the battle o' Culloden an' Glencoe an' the feuds between the rival clans like the MacDonalds an' the Campbells? No, 'tis no gentle place, this Scotland o' oor's."

Alec fell silent, and when Joanna glanced over toward him, his eyes seemed to be staring at the view but his thoughts seemed far away.

Alec was pondering his own words.

He had almost said too much, revealed more of himself than he wanted to. Why he should have done so he didn't know. Perhaps it was the spell of Marbrae, or was it feeling at ease with Joanna? Only Nathaniel knew just why he had left his home to set up practice in Port Strathy—best it stay that way.

He looked down at his hands and the hint of a shudder stirred his frame. Yes, he knew of violence . . . only too well.

"What's that?" asked Joanna pointing to a ridge about a mile off which stood out from the green valley which stretched out below them toward the sea.

Alec pulled himself out of his reverie. "That's Braenock Ridge. 'Tis a stretch o' rocky moorland, full o' little but brown shrubbery, an' is not good fer much. But there, can ye see . . . "

He pointed and Joanna followed the direction of his arm.

"Jist look, aboot in the middle o' it, ye can jist barely make it oot. 'Tis the last bits o' the ruin o' an ancient Pict village," he said. There was little to be seen other than some piles of rock covered with creeping ivy and surrounded by a few scraggly looking shrubs.

"History says one night a Viking ship landed in oor harbor an' the Viking warriors made their way inland an' fell upon the village, slaughterin' every man, woman, an' child in the place."

His voice caught on the words. But he determined to go on with the grisly tale. " 'Twas so sudden," he resumed, "that they had no chance t' defend themselves wi' as much as a single blow."

"How awful!" Joanna breathed with a slight tremble.

"An' all jist because they wanted somethin' t' eat. So the story goes, but I expect there was more t' it than that."

"They could have just taken it. They didn't have to kill everyone."

"But that's how it was. I expect the Picts would hae done the same if the tables had been turned. An' that same blood is mingled wi' the inhabitants o' the land today. An' many a Scotsman takes pride in that fierce, savage past. No, Miss Matheson, yer new friend Nathaniel . . . he's the exception. An' even he has that same blood flowin' through his veins."

"Why then is he such a gentle, compassionate man?"

"It's not bein' a Scotsman that sets him apart. It's his faith. Surely ye've noticed the way he talks aboot God an' the Scriptures?"

"Well . . . I guess I hadn't thought of it. But, yes, now that you mention it I do recall him referring to God. But he's not a churchy sort of man."

"Exactly my point. He's different. He neither fits the pattern o' bein' a rough Scotsman or a religious clergyman sort. He's jist . . . Nathaniel."

"Well then, what's so different about him?"

"Don't ye see? It's because he lives his faith. He doesn't spend all day talkin' aboot it or preachin' at ye or puttin' on airs. He jist rolls up his sleeves an' gets on wi' livin'. His faith is jist reflected in the kind o' person he is."

"It sounds like he's had quite an impact on you."

"Aye," said Alec slowly after a moment's reflection. "I suppose ye're right. I met him soon after I came to Strathy. He an' Letty sort o' took me in, ye might say. Kind o' like they have yerself'. An' I soon found I'd never met anyone like the man before. I couldn't help wantin' to be like him. He's honest, forthright, not afraid t' speak his mind, not afraid t' jump into the fray if he thinks somethin' isn't right. He doesn't care what the townspeople say aboot 'im, always wantin' the truth t' come oot more than anythin'."

Joanna looked at Alec, not sure if he had finished speaking.

He was gazing into the distance, absorbed in his own thoughts. The face intrigued her. Just now she noticed something she hadn't seen in it before. Little of the savage was evident. There was, in fact, a gentle flow to his features that reminded her of the very words he had been speaking about Nathaniel. Yet burning in his eyes Joanna could detect a remnant of a certain untamed, forceful energy, perhaps a fierceness not unlike the rugged coastline or the green mystery called Dormin.

"And what about you, Alec?" Joanna asked, surprised with her own boldness.

He did not answer immediately.

When the words finally came, they were slow and measured. Joanna could feel the deep sense of personal introspection in his tone—as if he was confronting an old dilemma which had already been round and round through his brain dozens of times but for which he had not yet discovered a satisfactory solution.

"The Bible says t' turn the other cheek," he began. "It says many such things. An' I believe the words. An' I see the fruit o' doin' them in Nathaniel's life. An' that's how I try t' live my life. But . . ."

He paused.

His eyes bore into the distant sea, as if the elusive answer might lie there. "I suppose tryin' isn't always enough. The words o' Paul the apostle aboot sums it up fer me—'the good that I would do I don't do, but the evil I would not do, that I do.' It's some comfort t' know that Paul struggled wi' what lay at the very bottom o' his bein'."

"I don't understand," said Joanna.

"It's jist that evil lies at the core o' us all, though not all hae had it come t' the surface an' . . . an' . . . weel, 'tis hard t' put into words." *Maybe someday*, he thought. *But not just yet.*

"I'm sorry . . . I didn't mean to pry."

"There's one thing else Paul says aboot it, though, that there's hope through Christ. I have t' remin' myself' o' that."

A heavy brooding silence followed Alec's words.

When he spoke again his voice was an obvious attempt to lift the mood and divert the course of the conversation away from himself.

"But ye haven't seen everything," he said, rising and offering his hand once more as he helped Joanna up from the rock where she sat.

"Look over in that direction, Miss Matheson," he said, turning for the first time toward the south, where the Lindow shrank in size as it disappeared from their sight in the distant hills of its origin. "Beyond all we can see, away t' the south and west, lie the Scottish Highlands."

Joanna quietly drank in everything. Then it became her turn to grow introspective. This whole land seemed like another world, from another time, another age. Yet suddenly, more than ever, Joanna found she wanted to be a part of it.

She wondered if she ever could.

18 / Flame Dance

Alec MacNeil had lived on Scotland's rugged northern coast for twenty-three of his twenty-seven years, the four-year break a result of his veterinary training in Edinburgh. He had been raised just west of Ramsey Head.

Alec's father had been a highly esteemed fisherman in his community and had died in a storm at sea when Alec was fifteen. The young boy had always intended to follow his father to the sea, and even during his teen years had already become a fisherman of no small skill. But soon after his father's death, the local veterinarian had needed an assistant and had taken young Alec under his wing. Realizing his mother and sister would require support from a safer and more dependable source than the sea, Alec decided to follow his new line of work. The old vet took a liking to Alec and offered to finance him through veterinary school.

By age twenty-two, Alec had everything he wanted—a profession he loved and a promising future. Most of all, he would be able to support his family. Things could not have been better for Alec and would have continued thus except for that night . . . that night which would always burn in his memory.

It had been a busy week. As he rode home from his final call of the day, he was nearly asleep in the saddle. His house was around the next corner and he was thinking of hot soup and biscuits when he jerked to attention, startled. He thought he'd heard muffled cries down the darkened side street as he passed. His vet's instinct forced him to stop and investigate. Some animal in trouble, no doubt.

But it was no animal!

In the dim light of the late fall evening, he could just make out the form of a man's arm raised to strike a helpless victim.

"Hey!" he yelled to distract the man as he ran down the alley toward them. On reaching them, Alec tore the man from his victim and in that moment, he saw a woman lying on the ground, dress torn, face bruised and a trickle of blood oozing down her cheek where the man had struck her.

It was his sister!

In unrestrained wrath, Alec spun around, viciously grabbed the man and threw him bodily against the side of the brick building. He raised his arm to strike him but the man slumped into a heap on the ground. He lay motionless for some time, and upon closer inspection Alec realized the man's head had smashed against the wall. He would never move again.

When the whole sordid incident came to public light, Alec was lauded as a hero. The dead man turned out to be an unsavory character from Aberdeen who was wanted there for numerous crimes. But none of this mattered to Alec.

He had killed a man.

In rage and violence, his own two hands had taken a life. It tormented him day and night. He lived in fear should his wrath rise again against another—perhaps next time, his victim would not be so culpable. And, too, there seemed a vague change in the attitude of his friends and neighbors toward him, an effort on their part to avoid arousing his anger.

Perhaps it was all in his mind. But when the position in Port Strathy opened up, Alec wasted no time in applying.

Jacob Greely, the vet in Port Strathy, needed an assistant; Alec fit the bill perfectly. The two struck up an immediate friendship and the older man hardly blinked an eye when Alec revealed his past. Jacob respected the lad all the more, not only for his forthright honesty, but also because his deed had so clearly disturbed the lad.

Then within a year, Jacob died, leaving his practice to Alec.

Alec loved his work, even on mornings like this when Billy, the stable boy at Stonewycke, pounded unmercifully on his door at 6:30 a.m. The lad had no way of knowing Alec had only moments before (or so it seemed) crawled back into bed after spending several strenuous hours with Hootons' sick Galloway.

"What can it be, lad?" Alec asked as he pulled on his overalls.

"Mr. Innes sent me, sir," Billy replied. " 'Tis Flame Dance. He's some sore ailin'. We never seen 'im like this. Mr. Innes says fer ye t' come right away."

Alec disappeared inside the house to pack the few items he thought he might need and then hurried to the stable to saddle his own smoke-gray gelding. He wondered what could be wrong with the great roan stallion, the late laird's favorite horse. He remembered when the stallion had been born four years earlier. Jacob had been alive then, but he let Alec officiate at the difficult delivery. The moment the newborn colt heaved its already massive bulk up on willowy legs, Alec knew the horse would be special.

And he had not been wrong. Flame Dance soon proved himself the fastest horse in the county, and that with little or no training. The laird developed something of an obsession, working tirelessly to prepare Flame

Dance for national competition. But the horse's racing career ended almost before it had begun when he began to reveal himself as a one-man horse. The laird brought in the best jockeys his position could buy, but all efforts at racing on the circuit ended in futility. Yet the laird so loved the horse that even the loss of potential glory could hardly quell the thrill of riding him.

A year ago Flame Dance had cut his leg, and from that time on Alec began to develop a special bond with the stallion. Just prior to the laird's death, Alec had actually ridden the great horse. Since that time he visited the estate at every possible opportunity, hoping to relieve at least a portion of the loss an animal must feel upon the death of a loved master. Inside, Alec harbored the secret hope that in time the magnificent animal might give to him the same affection he had previously given the laird.

Now what could be the matter? he thought as he galloped through the open gates of the estate, Billy already a quarter of a mile behind on his own horse. Alec slowed his horse to a trot and directed it past the house and around to the back where the stable was located.

The moment he walked into the horse's stall, his stomach lurched. He stopped, face deathly pale, and closed his eyes momentarily as he sighed a long, bitter sigh. Flame Dance stumbled about, his twitching flesh lathered with sweat from the agony he was in. His eyes were glazed over, staring blankly ahead, and he showed no signs of recognizing Alec.

"Dear Lord!" Alec groaned, "not this . . . please, not this." Then, aware of the factor's presence seemingly for the first time, he turned sharply toward Walter Innes standing near the stable door. "Innes," he snapped, "why didn't ye call me sooner?"

"I—I thought 'twas but a bit o' colic, Alec," said the factor, directing his eyes helplessly toward the ground. "I been drenchin' him, but nothin' seemed t' help the poor beast."

"Probably nothin' can," sighed Alec. "But get me some soap an' water, will ye?"

Alec opened his bag and took out a thermometer. He knew, however, he was only going through the motions. Still, he thought within himself, maybe—just maybe—Walter's diagnosis, not his own, might be right.

Innes returned with a bucket of soapy water and Alec began his examination. Flame Dance offered not a flutter of resistance, giving still another confirmation to Alec's initial fears. The examination took barely five minutes. At last Alec rose slowly. Now it was time for his eyes to avoid the factor's fearful and probing face. But there was no reason to put the horse through any further torment.

"He's got a badly twisted bowel," Alec said in his blunt and professional manner.

"What can ye do?" Innes asked desperately.

Alec swallowed hard. His throat had gone dry.

"Walter," he began, "ye know yersel' there's nothin—"

"Alec," cried the factor, "ye can't be tellin' me there's not a thing ye can do fer him! Surely ye can—"

"Walter!" said Alec with the raised voice of helpless agony. "The bowel's twisted. It'll just get worse till it kills him from the inside. An' it's an awful death. Ye know that, Walter."

"But," insisted Innes, "couldn't we jist—"

"Don't ye understand, man?" Alec interrupted again, this time with a finality in his tone. "I have t' put him doon."

A mournful wail followed from the lips of the factor. "Not him! There's got t' be some . . . first the laird . . . now his poor horse. Oh, I've ruined it all—"

"Listen, Walter. I'm sorry I spoke rough wi' ye before. There was nothin' anyone could have done." Alec tried to make himself believe his own words as if they might answer for his own inadequacies.

"No, 'tis all my fault," Innes persisted. "At first, I blamed the horse for the laird's fall, but 'twas me. I should have checked that saddle. I should have—"

"Stop it, Walter! The laird was too old and sick t' be oot riding. Ye canna blame yersel'."

"No. I'm guilty. He trusted me."

"Weel, ye're wrong," said Alec, "but I'm not goin' t' argue wi' ye. Hardly matters now, anyway. An' right now I have to take care o' the horse."

"Ye'll do it, then?" Innes asked. "I couldn't."

"Don't worry," Alec replied. "Leave if ye must."

The two men walked out of the stable silently. Alec went to his horse where he drew out his rifle from its pouch alongside the saddle. Innes disappeared somewhere behind the stables.

This is my occupation, Alec thought.

Every job had its moments of distastefulness, but what could compare with this? His stomach nearly failed him at the mere thought of what he was about to do. It never became easy, never failed to make him physically sick. But it was a necessary evil all vets had to cope with however they could. He had done it before. And he would have to do it again.

But it would never be easy.

This time he almost failed altogether. His sweaty fingers trembled as he tried to squeeze the trigger. All he could see was Flame Dance, that magnificent horse, in his glory—proud and mighty, full of fire and vigor. A vision rose in his mind's eye of the day he had first ridden him. A frosty morning, just cold enough so that the horse's every breath hung in the air, his throbbing nostrils sending great hot puffs of smoke-like energy into the chilly morning, while Alec laughed aloud on his back, urging him through the knee-high grass of the meadow.

Slowly the vision faded and the cruel chill of reality swept through Alec, sending a shiver up his spine.

Now the once mighty horse was . . .

Oh, Lord!

Alec groaned deep within. Perhaps he would never have been able to pull that trigger had Flame Dance, at the final moment, not glanced up at Alec through his final agony, with a glassy look of pain in his eyes. Was the poor animal begging for the mercy of death?

Finally, with tears stinging his eyes, Alec did what had to be done. It was his job.

An hour later, Alec reclined on a grassy dune a quarter mile from town. He had left the house as quickly as possible. He and Walter would bury Flame Dance later, after the emotions were settled somewhat. But for the moment, he had to get away. No doubt Walter, too, would need time to himself.

Often when he sought the solace of nature, Alec rode to Marbrae. Something about the awesome power of being so high above the landscape filled him with fresh vitality and peace. But today, there was no time for the long ride. He had an appointment in town and hardly needed a strenuous ride to tax him still further after the morning's events.

He sat, gazing blankly at the steadily rising tide, only vaguely conscious of the repetitive crashing of the waves on the sandy shore. A white and black pelican with an injured wing limped sadly by, yet he hardly noticed. His usually compassionate veterinarian's heart could hardly be moved today; it had already been stretched to the limit of its endurance.

He tried to pray.

"God . . ." he began, but the words fell silent even before they began.

Was it right to brood over the death of a horse? His emotions were nearly as taxed as if it had been a man. Was that the proper response, the spiritual response, what Jesus would have done had it been His horse?

But even as that question rose in his mind, another followed in its wake. Was it not said two sparrows are worth but a farthing? Yet not a single one falls to the ground without the Father's knowing . . . and caring.

So God, too, was grieved.

Alec found some comfort in that thought.

Yet it consoled him little, for he was the one by whose hand Flame Dance's life had come to an end. Once more he saw the great beast slump motionless to the ground where he lay as the fatal bullet found its mark. Again, the memory brought tears flooding to his eyes. He tried to remind himself what had been ingrained into him at Edinburgh's College of Veterinary Medicine—these were but poor dumb beasts. They did not understand nor respond to pain in human fashion. Under the circumstances it could only be a mercy to be given relief . . . only a mercy. . . .

Alec had not intended to fall asleep, but it is difficult to solve life's pressing dilemmas on two hours of sleep. When he began to come to himself, he wasn't certain whether the rustling of the breeze in the gray shoreline grasses had awakened him or if he had just slept his fill. The sun had risen high in the sky, but it was not yet noon.

Alec rolled quietly onto his side, expecting to see a rabbit in the grass. They were everywhere, it seemed, especially in the clusters of thick, high grasses that covered the dunes fifty feet inland from the water's edge. If it hadn't been the breeze that had startled him awake, surely some jackrabbit was making for cover. Instead as he turned he perceived the form of a woman, partially hidden by the low-lying hill of sand she was ascending. The sun pierced his eyes, and he could make out her silhouette against the blue sky, but none of her features. She had apparently not seen him.

Alec watched her slow movements through the soft sand, realizing at last that it was Joanna. His natural inclination in his present frame of mind was to remain silent. But then remembering their first awkward meeting not far from this very spot, he decided to speak.

"Ho . . . Miss Matheson!"

Joanna looked up, mildly startled.

"Hello . . . Mr. MacNeil, is that you?"

"Aye," he replied.

"I didn't know anyone was here. I haven't disturbed you, have I?" She too remembered that first meeting.

"No, not really."

"I was just out for a little walk," she said. "I came into town this morning with Nathaniel, hoping to have received some word from home."

"It must be hard fer ye not knowin'."

"Yes. I was certain Dr. Blakely would have had something here for me by now. I guess it would ease my mind even if he only could tell me things were the same."

"Weel, ye shouldn't let it bother ye that there's no news. The wireless is still new around here and poor Olive hasn't ironed out all the kinks in it yet. We dinna get many wires, but most of those that do come usually take forever t' get here . . . if they get here at all."

"Oh," Joanna said, her countenance noticeably wilted. "You mean I may not hear anything at all?"

Alec immediately saw his blunder. "Oh no, mem! Yer're sure t' hear . . . I mean, it doesna always foul up. Ye need not worry." His speech ended awkwardly and he fell silent.

Joanna continued to stand and they both felt more awkward than ever.

Finally Alec spoke again, attempting to alter the direction of the conversation. "Ye like the shore an' the beach then?"

"Oh yes, I love it. There was nothing like this where I was raised."

"There's nothin' like it t' encourage the Lord's peace when the mind gets muddled . . ." He looked out at the crashing waves and for a moment forgot to finish his sentence. His thoughts were still full of the awful events of the day.

"But . . . I've intruded. I'd better be going," said Joanna, moving away.

"Weel," said Alec, "ye might have intruded . . . but 'tis a welcome intrusion, I assure ye. When I came here I thought I needed t' be alone. But maybe I need some company after all. Wrestlin' wi' the paradoxes o' life is gettin' me nowhere."

"I doubt I can be of any help, Mr. MacNeil," she said, then smiled.

"Weel, the first thing ye can do, Miss Matheson, is t' leave off callin' me Mr. MacNeil. I've never been much comfortable wi' such formality. I'd be pleased if ye'd jist call me by my given name, Alec."

"And you'll return the favor?"

"Aye, that I will . . . Joanna," he said with a smile.

He took a moment to study her as she stood framed in the sunlight. Her auburn hair was piled atop her head with a few strands falling to either side of her face; her skin was creamy, in contrast to the rough-hewn toughness of the farm women he had grown accustomed to. She had already become used to her new surroundings and was no longer the insecure stranger she had been less than a week earlier.

"Weel," he said after a moment, ". . . sit ye doon, then, Miss . . . ah, Joanna."

They laughed together at his error. Then she sat on the sand near him, spreading her blue and white cotton dress about her feet. Still she found she could not read his face, the flicker of introspection that had momentarily settled there. He was not one to reveal too much of himself at a time.

A long silence ensued.

Joanna looked down at her folded hands. Alec had retreated into the privacy of his own thoughts, and again she felt awkward about having stumbled into his time of retreat. He looked past her toward the open sea. It had always been hard for him to speak his feelings, to share with another his innermost thoughts. He did not know why he should want so desperately to do so just now—except that his heart was too heavy to enable him to bear the burden alone.

"I had t' kill a horse today," he said at length, still gazing into the distance.

"I'm sorry," she said, tilting her face up toward him. "It must be difficult for you."

"He was a grand animal, Flame Dance. I helped deliver him four years ago. His name spoke o' much more than his colorin'. From the moment o' his birth, there was a spark in his eyes—a vigor . . . he was so alive! Ah, 'twas more life in that horse than his flesh could contain and he was so fast! Like a fire ragin' through dry grass."

"Perhaps he's finally free now," ventured Joanna, groping for words. Alec did not respond for some time and she wondered if the statement had upset him.

Finally he spoke, continuing to stare straight ahead: ". . . they shall mount up with wings as eagles; they shall run and not be weary. . . ."

He paused briefly, then went on.

"I know that wasn't intended fer horses, but can ye imagine what it would be like fer him—if indeed there be an afterlife fer beasts—t' run with wings? Even the wind would seem slow!"

"Remember him like that," Joanna said softly, with gentle encouragement in her voice.

He sighed, then turned his blue eyes toward her in gratitude.

"I will," he said. "Thank ye."

"You have a great love for animals, don't you?" said Joanna. "It's more than just a living for you."

"Aye, ye're right. 'Tis my way o' servin' God. I've always been better aroun' animals than people."

"Your religion is important to you, isn't it?" she asked.

"In a manner o' speakin'. But I dinna like t' think o' mysel' as a religious man."

"I don't understand."

"People can be religious aboot many things," he replied. "But I would hardly be doin' my faith justice to jist say I was religious an' leave it at that. An' I'm not so sure I am, anyway. I love God, an' I want t' serve Him and His creation, but not because I'm religious. I suppose it's because havin' once seen His love, what else could I do?"

"What do you mean, 'having seen His love'?"

"It's different for everyone, but mostly I think it's when ye come face-to-face wi' Him and ye realize He still loves and forgives ye no matter who ye are . . . or what ye have done . . ." His voice died away reflectively.

"My grandmother used to say such things, but . . ." She hesitated a moment before continuing. "But there are some things even God wouldn't forgive."

"I've never yet found that t' be so," Alec said softly, noting the momentary flicker of pain that had revealed itself in Joanna's eyes.

"I know I should feel differently," Joanna continued. "Both my grandmother and mother shared that kind of faith. My mother died when I was born. She was . . . very good. I would have wanted to be like her. But I never got the chance. It was because of me—"

She stopped abruptly and a flush crept into her cheeks. "I don't know why I'm saying all this."

"I'm sorry about yer mother," said Alec. "An' ye blame yersel', do ye?"

"No!" she almost shouted. "How could I?" she went on quickly. "I was only a baby."

"Then God?" His eyes seemed to penetrate her very soul.

"Of course not!" There was an unmistakable edge of defensiveness to her tone, but even that did not prevent a tear rising to her eye.

"Perhaps I *do* blame myself . . . I don't know," she went on after a moment's pause. "You seem to have something very special, Alec. Maybe . . . maybe someday I will come face-to-face, as you put it, with God."

"Maybe," he said, knowing this must have been her way of saying she had not yet chosen to follow God. Instinctively he felt enough had been said. He certainly felt no compulsion to preach to her. No one— least of all himself—could be talked into seeing God's love. She would have to meet Him for herself, however and whenever that moment came. Then and only then would she be able to deal with the inner turmoil of the guilt she felt. For him the encounter had come late one summer night alone on the sea. For Joanna it would come soon enough, when the time was ripe.

As if by mutual consent, they fell silent, each content to enjoy the tranquillity of allowing the other time for inner reflections. No word was spoken for perhaps five minutes.

With reluctance, Alec finally stood.

"Weel, I've got several more rounds t' make today," he said as he stretched his long limbs. "Do ye need a ride anywhere?"

"Thanks," said Joanna. "But I'll be meeting Nathaniel in a while. I think I'll stay here for a few more moments." She smiled.

"I'm glad ye happened along, Joanna. Maybe sometime ye'd like t' come wi' me on a round or two. They're not all so intense as a cow birthin' or a horse killin'. Sometimes it's right fun."

"I'd like that."

As Alec strode away down the beach toward town, he wondered to himself why he didn't ask her along now. But, then, it seemed she wanted to be alone.

There would come another time.

"I don't care what it takes . . . you get those papers!"

"But," answered one of the others, noticeably cowed by the lawyer's tone, "how far do ye want us t' go? I mean . . . ye don't want us t'—"

"Whatever it takes! Do you understand me?"

Palmer Sercombe stopped pacing around his inner office and glared at his two reluctant accomplices. The dimly lit china lamp cast but a shadowy light and only vaguely illuminated Sercombe's companions.

" 'Tis more than we expected, sir."

"Are you asking for more money?" Sercombe snapped.

"If I be understandin' ye aright, weel . . . we'll be takin' a greater risk, an—"

"Don't talk to me about risk!" the lawyer said, almost to himself. Then he turned his attention once more toward the other. "Twenty quid—and that's all!"

"Twenty apiece?"

Sercombe nodded. The other two exchanged silent glances of agreement.

"You'll get half now," the lawyer went on, "and half when the job is successfully completed."

He handed each of the men their share of the money which he had retrieved from his desk drawer, then escorted them out the rear entrance. "Don't come back here," he added. "I'll meet you tomorrow night behind the inn; nine o'clock. Have the papers! You'll not get a farthing more until the job is done."

Sercombe closed the door and bolted it.

What a seedy lot! he thought with disgust. But it was exactly what he had been looking for on his recent trip to Fenwick Harbor. It had been much too risky to use a local person; he should never have resorted to it. But he'd panicked the moment he'd laid eyes on Joanna Matheson's papers.

Perhaps there was good reason to panic.

But he was too smart for that sort of thing. From now on he'd make no more such mistakes. He couldn't afford to.

He sat down at his desk. Even alone in his office he did not slouch or lean back. He picked up a pencil and began to jot a few ideas down on a pad. There was still, after all, other work to be done. Soon, however, the brisk movement of the pencil slowed and then finally stopped. With elbows propped up on his desk, he held the ends of the pencil in both hands, thinking.

Everything had been going so well. What kind of despicable coincidence could have brought that confounded girl all the way from America!

And where in God's name had she gotten hold of those documents?

If only she had delayed a month, or stopped on the way to visit London.

Of course, her claim could be a ruse. Who could have put her up to it? Perhaps the deed was a forgery. Yet, the documents looked too authentic.

He had to get his hands on those papers!

But even with the Matheson girl's meddling interference, all was not lost. He merely had to speed things up. If he could get done in the next week what should have taken two or three, then he could relax. Even if she had suspicions, there would be too little time for her to do anything. The fact that she had gone to the Cuttahays played into his hand. She must, for the moment, see no reason to press the issue. She had not been back to see him and he had heard nothing about any further attempts to get into the house. The attack by his hired ruffians would certainly alarm her. But even if she were able to make the connection and trace it back to him, by then he would hold the documents and she could persist all she wanted—it would be to no avail.

Those two vagabonds had to be successful—there was no room for failure.

He had to have those documents. Everything hinged on that single fact—everything!

Suddenly the pencil snapped between the pressure of his fingers.

20 / Attack!

Joanna could hardly believe she had come all this distance only to find the lawyer away. Gordon Ogilvie had been called out of town on business and was not expected back for two days. She so hoped this old friend of the Cuttahays' might have been able to shed additional light on her grandmother's papers. Now she would have to wait; it seemed she had already been waiting a lifetime.

The inland village of Culden should have offered a tourist from America a pleasant day, with its unusual inn, ancient brick and granite cathedral, and hospitable Scottish residents. But for Joanna it proved symbolic of one more disappointing dead end.

Perhaps she should not have left without Alec.

After all, he had been kind enough to escort her to Culden. But she had no idea how long his calls in the area would take and had no desire to sit alone waiting all day in a strange town. Therefore, she opted to begin the two- or three-hour return journey alone.

She directed her bay mare at a leisurely pace. There was no real hurry to get back, although the thought had occurred to her to try once again to get into Stonewycke Castle. Perhaps this afternoon would prove a better time. Still, she was in no rush and only held a tenuous control of her horse's reins.

The road between Culden and the bridge over the Lindow was a lovely one—thickly forested on her left, and on the right, heather-covered meadows which sloped gradually upward toward distant snow-covered peaks.

The mare's gentle clip-clop on the hard-packed dirt surface of the road lulled Joanna's mind into aimless reflection. The events of these past weeks jumped into her mind in disconnected bits and pieces; try as she might, she could create no order out of the chaos that had happened. Jason . . . MacDuff . . . Sercombe . . . her grandmother.

Would she ever learn anything about her grandmother's past? Would she ever see Jason again?

All at once the image of Alec sprang into her mind. He was certainly not a man of the world like Jason Channing. Yet he had stirred an introspection she had not known before. That was a quality—perhaps even a gift—not every man possessed.

Preoccupied, she paid little heed to the two approaching riders. She would have ridden right by, except that as they drew near they hailed her to stop.

She reined in her horse.

"Mornin', mem," said one of the riders, lifting his wide-brimmed hat politely, revealing coal black eyes underneath, deep-set above a bushy brown beard. The man who spoke sat tall in his saddle; his companion—a shorter, stockier man—remained silent.

"Uh . . . good morning," Joanna returned reticently. Glancing nervously toward the one who had not yet spoken, an involuntary shudder tingled through her spine. A beard would no doubt have been a vast improvement to his scarred and pock-marked face.

"Ye headin' fer Strathy, mem?" asked the bearded rider.

"Yes."

"Not safe fer a leddy like yersel' t' be oot on the roads alone."

Joanna said nothing.

"We'd be mor'n happy t' ride along wi' ye—fer yer protection, mem."

"No need," said Joanna, afraid her uneasiness was showing. It occurred to her that this could become awkward if they continued to press her.

She gently reined her mare to the left and urged her gradually forward, trying to circumvent the riders, but as she did so the scarred man moved to block her path.

"We'd feel sorely guilty, mem, if anythin' was t' happen t' ye," the bearded rider said. A cold chill shot through Joanna as she noticed his hand slowly move to rest on the butt of a carbine strapped to his saddle.

When thinking about it later, Joanna was not sure whether it was good sense or sheer panic that prompted her to do what she did next. In any case, fear had by now nearly overpowered her, and she knew she must act quickly or face some terrible danger.

In a desperate instant of decision, she dug her heels unmercifully into the flanks of her horse.

The mare shot between the horses of the two men, leaving them momentarily stunned by the suddenness of Joanna's daring maneuver. Her heels kicked frantically, prodding the horse on. She lashed the reins across its neck. Daring to cast a hasty glance behind confirmed the worst of her fears—the two riders had already gained a full gallop and were matching her speed stride for stride.

Still she lashed with the reins, digging into the mare's heaving sides with her heels. But that she could hope to reach the Cuttahay farm seemed a slim—if not altogether impossible—prospect.

Joanna never rode so fast; she felt as if she were flying. But she was an inexperienced horsewoman and only sheer terror kept her grip tight and forestalled inevitable disaster.

She rode on, not turning again. She knew the two men were near; the thundering of their horses' hooves reverberated in her ears.

Suddenly a sharp blast pierced the air.

The carbine!

She had forgotten about it. The first shot had probably been intended as a warning. Wouldn't the wisest thing to do be to stop? Maybe she could reason with them.

Yet something drove her on.

In the distance, perhaps two hundred yards away, Joanna saw the narrow wooden bridge across the river. If she could just reach it first and then somehow lengthen her lead on the other side, maybe . . .

Sheer tenacity, however, bolstered with hope, could not have prevented the mare's tiring legs from stumbling over the large rock which lay in the middle of the road. At the speed she was moving it was impossible to recover in time. The horse crumpled to her knees and Joanna was thrown over her head. Springy shrubs at the side of the road broke Joanna's fall but she was momentarily stunned, bruised and cut.

The two riders, having drawn almost alongside to her right, galloped past, unable to rein in their horses, moving at full stride, for some distance. It allowed time for Joanna to scramble to her feet. Every muscle in her body ached, but she managed to plant her feet firmly beneath her and run for the brush at the side of the road. Half stumbling, half running, she made her way through the bushes and farther from the road. The farther she went the denser and taller the growth became.

Soon trees surrounded her and the forest thickened with tightly bunched trees and undergrowth. Shrubs, bushes, brambles, and ferns inhibited every step she tried to take.

She glanced back in haste, seeing nothing, but voices were not far behind. A branch across her way tangled her feet and sent her sprawling on her face. She struggled, groaning, back to her feet.

The voices came closer!

Joanna scrambled over a fallen log, sweating, moist dirt from the forest floor smeared on her riding breeches and face, unconsciously crying out in her desperation, yet afraid of uttering a single sound. Tears streamed down her smudged face as she struggled forward, heart pounding, each breath accompanied by a sharp pain in her chest.

Finally she had to stop . . . if only for a moment. She had to catch her breath.

Silently heaving deep draughts of oxygen into her aching lungs, Joanna listened intently.

Except for her own labored gasps there was silence all about. The light was dim; only occasionally patches of sunlight penetrated the thick, leafy foliage overhead.

"There she is!" a deep, angry voice shouted.

Alas, the short stop had given Joanna's position away. She saw him now—the tall one—some fifty feet away, directing his accomplice around her flank, trying to cut her off in two directions.

She turned and flew, to the limited extent speed was possible in the tangled underbrush, forcing herself to run as swiftly, yet silently, as she could. After a few minutes she paused once more. She heard nothing. Could she have at last eluded pursuit?

Then she heard the two men shouting. They seemed, for the moment to have lost track of her position. She crept forward, away from their sounds, now forcing herself to move as slowly and with as much stealth as possible.

A twig snapped beneath her foot.

Joanna froze in place, kneeling down instinctively.

Suddenly a shot rang through the silent forest, but it was far from its target.

Then Joanna first realized her extreme danger. If they caught her now, so far from the road, neither would have qualms about killing her and leaving her body where it would never be found.

She had to get back to the road!

Joanna resumed her snail's pace escape, bending low to avoid being seen. She feared she was lost, but tried to move in a wide arc and thus return to the road and to her horse.

It was her only chance.

A great fallen tree forced her to the left. She had lost all sense of direction. Now she could only plunge onward and hope she was headed toward the road and not deeper into this tangled maze.

Over the tree she climbed, then again toward her right . . .

All at once, no more than an arm's length in front of her, loomed the scarred face of her pursuer. His yellowed teeth gleamed as his lips parted in an evil grin. The scream that forced itself out of Joanna's mouth was hardly more than a cry choked down by terror.

"Now, mem, where's them papers?" he rasped in a cruel voice as he brandished a large knife in his left hand, its cold steel hovering dangerously inches from Joanna's throat.

"I . . . I don't have them," said Joanna, "they're . . . they're not here."

"Weel, where is they? Come now, ye don't want t' rile me, does ye?"

"I . . . don't have . . . they're not here." But Joanna knew he didn't believe her lie.

"Ye's angerin' me, mem!" he said. "I can get 'em my own way, ye know," he added in a tone which made her shudder.

He lunged toward her.

Instinct made Joanna duck to the right. As he recovered from his misplaced blow, she turned and flew, giving no heed to caution.

If he caught her now—she was dead!

With her life at stake, panic drove her with no thought of the noise she made or the desperate cries for help escaping her frantic lips.

Her sleeve caught on a branch.

She gave it a frantic yank, tearing the once-beautiful cotton fabric and leaving a large chunk behind. The hideous enemy was only a few paces behind. She expected at any moment to encounter his bearded partner or to feel the sharp, cold steel in her back.

Glancing back for a quick look she did not see the figure of a large man step into the path of her flight. With a sickening thud she crashed against him with her full weight and felt his strong arms enclose about her.

A familiar voice was calling her name but it was faint and distant. Her vision blurred by perspiration and exhaustion, mingled with loose strands of wild hair. Her mind grew fuzzy and her head faint. Where had she heard that voice?

Her knees buckled beneath her, and she knew no more.

Alec had scarcely a moment with Joanna before the attacker was upon him. He set Joanna's limp body down as quickly as he could—she would have to recover from her faint on her own. Standing, he spun about to face the scarred face of his antagonist. Alec grabbed the hand still holding the gleaming knife, attempting to twist the assailant's arm and wrest it from him. The battle was fierce, for though the enemy was a small man his strength proved almost equal to Alec's. However, in the end a groaning cry signaled his weakening and a moment later the knife fell on the forest floor.

Alec loosened his grip, but his compassion was unwise; the other broke away and sent a gnarled fist squarely into his jaw. He lunged at Alec, bringing him to the ground. But his advantage was short-lived. All the gathered centuries of Scottish temper rose in Alec's blood. He rallied and pounded his fist into the man on top of him, sending him backward.

Alec jumped to his feet and lurched forward, grabbing the man as he staggered backward and slammed his body into a nearby tree. His fist was raised to strike what would have been the decisive blow when he faltered. His heart pounded in his temples. His mind lingered between rage and fear.

Hesitating, he began to lower his fist.

Suddenly a shot ripped through the air, shattering the bark of the tree. The slug missed Alec's head by three inches.

Joanna began to come to herself only moments after Alec set her down. Even while struggling to regain her feet she remained in a daze. Then she saw the approach of the bearded man, rifle in hand, too late to scream a warning to Alec.

She lunged toward him just as the shot rang out, grabbing the villain's legs with her hands. He was knocked off balance and the gun flew from his hands. Alec quickly let his first attacker loose and turned his attentions in the other direction. The tall, bearded man was more nearly Alec's size and his muscular frame appeared as strong as his intent was evil. He quickly regained his feet, swore a vile imprecation at Joanna, and—now angered—strode toward his adversary and in an instant had delivered two powerful blows to Alec's midsection.

"Ye'll see what comes o' meddlin' where ye're na welcome!" he cursed with a growling voice. "We'll leave the two o' ye i' the forest fer rat's meal!"

In another moment Alec was fighting off both men. The shorter of the two located his knife where it had fallen and poised himself to send its razorsharp steel point into Alec's back the moment his friend had him sufficiently occupied.

Perceiving his intent, Alec backtracked keeping both men in front of him. The tall man sent a blow to Alec's head, dazing him momentarily. Almost at the same instant a stinging stab of pain pierced his right shoulder and he felt his warm blood flowing from the gash of the knife.

He kicked at the short man, trying to hit his knife hand with his boot while guarding his other side against his companion.

Another piercing shot brought the melee to an abrupt halt.

The three men fell apart and immediately Alec looked in Joanna's direction, where, pale and trembling, she clutched the carbine with quivering fingers.

The two attackers backed off, eyeing Joanna intently, and fled into the woods without a word.

Joanna dropped the gun, her body shaking as she at last let the pent-up sobs loose. Alec hastened to her side.

" 'Tis over, noo," he said, trying to soothe her as he gathered her into his arms. " 'Tis over . . . everythin's all right," he whispered over and over. But even as he did so he kept a wary eye peeled for any hint of recurring trouble. He stooped to retrieve the gun, just in the event its use should again become necessary. Holding it with his left hand, he clutched Joanna's quivering body with his weakened right arm. He brushed a strand of hair from her face and gently kissed her forehead. Gradually Alec felt Joanna's trembling tears ebb as she regained her strength.

He tried not to think of the sickness in the pit of his own stomach. The rage surging through him had been more overpowering than he would have believed possible. He shuddered to think what he might have done to the first man had not the gunshot from his partner interceded. He had lived in fear of a moment like this for years.

Could he have killed again?

The uncertainty was almost as horrifying as the act itself.

Almost without thought he took Joanna's hand and led her from the depths of the forest.

21 / Plans

Letty wrung warm water from the clean cloth.

Nursing a wound was something she could do, but understanding why such a wound would be inflicted was too much for her gentle mind. The moment she had seen Joanna and Alec, tears welled up in her eyes, not only for their obvious pain, but that two persons she dearly loved should have been so victimized.

It was past dinnertime when the two rode in together on Alec's horse; Joanna's had wandered off after its fall and they were too exhausted to attempt a search. They hoped the mare would find her way back. If not, they would return to the Dormin to find her. In the meantime, the Cuttahays rushed them into the house and immediately tended to their wounds—superficial cuts and bruises, but nonetheless painful.

Alec bore a deep knife gash in his right arm.

"We can be thankful 'twas no worse," said Letty after Joanna gave a brief account of the incident.

" 'Tis a shame the scoundrels got away again!" said Nathaniel in an outrage.

"Not *again*," Joanna corrected. "Neither of these men were the one you scared off in town the other day."

"But ye say they were still after the papers, lass?"

Joanna nodded. "They told me to give them the papers, just like that."

" 'Tis a good thing the lad came along. How did ye come t' be in Dormin right then, Alec?"

Alec had been silent since they entered the cottage.

"I left Culden just after Joanna and was tryin' t' overtake her when she was accosted," he replied in a sober tone.

"Weel," fumed Nathaniel, "I'd like t' get me hands on Tom Forbes."

"But Joanna said it wasna him," cautioned his wife.

"I'll warrant he knows somethin'! I should hae turned him o'er t' the Ballie soon's I saw that bandage."

Nathaniel paced the floor in silence for a moment. Then he stopped abruptly and faced the others.

"It's always back t' them papers," he said. "Someone's willin' t' kill fer them. Which makes me think mor'n more that what we all been

135

thinkin' aboot Joanna bein' one o' *the* Duncans 'tis true.''

"If only I could get *into* the house and talk to some of the people,'' Joanna sighed. "I feel certain someone would tell me something.''

"Maybe they *could*, lass,'' Letty interjected. "But the question is, *would* they? Walter's already shown himsel' t' be tight-lipped, an' though he's a good man, he can be stiff-necked when he wants. Comes o' that Highland blood o' his, I suppose. An' Mrs. Bonner . . . well, if she's under orders from Mr. Sercombe too, I expect she'll be bound t' obey. The only other body there is auld Dorey.''

"I doobt ye'd get a straight word from him,'' Nathaniel put in. "But I expect he'd have a mite t' say aboot the Duncans—he's been there near as long as I can recollect.''

"What's wrong with him?'' Joanna asked. "The way people talk, you'd think he was crazy.''

"Na, na. He's harmless, t' be sure,'' Letty answered. "Keeps t' himsel' an' tends his flowers. Stays in the castle or on the grounds mostly. I only recall seein' him in toon once—oh, must be years noo. Come right int' the Crearys' yard, he did. That was when Doug Creary's mama was still livin'. Weel, auld Mistress Creary stood on the porch an' watched as he began diggin' up the earth aroun' the front o' the hoose—guess she was jist too surprised t' say anythin'. Then he took some plants he had in his knapsack an' laid them int' the groun' an' planted some seeds. All this, mind ye, wi' oot a word spoken. He watered the plants an' then wi' a smile an' a tip o' his hat he strolled away leavin' Mistress Creary wi' her mouth hangin' open. In a few months the plants was a-bloomin' an' before ye knew it the Creary's yard—what used t' be the poorest in the valley—was nearly as pretty as Stonewycke's own. The other folk decided they liked the idea an' soon every yard aroun' was bright wi' flowers!''

Letty smiled joyfully and for a moment forgot the terrible events of the day. "If that be crazy, then it couldna harm us all t' have a bit more o' it.''

"If I could just have even a few minutes to talk with him,'' Joanna said.

"If he can talk at all,'' added Nathaniel.

"He spoke to me when I was there the other day,'' Joanna said hopefully.

"Did he?''

"Well, only one word. He seemed frightened. Then Mr. Innes drove up and he ran away.''

"Alec,'' said Nathaniel, turning toward the younger man. "Ye're oot t' the hoose now an' then. What do ye think?''

Until then, Alec had remained detached from the group. The muscles of his jaw rippled with inward tension.

Perhaps it was the pain in his shoulder, thought Nathaniel. But his quiet seemed to come from more than physical pain. Nathaniel had a suspicion, but he knew he could not offer a word of comfort to the lad without revealing his secret—which even Letty did not know. When the time came for Alec to tell, the decision would have to be his alone.

"Are ye all right?" Nathaniel asked slowly.

Alec lurched to his feet. "I jist need some fresh air," he said, and stalked from the room.

The cool, sharp evening air felt good. But it could not clear his muddled thoughts. Since that dreaded night in his hometown he had desperately avoided even the hint of conflict. And now he seemed caught up into the middle of a conflict more dangerous than he dared even consider. When he saw Joanna so battered and desolate, he had wanted to protect her, to come to her aid. For those few brief moments . . . he had wanted to kill! He still trembled at the thought.

And he knew that if he found her threatened or in danger, he would have to jump into the battle on her behalf again.

What was he to do?

What is expected of me? he wondered. *What does God require? What would have happened to Joanna if I had not been there?* He closed his eyes and clenched his teeth as the agony in his mind increased.

He heard the cottage door open and a soft footstep approached behind him. But he could not turn to meet it.

"I'm sorry," Joanna whispered. "I'm so sorry to have brought all this on you. I . . . I've been so thoughtless. You people have been so kind to me, and look how I've repaid you."

"No!" said Alec, spinning around to face her. "Ye must not say that . . . or think it, even. It's not ye? It's me. Ye've asked nothin' o' us. Ye had a need and we—I helped ye . . . an' I would do it again. I would hae to."

"I don't understand."

"Ye've brought nothin' on me. I brought it on mysel' . . . or maybe God has brought it on me. I've been runnin', an' what if I'd turned my back on ye too? I can't do that . . . I don't think that's what the Lord would want. An' yet . . . "

"Alec," said Joanna, "please, what's troubling you so?"

"Ye're probably thinkin' maybe I am a babbling idiot t' be speakin' like this. I thought I had it all worked oot in my mind. But—"

He stopped abruptly.

"Alec. What is it?"

"Four years ago somethin' happened—my sister was attacked. When I saw the man, I grabbed him an' . . . "

He stopped again and covered his face with his large hands, hiding the tears that had begun to flow.

"I . . . I," he stammered, "I *killed* him!"

"Oh, Alec!"

"They called me a hero, but I felt like the very devil. With my bare hands . . . I took a life."

He held his hands up toward her.

"These hands . . . hands that are supposed t' give an' protect life—these very hands . . ."

Again he covered his face in shame.

Joanna gently reached out, clasped his hands in hers, and said: "Alec, these are good hands. All I see in them are the tender, loving hands that gently placed that baby calf before its mother."

"But today . . . I think I could have killed again. I . . . I was so full of anger when I saw what they had done that—"

"But, Alec," she interrupted, squeezing his hands more tightly in hers, "you had no choice! Those men were trying to kill me. And they would have."

He shook his head in confusion, unable to speak.

"Alec," Joanna went on, "I saw what happened. You did what you had to do, and no more. When you had that man against the tree, you could have struck him again. But you didn't. Your anger didn't control you. You subdued it."

A long silence followed.

At length Alec calmed and raised his eyes to look at Joanna.

"Alec, thank you for what you did. You saved my life today. And after what you've told me, it means even more. But I'll not ask anything more of you or Nathaniel or Letty. I cannot involve innocent people any further in—"

"Innocent!" Alec said, laughing for the first time. "Lass, ye hae no say in the matter. We are boun' t' help ye."

"I'm afraid I couldn't ask you to help me with what I plan to do next."

"An' jist what would that be?"

As she had listened earlier to the discussion about Dorey, Joanna had found herself thinking once again about her initial reason for coming to Port Strathy—her grandmother's plea to find her family. That remained the one thing she still had to resolve. And to that end she knew one thing that had to be done. She would have to try again.

"I'm going back to Stonewycke tomorrow." Her words were flat and unyielding, braced against argument. Something was happening inside her. She felt a change. The old, timid, quiet Joanna was slowly giving way to a new, more confident Joanna. And she could not help but think the change a good one. Perhaps this decision was her way of helping the change along by asserting herself in a direction she felt she had to go. "I want to see this Dorey. Somehow I think he can tell me something."

"It could be dangerous. Ye know what's been happenin'. These men won't give up."

"It's something I have to do," she insisted. "My mind's made up."

"Then I'll be goin' wi' ye," said Alec.

She opened her mouth to protest, but before she could, he said, ". . . an' I've made up *my* mind."

She smiled.

"I'll be most happy for that," she consented.

Walter Innes had no reason to suspect the Cuttahays' luncheon invitation.

A widower, he was often the glad recipient of the generous hospitality of the neighborhood. This morning seemed no different, though it had been quite some time since he had socialized with anyone. Since the laird's death, he found he preferred to remain on the property, either at his own little cottage or at Stonewycke itself. But more than once he remarked to himself that "it was like closin' the byre door after the cow got oot." Still, there was Dorey and Mrs. Bonner, the housekeeper; and the house itself *was* in his care.

When Nathaniel had stopped by that morning, Walter suddenly found himself longing for company, especially the company of these friends who never failed to lift his spirits. And there was no doubt his spirits could use some help right now. It crossed his mind every now and then that maybe he was going as daft as Dorey himself. It would do him good to get out for a while; Mr. Sercombe was sure to understand.

He closed the gate and locked it—another new policy handed down by Sercombe, this one only yesterday. *A lot o' useless effort if ye ask me*, thought the factor to himself. The ancient cast iron gate was a mere formality as protection from intruders, for the surrounding portions of the iron fence had fallen into disrepair years ago, now supplemented in part by the thick, ten-foot hedge.

Walter turned left, and his lanky figure paralleled the hedge as he turned down the steep path into the rocky gorge along the side of the road. The footpath did not lead toward the town but offered a shortcut west to the valley in which the Cuttahay farm lay.

Yes, this was just what he needed.

The laird's death could not help but change the character of life at Stonewycke, but of late it had become almost like a prison. Not that it had ever been a cheery place, even during the laird's lifetime. But at least then everyone was free to come and go as they pleased. Now, however, no one came to the House—not even for deliveries. The lawyer's security precautions had turned it into a mausoleum. Walter had even considered giving up his post—he'd no doubt be losing his job soon enough anyway, once the property was sold. Yet he could not neglect the deep loyalty he felt toward the great estate.

Deep in thought, Walter walked across the grassy meadow on the other side of the gorge. He took no notice of the two furtive figures behind him, approaching the gate he had just locked. He did not see them test the lock, then, finding it secure, creep around the fence eastward to the breach just where the hedge began.

Joanna argued against the subterfuge.

But she trusted Alec; and when the Cuttahays went along with his suggestion, she consented, knowing they were doing it for her benefit. As she and Alec crawled through an opening in the hedge, seeing Stonewycke with all the potential secrets it might reveal so close, she forgot her earlier hesitation.

The house loomed before her in its ancient gray splendor. Stone laced with ivy, towers, parapets, and ramparts—possibly the very home of her grandmother. Buffeted by conflicting emotions, she walked slowly toward the door. If nothing else succeeded on her trip to Scotland, she could at least know she had touched a portion of the past she had come seeking.

"Do we try the front door?" Joanna asked.

"There still might be a few o' the servants aroun'," replied Alec.

He paused, then suddenly turned the opposite direction. "Come on," he said, "I hae an idea."

He led her around the house the way she had gone before, past the little rose garden, still farther to the stables and beyond, and through a tree-lined courtyard. When Joanna's eye caught a glint of the sun reflecting off the roof of a glass greenhouse, she knew their destination.

She had hardly had leisure to frame any definite opinions about the man she had assumed was the gardener. On her previous visit he had departed so hastily. And from what she had gathered from hearing others talk about him, she expected the man known as Dorey to be frail and rather simple-minded, with an empty stare in his eyes. But as she walked into the greenhouse, she instantly realized her presentiment could not have been more inaccurate. His trim broad-shouldered frame was bent now, but it hinted of past glory, as did his thick mass of snow-white hair. But his face! At a glance Joanna saw that it bore the mark of the aristocracy of the family he served; even his simple, homely work clothes could not hide the noble look of his aging face.

He looked up slowly as they entered.

Joanna saw that she had been correct, however, about the far-off gaze in his eye; it was so different from the look of alarm which had greeted her when they met briefly before. He turned toward them, stared directly forward, but appeared to take no notice of their presence.

"Primula Scotica," he said, as if continuing an ongoing conversation with himself that they had interrupted. "Lovely, isn't it?"

Joanna looked toward the tiny, purple-red blooms in the wooden planter where the man's deft fingers gently loosened the soil.

"Yes . . . it is," she answered, feeling suddenly awkward.

He looked at his visitors again, glancing back and forth, finally resting his eyes on Joanna. Forcing his vision into focus, a brief questioning frown crossed his brow, then just as quickly disappeared. The distant, glazed look reappeared.

"Do you know flowers?" he asked.

Joanna shook her head.

"The Scottish primrose—not many in this area, but mine are doing well. The ones you see in the valley are a different variety. But this strain is very rare." His voice lacked the heavy brogue she had already grown accustomed to; if she knew anything about accents, she would have identified an Oxford ring in his. "I suppose I shall have to try them outside the nursery eventually, but . . ."

His soft voice trailed away in a few mumbled words and he returned his attentions to the plant he was cultivating.

"Even the most delicate o' flowers can be hardier than they look," Alec ventured. Dorey looked hard at him for a moment.

"Yes . . . perhaps," said Dorey, then paused. "I . . . I know you, don't I?" he added in an uncertain tone.

"I'm Alec MacNeil—I've tended some o' the laird's animals."

"Ah, yes. You're the young vet."

Just as quickly as the promise of dialogue had begun, Dorey lowered his eyes and began to putter about with some of the other plants on his workbench, offering not another word. He sprinkled a handful of fertilizer into the pot of a brilliant orange azalea, worked it deftly into the soil, gave it a swash of water, and stood back to admire his work. Then he turned his attention elsewhere, picked up several small pots containing leafy plants Joanna did not recognize, and carried them to his worktable. Gently he loosened the velvet-like green foliage and commenced the operation of transferring them to larger pots.

Joanna and Alec watched with fascination, neither feeling an inclination to disturb the serenity, content for the moment to observe Dorey's skillful ministrations. So complete was his absorption in his work, Joanna was certain he had forgotten they were present. Joanna was wondering how she might reinstate the conversation when Dorey broke the silence.

"Was there something you were wanting?" he asked, not looking up from his work.

"We—we hoped just to have a visit with you," answered Joanna cautiously.

"I have no visitors." His voice sounded almost apologetic.

"We didn't mean to intrude," said Joanna, "but I've wanted to meet you, and the last time I was here—"

"Then . . . I don't know you?" he said, glancing up and eyeing her intently. "But I thought . . ." He paused and a cloud of perplexity crossed his face; then he looked back down and never completed the sentence.

"My name is Joanna. I've come from America."

"America?"

"Yes . . . I arrived only a few days ago."

"But surely . . . it's Alastair you'd be wanting to see. He's gone now . . . dead, you understand. He was the laird, you know . . . I am his houseguest. I'm afraid the place is just not the same without Alastair. You will be disappointed, I'm certain—but of course you are welcome. It's too bad, though. Alastair always loved visitors."

"What will you do now that the laird is gone?" Joanna asked.

"Do? Well . . . tend my flowers just like I've always done. They will always need tending, you know."

"Will you stay here?"

"I have no place else to go. It's been so long—"

"I mean will you stay here, at Stonewycke?"

"Oh, the house. Yes, of course. Palmer has arranged everything for me. A very generous man. I don't deserve it, but he knows I could never leave. I know I'm only a guest, but this is my home."

He stopped and looked hard at Joanna, as if trying to remember something.

"Yes, I shall stay. Nothing will change. It won't be the same, but still nothing will change. That's the way it is here—always the same, always . . ."

His voice trailed away again as he plucked off one of the delicate primrose blossoms and held it up toward the light in admiration. "There is none lovelier, don't you think?"

"Yes," agreed Joanna, trying not to allow her voice to betray her disappointment that the conversation had turned so abruptly back to the flowers.

"Yours are especially lovely," she added.

"Thank you. I work with my flowers . . . and I love them."

Neither Joanna nor Alec said a word. Dorey continued, however, taking no notice of them.

"Sometimes it takes such an effort to think. Maybe that's why it's so peaceful here. I don't have to think. I can just visit my flowers and work in the nursery. I suppose it's odd that I would find peace here, you know . . . after . . ."

He paused, wiped one eye with the back of his sleeve, then looked down at his hands. "Oh no!" he exclaimed, seeing the delicate blossom crushed between his fingers which had steadily tightened as he spoke, "I've ruined it!—I was going to give it to you . . . I know how you love them . . ." The confusion once more passed over his face and halted his words. Then a look of frustration grew out of it and he said, "But why have you come here?"

"I hoped we could be friends," she said.

"Friends . . . why me? I don't understand?"

"I came to Scotland all alone. I hoped to find my grandmother's family here."

"Family is important," he said, seemingly recovered. "I have no family either. There are some relations in London, but they hardly count."

"Were you related to the laird?" asked Joanna tentatively. She debated within herself how far to push the discussion.

"Related? I'm his houseguest—the laird's. He's dead, you know. Quite a scholar was Alastair—ancient Greece . . . loved history. But it's quiet here now. Even the servants are gone—except the housekeeper, and Innes. Palmer says this is best—too much activity isn't good for me, he says. And I have my flowers. Alastair had this nursery built for me."

"That was kind of him," said Joanna.

Dorey returned to his repotting with vigor. After a lengthy silence, Joanna swallowed, took a deep breath, and prepared to ask her next question.

With her heart thudding in her chest, she said: "Did he have a sister?"

"Sister . . . who? Alastair?"

"Yes. Did Alastair have a sister?"

"Sister. . . ?" he repeated.

Joanna waited but soon realized either his mind had wandered off again or he did not intend to answer her question. He bent over his workbench, to all appearances oblivious to her words. Joanna proceeded:

"I didn't want to bother you, but . . . well, since you have lived here so long, I thought you might be able to tell me something. You see, my grandmother's name is Margaret Duncan—"

Joanna did not finish her sentence.

As he stood straight up the look on Dorey's face stopped Joanna short. With the words he winced and a momentary frown wrinkled his brow. Then, just as abruptly, his countenance went blank. His attentions returned to his table and his hands accelerated their activity, moving frantically at their work.

"Sinningia," he said. "They'll have a lovely red and white blossom. Need plenty of light and humidity. You wouldn't think a tropical plant like this could grow here, would you? But of course, it must stay in the nursery. And I must watch over it—"

"Please . . ." Joanna implored.

"Joanna," Alec gently interrupted. "Perhaps we could come another time t' visit."

"Another time," said Dorey. "Yes . . . another time. That would be nice, young man."

He looked at Joanna again. A trace of knowing passed through his eyes and his lips formed a faint smile—the first she had seen. "Yes . . . you are always welcome here," he went on. "I'm glad you've come back. You must come again—we'll have tea. But now I must go . . . yes, I really must go . . ." and with those parting words, he hurried past them out of the greenhouse.

23 / News from America

Olive sighed heavily as she lifted her hand to knock on the Cuttahays' door. She didn't like telegrams—they never brought good news. She hadn't been at all thrilled when the laird installed the telegraph machine in Port Strathy and even less when the duty of tending it fell to her. It had been a plague ever since; the only good thing about it was that precious few messages ever came over it.

Now she bore a message for Joanna and she knew the contents would further burden the already troubled girl.

Letty answered the door.

Joanna sat by the fire still pondering her visit with old Dorey. She had had such high hopes for the encounter but like everything else, it had ended in disappointment. The old man was probably crazy just like everyone said and would not or simply *could* not tell her anything. Whatever her grandmother had sent her here to find seemed bent on eluding her—first, through the death of Alastair, her only link with the past; now, through the disorientation of an old man.

Yet her grandmother had passionately urged her to come here, with good reason—though Margaret Duncan could not have guessed at these recent developments. Something terrible was happening, but what it was and how it involved her grandmother, Joanna did not know. If Margaret was truly Alastair's older sister, then she should have been the heir. But still . . .

Her thoughts drifted off unfinished as she became aware of Olive's presence.

"Joanna, dear," she said. "This came for you today." Her voice sounded grave.

Reluctantly, Joanna reached for the paper Olive offered. She opened it and saw Olive's precise printing:

JOANNA
YOUR GRANDMOTHER HAS GONE HOME STOP HAVE MADE ALL THE ARRANGEMENTS STOP NO NEED TO CUT YOUR TRIP SHORT STOP

DR. BLAKELY

"It's so cold and impersonal!" Joanna said. Olive had thought so, too, but she had excused it as a typically medical approach to a crisis.

146

For a moment Joanna could think of nothing else, her mind seeming to have frozen. She looked up at Olive, her face blank. Then slowly her countenance contorted in grief as the reality of the message dawned upon her. Olive put her strong arm around Joanna, and Letty rushed up to offer what comfort she could.

"I'm sorry, lass," Olive said.

"Is it her grandmother?" Letty asked Olive. The storekeeper nodded. "Oh, dear child!" Then when Letty read the printed words, she squeezed Joanna's hand. "I ken 'tis hard fer ye right now, Joanna, but like these words say, she's with her Lord now. Try to take comfort from that."

"I should never have left," Joanna cried.

"You only did what she wanted," Olive said.

"She shouldn't have died all alone . . ." Joanna answered. "And what good have I done here, anyway!"

Joanna walked to the fire and stared into the flickering flames. She shivered despite the warmth. *It's over*, she thought. *My grandmother had one last hope, and I failed her. She died knowing her home would never be restored to her.* Now Joanna realized that must surely have been what her plea had been all about. Her grandmother was dying when Joanna left; the doctor had as much said there was no hope. Yet Joanna had maintained in her heart the smallest of hopes that she might find something in Scotland that would bring healing to her grandmother.

That would never happen now. This message rang with an awful finality. What did anything else matter? From the beginning all her efforts seemed destined to end in futility. She should never have made that promise and thus raised the woman's hopes. Maybe she never realized what a failure her granddaughter was. *Perhaps I can go home and forget all my failures*, Joanna thought miserably.

Home! At the thought Joanna cried anew. Her grandmother was the only home she had ever known; with her gone . . . she had no home. She had begun to feel attached to this place, these people, but she had no reason to stay now—besides, she would only bring trouble on them too.

She turned around to face the two women who had become her friends. As she looked on their kind, sympathetic faces, she knew she had grown to love them. How could she leave this place?

"I'm so thankful you two are with me now," she said, trying to form her quivering lips into a smile. "It's going to be so hard to leave . . ."

"Leave, child?" Letty interrupted, sounding almost as dejected as Joanna.

"I came here at my grandmother's request," Joanna replied. "Now that she's gone I don't see the purpose of staying."

"Do you think her death makes your promise any less binding?" Olive asked, her natural gruffness making her words sound sterner than she perhaps intended.

"I was doing this for her . . ." Joanna began, but suddenly she recalled that part of it had been for herself also. Still, she had already been too selfish.

"If your grandmother was Lady Margaret Duncan," Olive went on, "and I think we can be pretty certain she was, then there is more to this than simply fulfilling a dying woman's last wish. This land meant so much to her that she spent her last words on it. And now something wrong is happening here. Stonewycke needs you, Joanna, now, more than ever before."

"What can I do against all the violence and threats?" was Joanna's anguished response.

It was Letty who gently replied, recalling the dear memory of her own mother's stories of times long past. "Ye can do what anyone wi' Ramsey blood in her veins would do," she said. "Ye can do what Lady Margaret herself would hae done if she had seen her people threatened. Joanna, hae ye considered that it's not mere chance that ye hae come jist when ye have?"

"I don't want to fail her," Joanna replied.

"Ye willna, lass. I ken ye willna."

"I suppose I don't have much choice." Joanna blinked back a fresh rush of tears. "And I truly don't want to leave this place just yet. I'm growing to love it so."

Then the three women embraced one another and wept together. There were tears even in Olive's shrewd old eyes.

The fire flared with a noisy spattering of sparks.

Sandy Cobden tossed another log into the hearth. The conversation was lively that evening among the small gathering of locals in the Bluster 'N Blow's common room, and the ale had begun to flow freely.

"If I hadna seen't wi' my own eyes I wouldna believed't!" boomed Rob Peters as if he were still shouting orders aboard his herring boat.

" 'Tis no more'n Mr. Sercombe promised," said Sandy from behind his counter.

"Aye. But I always say, 'Don't count yer chickens afore they be hatched.' "

"Weel, it sounds t' me as though they be startin' t' hatch. So maybe we can start countin' noo," put in Doug Creary. "One thing's aye fer certain, those men were excavatin' the new harbor, sure's day."

"Things'll be changin' here noo!" added Sandy, and he poured another round of ale as if to celebrate.

"Aye . . . change fer sure," MacDuff's voice drawled with uncertainty. "Maybe more'n we're wantin'."

Nathaniel had listened in silence. His chief purpose in coming that night was not to socialize with his neighbors but to gather information. After his chat with Walter Innes and Joanna's visit with Dorey, he felt the time had come for him to put his shoulder to it, as he said, and find out whatever he could. The news of the arrival of workmen from Aberdeen had certainly been unexpected and had thrown the whole town into an agitation of excitement and speculation.

"Ye never know," he finally interjected into the discussion. "It may be that MacDuff's right. Not all change be fer the best."

"That's easy fer ye t' say, Nathaniel," said Rob. "Ye havena had t' risk life an' limb comin' in an' oot o' that harbor every day. I say 'tis high time somethin' was finally done aboot it." As if to seal his words with a stamp of authority, he lifted his mug to his lips and took a long draught of ale, then set it down on the thick oak table with a resounding thud.

" 'Tis jist a shame the poor laird had t' die fer it t' happen," added Creary.

"Aye, but it shows who cares fer us, after all," said Rob.

"Sercombe?" Nathaniel said with a dubious scowl.

"Don't bite the hand that's feedin' ye, Nathaniel," returned Rob.

"Weel," said Nathaniel, " 'tis true enough that one hand may be feedin' me, but 'tis the other hand I'll be worrin' aboot."

"Are ye tryin' t' malign the word o' Sercombe?" snapped the innkeeper.

"Not a bit o' it, Sandy," Nathaniel answered, realizing he'd been foolish to make an empty accusation. "I'm jist sayin' the land's not sold yet, so let's hold back oor celebration till then."

The conversation continued on, filled with speculations—some founded, others groundless—on the extent and specific form of the anticipated improvements. Each carried his own set of notions, based more on his personal needs and wishes than on any foundation in fact. On one thing, however, they were all agreed—a great day was coming to Port Strathy. Before long, one of their number stood and toasted the health and long life of the lawyer they had been fortunate enough to have take an interest in their town—Palmer Sercombe. He took his seat to the resounding cheers from his companions, and they continued thus, long into the evening through several more pitchers of Sandy's finest dark ale.

Nathaniel had chosen to hold his peace and had just decided to take his leave when the door of the inn opened and Tom Forbes walked in, wearing mud-splattered riding boots and breeches and a heavy, dark-brown leather coat.

"Hey, Tom," called Rob Peters, "come on over an' join yer friends fer a drink or two!"

Forbes said not a word, waved off the invitation with a tired look, and slunk toward a corner table where he sat down alone. His wide-rimmed hat cast a dark shadow over his face. Nathaniel eyed him intently, but Forbes seemed to pay him no attention, possibly never having realized it was Nathaniel who had driven him away that night in the alley.

Deciding to remain a while longer, Nathaniel turned his attention to Rob Peters' outline of how the new harbor ought to be constructed, while MacDuff—farmer that he was—proceeded to refute every point. There were several suggestions as to the best possible location for the new fish processing plant and then the discussion digressed so far afield as trying to decide who the foreman should be. Peters thought he might give up fishing altogether and operate his own schooner service to Aberdeen. MacDuff suggested that if any improvements were made, they ought to first make the roads fit to use.

Just then, two men entered the common room, glanced around, then walked toward Forbes's table and sat down. The talk at Nathaniel's table grew immediately hushed in the presence of the two strangers.

"Couple o' workmen, I'll warrant," said Rob in a muted tone.

"That tall un's a rum 'un, he is," whispered MacDuff, glancing over his shoulder at Forbes's companions.

But Nathaniel scarcely heard a word. The moment they had appeared his heart gave a leap. No shadows could hide the bushy black beard of the one or the scarred face of the other. They were speaking in whispers; Nathaniel strained his every nerve to make out their voices, but he could only make out periodic snatches of the conversation.

". . . hardly my fault," Forbes was saying, " . . . ye jist bungled the job, that's all . . ."

"Ah! we had the lass," the bearded man replied, "till that meddlin' big fella . . . if he hadna . . ." By now, the conversation at Nathaniel's own table had again risen to an excited pitch and drowned out the remainder of the man's speech.

"Do ye understan' what ye're t' do this time?" Forbes was saying when again Nathaniel was able to discern their voices.

"Mr. Sercombe—"

"Quiet, ye fool!" snapped Tom, loud enough for anyone to hear. But no one took much notice.

"Ye can count on us, man."

"I hope ye're right. If ye blunder't again, there'll be the devil fer us all t' pay . . . likes no mistakes . . . kind o' man he is. Now—get out."

"How 'bout a glass o' ale first?" suggested the short, scarred man who hadn't spoken till now.

"Get out, ye idiot!" Tom nearly shouted.

The two men rose and skulked from the inn.

After a few moments, trying to appear oblivious to the recent proceedings at the corner table, Nathaniel rose, bade his farewells to his tipsy friends, paid Sandy his tab, and slowly exited the Bluster 'N Blow by the back door, where, he said, he had tethered his horse.

The cold night air rushed against his warm face. Hurriedly, he crept around the edge of the inn to a point where he could keep an eye on the front door. In another five minutes, out walked Tom Forbes, who turned up the street toward the few shops.

Once he judged himself a safe distance behind, Nathaniel set out behind, keeping a sharp eye on his quarry and a careful mind on his feet so he made no unnecessary noise. Past the chandlery and Miss Sinclair's store Tom walked. It came as no surprise when he halted in front of the lawyer's office, looked quickly about, rapped three quick times on the door, and then entered the darkened room noiselessly.

Hesitating only a moment, Nathaniel stepped out from the shed he had crept behind, hastened to the buildings, skirted the outside wall of

Miss Sinclair's store, and at length arrived at the back alley which ran past the row of buildings. In a moment, he arrived at Sercombe's back door. The shade was drawn and there could have been at most a single candle inside illuminating two larger-than-life figures against the window. He leaned his ear up to the edge of the window and listened.

". . . it may be our only recourse," came a voice Nathaniel quickly identified as Sercombe's.

"I know they're bunglers, but I say let's at least give the two Fenwick boys another chance." That voice was Forbes's. "No one knows them here . . . an' ye canna be implicated yersel'."

"It hardly matters now that the Cuttahays and that cursed vet have seen those documents."

"But ye said yersel' they couldna do a thing wit'oot the papers in hand. If we can jist get 'em—"

"They might still find a way."

There followed a long silence.

"All the same," he continued, "if she's out of the way, those papers would be meaningless."

"Gettin' the papers is one thing. Murder's another. I'll have no part o' that. I told ye that in the beginnin'."

The lawyer made a hollow attempt at a laugh.

"Come now, my friend. You had no trouble with the laird."

"That was different," Forbes said. "He was old . . . his time had come. An' besides, the old fool deserved what he got. An' I didn't kill him—if he'd been a better horseman—"

"A moot point, I'm sure," Sercombe laughed. But he instantly sobered. "Remember, my friend. We all—including yourself—stand to lose a great deal if this thing is delayed. Our buyer will be here soon—in a matter of a few days. I want no loose ends muddling up our end of the deal. And from now on, don't use the front door. In fact—we had better not be seen together again. I see no need for further interviews—*if we each hold up our end!*"

Suddenly, Nathaniel heard the latch of the rear exit rattle. He scrambled for a place to hide and crouched behind a garbage bin just as the door opened. Had Forbes gone toward the left instead of the right he would have nearly stumbled over Nathaniel's bent body. For the time, however, Nathaniel remained hidden and whispered a silent prayer of thanks.

He waited until the footfall of Forbes's retreating steps could no longer be heard. In another minute, the candle in the lawyer's office was extinguished and he heard Sercombe exit through the front of the building, locking the door behind him. Nathaniel waited another few moments, then rose, straightened his stiff back, and carefully crept around the building the way he had come.

The street was deserted. In the distance, the voices of his friends at the Bluster' N' Blow could still be heard. He hastened back to the inn, retraced his steps around back, untied his horse and led it away. Once out of earshot of the inn, he mounted, dug his heels into the horse's flanks, and raced home as fast as his horse could carry him.

He had to take immediate precautions against another attack. He only hoped he wasn't too late and admonished himself for delaying so long following Forbes. What if the two men were at his home this very moment!

Nathaniel could have spared his horse the frantic gallop. But he had no idea that even as he led his horse away from the inn, the two men had doubled back and were enjoying another round or two of ale.

Whatever their intentions, they would not accomplish them until their thirst was well quenched.

25 / A Second Legal Appraisal_____

Nathaniel galloped up to the house, dismounted in a thick cloud of dust, and rushed inside.

Joanna sat in Letty's cozy kitchen sipping tea, still feeling numb from Olive's recent news. Letty busied herself over the breadboard, despite the hour, uneasy over Nathaniel's long absence and unable to retire until her anxiety had been stilled.

As Nathaniel burst through the door he glanced to the right and left, taking in the peaceful setting, and simply uttered, "Thank God!" He took off his hat and collapsed in a chair. Alarmed by his obvious apprehension, the two women plied him with questions. But try as they might, neither was able to draw a word out of him as to what had happened in town to cause such concern.

"It's time we was all in bed," he said at length, and they finally consented.

As Nathaniel lay quietly down beside his wife a few minutes later, his eyes remained wide open. The moment he heard the deep steady rhythm of Letty's breathing—the signal she was finally asleep—Nathaniel eased himself out of bed. He dressed, tiptoed back out into the living room, placed another log on the dying fire, and took his rifle down from over the mantle. He checked to make certain it was loaded, then sat down in his favorite rocker—the gun lying across his lap in readiness—with his back to the fire and his face toward the door.

Nathaniel rocked back and forth and waited. Gradually his eyelids began to droop. A man of great energy and superb health, the strenuous day had finally caught up with him.

All at once Nathaniel started forward.

He hadn't meant to drift off. How long he had been asleep he had no idea. It was the dead of night and the eerie silence hung heavy. But there could be no doubt—the soft thud of a footstep on the porch had awakened him.

He clutched the handle of the rifle.

The front door opened with a creak, and through the opening the light of the moon streamed into the cottage. In its glow Nathaniel could make out the silhouette of a tall, bearded man . . . a figure he had seen only once before—tonight at the inn. Almost immediately he could smell the stale scent of ale about him.

The moment for action had come.

Leaning forward, poising himself in preparation for battle, and saying to himself, "In the name of the Father, Son, and Holy Ghost, Amen," Nathaniel sprang from his chair with a bound and rushed toward the enemy screaming, "A diabhuil mhoir, tha thu ag deanamh breug!"

Before the terrified burgler could recover his dazed wits, dimmed by alcohol and further sedated by the conviction that the entire house was asleep, he received a punishing blow from the butt of the rifle squarely in his chest.

Stunned, he staggered backward and, mistaking Nathaniel for Alec—whom he already had reason enough to fear—turned and fled the house, knocking down his bewildered partner as he scrambled back through the door.

Shouting a torrent of whatever Gaelic he could recall from his childhood, Nathaniel bolted after him and discharged two deafening shots over their heads. Their imaginations heightened from the liquor (of which they had had considerably more than two rounds), the suddenness of the attack, and the alien sound of Nathaniel's high-blooded Gaelic shrieks, the two hoodlums sprinted down the road. In mortal terror that a demoniacal madman was pursuing at their heels, they did not stop until they dropped, exhausted, half a mile from town.

And ever after—though not around Port Strathy—when recounting the incident, they swore the maniac had fired a minimum of ten shots directly toward them and they had only escaped with their lives as a result of their shrewd maneuvers and the speed of their retreat.

It took over an hour to settle down Joanna, Letty, and assorted clamoring farm animals after the chaos of shouts and gunshots. Reiver scampered about the precincts of the farm barking encouragement to the other animals and warning to any and all future trespassers. But there was no further activity that night.

In the morning Joanna refused to heed Nathaniel's warning to remain in the house. The memory of events during the night, supplemented by Nathaniel's graphic recounting of his evening in town, sent a cold shiver down her spine, but it only hardened her resolve. No longer could she play a disinterested role in this drama which seemed determined to envelop her. She had grown attached to this town and its people and she would not shrink from her duty.

In the meantime, she had to get the documents to safety. No one—Nathaniel, Letty, Alec, or herself—would be safe until they were out of the house and secure.

"We must see Ogilvie," said Nathaniel the next day. "He's a good man. He'll know jist what's t' be done."

"I'll have t' get t' Culden in secret," said Alec. "They may be watchin' the hoose."

"*You?*" exclaimed Joanna. "I'm not going to put you in any more danger on my account. I'll go see Ogilvie."

"No, no, lass, the lad's right," replied Nathaniel. " 'Tis best that he does it."

"Maybe I'm being foolhardy," insisted Joanna, "but I'm going. If Alec wants to go too, that's fine. But I'll not stay here while he goes alone."

The Cuttahays looked at one another. Alec sighed, knowing her mind was made up.

"And besides," added Joanna, "I want to hear for myself what he has to say. They are my own grandmother's papers."

"If ye must hae it that way," said Nathaniel at length, "ye must go at night. That's yer best chance t' slip away wi' oot bein' seen."

After an early evening slumber, they arose shortly after midnight, had a cup of tea and some oatcakes, and set out for Culden. Alec led by the most circuitous route possible, avoiding all main roads until they reached the river. After crossing the Lindow bridge, they rode past Dormin, and Joanna could not shed the eerie chill that assailed her at the memory of her last time along this very road.

It was some time before dawn when they finally rode slowly into Culden and through its main street. All was still and every door was yet barred against the night. The clip-clop of their horses' hooves echoed through the vacant streets.

They rode past Ogilvie's store-front office, knowing he would never be there at such an hour. Alec led the way to the lawyer's residence, a substantial stone house several streets off the main thoroughfare. They dismounted, tied their horses, and walked to the front door, feeling for the first time a bit sheepish about what they were compelled to do. But the harsh reality of the truth finally enabled Alec to raise his hand and give a sharp rap to the solid wood door. Several moments passed and Alec knocked again. Finally they heard the soft shuffling sound of slippered feet approaching the door.

Gordon Ogilvie opened the door, bleary-eyed, clad in woolen robe and carpet-shoes, and scrutinized the two before him with mingled puzzlement and annoyance. A slight middle-aged man with sparse salt-and-pepper hair, he was wearing wire-rimmed spectacles well down on his nose.

"What in the name of—"

His voice creaked over the words and he paused to clear his throat.

"Do you realize it's the middle of the night!"

"More near t' mornin' than ye'd think, sir," Alec replied.

"Alec MacNeil?" Ogilvie said, still puzzled. "I have no animals, as you know. Not that I'm unfond of them, but the little beasts always set me sneezing."

"Fish make fine pets," Alec suggested.

"Oh, do they?" Ogilvie hinted at a smile. "But not overly affectionate, I'd imagine."

Alec laughed outright.

"Well, young man," Ogilvie went on. "I trust you haven't awakened me at this ungodly hour to discuss the merits of piscatorial housepets."

"No, sir, that I haven't," Alec said. "And we're truly sorry t' intrude on ye like this—but ye'll see 'tis important when we tell ye why we've come."

"Well . . . come in, come in."

The lawyer ushered them through a tall-ceiled room, down a carpeted hallway toward the back of the house, and into the kitchen.

"Come, sit here at the table," he said. "I think I can get a fire going in the hearth—see, it's still quite hot." He worked on the fire with a poker and a few chunks of dry wood while Alec and Joanna seated themselves at a large, round oak dining table.

By the time he again turned to his guests, he was out of breath. "Now," he said, "what seems to be the problem?"

With that, Alec introduced Joanna and between them they provided the lawyer as complete an account as they could of the events leading to Joanna's coming to Scotland and all that had happened since her arrival.

"My, my, my," was all he said once they had finished. "This must be an extremely difficult time for you, Miss Matheson. Please accept my sincerest sympathies over your grandmother's parting."

"Thank you, Mr. Ogilvie," Joanna replied. "It has been hard, but I suppose it's helped knowing there might still be something I can do for her."

"Yes, that is the best way to look at it." He rubbed his chin thoughtfully for a while, then he added, "I daresay, I could use a cup of tea—will you join me?"

Ogilvie busied himself filling a kettle with water, muttering something about his housekeeper being away, then set the kettle on the stove.

"It is a shame all this other business has come up to interfere with your original plans." He took cups from the cupboard and poured cream into a small pitcher. "Mr. Sercombe is a colleague of mine. Of course,

I hardly know the man, and can't say he's been a favorite with me. But then, that wouldn't help much in a court of law, now would it?'' He chuckled lightly. "And as I said, he's an associate of the bar. I would hesitate to interfere where there wasn't some rather solid evidence. Do you see what I mean? The best thing for you to do, and this would be my recommendation, Miss Matheson, is to forget trying to prove anything against Sercombe and concentrate on affirming your own position.''

"My . . . er, my . . . position?''

"Yes. Isn't that what this is all about, your descent from James and Atlanta Duncan?'' asked Ogilvie.

"I . . . suppose I really haven't had a chance to think of that.''

"Yes, of course—you've only just heard of your grandmother's passing. But, my dear, as difficult as such considerations might be at this time, you must understand that if you hope to stop Sercombe, you need to think in these terms.'' He paused as the hissing kettle occupied his attention. After a moment, he continued, setting cups before his guests. "In other words, Miss Matheson, if you are the great-grand-daughter of James and Atlanta Duncan, then the implications are abundantly clear.''

"You don't mean . . .'' Joanna began, but found she was unable to say it.

"I mean, young lady, that you are in the direct line of descent. You mentioned some documents you possess concerning the property; there are no other claimants that I'm aware of. It's all very straightforward and direct,'' he concluded, dumping three teaspoons of sugar into his tea.

"Are you saying,'' Joanna stammered, "that I . . . I could be the heir to the estate?'' At last the unspoken question had been voiced.

"Certainly. That's what this early-morning meeting is for, is it not, to talk about proving your claim?''

"Yes, Mr. Ogilvie,'' put in Alec. "But ye see, 'tis still so new to Joanna.''

"I know,'' replied Ogilvie. "And you must forgive me if I sound rather heartless and cold. But my dear Miss Matheson, it appears as if time were rather crucial here. And as difficult as it may be, you might well be called upon to lay aside your grief in favor of some, shall we say, affirmative action. Your grandmother knew she was dying when she issued her request, yet she felt nothing could stand in its way.''

Joanna sat dumbfounded, allowing the full weight of the conversation to sink in.

"I didn't come here seeking the property,'' she said at length.

"That is all well and good, my dear, but it may be your only way to stop these—well, what you seem to consider dubious schemes. Sercombe is a most cunning man. He's never careless. If what you imply is true, I'm certain he's taken every detail into account—everything, that is, except an unknown heir turning up out of the blue. And that will be the only edge you possess."

"And if I'm not the heir at all . . . if this deed isn't authentic—"

"Nothing is certain. And there's no use speculating." He lifted his cup and took several sips before continuing. "Perhaps we ought to have a look at those documents before we make any more wild conjectures."

Joanna brought out the ancient papers she had carefully folded in her purse. They seemed even more frail now than when she had first discovered them. She handed them across the table to Ogilvie who spread them out before him.

The lawyer scrutinized the papers for some time without saying a word. He tapped his finger against his mouth, and an occasional *hmmm* escaped his lips. Periodically an eyebrow cocked as he continued to peruse them in silence.

At length he looked up and drew a deep breath.

"It's little wonder someone is after these papers," he said. "If you had not appeared here just now, with these papers, Sercombe would have been able to go ahead with his plans with little to impede him. He is, after all, the family lawyer; he has power of appointment; there has been no heir. It is, I must confess, all rather convenient for him. But now, with these documents, that's another story."

"Is it simply the possibility of my being the heir?" asked Joanna.

"That's only part of it. You see, a deed is . . . well, it is after all a *deed*. And this one appears to be . . ." Here he paused and once more tapped his lips thoughtfully with his finger. "This quite appears to be the original deed drawn up by King George himself when the Ramsey lands were reinstated to them following the Jacobite Rebellion. You see, the Ramseys were among those staunchly loyal to Bonnie Prince Charles who, as punishment for their participation in the rebellion, had their lands confiscated. Then some forty years later as a conciliatory gesture, George reinstated the lands to the heirs of the rebels. You will note the date here—1784."

"Can we stop the sale with this deed, then?" Joanna asked.

"If the deed was left with your grandmother fifty years ago, no doubt no one even knew of its existence. And it is likely another was since drawn up, perhaps by Sercombe himself using the authority of his power of appointment. I imagine such a document is already in his hands if the transfer to the new buyer is to take place as imminently as you say."

Ogilvie paused to refill their cups with tea.

"Do you know anything about the new buyer of the land?" he asked. Joanna shook her head.

He glanced toward Alec.

"Nothing, sir," he said. "We've all heard rumors, ye know."

"Ummm . . . I see," said the lawyer slowly.

"So where does that leave us, Mr. Ogilvie?" asked Joanna.

"I would say it leaves our friend Palmer Sercombe in a rather precarious position," he answered, with the faintest gleam in his eye. "Your possession of this deed, and if you can prove your position in the Duncan family—which, of course, you must be able to do to verify that these papers aren't merely a fraud—well, it quite puts Mr. Sercombe out in the street, so to speak. It may well even nullify his power of appointment."

"It's all coming so fast," said Joanna, "I . . . I just can't understand it all."

"My dear, your grandmother was Margaret Duncan, is not that what you told me?"

"Yes."

"As the eldest child of James Duncan, she should have inherited the estate—surely you have realized that?"

"Yes," answered Joanna tentatively. "But I thought she was disinherited or relinquished it by going to America."

"Do you know that for certain?"

"I don't know anything for certain."

"The fact that she held the deed, you see, that's the crucial point. By being the natural heir in the blood line of the family—as her birth had made her—the property was hers. And the fact that she held the deed, well that authenticates her right beyond the shadow of a doubt."

"But it hardly matters," interjected Alec. "Even if Alastair was the legal heir . . . even if his sister had let go any claim on it, Joanna would still inherit. He had no children. She still stands next in line."

"Ah, yes, but then you would have Sercombe's power of appointment to contend with. If Alastair, as the true heir, had turned over power of appointment to him, then he does have legal right to do what he chooses. But if Alastair wasn't the rightful heir, then a power of appointment issued by him would not be binding, at least with regard to the disposition of the estate."

"There is one other odd thing about this deed," the lawyer went on, perusing the document once more, a finger held thoughtfully to pursed lips. ". . . yes, quite odd."

"What is it?" asked Joanna.

"No doubt it escaped your notice, but there is a signature here at the bottom—*Anson Ramsey.*"

He paused and Alec and Joanna waited for him to continue.

"This deed was drawn up in 1784, probably because at that time lands were reinstated to certain rebellious factions of which the Ramseys were a part—namely, the Jacobite Rebellion. The names are faded now, but you can make out the signatures of Robert Ramsey and the King. But below them is Anson Ramsey's signature."

"Who was he?" asked Alec.

But Joanna remained silent. She knew the name only too well. She had gazed over and over at it on her grandmother's family-tree embroidery.

"Anson Ramsey was Robert's son and heir," Ogilvie replied. "Still, I see no reason for his name to appear on a deed, unless . . ." His finger found its way once again to his pursed lips.

"What was he like?" Joanna asked when Ogilvie's sentence trailed away unfinished.

"His whole tenure as laird was rather peculiar. He was extremely beloved of his people. Of all the lairds, since the Ramseys came to Strathy, he was one of the few who actually made this area his home. He was a good man, most benevolent toward his subjects. There was great prosperity here during his life, largely due to his influence. The one flaw in his life proved to be his two sons. They were both said to be scoundrels. Then when he was still in his prime, Anson died a rather sudden and untimely death."

"Was he . . . murdered?

"It was a hunting accident. But there was considerable speculation as to whether it was truly an accident. It happened between Dormin and Culden. He and his sons were alone. Nobody really knows what occurred. There were rumors he had threatened to disinherit his sons if they did not begin to act worthy of their station. But I wonder about his signature here. And under his name are the words: '*In accordance with the 'title transfer' to be presented forthwith.*' "

"Was the land transferred to someone else?"

"Yes, it does rather sound that way, doesn't it?" said Ogilvie. "But if that were the case, knowledge of it must have been lost. Because the land remained with the Ramseys. His son, Talmud, inherited the land in due course, after his father's death. No, I just can't say what this means."

"Sounds t' me as if he was plannin' t' transfer it," said Alec. "Maybe he jist never got aroun' t' it."

"You may be right," said Ogilvie thoughtfully. "If there was a 'title transfer' document, that would certainly tell us more. But I doubt such a paper even exists. Possessing this deed with other necessary proofs, Joanna is most certainly the heir. But if the property was later transferred, well . . . that might change everything.''

"What if Sercombe has it?" suggested Joanna. "He has been the family lawyer for years."

"Yes," said Ogilvie slowly, "that could certainly change your position dramatically. And that might, after all, be Palmer Sercombe's ace in the hole, as it were."

26 / Nathaniel and Letty———————————

The return ride to Port Strathy was long.

A solemn silence hung over the two as they plodded along. Perhaps the need for sleep had overtaken them after their stealthy midnight journey. Perhaps the threatening overcast sky cast a pallor over their spirits. Or even more, perhaps the thoughts of each were occupied with Ogilvie's assertion as to Joanna's position in Port Strathy's affairs. Joanna herself was not sure whether the visit with the lawyer was cause for celebration or sackcloth. She had learned a great deal, to be sure. Yet she still had no specific direction to follow. In the meantime, the lawyer had promised to look into a few details on his end—discreetly of course.

It was shortly before noon when they reached the Cuttahay cottage.

The clouds had amassed thick and menacing, and the two narrowly escaped a sound drenching. With weary bodies they approached the door. What a relief it would be to sit down in front of the fire with a warm cup of tea!

Unexpectedly Olive Sinclair met them at the door. Whatever greeting she uttered was lost to their ears as they saw beyond her the tidy little cottage in complete disarray.

"What happened!" Alec groaned, brushing past Miss Sinclair. "Nathaniel . . . Letty!" he called, seeing neither of his old friends, his voice trembling with fear.

Quickly he spun back around and faced Miss Sinclair, "Where are they?"

"They're all right," she answered. "They're resting in bed."

Alec turned again and started toward their bedroom.

"Wait, Alec," Olive called after him. "Just calm yourself, lad, and let's sit down and I'll explain everything to you—at least as far as I can."

"Hoo can I sit when I ken somethin' dreadful must o' happened?"

"Well, stand then! But you'll not be disturbing Nate and Letty after my just getting the two of them to sleep." Her rising voice peaked until it threatened to wake the sleeping couple with none of Alec's help.

Apprehending her firm resolve, Alec yielded and slumped into Nathaniel's rocking chair. Joanna, who had been standing in the doorway during the exchange, moved into the room, trembling, and stood silently before the fire, horrified at this latest outbreak of violence.

The table in the kitchen was overturned, as were most of the pieces of humble furniture in the living room. An overstuffed couch, the one item of luxury that the Cuttahays owned, had apparently been slashed with a knife, its cotton and feathers scattered about the floor. One of the room's large windows was broken, but no glass was to be seen; Olive explained that a stool had been thrown through it, sending the breakage to the ground outside. The single indoor plant, an ancient green and yellow sansevieria, lay in three pieces on the floor, its pot shattered, dirt scattered about the room.

"I came here two hours ago," Miss Sinclair began. "I found the place much as you see it now, except that Nathaniel, poor soul, was in here bent over Letty—weeping."

Alec jumped from his seat, but Olive reached out a hand and grabbed his arm.

"Don't worry, lad," she said, "she'll be all right. But Nathaniel was afraid to leave her alone to get help. 'Twas only by chance I happened along. I fetched the doctor. Letty's arm was broken, and he set it. Nathaniel had a mild concussion; he had been unconscious for a time."

"How?" said Joanna, finally finding her voice.

"Nathaniel says they broke in just after breakfast. He said they were after the two of you, but once they realized you weren't here they seemed bent on destruction. He said one of the men yelled, 'See what comes of meddlin' where you're not wanted, old man!' Something like that."

"Did he know who they were?" asked Alec anxiously.

"They had scarves over their faces. He wondered if one might have been Tom—you know, Tom Forbes. Wasn't sure of the other. But then, it could have been the two men he feared off the night before. He just wasn't sure; they burst in so fast and started beating on the two of them— the poor dears!"

"Oh no!" Joanna moaned, covering her face with her hands. "What have I done? What have I done? None of this would have happened if I hadn't—"

Alec was at her side in a moment. "Now ye can't go blamin' yersel', lass," he said.

"Then who else?" Joanna replied. "I should have known—"

"We both should hae known," said Alec.

"Only the Lord himself knows what's going to happen," said Miss Sinclair. " 'Tis no use crying about it now. Letty and Nathaniel will both be fine, and praise the Lord for that! And that's mostly what matters. What's happened has happened. We just need to look forward now. Come and sit down; we need to have a little talk."

Alec led Joanna to the rocking chair where she sat down. Alec gathered his long legs beneath him and sat on the floor. Miss Sinclair laid another log on the fire, where it crackled into flame, then pulled a three-legged stool in front of Alec and Joanna and lowered herself stiffly onto it.

"Am I to take it, lass, that the two men were after you or your documents?" she asked.

Joanna nodded. "It's a nightmare."

"It can't go on," said Alec angrily. "I've got t' do somethin' t' stop those men."

"But, Alec," insisted Joanna, "it's not your fight. It's *me* they're after."

"It's bigger than just yourself," said Miss Sinclair. "There's something afoot here that involves us all. That's why I came out here this morning. Sercombe left town at dawn today. I hate rumors, but in my business I can hardly escape them. And folks are saying he's off in Aberdeen to fetch the bloke who's buying all the land. Most likely they'll be back in four days and everything will be about over then. The transfer of the title is supposed to be taking place just a few days after that. I heard something about a public gathering when the signing'll take place and the money'll be delivered and all that."

"I just don't know what to do," sighed Joanna. "We saw a lawyer in Culden today, a Mr. Ogilvie."

"Good man, he is," Olive assured her. "Yes, a fine man. You can trust him."

In deep thought Alec finally burst out, "Joanna, I know ye're reluctant, an' ye're a woman, an' ye think folk won't accept ye 'cause ye're new here, but the time's goin' t' come when ye're goin' t' have t' make public who ye are. The people have t' know."

"I . . . I don't know," said Joanna.

"No!" Alec nearly shouted. "This has gone too far. It must be stopped."

He jumped to his feet and stalked across the room. "I know I've had t' wrestle wi' my own stormy nature an' my desire t' be like the Lord. An' ye've helped me t' get it worked oot within mysel'. But there's a time fer doin' what's right an' fightin' wrong, e'en if ye hae t' set aside yer meekness fer a time. An' if I hae t' go t' Sercombe an' Tom Forbes an' the other bla'gards an' wring their necks t' find oot what's afoot, then so be it! I jist can't sit by—"

Suddenly he stopped, sighed deeply, and turned toward Joanna. "I'm sorry. Maybe I'm bein' a bit hasty. I jist can't stand t' see people I love hurt, but I'll wait fer ye, Joanna. We'll do what ye think best."

"Oh!" moaned Joanna. "I just don't know what to do!"

"You have to do what's right, that's all," said Olive. "Stand your ground."

"But how do I know what's right?"

"Trust in the Lord to show you." Olive laid her coarse hand on Joanna's arm.

"But I don't even know what that means," replied Joanna with a frustrated voice. "Don't you realize? I'm not like you or Nathaniel or Letty. I don't know *how* to trust your Lord. I thought I was doing the right thing by going to Culden with Alec. But just look at what came of it. It's all my fault that this happened to Nathaniel and Letty."

"Joanna—"

"But it is my fault! It wouldn't have happened if I hadn't come here."

"The Lord's hand was in your coming. You can't blame yourself."

"I should never have come! I'm just causing trouble. That's all I've ever done all my life."

"Don't talk like that, Joanna," said Olive tenderly. "The Lord loves you. He just wants you to trust Him to do the work He has for you. You can't do that until you accept His forgiveness. And then you must forgive yourself, child. That's what life with our God is all about—forgiveness. We're all sinners before Him, you know. But He can wash the past all clean."

"But I told you . . . I don't know how. I haven't had any practice. I don't even know what it means to trust Him."

"Have you never given your heart to the Lord, child?"

"No—I suppose I haven't," replied Joanna.

"You can't live by trusting Him till you've given yourself to Him," said Olive.

"But I don't know how to do that."

"Oh, 'tis simple, child. You just have to open your heart and tell Him you need Him and invite Him to come in and live with you."

Joanna turned thoughtful for a moment, then burst out. "Maybe I could do that if I didn't feel so guilty about what happened to Nathaniel and Letty!"

And with the words she ran from the house.

Alec started toward the door after her, but Olive placed a restraining hand on his arm.

"She needs to be alone, Alec."

"But I can't let her oot alone after all that's happened."

Just then they heard the creaking of the byre door as it opened, followed by the wooden thud of its closing.

"She'll be nearby, lad," Olive replied, looking steadily at Alec.

After a few moments, Alec turned back inside, and together the two began to set about restoring order to the ransacked cottage.

Guilty!

The word rang through Joanna's mind as she ran from the house, tears streaming down her face. It had fallen from her lips so carelessly. Yet now that she had spoken it she realized that the same feeling which had haunted her all her life was at the root of her present troubles. She had never been able to conquer the guilt she felt about her mother. And now there were more lives being ruined because of her!

She was weeping by the time she reached the barn, but she had to get away, to escape . . . from everyone, to hide from the world so they couldn't see the shame and stains of guilt which blackened her soul. Sobbing as she ran, the warm tears stung her eyes and blurred her vision. The homey warmth of the barn with the rich aroma of friendly animals and honest work should have been comforting, but she was hardly conscious of her surroundings. If only she could run, and run, and run and never come back, never see anyone again. Then no one else would be hurt by the curse of injury and pain which she seemed to carry with her wherever she went.

Oh, God! she thought. *How can they talk of trusting God, of doing right, of standing up for truth when life is so cruel? Oh, if only I hadn't come here! I do nothing but cause pain wherever I go!*

What had she gotten herself into? She never meant to cause trouble. She had only wanted to fulfill her promise to her grandmother. Now it seemed everything was crashing in upon her. Because of her, violence and pain had come to the once sleepy little village of Port Strathy. Some curse was upon her; it followed her and touched all those whom she contacted. She alone was guilty; some unknown evil was part of her very being!

Suddenly Olive's words rang through her mind: "The Lord loves you. You can't do the work He has for you until you accept His forgiveness. You can't learn to trust Him till you've given Him your heart."

Joanna stopped and threw herself down on a mound of straw.

"Oh, God!" she wept. "I want to know you like they do. I want to learn to trust you. God—help me!"

She could not go on, but hid her face in her hands and wept in bitter sorrow. How alone she was! How far from home! She had no mother, no father, no grandmother. Not even a home!

All at once a small voice—was it just a thought in her mind, or was someone speaking to her?—seemed to say: *"You are not alone, child. I love you."*

Joanna looked up and swept a sleeve hurriedly across her eyes. She was alone. She glanced about, as if not believing the words she had heard in her mind. Then she recalled something her grandmother read to her so very long ago: *Yea though I walk through the valley of the shadow of death, I will fear no evil: for thou art with me . . .*

Joanna strained to hear more as if all the words she had ignored as a child would suddenly come back to her. "I don't deserve such promises!" she sobbed.

Then other words tumbled into her brain; she had heard them more recently: *He loves and forgives ye no matter who ye are . . . or what ye have done*. She thought for a moment of Alec and what he had experienced to bring him to that place.

No matter what ye have done . . .

"Did Alec mean I don't have to deserve you, God?" she found herself asking.

And that same voice within her seemed to resound, *"Yes!"*

"Oh, God," Joanna wailed. "I want to be clean! I want to know you! Help me know how."

But even as she uttered the words she realized she already knew. Hadn't Olive said it was simple? Hadn't she told her how?

"If only it could be true!"

At last the years of pent-up self-condemnation was released and Joanna wept with bitter remorse. When the deep and agonizing wells of guilt and sorrow had spent themselves, she sat up, glanced around, and—though her eyes were red-rimmed and her voice still quivered with sobs—she felt strangely steady. Then she folded her hands in prayer, following the habit her grandmother had taught her as a child, breathed deeply, and said: "Lord, I need you so desperately! Won't you please come into my heart and stay with me, and show me how to live?"

An hour later the kitchen door opened.

As Olive turned toward her she knew immediately a change had come upon Joanna. Her eyes were still puffy and red, but her face glowed with the release from the bondage of her past.

"You were right, Olive," she said softly. "He has forgiven me."

"Aye!" replied Olive with a smile. "And has He shown you what you're to do?"

"No. Not yet. But I'm sure He will. He has forgiven me, and for the moment that is enough."

The sleek black motor car wound its way cautiously through the narrow city streets.

The few automobiles found this far north were scarcely larger than the buggies and carriages the streets had been designed for, and maneuvering a full-sized Rolls Royce through horse-carts and staring crowds proved no easy task. An unrelenting rain pelted the auto, and the chauffeur gritted his teeth as he peered through the smeared window, wondering if he had missed his turn.

The two men in the backseat sat oblivious to the driver's misery. With higher things on their minds, they were accustomed to leaving such trivial worries as the weather to their lessers.

Palmer Sercombe stroked the rich leather seat with his palm.

He enjoyed this, he had to admit. And the convenient portable bar from which his companion served their drinks was impressive indeed. It was the finest Scotch he had ever had the pleasure of drinking.

Sercombe had long been associated with wealthy, powerful men. Yet somehow it had never been enough only to rub shoulders with wealth. As he scanned the luxury all about him, he felt a tingle of satisfaction knowing that soon—yes, very soon—he would possess the means to command his *own* power—wield his *own* wealth. He had waited many years for this moment.

It would be his finest hour!

His face broke into a grim smile of triumph.

But first things first, he thought as he returned his attentions to his companion, a businessman in a gray three-piece suit.

"Am I to understand," he was saying, "that there is danger the deal may fall through?"

"Not at all," the lawyer replied.

"Your wire sounded urgent."

"I only felt we should take steps to move along more quickly. I have drawn up all the necessary papers—they will become finalized in a week."

"Why the haste? I didn't expect to be called away from London for several weeks more."

"A small problem has cropped up. Nothing but an annoyance. It's being dealt with—in fact, by this time it should have already been taken care of."

"A problem?"

"Some papers I need. Actually, we don't need them to continue; it would just be more, shall we say, expeditious if I held them firmly in my possession prior to the close of our escrow. And those papers should be in my office even as we speak. Two of my local colleagues were sent to retrieve them the morning I left."

"What makes these papers so vital? I thought we had everything necessary before us when we met last time in London."

"Yes, of course. But a woman has shown up."

"Don't they always?"

"I'm afraid this one may try to lay claim to the inheritance."

"You assured me there were no heirs . . . no sticky difficulties that would come back to haunt us."

"I'm sure she will prove nothing but a fraud. We will see to that. But she has certain documents—"

"You've seen them?"

"Yes."

"And you let them slip away? I thought you had more backbone than that."

"Don't worry. She will have been eliminated before we arrive."

"You'd not be fool enough to kill her!" The man seemed more shocked at Sercombe's stupidity than at the prospect of murder.

"We both stand to lose a great deal here. I plan to do what must be done."

"Well, do what you want. But just remember—I didn't hear a thing."

They nursed their drinks in silence for a few moments.

At length Sercombe said, "I thought we might have a bit of a public show with the signing of the papers. A town meeting, banners, couple of speeches—that sort of thing."

"Is that really necessary?" asked his companion with the tone of a parent humoring the whims of a child.

"We must make a show of good faith—I don't want to be hounded the rest of my life by disgruntled tenants. I plan to make some token improvements. They are simple-minded people. They have no concept of the true value of the land. We'll repair their harbor, as we've discussed, hand out some cash indulgences—"

"What does all that matter? The whole place will be under water within three years."

"And remember," said Sercombe with a smirk, "I never heard a thing."

"I don't care what you hear or don't hear."

"It won't all be under water, only the low-lying inland areas. Port Strathy will still be there, and so will its people. We have to make attempts to mollify them."

"Everything I plan to do is all legal and aboveboard; which is more than I can say for you. Actually, what I'm doing will benefit them more than your farcical little harbor."

"Unfortunately, two-thirds of the population won't be around to reap those benefits," Sercome chuckled wryly.

"A minor point!" The man's white teeth gleamed through a cunning smile. "A stint in Glasgow or Edinburgh will do the poor devils some good."

The car swerved and skidded on the slippery road. Sercombe's companion rapped sharply on the window separating the driver from the rear seat.

"These provincials can't even drive properly!" he muttered with disgust.

29 / Doug Creary's Sow_____

For the next three days things settled into as much of their old routine as could be expected. Alec saw to a number of chores he had neglected and resumed his rounds throughout the neighborhood—keeping, however, as close an eye on the cottage as he could manage.

With a relieved sense of quiet joy, Joanna filled her days ministering to Nathaniel and Letty. When the following morning dawned, Letty was much improved and insisted on rising to fix breakfast. A good part of Joanna's energies had to be expended to convince her to remain in bed. Her next most difficult task was to prevent Nathaniel—notwithstanding the headache which lingered from the blows he had received—from going out to perform his usual chores.

In the end he agreed to rest for one day. But no more.

This provided Alec the opportunity to lead an exhuberantly enthusiastic Joanna through all the morning rounds of cow-milking, stable-cleaning, and pig-feeding. As she tromped through the stalls in Letty's knee-high rubber boots, not even the pungent smell of manure sloshing beneath her feet could dampen the eagerness she felt to be on the giving rather than the receiving end of the Cuttahays' goodwill.

A cheerful smile remained on her lips and a song in her heart throughout the day, and the next, taking the old couple tea, sweeping out the house, restoring order, and maintaining a warm fire glowing on the hearth. Her freedom from the burden of self-blame allowed Joanna to receive the benefit in her spirit of such ministry of love and caring. Truly the healing of her deep emotional scars had already begun. Alec repaired the broken window and Joanna prepared a huge pot of stew, not without a good deal of verbal assistance from Letty in the bedroom. By then Nathaniel, who could not be confined a moment longer, was up and about in tolerably good spirits.

Had she been able, Joanna would have instantly traded all possible claim to any inheritance for a future with this simple couple.

Four days after the attack on Nathaniel and Letty, Alec stopped by to help Nathaniel with his livestock. However, the work was prematurely interrupted as Douglas Creary's son came running up, out of breath, calling for Alec. There was an emergency with their pig.

"Take the lass with ye, son," suggested Nathaniel. "We'll be fine here."

Alec eyed him for a moment, then ran inside to ask her.

She declined on the Cuttahays' behalf. She must stay, she said; they needed her.

But the two older people protested so vehemently Joanna realized they might feel worse if she remained behind. At length, therefore, she consented.

"There's little time t' lose," said Alec. "My horse is ready t' go, an' 'tisn't far. We'll ride together. Letty'll want the boy t' rest awhile before he follows."

They rushed outside, and Alec took Joanna's hand and helped her onto the horse's back; then he swung up into the saddle behind her, took the reins firmly, and off they galloped.

In the high delight her spirits had enjoyed the last few days, the ride into town on horseback was exhilarating. The wind blowing in her face, the surging power of the horse's muscles flexing beneath her—all intoxicated her still further. And Alec's proximity as he urged the horse on contributed as well to the mood of joy and abandonment she felt welling up within her. She leaned back until she felt her back against his great strong chest. His forearms tightened around her waist. With her hair blowing back in Alec's face, Joanna let out a spirited laugh from the sheer ecstasy of the moment. *He may be what my school-friends in Chicago would term a "country bumpkin,"* she thought. *But underneath that crude, homespun exterior lies a tender and compassionate man, with just enough humor and impulsiveness to make him interesting. What girl in her right mind wouldn't be proud to—*

Her thoughts were interrupted by shouts from the house in front of them.

A poor cottage with thatched roof and chipped paint confronted Joanna. She took special note of Dorey's garden situated bravely in front in full color with another spring. Doug Creary and his youngest son stood on the ramshackle porch and extended a friendly greeting. Creary was a tall, lean man in his mid-thirties. His skin was coarse and deeply tanned from years of exposure to the elements, but there was a welcoming sparkle in his eyes. It reminded Joanna of the warmth she had seen in his wife's greeting the first day she had arrived in Port Strathy.

He said very little as he led them around back to the pen where his sow was confined.

The animal lay on her side, howling in obvious misery. Alec immediately began his examination amid her ear-piercing cries.

"I canna tell ye what's wrong wi' her," said Doug. "She's been bellerin' like that since early this mornin'."

Alec examined the animal's body and when he touched its right forefoot, the shrieks rose to such a crescendo Alec feared she would disturb the inhabitants in faraway Aberdeen.

"There . . . that's it!" he cried.

But when he gingerly lifted the foot, the pig showed her strength was by no means yet spent.

"Hold her, Doug!" he said, struggling to keep her from throwing him off and escaping.

Alec probed further while the racket continued. Finally he withdrew a thorn the size of a small nail.

"All right, Molly . . . the show's over," Alec said, dumping some powder into the wound. "Ye'll be feelin' yer old self now."

"Glad ye saw fit t' come, Alec," said Doug. "She's a braw sow, she is."

"I'm sure ye canna afford t' lose her, then."

"Aye, ye speak the truth there. But things look t' improve aroun' here real soon. Why, Rob Peters be thinkin' o' settin' up a schooner service, an' ye know what that'll mean."

"I'm not sure I do," Alec replied.

"Why, his troller's goin' t' be up fer sale an' I'll jist ha' enough t' buy her." Doug's face beamed as if the troller were already in his possession.

"Sounds like ye've come into some good fortune," said Alec. "Congratulations!"

"Thank ye, Alec. But ye must o' heard aboot the money?"

"I heard talk o' a new harbor."

"But that's not all!" exclaimed Doug. "Each o' the tenants are set t' get fifty poun's. Fifty poun's, man, did ye hear me! All o' us!"

"That's a lot o' siller, no doobt, Doug."

"Port Strathy's finally goin' t' take her place amoong the great fishin' ports, an' that's the truth. We're goin t' make oor mark. We all could stand t' do right well, an' fer a long time."

Alec glanced at Joanna. They exchanged an unspoken sign their host did not notice.

As Alec and Joanna made ready to depart, Rose Creary came out of the house, with her little smudge-faced daughter clinging to her apron. Rose held a tiny bouquet of nasturtiums and daisies bound together with a faded red ribbon. She held them out to Joanna with a look of bashful admiration on her face.

" 'Tisn't much," she said. "But we're right honored t' hae ye visit oor home."

"How sweet of you!" exclaimed Joanna.

To her surprise, Joanna felt a tear rising in her eye. "They're lovely," she said. "Thank you so much."

As they rode away from the Creary home, Joanna's mood was peaceful and subdued. There would be no need to hurry now and they could enjoy a leisurely ride back out into the country. She could just sit, with Alec's arms around her, and drink in the serenity of being with him and no one else.

"Why don't we swing by Olive's?" suggested Alec. "I'm sure she'd want t' know Letty an' Nathaniel are doin' jist fine."

"Ummm," purred Joanna, turning and casting him a satisfied smile, "whatever you say. I'm yours for the rest of the day!"

Alec laughed and turned the horse toward the center of the village.

Arriving at the store, Alec swung down off the horse, took Joanna's hand and eased her to the ground, unaware of two piercing eyes taking in the entire scene from inside the building. He tethered the horse at the rail and led the way to the store's front door.

Just as they were about to enter, the door swung open and an elegantly dressed stranger stepped onto the walk. Taking no notice, Alec continued on into the building, not realizing Joanna had stopped dead in her tracks as the stranger had flashed his coal-black eyes full upon her.

"Good Lord!" he breathed, "it *is* you!"

Joanna was dumbstruck, her face suddenly grown deathly white.

In silence Joanna allowed Jason Channing to lead her by the hand away from the store.

"I thought I would never be able to get you alone," he said.

"Don't you think you were a bit rude to Alec?" said Joanna haltingly, finding her voice for the first time since seeing Channing.

"Rude! My dear, you have to be direct with these simple folks; I'm sure he hardly noticed."

They walked toward the harbor, past the Bluster 'N Blow, and to the water's edge. There Channing turned and led Joanna away from town along the seafront.

"Regardless," he went on, "do you realize how long it's been since I saw you last? It seems like years! I've thought of nothing else. So at least allow me to be excused on that basis."

"Really . . . Jason," said Joanna, recalling immediately the discomfort of his flattery. *Oh, why did I let him take me away from Alec?* she thought.

"Joanna, you are so beautiful." He paused and turned toward her, lifting his hands to cup her cheeks between his palms. "How could I erase the lovely vision of you from my mind?" He sighed. "Oh . . . how I've missed you!"

"How did you find me?" asked Joanna, squirming to back away. Why were this man's attentions so disquieting? *Please, God, don't leave me now!*

"What does it matter?" he replied. "What is important is that I *have* found you. Fate has led me to you. How can there be any doubt we belong together?"

"I . . . I don't know, Jason. A lot has happened to me since I came here."

"That's what you wanted, wasn't it? Adventure . . . that sort of thing?"

"No, it's more than that. I'm not the same person I was when I came."

"Nonsense. You're still my shy, little Joanna—just like the day I found you."

"No, Jason, I've changed. I've grown. There are things I care about, people I have grown to—"

176

"Don't tell me you're in love with that yokel I saw you with!"

"What? Oh, Alec . . . in love—no, of course not," replied Joanna, notably flustered.

"Then what can possibly stand in our way? Joanna, I love you . . . I want you. I have longed for this moment when we would be together again."

He pulled her toward him, wrapped his insistent arms around her waist, and kissed her. His lips were warm and vibrant. Momentarily she relaxed and returned his embrace, but then eased herself gently away.

"Oh, come now, Joanna. Surely by now you've had enough of those little games you were playing on the ship. You've had time to think, to grow up. I was patient with you then because I knew all this was new to you. But you're a big girl. It's time you learned about the real world."

He kissed her again, and again. This time she did not pull away.

"And you know you love me too," he said at length.

Joanna did not reply. Maybe he was right. Did she even know what love was? *Oh, Lord*, she thought, *what am I to do?*

"Why did you come to Port Strathy?" she asked softly, making conversation.

"Ah, Joanna," he replied. "Let's reserve all the talk for another time. Come with me." He turned, took her hand, and led her back the way they had come.

"Where are we going?"

"To my room at the inn."

Something about his evasive tone put Joanna on her guard.

"But you still haven't told me why you came," she said.

"Is that a note of suspicion I detect in your lovely voice?" he said, his smile full of merriment. "Come to my room. Let's celebrate our reunion. Then we can talk about it. You can ask all the questions you like. Besides, you should know I came to see you. I told you before—I make a habit of going after things I like."

Sensing a reluctance in her spirit toward this man whose vows of love tempted her, Joanna stopped. Something clicked in her mind.

"You're here about the estate, aren't you?"

"What does it matter?"

"It matters to me," she persisted. "You are the man we've been hearing about!"

"You know I hate to mix business with pleasure," he said, pulling her toward him once more. But this time she stiffened, not yielding to his embrace.

Affronted, he added, "What simpleton here cares anyway!"

"I care, Jason. This place is special to me."

"Yes, I can see where it would be," he replied, his hidden motives gaining the upper hand over the oily blandishments of his charm, "if you can get your greedy little hands on it." Derision marked his tone.

"It's not like that at all. How could you suggest such a thing?"

"I knew there was some claim to the inheritance. Before this moment I only had the vaguest suspicions, though I should have put two and two together."

His lips cracked into a wry smile. Joanna was silent.

"It seems as though we've become competitors. But I'd much prefer to think of us as business associates—beautiful partners."

"What do you mean?"

"I could pull some strings—make sure that inheritance was in the bag for you. Then I wouldn't have to shell out a dime to Sercombe—or should I say shilling? No matter. Anything we'd make after that would be clear profit. We could make a bundle, you and I, Joanna."

"What are your plans? What are you going to do with the estate?" The man's words suddenly sounded foreign, distant from the simplicity of the new life she had discovered.

"Technically, nothing. It's the water rights that interest me—the river will do the rest."

"The river?" asked Joanna, confused.

"The Lindow. It's a sweet little deal. I've been wanting to expand my operations into Europe. All I have to do is create some hydroelectric power up here—and you name it, I can do it. Labor's cheap . . . no nasty unions to contend with—"

"Electricity? But there is no electricity here."

"Not yet. But it's coming. Haven't you heard—this is the industrial age, Joanna. I'll make electricity here, and industry won't be far behind. And I'll be sitting right—"

"Do I understand you?" interrupted Joanna with rising emotion. "You're going to build a dam on the Lindow?"

"For openers."

"And the valley, the farms?"

"Are you kidding? You know how dams work. Don't be naive, Joanna! It's going to be one big lake—Loch Channing . . . how does that sound?"

He burst into a laugh.

Joanna barely heard him, for a vision suddenly sprang into her mind. It momentarily confused her, for there in her mind's eye were Jason and Alec standing side by side. Could there be two more divergent personalities? Jason, with his polished glamor, flashy smile, and smooth-talking assertiveness—a man who nearly eclipsed Alec's simple countenance. Yet what were these compared to Alec's forthright honesty? He was a man who had only his obscure little cottage and horse to call his own, a simple vet with mud and manure on his boots, whose days were spent giving of himself to the neighbors who depended on him. But did he not have more than money, prestige, or power could ever hope to gain? She suddenly realized that her newfound faith was causing her to reshape her priorities—to really see what was most important in life.

Joanna's thoughts were interrupted as the sound of Channing's laughter brought her mind back to the present.

"Listen, sweetheart," he was saying, "if you work with me on this, I can guarantee you'll be on easy street for as long as you like. But if you work against me," and here his voice lowered to a whisper which could hardly be distinguished from a growl, "you'll have nothing. And I mean nothing—at all."

For a moment Joanna's lips moved silently, unable to form the words stuck in her throat. Her head was spinning. How could she ever hope to resist such a powerful man? How could she ignore the vacillating emotions that threatened to overwhelm her?

"Why did you choose Port Strathy?" she asked in a voice that sounded so small, trying to maintain her composure.

"I met Sercombe in London last year. I happened to mention I was interested in foreign investments. One thing led to another . . . you know the routine."

"And what does he plan to do with the money?"

"I don't care if he plans to buy a yak farm in Madagascar."

"But he's going to keep the money, is that it?"

"You don't think he's a complete idiot! But why all the questions? Is this an inquisition or something? It's hardly your concern if you join forces with me. I'll take care of all the details."

Joanna opened her mouth, then closed it and was silent.

She had to get away to think!

". . . why all the questions?" Channing had asked, and the phrase rang in Joanna's mind.

Finally the words she had sought surfaced and she spoke.

"Because, Jason, you don't expect me to make a decision without all the facts?"

"There's really no decision for you to make, you know."

He paused, as if thinking what tactic to use, then continued. "Oh, come now, Joanna—you know how right we are together. Let's stop arguing and go to my room. We'll have a drink or two, relax, and see what happens. All this can wait till later. What happened on the ship was a long time ago. You can't refuse me again."

"Oh, can't I?" she said with a marked edge to her tone.

"You're turning into quite a woman, Joanna. I like that! Come."

He took her hand to lead her into the inn.

All at once Joanna visioned all the people she had met since arriving in Port Strathy—the Cuttahays, Olive, the Cobdens, the Crearys. In a flash she saw their cottages, their flower beds, their struggling gardens. Dorey's face came into view, then a picture of Doug Creary's pig and the look on his son's face while watching Alec work. If Channing had his way, all this would be gone—the simple life, the valley, the awful, beautiful forest called Dormin, the barns, the fields, the flowers.

Was this her land?

Were these her people?

Was she indeed one of them? Had she been led here to fight on their behalf? to preserve a way of life which gave meaning and purpose and joy? Did God truly have a hand in leading her here, to these people, to somehow fulfill a destiny among them?

A resolve began rising within her. If this were her chosen path . . . if God had indeed led her to this place, to this moment, for a purpose, then there could be no doubt that He would also give her the strength to do what He was calling her to do.

Silently Joanna sent forth a prayer: "Oh, Lord, now more than ever I need your guidance! Give me strength. Help me do what you want me to."

Then she turned and faced Jason Channing with a boldness she had never before known.

"Jason," she said, "I can get the inheritance, with or without you. If you want to work with me, you would have to make major changes in your plans."

"I don't make concessions," he replied flatly.

"It seems we agree on one thing," she answered. "But I have no intention of letting you get your hands on the land. Sercombe may be a swindler. But what you intend would destroy these people's lives, homes, history—their whole meaning."

"So we're feeling rather noble about it all I see," he said. "No one's going to be left homeless in the streets. So they have to relocate—it won't kill them. That's progress. It happens all the time."

"You don't have any concept of what this land means to them. Some of these families have been here for generations."

"These are new times, Joanna. This is the modern age. Times are changing."

"Well, these people have something here—something far more valuable than your progress, your industry, your wealth. And I won't let you take it from them, Jason!"

She moved away from him and turned to walk back toward the store.

"Joanna," Channing called after her, stunned and angered at her rebuff. "Joanna! I believe I told you once, but I'll tell you again—I *always* get what I want!"

She stopped and turned to face him.

"Not this time, Jason," she said steadily, then continued down the path.

"You're making a big mistake!" he called after her. But she did not look back again.

Joanna rode as fast as the horse would carry her.

The slope of the grassy hill was hardly steep and the mare was able to keep moving at a full gallop all the way to the top. Still Joanna urged her on. Her hair streamed out behind her. She could feel the perspiration from the horse's back.

All at once she reeled in, jumped to the ground, and ran on foot, still higher up the slope, till her lungs cried out for rest and the sweat gathered on her forehead, back, and arms. Exhausted, she threw herself on the grass laughing. Within moments, however, the sounds had turned to sobs. Inexplicably and uncontrollably she wept aloud, unable to stem the confused array of emotions pouring out of her.

Her mare approached cautiously, nuzzling its moist nose into Joanna's tear-streamed face.

"Watching a grown girl cry?" she asked, sniffing, then wiped her eyes with her sleeve.

A low, rumbling whinny was the horse's only reply.

"Come here," she said, rolling over and giving the huge horsey head a hug.

She sighed deeply. The tears had done their work and swept away the black clouds of doubt and uncertainty.

Leaving Channing, Joanna had found Alec waiting for her at Olive's store. They rode back to the farm in silence. She knew it was cruel to give him no explanation. But at the moment there were simply no words she had to offer. She would tell him all in time.

"I have to be alone for a while, Alec," she had said when they reached the cottage. "I have to think."

In silence he saddled Nathaniel's mare and watched her ride off over the meadow and up the hill on the other side. Alec was too strong to be hurt, but he was too human not to feel the chill of her silence as he stood viewing her retreat.

On the top of the little peak, Joanna stared at the valley beneath her. The Cuttahay farm stood a mile away. To her right she could barely make out the outline of Stonewycke Castle. Port Strathy lay at the ocean's edge two miles distant between the two.

It all comes down to this, she thought.

This valley . . . this land.

She had come here on a vague quest with nothing but an old woman's words and a few antique relics—no friends, no prospects, hardly even a future. Now it seemed she had more than she bargained for, more than she was prepared to handle.

She sighed again.

What was she to do?

Lord, she thought, *how am I to know what to do? Help me hear your voice . . . make everything work out right for these people*.

Then as she silently sat reflecting on the scene spread out before her, the memory of Olive's words came flooding back into her mind: *The Lord loves you. He just wants you to trust Him to do the work He has for you. You can't do that until you accept His forgiveness*.

I've done that, Joanna thought. *I've accepted His forgiveness and He has cleansed away the guilt which has clung to my soul since before I can remember*. But now it seemed something more was required of her before she would be able to hear His voice telling her what she was to do next.

All at once the rest of Olive's words came back; she had forgotten them until now:

And then you must forgive yourself, child. That's what life with the Lord is all about.

How could Olive have known? It was only now just becoming clear to Joanna herself what had been at the core of her trouble all along, what had kept her shut tight to any intrusion by her father, her grandmother, even God. The blame she had placed upon herself for her mother's death, and even her father's had steeled her heart against the acceptance of forgiveness. For at the bottom of her deepest self, she knew she wasn't worthy.

That night in the Cuttahays' barn she had at last been able to unlock her heart and open it to receive God's forgiveness. Not because of any worthiness on her part—she knew now that didn't matter—but because God forgave her without conditions.

Yet she had still not released herself. How could she serve God until she realized He was in control of *everything*? Even her father and mother had been in *God's* hands, as were all these folk in Port Strathy. What had happened had not been *her* doing.

Is that it, Lord? thought Joanna. *Have I accepted your forgiveness, but still haven't forgiven myself?*

The only answer was the gentle breeze flowing through the grassy field. Yet even as Joanna framed the question, she knew that Olive's words reflected the truth she needed to hear. Why should the Lord speak again, when the answer had already been given through the words of her friend?

"Help me, Lord," she sighed. "Help me do what I must do."

In reply the thought came, *For this you do not need my help. I have washed you clean. Now you must accept it.*

Drawing in a deep breath, Joanna rose to her knees, and then at length said, "If you find me worth forgiving, Lord, then it is faithless of me to do anything less. Dear Lord, I do—"

She paused, hardly able to force the words out.

"—I do . . . *forgive myself!*"

The tears which followed were quiet tears—tears not of joy or elation, but of release, of letting go of a lifetime of condemnation and guilt. In her deepest heart, Joanna knew that the Lord's healing of her past had now begun in earnest. For the first time in her life she felt whole.

And for the first time since arriving in Scotland, she felt ready to do what had to be done for these people. God had led her here not only to work His healing in her soul, but so that she might do what had to be done on behalf of these people she had grown to love. And though she had no way of knowing it, God had led her here in answer to her grandmother's prayer for one she loved. For though the generations come and go, God's work of reconciliation goes on unceasingly, and the prayers of His children do not go unheard.

Out of the midst of her thoughts, suddenly Joanna recalled words she had heard long ago. She wondered that it had taken so long for them to have meaning for her: ". . . and lo I am with you always, even unto the end of the world."

She sat upright.

"Was that your word, Lord?" she asked herself. "Will you be with me no matter what?"

I am with you . . . I will lead you.

The phrase resounded in her brain like a cymbal.

"There could be no other way I would be able to face this crisis," Joanna murmured aloud.

I will lead you! came the same small voice within.

Joanna rose, took hold of the mare's rein, and began walking down the hill, feeling a welling surge of courage, optimism, and strength. *I will lead you.* The promise spun through her thoughts . . . *I will lead you!*

She turned her gaze out to the sea and thought of the Vikings Alec had so graphically portrayed—a strong people, men of courage and stout hearts. Brutal sometimes, yes—but nevertheless men of might and valor. She thought of the ancient Highland chieftains she had heard about— men whose loyalty to clan and principle knew no bounds.

Were these stalwart men her own ancestors as well? Did she have their heroic blood flowing through her veins?

Yes!

She was certain of that now.

This was her homeland. These were the roots from which she had sprung. She took pride in these people and their simple virtues and their robust characters because she was one of them!

A resolute determination arose within her.

She *would* see this fight through to the end! If her lot in life was to lay claim to her destiny as the last of the Duncan line, then so be it. She had not come here by accident. The Lord's hand had been on her all along, since her earliest days, since before she was born, preparing her for this moment.

She jumped onto the mare's back, dug in her heels, and galloped down the hill toward the farm, with the words *"I will lead you"* ringing in her mind.

The following morning the rain clouds, which had only produced intermittent showers for two days, at last released their pent-up floods. It poured all through Nathaniel's chores, and when he finally burst into the house shortly after 10 a.m. he was drenched to the skin.

"Aye, ye're finally gettin' t' see a full-scale northern storm," he said to Joanna. "An' jist wait till the dead o' winter! Then ye'll really see a sight o' weather!"

"But it makes the cottage so cozy," replied Joanna.

"I'm grateful Alec was able t' get that window fixed in time," added Letty. "This storm would hae been a mean one wi' a hole in the wall!"

Letty was still reduced to performing only the simplest of tasks on account of her arm, so Joanna busied herself in the kitchen. She still had no clear picture of what she was to do next. But after yesterday's experience on the hillside, her confidence remained high and her spirits buoyant. She had faith the next step would be revealed at the proper time.

Shortly before 2:30 came a sharp knock on the door.

Amazed anyone would be out on such a day, Nathaniel rose and went to the door. There stood Walter Innes, water dripping from his wide-brimmed hat.

"Walter, whatever brings ye oot i' such a squall?" exclaimed Nathaniel. "Weel, come in, man, come in!"

"I'm deliverin' a message," said the factor, running a wet hand across his equally wet face.

"Weel, at least ye can dry off afore ye give it t' us," insisted Letty. "Come over an' stan' by the fire."

Innes complied, although he was too wet for the fire to accomplish much in the way of drying his clothes.

"Weel, what's yer message, Walter?" asked Nathaniel at length.

" 'Tis not fer yerself', man," the factor replied. "My message is fer Miss Matheson."

"Me!" exclaimed Joanna.

"Aye, mem. It's from Dorey. He wishes ye t' join him fer high tea this afternoon—that is, if ye're not mindin' the weather."

The rain notwithstanding, the words were scarcely out of the factor's mouth before Joanna had disappeared, only to return a moment later with coat and hat. This was her opportunity, and she didn't need to be asked twice! The chance to visit again with the strange old man—gardener or houseguest, or whatever he was—was too exciting to let pass. Surely he must know a great many of Stonewycke's secrets. Joanna only hoped this time they might be able to speak more freely.

She hardly felt the rain.

And it would have made no difference, besides. Walter Innes' message had come as a sweet breath of wind from the high places. Joanna tingled with anticipation to see what would come next.

This time she entered the property by the front gate, as a guest rather than a housebreaker. She felt a shiver of awe as she approached the great carved door, knowing that somehow the mysteries of her personal history were held within its walls. The factor clanged the bell announcing his entry, and it sent sharp peals of command reverberating inside. Without waiting for an answer, he lifted the latch, swung the massive door forward with a creak, and led the way inside. Hastening toward them was a dumpy little woman with graying hair. Arrested in mid-flight, she stopped, motioned to the factor with a nod of the head, which he returned. Neither spoke a word. Innes went no farther, but the housekeeper proceeded to lead Joanna through one massive hall after another, all draped in dark brocades and velvets and filled with austere furnishings that looked to be from another age altogether.

Finally they came to a halt before two matching doors. The housekeeper slowly opened both, revealing a spacious banquet hall. The long table in the center was bedecked with candelabra, bowls of flowers, and settings of fine china and glassware. It was clearly large enough to seat fifty, but today only one lone banqueter sat at the far end of the table. The man known as Dorey appeared forlorn as he looked up at his guest with a wan smile.

Dressed in formal attire, with the house and its servants apparently at his command, he can be no mere gardener, Joanna thought. The mystery of his strange presence deepened as she entered, for his bearing and carriage were altogether different than the two previous times when she had seen him in his rough work clothes. The noble look she had caught in his eyes once or twice now returned full force. But even more than that, a change had come over him. Although he was more than sixty-five years of age, a light seemed to be burning in his eye, as if he had just awakened from a long sleep.

"How good of you to come," he said. He rose and went to her.

"Thank you for the invitation," replied Joanna, smiling as he took her hand.

"What else could I have done? I'm afraid I may have been rather rude when you last came," he said. "Not one of my better days."

"Not at all," said Joanna. "We barged in on you uninvited; you were perfectly—"

"No matter," he interrupted. "Come and sit down . . . please."

He led her to a seat near his. "Wasn't it good of Mrs. Bonner to prepare this for us? We're not much accustomed to guests here anymore. There was a time, though, when this great house boasted grand banquets and parties. But I'm afraid those days are past . . . gone . . ."

He spoke in a detached tone, as if it were a great effort to speak at all.

Mrs. Bonner began to serve their meal. Fresh baked salmon, piping hot wheat bread with creamy butter churned only that very morning, barley soup, and fresh garden vegetables. Joanna was hardly hungry enough to do such a feast justice; she had still not fully adjusted to the unusual eating schedules she found in Scotland. In addition she found difficulty in calming her inner excitement in wondering if there was more on Dorey's mind than a simple social visit. But her host seemed neither to notice nor to mind her scanty appetite.

The main course was followed by a tray of delicate pastries and sweetcakes. Dorey chatted about the house; but his talk focused mainly on trivial memorabilia—occasionally fading in and out of the present, but for the most part remaining considerably lucid.

"That chandelier there, you see, above our heads. It was shipped from Italy over seventy-five years ago. Every piece was broken and had to be replaced. It took over two years to finally get it in place."

"You seem very familiar with the history of Stonewycke?" Joanna ventured.

"Ah, yes, I suppose I am," he returned.

"More so than a mere houseguest would be, I should think," she ventured still further. "How long have you been here?"

Dorey's face seemed to go blank for a moment, then he said, "How long. . . ? I don't know. Most of my life, I suppose. It was all so long ago. I lose track of time. The mind forgets, you know."

Joanna nodded. Before she could decide what to say next, Dorey resumed in a new track. He told of past lairds and ancient battles that took place when the great house was more than simply a residence, but rather the chief line of defense for the surrounding valley.

"Of course that was long before our—I mean before my family . . . I should say the laird's family, came to possess the property. It was given by the king, you know."

Joanna gave a half nod, unsure if she had heard him aright.

"Then you are related to the laird's family?" she said.

But Dorey went on as if he hadn't heard, "Ah, if this old house were a living organism, it could stand proud. Would that such could be said of us human beings. I suppose it's only fitting that a majestic house like this can survive hundreds of years, while mortal life spans only . . . a fleeting . . ." but his voice trailed off as he rose and turned away from the table.

Motioning Joanna to follow, he led to a much smaller room adjacent to the great hall, warmer and more homelike than any she had yet seen. A fire crackled cheerfully in the hearth. They took chairs on either side of the fire, and sat down.

"I once thought," Dorey continued, "that survival was the cruelest form of punishment. Perhaps that is why, in the end, I allowed myself to survive. This great house here," he paused to sweep his arm around in a great gesture, "this place became to me like my nursery is to my flowers."

He stopped and rose, and restless, walked to the room's large picture window and stood mesmerized by the huge drops pounding against the pane of glass. *This is certainly no madman*, Joanna thought to herself. Whatever notions the townspeople had, this was surely a man who had been misunderstood.

The silence was long.

At length Joanna gathered her newfound courage.

"Mr.—"

"Do call me Dorey; everyone does, you know."

"But, Dorey," she began again, "I don't even know your real name."

"It's unimportant," he replied. "No one has used that name for years. I even begin to forget it myself."

"But you know that Mr. Sercombe plans to sell the land . . . this house? . . . the whole estate of Stonewycke?"

She held her breath, but Dorey's response did not indicate shock at her words.

"Yes . . . these things happen. Time marches on . . . generations pass. Besides, there is no heir; something must be done, I suppose."

"No heir?" Joanna repeated, at last approaching the question she had been wanting to ask since her first day at Port Strathy. "But surely there are other Duncans—"

"I am not in the line," he interrupted. "I am but a distant cousin."

Joanna sat upright, masking her shock at his words as best she could. "But . . . but . . ." she stammered, "what about the others? Was the laird—was Alastair left without anyone else?"

"I told you, there is no heir," he repeated.

"I . . . I believe my grandmother was born in Port Strathy," said Joanna. "She died recently and her last words were of her girlhood home. That's why I came, hoping to find others of the Duncan name. Relatives."

"There are no more Duncans."

"But I thought you just said—?"

"Only a second cousin . . . it's a distant family tie—from all the way down in London. I don't even deserve the name."

"Then you *are* a Duncan?" said Joanna, trying desperately to hide the emotions mounting inside.

"From a distant branch of the family," he repeated.

"But if there is no one else, it seems the descent would ultimately fall to you?"

"I could not—"

"Is it because people say you're unfit?" said Joanna gently.

"I would not take the land, even if I were fit," said Dorey, speaking with a firmness Joanna had never heard from him. "James Duncan would turn over in his grave." He gave a dry chuckle. "Now that would be the bitter irony, wouldn't it, for me to inherit the old rascal's estate?"

He laughed again, this time more loudly, thoroughly enjoying the idea which had apparently struck him for the first time.

Then he stopped abruptly, turned and stared into the hot embers of the dying fire, as if he were fading again into a distant memory of the past.

"No, better it go to strangers . . ."

His voice trailed off.

When he spoke again, his tone had returned to the soft, far-off sound. He seemed to have forgotten the estate altogether and the look on his face spoke of remembered pain.

"He had no right to do what he did, you know."

Glancing up, Joanna realized he was crying softly. She was afraid to speak. He was now clearly floating in and out between the present and the past.

". . . then she was gone. It was too late. I fell apart. The man had played a cruel trick on me. But he must have told you all about it—"

"No," he said suddenly, glancing up at Joanna; " . . . there, I've gotten it all wrong again, haven't I?"

He stopped short, staring at Joanna for a few moments, and then his face seemed to come back to reality.

Hardly knowing what to say, Joanna tried to pick up the previous threads of the conversation. "But if the estate is sold to strangers, what if they let it run down?"

Dorey turned toward her, confused again. He had an agitated look in his eyes, and his mouth was contorted in confused questioning.

"But . . . but you," he stammered in bewilderment, ". . . that couldn't—I mean, you would never let . . . you love the land, don't you, Maggie?"

The response poised on the tip of Joanna's tongue died the moment she heard the name.

"I . . . I—" Joanna faltered, but no more sounds would come.

The final word Dorey had spoken dashed against her ears like a brick, a blow that pierced directly to her heart.

"You love this land," Dorey went on, now wandering in the private world of his own rekindled memory, suddenly awakened after being blanked out for over forty years. "How you must have suffered when you left. Your mother suffered too, you know. She knew neither James nor Alastair cared for the land. They only sought the power of it. She longed for you to return . . . never stopped hoping. That was why she gave you the deed. She was certain it would bring you home in the end. She came to care about me, I think, for your sake. That was why she invited me here. She and Dermott tried to make life comfortable for me, after—you know—after my mind closed to everything that had happened. It could have worked out . . . in time . . . I could have followed . . . could have found you . . . if that father of yours hadn't driven you away so that you died before I could come—"

He paused, his voice rising in anger.

Longing to hear more, Joanna squirmed from the intrusion into a private conversation of which she was not a part.

"—he had no right," the old man went on. "I never told you this, but when he found out that—"

"Dorey," Joanna said, interrupting him.

Startled, he glanced toward her.

"Dorey," she repeated, "I'm not Margaret."

He stared deep into her eyes, blinked, then scanned her face, as if seeing her for the first time.

"No . . . no, of course you're not," he said. "My mind . . . it's filled with cobwebs, you see. Things seem so confused. No, you aren't. But . . ." His voice drifted off once more.

"I would like to hear more about my grandmother," said Joanna softly after a moment. "That is, if you'd like to talk about her."

"Your grandmother?"

"Yes. My grandmother was Margaret Duncan. She died recently. That's why I'm here."

"Died . . . recently? But I thought . . ." He stopped for a moment, then went on. "But there's so much I don't understand. Was I confused about that too?"

He glanced around the room, then rested his eyes once more on Joanna. They were full of tears.

"I haven't spoken of Maggie, even thought of her, in years," he began once more rational and clear-eyed. "Seeing you, I suppose, triggered some deep memories—you look so much like her, you know. What would you like to know about her?"

"Whatever you want to tell me."

"Oh, she was a joy—so young and vibrant . . . sweet, like the very land she loved."

"You and she were . . . close?" Joanna asked tentatively.

"Oh yes. Atlanta hoped the promise of the inheritance would make her return. Atlanta always expected her to come to her senses and return to claim it. She was certain the thought of her brother being the laird would send her home."

"Why did she leave Scotland?"

He winced and glanced away momentarily.

"Oh Lord . . ." he began, then swallowed and groaned softly. "I made her leave! I—whom she trusted and loved. I forced her from home . . ."

He paused, then seeing the puzzled expression on Joanna's face, summoned the effort to continue.

". . . I thought it was for the noblest of reasons, but it all turned on me like a wild animal."

He buried his face in his hands.

"In the end, she believed I had deserted her . . . for that I shall never be able to forgive myself."

He slumped back into his chair; his shoulders shook in silent sobs.

Joanna could not speak. Every thought that came to her lips melted away, hollow and useless.

"I hated James for a while," Dorey went on, as if now that the gate was open the tide of his words could not be stopped. "But mostly . . . I hated myself. It is a coward who hides behind words like safety and honor and wisdom. She was the brave one! And I even grew to hate God. I could not forgive Him for the loss of the only precious being I had ever known . . . oh, Maggie!"

His voice caught in a sob.

Joanna rose and walked slowly toward him, then laid a gentle hand on his shoulder.

"She loved you in the end," she said softly, the meaning of her grandmother's last words suddenly becoming clear to Joanna. "She spoke of you before I left her."

"I didn't deserve it," he replied. "What kind of man sends his wife—"

"Wife!" Joanna interrupted, "I thought she was married in America."

"Our time together as husband and wife was brief . . . too, too brief. James was in a rage when he found out. He hated my family . . . disdained me. And in many ways I was deserving of it. He had higher hopes for his daughter—George Falkirk, the son of the Earl of Kairn. I . . . should never have intervened. But then the rascal was no better than I . . . poor Maggie. She deserved better than either of us."

"But she loved you—" said Joanna, trying to comfort him. He cut her off.

"Love is not always enough."

Were they talking about the same Margaret Duncan?

This love of Theodore Duncan's youth seemed so different from the woman Joanna had known and grown too late to love. Yet here they were, knit together in a bond of love for the same woman. For Joanna knew that Dorey loved her still.

He shook his head bitterly.

"How my sins have hounded me!" he went on, clearly in agony at the memory. "I tried to hide from them, but they caught up with me. No . . . love is never enough . . . Oh, God, why?" he shouted in an agony of anger and remorse.

"Dorey," said Joanna, not sure how to express the thoughts that were so new to her, "if your sins have followed you, perhaps . . . it is because God could not let go of you . . . because He loves you and wants you to find forgiveness."

"I deserve none," replied Dorey, who began weeping anew.

"Then maybe it is you who need to forgive. God cannot give you the forgiveness He has for you until you stop blaming Him for what happened. None of us deserve forgiveness. But God loves us enough to give it anyway."

Joanna was surprised at her own words, but they seemed to flow of their own volition.

"Would that it were true . . ." His voice trailed off in despair.

"Dorey . . ." Joanna said, and as she spoke she reached up to her neck and loosened her grandmother's locket which she had worn constantly since arriving in Scotland. She unfastened the catch and held the open locket to him.

"This is you, isn't it?"

The old man nodded.

"She wore it until her last days," Joanna said.

"Oh, dear God . . ." The man sobbed as he tenderly wrapped his fingers around the precious reminder of his youthful love.

He lifted his head to face her. "At least there's one thing," he said. "There's you. Perhaps it is true that God is merciful. I thought she was dead. That is what they told me. She, along with the child . . ."

His voice trailed away as he gazed steadily at Joanna.

"The child!" Joanna could barely form the words.

"The child . . . who was forever lost to me . . . the child I would never see."

"Whose child, Dorey? I don't understand . . . whose child? I have to know."

"Why, Maggie's, of course. When she left she was carrying our child. But I would never see the baby . . . our baby."

"Dorey," said Joanna, the tears flowing from her eyes, "*my* grandmother had only one child—my mother."

"I . . . I should have known . . . the first day you came . . . the moment I laid eyes on you."

Weeping, Joanna fell to her knees at Dorey's side, laying her head on his lap with her arms around his bent frame. He patted her hair tenderly with his gnarled hand and gently stroked her tear-stained cheeks. A single tear made a lonely track down his face, but his heart beat with joy at the loving reunion that had come after more than forty years of waiting.

This was more than Joanna had dared hope for when she set foot on that ship in New York harbor as an innocent young girl cast adrift into the world. Even now she was afraid to believe what she knew in her heart was true, that here—thousands of miles from what had once been her home—she had found her grandfather!

33 / Joanna's Resolve

The sweet smell of hay filled Joanna's nostrils.

Nathaniel had finished his morning's chores and his cows had been led out to pasture for the day. The barn stood silent as the late morning's rays of sun filtered through the cracks in the siding. Joanna sat high atop a stack of baled hay reflecting on the events of the previous day. Nathaniel and Letty had been understandably overjoyed as she had recounted her talk with Dorey. And that evening they had enjoyed a festive time of celebration, welcoming Joanna into her Scottish heritage as full-blooded kin to Port Strathy's leading family.

Indeed, as that family's heir apparent.

But this morning, after the excitement had settled, Joanna discovered a streak of melancholy running through her she couldn't explain. Was it the letdown after reaching a cherished goal? Or was it the weight of responsibility she now felt resting on her shoulders?

Now, as she sat in the empty barn collecting her thoughts, tears came to her eyes. Were they tears of joy—or tears of fear?

She didn't know.

Yes, she was happy. But at the same time, the awe she felt sometimes overpowered her—an awe that occasionally took the form of apprehension over the future, and at other times as thankfulness to the God she was only beginning to know.

He had led. She knew He would continue to do so. As she looked back over her entire life she could see vividly that He had been with her all the way. Even through all those years of pain and loneliness. She had never really been alone. He had been preparing her for this moment.

Joanna heard the rusty latch of the barn door lift and the door swing open. Without glancing up she instinctively knew who was there.

"I thought I might find ye here," Alec said when he spotted her where she sat. "Letty told me everythin'. I'm happy fer ye."

"Thank you, Alec," replied Joanna softly with a smile.

"I haven't seen ye since . . . since we came back from town together two days ago. Ye was pretty silent on the ride here. Is . . . is everythin' all right?"

Joanna did not answer for a moment.

"Yes," she said at length, "yes, I'm fine. There have been so many things on my mind."

"I didn't mean t' pry. I jist sometimes . . . it's jist hard to tell what ye lasses are thinkin'."

"If you try to worry about what a woman is thinking, Alec, you will always be confused! Don't you know—that's how we of the fairer sex keep you men on your toes."

Alec's face spread into a broad grin. "It is good t' see ye laugh again. Ye was so somber before."

"The man you saw me leave Olive's with . . . he has caused me no small amount of emotional uncertainty."

"I could see," said Alec, shifting uneasily on his feet, "that he was some taken wi' ye."

Joanna sighed. "Yes, I suppose you're right," she said.

"And yersel'?" said Alec.

"Me?"

"It seemed the two o' ye knew each other right well."

"He was on the ship I sailed on from New York. His attentions swept me off my feet for a while—I thought I was in love with him."

"And were ye?" asked Alec stiffly.

"I don't know. Maybe I was . . . for a while. But that was before—"

She stopped and glanced quickly down to where Alec stood. She hadn't intended to say anything, but out it had come.

Though showing nothing on his face, a pang of hope shot through Alec's heart at her words. "Before what?" he wanted to shout; but he kept silent.

"Oh, Alec," Joanna hastened on, diverting the conversation. The time would come to explore her present feelings. But that time would have to wait. "Alec . . . what will happen to Dorey if I lose the estate? Jason will surely destroy the place if he gets his hands on it."

"The Lord will take care o' old Dorey," said Alec in measured tone. "But don't ye worry. Ye'll not lose the estate."

"How can you be so sure?"

His eyes seemed to pierce her as he said, "I've come t' know a little about ye, Joanna, in the short time we've been together. Ye're not the same uncertain girl that first came here. An' I know this—ye won't allow it t' happen."

"If only I had more say in the matter! But what if I turn out to be completely powerless? If only—"

She looked away from Alec for a moment, then back.

"You don't know how stupid I've been. I'm afraid I've incurred the wrath of a very powerful man—a man who isn't accustomed to losing."

"The man ye was with the other day?"

"His name's Jason Channing. He's the man who's buying the estate—a friend of Sercombe's.

"But what could this land mean t' the likes o' him?" asked Alec.

"The land means nothing to him—nothing except a way to make money. But what matters even more to him is winning. And he'll fight this to the bitter end because I did something to him no one else has done—I turned him down. I said *no*."

Noticeably relieved Alec said, "There, ye see. Ye're turnin' into a mighty strong Scots woman, ye are, Joanna Matheson. Ye'll do what ye need t' do. An' I'd put my money on ye t' win this one!"

"Thank you, Alec," said Joanna. "But don't forget. Whatever victories we may gain in this before it's over are half yours. You've been with me from the start."

The sound of urgent approaching hoofbeats halted their conversation. Alec turned and ran to the door of the barn. Joanna scrambled down from her perch and followed close behind.

It was Walter Innes.

"Innes!" shouted Alec, hurrying out to meet him, "ye've got yer poor horse in a heat o' lather."

"I know," the factor apologized. "But I figured it'd be quicker t' ride o'er the shortcut than t' take the motor car, an' I thought ye'd want t' know immediately." He swung down, removed his dusty hat, and wiped his brow with a broad sweep of his forearm.

"Know what?" asked Joanna stepping forward.

Walter approached the two, then with an awkward bow addressed Joanna: "My Leddy," he said, "I had a talk wi' Mr. Dorey an' he told me who ye are. This is a great day fer Port Strathy—'tis all I can say, an' I'm prood t' be the factor o' yer house. But—"

He paused.

"I'm afraid you're assuming quite a lot, Mr. Innes," said Joanna. "It's hardly my house. But nevertheless, I thank you for your kind words and your support."

"But," Innes went on, "weel, My Leddy . . . I only hope . . . that is, weel, I'm afraid somethin's wrong."

"What is it, man!" Alec exclaimed.

"Mr. Sercombe was at the house this mornin'. I was oot—chores, ye know. But Mrs. Bonner, she says they had a bit o' a row, they did."

"Who?"

"The lawyer an' Mr. Dorey. Mr. Dorey said he wasn't happy aboot the sale an' wanted t' hold up the proceedin's. Especially, she said he told Mr. Sercombe, seein' as there was now an heir. Then Mr. Dorey said he could prove beyond doobt that Miss Matheson," here he paused and nodded toward Joanna, "that she was the heiress o' the estate. Weel then Mr. Sercombe jist laughed in his face—laughed right in his face! Mr. Dorey kept insistin' an' finally Sercombe stopped his laughin'. Mrs.

Bonner says he became downright surely. Then he—Mr. Sercombe that is—shoved poor Dorey aside and went running all through the house, lookin' fer somethin'. He searched high an' low, gettin' angrier an' angrier the whole time. Mrs. Bonner, she says she was afraid t' say a word. He threw rooms an' doors an' wardrobes open and rummaged through drawers, but whatever he was lookin' fer he must not o' found it 'cause then finally he grabbed Dorey by the arm and led him from the house. She says Dorey seemed calm enough, as if he wasn't afraid o' the man. But Mrs. Bonner, she didn't know what t' do an' as they was leavin' she said, 'Where are ye takin' oor Mr. Dorey?' Sercombe jist smiled one o' his cunning smiles an' said, 'Don't ye worry about a thing, Mrs. Bonner. We're jist goin' t' my office so Dorey an' I can discuss the matter further,' an' then they was gone.''

"But you don't believe Sercombe?'' Joanna asked.

"I hardly know what t' believe, My Leddy. Mr. Sercombe has always been most kind t' me, an' t' Mr. Dorey too. But up till noo he's always been firm about keepin' Mr. Dorey at the house—any business was always taken care o' there.''

"Dorey is in danger,'' said Joanna with growing alarm. "I know that man means no good to him.''

"Nothin's goin' t' happen t' Mr. Dorey, My Leddy,'' Innes replied. "Ye can thrash me good if it does. But one thing I can tell ye fer certain. Nobody—not Mr. Sercombe or anybody—will be talkin' Dorey into anythin' against his will. Why, mem, since ye was there yesterday he's been a new man. I think he's but lapsed back into his old self only once.''

"How was that?'' asked Joanna.

" 'Twasn't nothin' t' worry about. He jist says t' me—it was last night, a bit late—he says, 'Baxter'—that was the factor before me—'Baxter,' he says, 'where does the Lady Atlanta keep her private papers? I know it's none o' my business, but . . .' Then he must o' realized I wasn't Baxter at all, an' he stopped. Then said he had t' tell ye somethin', Miss Matheson. That was all there was t' it.''

A moment's silence followed. Joanna glanced at Alec.

"First thing we must do,'' said Alec, "is t' make sure Dorey's safe. I'm ridin' into town t' see if he's at the lawyer's office. Walter, ye stay here with Joanna an' the folks.''

Walter nodded his approval.

Alec mounted his horse.

"There's one more thing,'' added Walter. "I dinna ken if the one thing has t' do wi' the other. But jist aboot the time when Sercombe was at the house, I was headin' into the stables t' do some work. At the time I didna know the lawyer was wi' Dorey. Weel, who should I find but that good fer nothin' Tom Forbes, snoopin' around in the stables—diggin' through the hay an' muck like a scavenger. Soon as he saw me he lit off like a hare. Anyway, I don't know if it means anythin'."

"Oh, it means somethin'," said Alec with a knowing look. "I only wish I knew what."

"Alec," said Joanna, grasping his arm, "be careful."

"Don't ye be worryin', lass, I will be." He smiled, laid his hand gently on hers, then quickly swung his gray gelding around, dug his heels in and galloped away.

Joanna spent the remainder of the morning and the early afternoon wandering idly about the cottage, roaming about fields close by, with now and again another peek inside the barn. But she could not keep her mind on any task. Her instincts told her Dorey was in trouble, and she couldn't still the anxiety in her heart. At every sound she glanced up and ran to look down the road, thinking it might be Alec returning with news.

About two o'clock Joanna walked aimlessly into her room to gather up some laundry, when her eyes fell upon her grandmother's music box sitting on her dresser. She hadn't listened to it, even noticed it, in days. She ran her hand along the finely carved walnut top, then opened it and wound the key. The delicate strains of Brahms' lullaby floated to her ears like a balm of peace.

The images the nostalgic melody raised in her mind were now clear and well defined. They had names, personalities, histories. There were mental pictures of actual landscapes. There were real faces.

"Oh, Grandma," Joanna whispered, reaching for a handkerchief to wipe the moisture from her eyes.

Her mind had been obsessed with Maggie Duncan, yet that young girl was far removed from the woman Joanna had known. Even now, when the word *grandmother* came to her lips, she could only visualize the nearly unconscious woman lying on her deathbed.

Margaret Duncan's frail voice and cryptic words drifted back to Joanna's mind, as clear as if she were still alive: ". . . don't let them take it, Joanna—it's yours!"

What else had she said?

Joanna remembered she had spoken of someone. She had paid so little attention then, because the words meant nothing. Now she realized her grandmother had been talking about Dorey. But what else . . . hadn't she also spoken of her mother?

". . . before I left . . . my mother . . ."

Desperately Joanna tried to recall the exact words.

"Find it . . . the treasure . . . in the nursery . . ."

Joanna snapped the music-box lid shut. A heavy fog lifted from her brain. Why hadn't she thought of it sooner?

"Of course!" she said to herself. "Something is at the house! Something so important it was all my grandmother could think about as she slipped into a coma."

Joanna jumped up from where she sat on the bed. She knew what she had to do. She didn't know what it might be. But whatever her grandmother had been speaking of—she had to find it . . . before it was too late!

She opened the drawer and set the music box inside. Her eyes fell on the folded embroidery she had also brought with her from her grandmother's locked bureau drawer. The sight sent a shiver up her spine. For this was not *Margaret's*, it was *Maggie's*—a sweet young teenager, in love and heartbroken. She tenderly unfolded the linen and now saw— as if for the first time—names that had come to mean something to her. From the hand-stitched family tree stood out the names of Robert, Anson, Talmud, Atlanta, and others.

And the blank spot where the name had been neatly torn away— where the name *Margaret Duncan* should have been, directly beneath the names Atlanta and James—had Margaret herself ripped out her own name? Was it another impulsive act of this youngster, feeling perhaps the sting of her father's rejection?

Grandma, thought Joanna. *You do deserve a place there. I will personally embroider your name in the proper place where it should have always been. You shall take your rightful stand in this family.*

Refolding the linen, she caught up her coat and tucked it inside. She then slipped from her room unnoticed, outside, and into the barn. Perhaps it was foolhardy to go off alone. If Nathaniel or Walter saw her go, they would insist on accompanying her.

But she had come to Scotland alone, perhaps to find meaning in her life. And notwithstanding the deep and loving friendships she had made, she now had to stand and carry out this final part of her mission alone as well. Her very being as a woman demanded it. Come what may, her mind was set; she had to learn to stand on her own two feet.

Besides, she consoled herself, *no doubt by this time Alec and Dorey would already be back at the estate.* So she would not be alone in her search after all.

Saddling the mare she reflected on how she had hated her riding lessons in Chicago. Now she was thankful she didn't have to worry about not being able to ride a horse. She led the mare out the barn's back door, walked her about half a mile to the east away from the road before she mounted. Then she mounted, doubled back, and rode toward the town, paralleling the road about a quarter mile to its east so as not to be seen. Reaching Port Strathy, she wound through the southernmost back streets and alleys, arriving finally at the road out of town toward Strathy summit. Because of the steep, rugged incline, she was forced to stay on the road by which she had first entered the village. But she saw no one, rode on, turned south toward Stonewycke, and rode the entire way without meeting a soul.

Once again the great iron gate towered before her.

Joanna tested the lock; it was open.

She swung the gate wide and walked in.

"The nursery . . ." The words resounded in her mind as she made her way up the cobblestone path. What did her grandmother mean? There was the greenhouse of which Dorey was so proud. But hadn't that been built by Alastair? Was there perhaps an older greenhouse, even a garden then called the nursery?

If only Dorey were here to guide her!

The full implication of searching such an immense place suddenly struck her. It could take days, even weeks! Especially as she had no idea what she was even looking for! What did the words mean?—*"You mustn't let them take it; it's yours . . ."*

Entering the courtyard, Joanna instantly saw that Alec's horse was nowhere to be seen. Dorey was undoubtedly not here, either.

She walked boldly up to the door, clanged the bell, and waited.

There was no response.

She rang again, but silence was the only reply. The place was utterly deserted.

What if Sercombe had spirited Dorey off, hidden him away, and then returned to the house to continue his search at his leisure? That would explain the open latch at the gate and the forlorn emptiness. Certainly he would not have allowed Mrs. Bonner to remain while he did his dirty work.

A churning formed in the pit of Joanna's stomach. No doubt, Sercombe was either in the house at this very moment, or he was planning to return. Why else would he have taken Dorey away?

She gingerly tried the door's latch.

The door swung open and she stepped inside.

"Well, here I come, Mr. Sercombe," she murmured aloud. "You'd better be ready for me because I'm not turning back now!"

The door shut with a bang and Joanna stood motionless till the echo resounding through the vast, cold hallways died away. She cocked her ear and listened. No sound was to be heard.

At first, she walked aimlessly about, gathering courage. The high ceilings, the walls draped with rich tapestries portraying ancient events, the ornately carved chairs and hall-trees and sideboards, the tiled floors, above all, the awesome silence, combined to create an atmosphere more like that of a cathedral than a home. What a contrast this was to the Cuttahays' warm, cozy little cottage! Here it would be sacrilege to lay a finger on a single piece of china. It was hard to imagine people actually living here.

Dorey's comment came back to her about banquets and gay parties. The sounds of a string quartet drifted into her consciousness. The room was filled with brightly dressed women and men in tails and top hats. Carriages were pulling up outside in a steady stream. The sounds of laughter could be heard. Now the host escorted the hostess to the dance where they led the company in a Haydn minuet.

What a gay ball it was!

Just then the bell sounded and the butler announced: "Ladies and gentlemen, the Lady Joanna Matheson . . ." She stepped forward, in shimmering ball gown and jeweled tiara, to take the hand of . . .

Joanna's vision faded. All that remained were the solitary footsteps of a young child racing through the long hallway. "I wonder what it was like to grow up here?" Joanna wondered.

Then all fell silent once more, and Joanna was left alone with reality. Forward she walked, approaching the great wooden staircase. Up it she climbed, then proceeded down the hallway in which she found herself. Turning into room after room, sometimes only for a moment, occasionally for a more thorough look, she began to explore the house of her ancestors. Not knowing where she was going or what she was seeking, she allowed impulse and instinct to guide her. On she went, through more rooms—some small, others huge, many empty—through a magnificently stocked library, and up another flight of stairs to the third floor, down several long hallways. At length she came to a narrow backstair. Following it she found that it led to a large, empty tower room. Descending the backstairs the way she had come, she came out again on the second floor.

For the first time Joanna felt a sense of bewilderment. She had turned in so many directions she was no longer certain of her bearings. She had come back down to the second floor but hadn't seen this hallway before. It must lead toward the main staircase up which she had ascended earlier. As she made her way along, Joanna continued to scrutinize the rooms on her way. She paused a moment in one of these. The afternoon sunlight streaming in drew her to the window which was toward the southwest corner of the mansion. Gazing out she was met with a curious sight. She found herself looking out toward the rear of the house and from her high vantagepoint she could see what appeared to be a walled garden. But it was wild and tangled and unkempt. She wondered at the sight, for the rest of the grounds were so meticulously groomed by Dorey. How odd that this particular spot should have been overlooked! The first chance she had she would explore it, but for now she had to return her attentions to the inside of the great house.

Leaving the room she proceeded on, but there was something so solemn about the place that she had not yet been able to bring herself to touch anything.

All at once the hallway ended abruptly. Issuing from its end, in both directions were two smaller passageways. By this time she was so disoriented that she had not a notion of which would be the more likely to return her to the house's main staircase. About to follow the one to the left, she became aware for the first time of two massive oak-paneled doors which stood directly in front of her. How could she have missed them as she approached down the wide hallway?

She tested the doors, found them unlocked, and stepped inside.

The room in which Joanna found herself was decidedly different than any she had yet encountered. It was a large room, but the lowered ceiling gave it a warmer feel. The furnishings possessed a distinct Mediterranean air—spindly and delicate compared to the massive wood furnishings found in the rest of the house. At the opposite end, French doors opened onto a veranda, from which descended a narrow, circular stair to a little courtyard full of an assortment of nicely trimmed shrubs and small trees. Dorey's care had clearly kept it lovely, though probably none but his own eyes had seen it for years.

Joanna wondered whose hand had chosen this unique decor. Could it have been Atlanta Duncan herself? It was not difficult to envision her great-grandmother on a shopping trip in Italy.

Atlanta . . .

All of a sudden, Joanna was aware she was trembling. Could *this* be Atlanta's room? If so . . . what secrets might it contain?

She walked about with a feeling of awe and reverence.

Then the words flooded back upon her memory:

"*. . . my mother . . . the day I left . . . gave me . . .*"

All at once Joanna could not content herself simply to gaze with wonder at all these ancient possessions. She had to stir up the settled dust of the past and unravel whatever mysteries this house contained.

Her eyes fell upon a small French provencial secretary to the left of the French doors. It held only three drawers. Joanna had to force each one open; she must have been the first in decades to attempt such an exploration. At least she had beat Sercombe to this room!

The first drawer contained envelopes and blank sheets of stationery embossed with a family crest; there was nothing else save a few dried-up pens.

The next drawer held more promise.

It was stuffed with several stacks of letters with strange names—an M. Browne of London, Clara Seaton of Suffolk, and a Richard Bosley of Glasgow. Most of the dates on the letters ranged between 1860 and 1870, but Joanna soon realized they contained nothing but the typical chit-chat exchanged by friends. The correspondence from Bosley proved the sole exception. It was a bill for certain remodeling done at the house, dated June 5, 1870. The rest of the letters told Joanna little. But they left one thing certain—every one was addressed to Atlanta Duncan, and one, much older than the rest, to Atlanta Ramsey.

Joanna had indeed penetrated the old matriarch's personal desk— her own great-grandmother.

The third drawer was empty.

Joanna closed the secretary and wandered slowly about the room. Undoubtedly because of the remarkable collection of works in the library, Joanna all at once realized she had not seen a single book in any of the rooms she had been in thus far. But here, a tiny but impressive set of leather-bound editions was enclosed in a fine walnut bookcase. On the top shelf sat a complete set of the works of William Shakespeare—bound in red morrocco with gold lettering and gilt edges. Below sat several glass and porcelain trinkets and a large black family Bible.

Joanna walked toward the case, stared for a few moments at the beautiful set of books, and absently began pulling down the volumes and flipping through them one by one while her mind was occupied elsewhere. She withdrew *A Midsummer Night's Dream* and *Macbeth* and *Romeo and Juliet*.

Replacing them, she lifted the family Bible and opened its leather-bound board covers. Her first instinct was to find the page showing the family tree. A hasty glance told her she would have to return for a closer inspection later. Then she flipped quickly through the remainder of the book. It gave the appearance of being new and scarcely used. However, toward the middle of the book, the pages fell open naturally to the twenty-third Psalm where several folded pieces of paper dropped out and to the floor. Joanna stooped down to pick them up. She gently unfolded the pages, yellowed with age, and immediately recognized the crest she had seen on the stationery in the secretary. The letter was written in a beautiful feminine script and began:

My dear daughter Margaret . . .

Joanna swallowed, took a deep breath, and tried to still her racing heart before continuing.

". . . how I regret the events which led to your untimely estrangement from your home and family. I wish with every fibre of my being that we could turn back the clock to those joyful days before our unhappy tragedy. You must remember how glad those days were, even if you care to remember nothing else. How you delighted in our rides over the grassy hillsides and our picnics on Ramsey Head! Ah, listen to the rambling of a sentimental old mother—but those are the memories I cherish in the depths of my heart. And I know we could recapture those days if you would but return.

There, I have said it!

You may think it cruel of me to ask you to return to the bosom of your sorrow, but ask I must. This is where you belong, my dear Margaret.

Your father is gone, dear. I do not ask you to grieve for him, but rather to think that now you could find happiness here once again. Especially in that I also bring you the joyous news (which perhaps Mr. Connell has already done) that your Ian is alive! Oh, Maggie, please return! For this is your home.

But perhaps even more than these things, dear Margaret, you cannot allow the land to pass to Alastair. The land is yours, daughter, it has always been and always will be. I have made sure of that. You need only to claim it. Alastair is an alien to the land, as was his father; but I know that for you, the land is your very soul—as it has always been for me.

Margaret, I am at my wits' end with fear of what will happen to my beloved Stonewycke. I have pledged to myself never to reveal a secret that has been for generations hidden, indeed, thought lost forever. I feel more closely akin to my grandfather Anson than I ever thought possible. I know now what drove him to do what he did, for often I was nearly driven to the same extreme and I used my knowledge of Anson's intention to work my will over your father many times. But now he is gone and I have hidden it, and I look only to you to carry on the legacy of the Ramsey name, if only you will return to claim your heritage, and the love both Ian and I share for you . . .

There the letter ended.

Joanna turned it over, vainly hoping to discover more. But there was nothing else. Atlanta Duncan's poignant pleading with her daughter apparently progressed no further than an ancient burial in the depths of her daughter's favorite psalm. How could Joanna have known that before completing the letter, Atlanta had received word that her daughter was dead?

Joanna read the words of the twenty-third Psalm of David with renewed insight: "He maketh me to lie down in green pastures: He leadeth me beside the still waters. He restoreth my soul . . ."

Joanna sat on the elegant, dusty divan. She reread the letter. What might have happened had Margaret received this letter? How differently things might have turned out!

And there was that name Anson again . . . what could it all mean? Once more her thoughts drifted toward her grandmother's cryptic words, and now, here, her own mother added still further to the mystery.

Joanna rose and leisurely returned to the secretary. Perhaps she had overlooked something. There had to be at least one clue—it was Atlanta's desk, after all.

Tiring of the seeming hopelessness of her quest, Joanna sifted aimlessly through the stacks of envelopes, bills, letters and miscellaneous old papers. There was a letter *from* Atlanta to the same Bosley. She was about to pass it by when it suddenly struck her—wasn't it a bit odd that the services of a carpenter from Glasgow would be enlisted for minor remodeling? Glasgow was a great distance from Strathy.

He could have been a family friend, Joanna thought. *Or simply the best in his particular field of work.*

The letter from Atlanta to Bosley revealed nothing, simply a settling of accounts. But it was followed by one from the Glasgow carpenter dated 1846, over twenty years before the bill she had first seen. She withdrew the single sheet from its envelope and read, in the most businesslike format:

"We are happy to report that we can commence work on your new nursery in two weeks—"

Joanna gasped with growing excitement as she continued:

"We feel certain we will have the job in question complete well before the blessed event. In our estimation only one wall will have to be removed and the window you requested—"

The letter fell from Joanna's hand.

Of course!

She had been so preoccupied with Dorey and plants and greenhouses that a child's nursery had never occurred to her. How could she have been so stupid? It was so clear!

Margaret had no doubt been speaking of her own childhood room; she had been born in August of 1846.

"That's it . . . that's it!" Joanna shouted jumping up from the divan. "It's in the *nursery*!"

Hastily she scanned the remaining contents of the drawer, hoping to find a drawing or some plans for the work or something which would give her an idea of where to look. But there was none.

She ran from the room and looked left and right, down the narrow passageways, and then straight ahead along the wide corridor down which she had walked from the back staircase. If she had been in Atlanta's room, no doubt the nursery would be close by.

Joanna hastened to the room directly next to it, apparently another bedchamber. It contained a heavy four-poster bed, wardrobe, and bureau. A brief glance at the contents revealed nothing of promise.

She ran down the hall to the room on the other side of Atlanta's. At first glance it appeared nearly as uninteresting, although considerably smaller.

It was little more than an alcove containing a setee, a velvet-covered highbacked chair, and low round table in front of the setee. Joanna shook her head in dismay and turned to leave. Whatever made her think a nursery would have been kept all these years? Even if Atlanta had kept it intact from sentimental reasons, surely Alastair would long since have dismantled its memories. Any secret that lay hidden within the nursery had no doubt been carried off with the rest of the furnishings long ago.

Glancing behind her for one final sidelong sweep of her eyes, the room's only window arrested her attention.

That's odd, she thought. The window was not only twice as high as it was wide, but also the glass appeared to run right up against the wall at the corner. "They certainly didn't plan that window very well."

She turned back into the room, walked toward the window, and pressed her face against it. The glass appeared to continue on, through the wall which ran perpendicular to the exterior surface, and into the next room.

Well, the adjoining room that shares this odd window bears looking into, she thought.

Back out into the hall she hurried, turned to her right, and found she had to walk some twenty feet before coming to another door. When she looked inside, to her surprise, she discovered no window butting up against the righthand wall at all but a single large window centered exactly in the middle of the wall. In addition, there was no conceivable way—at least according to her first judgment—that this room could have filled all the space between the rooms she had traversed in the hall.

Joanna stepped back out into the hallway, puzzled, and was about to return to the smaller room from which she had just come when a paralyzing sound seized her attention.

She strained to listen. It was unmistakable—the pounding of approaching hoofbeats!

Sercombe!

Panic gripped her. She would have no chance alone, especially if he found her here, searching the house. And what if those other two men were with him?

Joanna crept down the hall as noiselessly as possible. The hoofbeats soon eased. Somehow Joanna reached the back staircase. Should she go down and seek a hasty escape from the house? If Sercombe was not alone they might have all the doors blocked. They certainly would have seen her horse by now.

Below, she heard the tramping of heavy feet upon the tiled floors. She quickly made for the third floor and the tower room.

35 / Alec and Channing _____

Alec rode hard.

Leaving Joanna and Walter Innes at the Cuttahays, he made for Port Strathy in a full gallop, his indignation rising with each bend of the muddy road. He reached the town's outlying cottages in ten minutes but did not slow until he rounded the corner of the main street. In a flurry of earth and a clatter of hoofs, he reined in his mount directly in front of Sercombe's office. With a single motion, he swung down and covered the distance to the office door.

It was locked.

He shook it, but the door did not even give a hint of submitting to his strength. He kicked at it. Then he wiped away a layer of dust from the window and peered inside, but all appeared dark and lifeless.

Alec hurried next door to inquire of Miss Sinclair anything she might have seen of Sercombe's movements. She had not seen him all day.

In frustration, Alec heaved his tired frame upon his horse. He thought for a moment, then dug in his heels and sped eastward out of town toward Stonewycke. Perhaps Dorey had been taken back during Walter's absence. Near the top of the hill on the main road, he slowed his pace. He could almost feel the fatigue rippling through the gray gelding's muscles—the animal had to rest. Alec plodded on up the hill, slower but undaunted.

At Stonewycke nothing stirred. No horses were in sight; Mrs. Bonner was gone; and a ride around the entire grounds revealed nothing. Dejected, Alec returned to town where he cantered up and down the streets, asking those he encountered if they had seen Sercombe or Dorey. After two hours of fruitless search and inquiry, he guided his tired horse back to the Cuttahay farm.

When he arrived, however, he discovered that now not only was Dorey missing, but Joanna as well, with neither Walter nor Nathaniel able to offer so much as a clue about when she had left or where she had gone.

"What if they've captured the lass, too?" he said more in frustration than anger. "How could the two o' ye let her oot o' yer sights?"

Alec spurred his beleaguered horse back toward town.

Once again he rushed straight to Sercombe's door; this time he was not disappointed. A light was visible inside.

Alec stormed the door and threw it open without pausing to knock. "Sercombe, ye bla'guard!" he shouted, "ye've gone too far, an' now ye'll have t' answer—"

"Who do you think you are!" came a voice from the opposite side of the room, where Jason was reclining easily on the velvet setee.

He stood to face the intruder.

"You!" exclaimed Alec. "Ye're no better than that scoundrel lawyer friend o' yers. But ye're through here, the both o' ye!"

"My, my," Channing said in a measured tone. "I thought you country bumpkins were supposed to know your place. But it appears I'll have to put you there myself."

Alec bristled, but he resisted the urge to throw himself at this gentleman whose exterior appeared so refined.

Instead, he simply said, "Where's Sercombe?"

"I can hardly think it to be any concern of yours."

"I'm makin' it my concern, an' ye better too, if ye know what's good fer ye," came Alec's fervent reply.

"Is that a threat?" Channing's calm voice was betrayed only by a dark glint in his eyes.

" 'Tis but the second time I've laid eyes on ye, Mr. Channing, but I'm likin' ye less an' less with each passin' minute. Even so, I don't figure I have a battle with ye—jist yet, at least. But ye're pushin' me t' my limit."

Channing threw his head back in laughter.

"I thought you hillbillies had no limits," he said, then laughed again, amused at his own clever wit.

"If ye know anythin' concernin' the whereabouts o' Dorey or Miss Joanna, ye better tell me or it'll go the worse fer ye," said Alec.

"So that's it!" exclaimed Channing in mock delight. "It's jealousy for the pretty young hussy that makes you—"

At last the dam of Alec's patience gave way.

With an explosive burst, all the fury of his Viking blood surged within him. He took the distance between them in two strides and with his powerful hand grabbed the adversary by his immaculate white shirt and lifted his feet off the ground.

Undaunted, but struggling to control his trepidation, Channing growled, "You scum! You will pay for this foolish attack!"

He thrust his hands into Alec's face, freed himself momentarily, and sent a well-planted fist smashing directly into Alec's nose.

Stunned, Alec reached up to feel the blood starting to flow. A second punishing blow fell on his right ear. Heartened by his apparent success, Channing charged with redoubled effort. Alec retreated, trembling at his outburst but still finding strength within to form a silent prayer for restraint.

" 'Tis Sercombe I'm wantin'," he said in forced tones.

"Stand and fight, you coward!" yelled Channing.

"I tell ye, my fight's not wi' ye, much as I would relish givin' ye the thrashin' ye deserve," fumed Alec.

"You yellowbelly," taunted Channing, "it's I who am thrashing you!" Channing delivered another blow to Alec's midsection.

Alec clenched his fists trying to control the passions within him. "I'll not be fightin' ye, Mr. Channing—ye're not worth it."

"You coward!" raged Channing and he prepared to strike again.

But at that moment, the door swung open and Palmer Sercombe entered. Alec whirled about and faced him squarely.

"What is the meaning of all this!" Sercombe exclaimed.

"Mr. Sercombe," said Alec, trying his best to calm the hot rush of his anger, "I want no more o' fightin' today. I dinna want t' do anythin' we'll both regret. But what have ye done wi' Dorey? An' where's Joanna Matheson?"

"None of this is any of your concern, MacNeil."

"I've made it my concern. Now where are they?" said Alec advancing, "Or I'll measure yer length on the floor there!"

"Mr. Duncan is in my charge. I hardly need to inform you of the arrangement set up legally by the laird himself before he died. And I shall therefore do with him what I deem in his best interests. And any attempts on your part—"

"Yer legal arrangements mean nothin' t' me! Ye're a scoundrel, Sercombe, an' I'll see ye hanged if—"

"Tut, tut, my friend," said the lawyer coolly. "Don't threaten me. I have the law on my side. You interfere with the proceedings of justice in this matter and I'll bring in the constable to have you arrested. Then we'll see who hangs!"

"I tell ye, ye bloody charlatan, if ye hurt either o' the two o' them, ye'll hae t' answer t' me an' these bare hands o' mine! After that they can hang me if they will. But ye'll not be watchin' me swing, for my body'll be followin' yers t' the churchyard!"

Sercombe laughed a low, cutting laugh. "Don't worry, my friend," he said, "old Dorey is fine. I wouldn't harm a hair on his old gray head. I've simply withdrawn him from the house, for his own protection, to keep him away from hotheads like you."

"And Miss Matheson?" said Alec, retreating a step.

"As for your pretty American filly, I haven't laid eyes on her. For all I know she's taken up residence in the house on the hill she seems so bent on calling her own. Why don't you look for her there? But it will be her only chance to see the place. Before long, it will belong to Mr. Channing, and this foolish little charade she insists on playing will all be over!''

Realizing Sercombe would tell him nothing more, Alec took one final look of disdain at the lawyer then strode from the office, mounted his horse, and galloped up the street, directing the gelding east and up the hill.

Sercombe walked to his companion, who was rubbing a bruised and swollen fist.

"I've just had a most enlightening discussion with our friend Theodore Duncan," he said. "He revealed some rather interesting prospects. We have to get up to that house and conduct a more thorough search than I was able to this morning with people about. Seems this Matheson girl may be more of a threat than we'd thought."

Joanna flew up the back staircase two steps at a time.

At the top, she stopped, crumpled to the floor and tried to still her heaving chest and pounding heart. She listened once more.

The footsteps drew closer.

Was it her imagination, or did she hear someone calling her name? The distant voice sounded alien to her terror-stricken senses. But there it came again—it was her name, muffled by the walls and corridors and rooms and ceilings of the great house.

"Joanna . . . Joanna. . . !"

She stood and crept silently down the stairs, straining to hear better.

"Joanna . . . Joanna! Where are ye, lass!"

"Alec!" she cried, hardly able to contain her relief. "Alec, I'm here!"

Joanna ran down the stairs again to the second floor, turned and raced through the maze of corridors, finally reaching Alec just as he reached the landing of the main staircase on the second floor.

"Alec," she said breathlessly, running into his arms, "it *is* you. I was so afraid . . . I thought—"

" 'Tis all right," he soothed. "I'm jist relieved ye're all right."

"Is Dorey . . . with you?" she asked.

He shook his head. "No, I haven't found him yet. But Sercombe says he's fine and I think he's tellin' the truth. But what do ye mean goin' off alone like that?" He continued without waiting for an answer, "Poor Letty is nearly beside herself . . . not t' mention the rest o' us."

"I'm sorry," Joanna replied. "It was something I had to do and I saw no reason to involve anyone else. But, Alec," she continued excitedly, "I think I've found the nursery!"

"Ye have! Weel, where is it?" he said beginning to forget his own anxiety as he was swept up in her excitement.

"Here . . . in the house. Upstairs. It's a baby's room. And I think I've found it!"

"Let's have a look."

She ran back up the stairs with Alec at her heels. After a confused moment or two they reached their destination. "I'm not positive this is it," she said. "And it's walled off, so I haven't actually been inside. But it has to be."

Alec gave her a puzzled look.

"Come on," said Joanna, taking his hand. "I'll show you!"

She led back down the corridor and to the alcove next to Atlanta's room.

"You see this wall. Fix its position in your mind. Now come next door."

Joanna half ran to the adjoining room. "Look, no window. If this was the back of the same wall we just left, we would see the remainder of the window coming out from this side."

"Very unusual," Alec admitted.

He paced off the distance between the two doors, did some additional measuring in each of the rooms, and finally announced, "There's twelve feet unaccounted for . . . must be that much space between these two walls unseen and hidden, with no door—"

"The nursery!" exclaimed Joanna. "I just know it, Alec!" Her eyes shone with excitement.

"But why would it be blocked off?"

"Who knows? Maybe Atlanta kept it up for a while in hopes her grandchildren would occupy it. Maybe after Margaret left she wanted to preserve it as a reminder of happier times. Maybe she purposely wanted to seal some secret there. Perhaps her husband sealed it up out of spite. But I know that whatever my grandmother was telling me has something to do with that room. We *have* to get inside!"

"It's walled up. What would ye hae me do, knock down the wall? Hoots!"

"Why not, Alec? Why not!" she implored.

"But . . . but, Joanna. It's a *wall*. If anyone was t' find us here—"

"I have to get in there. Don't you see? And besides . . . it may be my house, after all."

A hint of a smile lit her eyes as she spoke.

"Weel, Dorey would certainly raise no objection," said Alec, a grin gradually creeping over his face. "I'll run down an' get some implements from the tool shed—My Leddy!"

"Please, Alec," said Joanna with a laugh. "I can take that from Mr. Innes, but not from you. And I'm not 'the leddy o' the house' jist yet, ye know!"

Alec laughed, delighted at her attempt at her mother-tongue, and raced off.

Joanna seated herself on the velvet chair in the alcove. Her thoughts drifted back to her grandmother's final days and hours. Was she at last poised on the threshold of fulfilling the woman's final wish? What would they discover behind that fateful wall?

It hardly seemed two minutes before she heard Alec's footsteps clumping back up the stairs, accompanied by the clanging of two picks and a heavy, iron crowbar. Joanna moved the chair to the opposite side of the room. Together they lifted the setee and carried it away.

At last, Alec lifted the pick, stood before the wall a bit hesitantly, looked at Joanna with a final questioning gaze as if to ask, "Are ye sure?"

Understanding his doubt, she simply nodded.

Raising the pick high in the air above his shoulder, and warning Joanna to stand well back, Alec swung down the handle with all his might. The pick's tip crashed into the wall with a resounding thud, but penetrated much deeper than Alec had anticipated.

" 'Tis not stone an' mortar at all!" he shouted. " 'Tis only some framin' boards an' a couple coats o' thin plaster. They must not o' intended it t' be a permanent change. I'll be through this in no time!"

Alec struck the wall three more times with powerful swinging blows, then paused. Already he had enlarged the hole to about a foot in diameter.

"Can you see anything?" asked Joanna, coming forward.

"Not yet. The dust o' the crumblin' plaster'll have t' settle before we can see inside."

"Pound out some more," insisted Joanna. "I want to go inside."

"Then turn yer back. I want no chips flyin' off an' strikin' ye in the face," said Alec, and once more raised the instrument high overhead.

This time he did not stop until he had demolished a two-foot-wide by four-foot-long hole through to the other side. He set down the pick and chipped away the rough edges by hand.

"That's enough . . . that's enough!" cried Joanna. "Let's go through!"

Joanna bent low and poked the upper portion of her body into the hidden area between the two rooms. That they had indeed discovered a walled-up nursery there could no longer be any doubt. But it was nearly black inside, the only light coming from the hole they had made, and that, with their bodies before it and in it, provided too little to see a great deal.

"We'll need a candle," she called back to Alec. "They've walled up the window on this side too."

"I'll run an' fetch one," said Alec. "I jist happen t' know where Mrs. Bonner keeps a few."

He disappeared but was back before Joanna had the chance to miss him. Carefully he lit the wick, handed it through the hole to Joanna, then crouched down to follow her through it.

At last they stood in the small darkened chamber. An eerie silence fell upon them as they looked about in the semidarkness. Several child-sized chests and dressers lined the walls, a sideboard with two faded stuffed toys lying on top of it. There was a single bed at the far end, opposite what would have been the window. It had clearly been used by a young child—probably a girl, judging from the decorative frills on the lace canopy above it. A certain mournful nostalgia seemed to pervade the place, covered with the undisturbed cobwebs of decades of disuse. A thin layer of dust lay over every inch of the room, like a freshly fallen sheet of fine November snow.

Neither Joanna nor Alec spoke a word.

As they reverently made their way around the neglected nursery, the shadows from the flickering candle in Joanna's hand cast up ghostly phantasms of the past. A number of pictures adorned the walls: an exquisite copy of Raphael's *Sistine Madonna*, a large framed linen tapestry displaying a family crest and genealogical record, a copy of Gainsborough's *Blue Boy* with *Pinky* beside it and a number of other prints and stitcheries. Joanna was immediately drawn to an oil original portrait, still displaying vivid colors, of a mother and daughter. It hung above the head of the bed and she immediately knew it must be a painting of Atlanta and Margaret when the latter was about nine.

Joanna held the candle up close to the painting, studying the two faces, with a growing sense of fulfilled belonging stealing over her quiet spirit. With moist eyes, she turned to Alec.

"This could be a painting of me. It's remarkably similar to what I looked like as a young girl."

They walked throughout the room a second time, taking time to absorb what was contained in it. The most striking feature remained merely the atmosphere of hushed antiquity, an unearthed Egyptian tomb which had been preserved as lifelike as possible.

"There's something here, Alec, something we're meant to find. I know it . . . I can *feel* it."

"Do ye hae any idea what we're lookin' fer?"

"No. But it's almost like I can feel my grandmother reaching out to me and saying, as she did before I went away, 'It's there, Joanna . . . it's there. You have to find it!' "

"If only we had some idea—"

"We'll find it. I know we will." There was a certainty in her voice that came from something more than wishful thinking.

Silence fell again, but another ten minutes of exploration yielded nothing. At last Joanna sat down on the floor next to the doorway they had broken through the wall.

From this vantagepoint, Joanna's eye fell on *Blue Boy*. It had always been one of her favorites. Her eyes moved to the right to take in the huge, brightly flowered tapestry. Something about it suddenly struck

Joanna; she had overlooked its familiarity the whole time they had been in the room. She could never have seen it before. Yet she was sure, impossible as it seemed, that she was not laying eyes on it for the first time.

She stared directly at it for several long moments. Around the outside edges were ornately woven leaves and flowers, of a multitude of hues and colors. The top third exhibited the family crest with the single word Ramsey beneath it in the most intricate Old English script imaginable. Underneath was a line-drawn family tree.

Then Joanna snapped to attention.

She jumped from the floor and hastened to the tapestry, held the candle aloft and close, and squinted to read the tiny names woven with thin black thread into the fine linen fabric.

"That's it! Of course. Alec, this must be it! This is the *original* of the family tree. Margaret must have copied this in making the smaller one. This *had* to have been Margaret's room!"

"But what's the secret?" asked Alec.

"I still don't know!" said Joanna excitedly. "Wait a minute . . ." She reached into her coat pocket. There lay Margaret's embroidery where Joanna had placed it before leaving the Cuttahays.

She handed the candle to Alec, then held up the sampler.

"It's just the same," she breathed.

"Could that hae anything t' do wi' yer grandmother's secret?"

"I don't know. Let's take the big one down and take it out into the light. If it has something to tell us, we'll be more likely to see it there."

Back in the alcove, they scrutinized the tapestry for a moment.

Then Joanna saw it. Something was wedged in front between the tapestry and its frame. She tried to pry it out with her fingernail, but succeeded only in breaking the nail. Alec was more successful with his pocket knife. It was an old, rusty key.

Slowly Alec shook his head. "If that's yer grandmother's secret, lass . . . in a place like this it might take forever t' find where it fits."

"There's got to be something else!" Joanna said. She looked behind the tapestry which Alec had braced against the setee. Its back was covered with thick, old paper. Smoothing her hand over it, the paper gave slightly under the pressure of her touch. She stood in silence for a moment as if resolving a dilemma in her mind. Satisfied at length with her decision, she set to work.

She ran her fingers along the edges of the paper where it was attached to the frame. Suddenly she stopped where the paper seemed more loosely adhered than in other places.

Doubtful, she looked at Alec.

"Go on, lass," he encouraged. "It can easily be fixed. 'Tis too late t' stop noo."

Joanna began to pry away the paper, with the feeling that she was desecrating something precious. But she reminded herself of her grandmother's words. Only half of the paper was lifted away from the frame when the envelope fell out onto the floor. With trembling fingers, Joanna picked it up and opened it. An aging parchment document was inside.

Together, she and Alec hastily read the document. After a moment Joanna looked up to Alec. Their eyes met, but no words were necessary. The document said it all.

"We have to get this to Ogilvie," was all Joanna could say. "This changes everything!"

"If Sercombe knew about this—" Alec began, then stopped abruptly.

"What is it?" asked Joanna.

"I heard something."

They listened. Now Joanna heard it too—the unmistakable sounds of horses riding across the cobblestones. There were at least two, perhaps more.

"That's not Dorey," Alec said, "not ridin' so fast."

"Sercombe?" asked Joanna in alarm.

Alec nodded. "He's searched this house once. An' now wi' Dorey an' Mrs. Bonner gone, he intends t' try it again."

"He couldn't possibly know about this?"

"I dinna ken what the rascal knows. But he's a clever one, an' covers all the angles. I wouldn't trust the likes o' him as far as I could throw him. We've got t' get oot o' here."

"But my horse is in front. They've already seen it! How can we possibly get away?"

"Mine's oot back," replied Alec. "I think I can find the back way oot. Come on!"

Joanna slipped the key and the document into her pocket, then they sped from the room, carefully closing all the outer doors to conceal their activity, and stole down the corridor to the back stairway.

The sounds of horses had stopped; below and behind them they could hear the footsteps climbing the main staircase. Down the backstairs Alec and Joanna crept, as quickly as they dared. Reaching the ground floor, Alec grabbed Joanna's hand, led her through several narrow corridors, turning first to the right and then to the left in regions of the house she had never seen, and at last to a small service door which opened behind the house near the stables.

"Come," said Alec still leading, "my horse is in there."

In a minute he was in the saddle, swung Joanna up behind him, and then prodded the horse carefully forward. As they rounded the back of the great house, Alec said, "Now hang on, I don't want t' lose ye!"

He grasped the reins tightly and dug in his heels. The horse reared slightly, then exploded around the front of the house and out the gate, with Joanna behind, clinging tightly to Alec.

"Mr. Sercombe . . . Mr. Sercombe!" shouted an alarmed Tom Forbes as they shot past his lookout post at the front door, "they're here! They're gettin' away!"

He rushed through the door, still shouting.

Scarcely slackening his speed, Alec turned his horse from the main road, down the path through the ravine, up the other side, and then away across the open pastures like the wind, toward the Cuttahays' cottage. There he hastily saddled two fresh mounts for himself and Joanna, and told Walter Innes to stay until they should return. They remounted and were off once more with Alec shouting over his shoulder, "We'll be back as soon's we can . . . an' Walter, ye'd better make sure ye hae a gun."

Two hours later, Alec and Joanna sat across from Gordon Ogilvie in the sitting room of his home after their hot and tiring ride.

"Are you sure you want to be riding back this late?" the lawyer asked as he replaced his cup in its saucer and dabbed the corners of his mouth with a napkin.

" 'Tis best we stay where we can keep an eye on Sercombe," Alec replied.

"Ah, yes," said Ogilvie with a glint of knowing in his eyes. "He'll bear some extra watching now."

"I'm afraid for Nathaniel and Letty," added Joanna. "We have to get back as soon as possible."

"I can hardly believe what you've found," Ogilvie went on, "though I'm sitting here staring at it with my own eyes. Who would have thought —why, I've scarcely ever heard of—well, if it doesn't stop Sercombe, it should certainly slow him up a mite."

"Let's hope so," said Joanna, "but are you certain we're not too late?"

"Almost a hundred years too late, judging from this document," Ogilvie reflected. "But I shouldn't think that makes it any less binding. I'll have to send off a wire or two, confirm legal precedents and all that sort of thing, maybe even a trip to the county seat if I can't do it by wire."

"Is there time?" asked Alec anxiously.

"I don't know. It would be best if I could go to Aberdeen, but there certainly isn't time for that. I should be able to have confirmation in time for the meeting—two days from now. Didn't you say that's when the signing is to take place?"

Joanna nodded. "But don't you think," she said, "that what you've discovered about Channing's plans would be enough to stop the proceedings?"

"No doubt that would make the townspeople turn on Sercombe. But their displeasure, no matter how scathing, won't have any legal effect on the sale, short of causing a riot."

He leaned back and took a sip of tea. His fingers unconsciously sought his spectacles and adjusted them on his nose, as if the ritual would somehow uncover something he hadn't yet seen.

"I opposed Sercombe once," he said, turning his gaze out the window for a moment's brief retrospection. "It involved a questionable boundary between the Duncan property and one of my clients—a minor dispute, really. But I think he's been resentful of me ever since."

"Why . . . what happened?"

"The court sided with me. He directed some very caustic remarks toward me afterwards."

He leaned forward, fiddled once more with his spectacles, and returned his attention to the paper on the table before him.

"No," he went on with a weary sigh, a rare momentary glimpse into the lawyer's age, "there has to be a legal way to block him. Otherwise, believe me, he'll make mincemeat of us all."

"And is this legally binding?" asked Joanna.

"Your birth certificate and other proper documentation would be best, of course. But by the time we had those the sale would be over and we could do nothing. This is the only chance we have. You can only be thankful you found it first."

"We best be goin'," said Alec, rising.

"I'll do what I can," stated Ogilvie, who did not sound as though he looked forward to the work but whose latent spirit of competition was slowly being roused against his former adversary.

"Thank you, Mr. Ogilvie," said Joanna.

"We'd best meet at the Cuttahay farm the mornin' o' the meetin'," said Alec.

"Very well," returned Ogilvie, showing them to the door. "I shall be there bright and early two mornings hence."

As his two visitors mounted their horses and rode off, Gordon Ogilvie shook his head and tapped his fingers thoughtfully against his tightened lips which already seemed to be ruminating on the possibilities. "My, my, my . . ." he breathed.

The excitement of the day had brought with it a certain exhilaration which sustained Alec and Joanna's stamina during the hasty ride to Culden. But conversing with Gordon Ogilvie had slowed the flow of blood in their veins and by now their reserve of energy had been nearly spent.

It was evening when they rode out of Culden, the shadows had begun to lengthen, and the gloaming bathed the landscape in its pink and orange shades. To their left the Dormin already lay thickly shadowed. As they rode past Joanna resolved that once all this was settled she would explore the forest under more pleasant circumstances.

They crossed the narrow wooden bridge over the Lindow and now their eyes were drawn to the Marbrae's summit to their right. They rode some distance on when Alec reined in his horse and stopped.

"Let's ride up the Marbrae," he said, turning to face Joanna. "The view at this time o' the day is one ye hae t' see!"

"I'm so tired," replied Joanna.

"It'll take but a few minutes each way," insisted Alec.

Nodding her consent, Joanna followed as Alec turned off the road and led them up the path they had walked together once before. Up the steep terrain and over the rocky ground their sure-footed horses took them until at last they stood on the peak. Dismounting, they tied their horses to a scraggly bush and walked slowly about, gazing downward in all directions.

Everything appeared so different in the evening light. The harbor and town lay beneath the fog which was inching its way inland. The farms of the valley were silent from this distance. The Dormin was by now but a dim blob below them and far off in the east the sun's last reflections of the day bounced irregularly off the geometric walls and windows of Stonewycke.

"What will ye do," asked Alec softly, at last breaking the silence, "if things don't work out?"

"What do you mean, at the meeting?"

"Aye, if Sercombe should win after all?"

"I don't know. I've tried not to think about it."

"I know ye hae said ye no longer hae a home in America. But that's still yer home."

"Not anymore, Alec."

"But if this town, this valley, should go t' Channing . . . what would there be fer ye here then? Unless ye . . ."

He floundered over the words but somehow they weren't coming out the way he had intended.

Joanna looked at Alec for a long moment. Then she turned toward the setting sun. She hadn't wanted to face these decisions. What if she had no home here after all?

"There's my grandfather," she said at last.

Why couldn't she say what was really on her heart?

"Aye, Dorey'll be needin' ye, an' that's a fact," Alec replied. He felt ready to burst with the swelling emotions within him. *Speak what ye feel, man!* he shouted inwardly.

But there remained one uncertainty still gnawing at him. He *had* to know.

"An' Mr. Channing might be seein' fit t' stay," he blurted out. He regretted the words almost before they were said.

"Mr. Channing!"

Joanna spun around, her face a distorted picture of mingled surprise and anger.

"He's a gentleman o' some means," Alec stammered. "Many women'd be glad t'—"

"Alec MacNeil! how dare you!" interrupted Joanna. Her anger now flashed unvented. "That you would even think I'd have anything to do with that—that . . ."

She exhaled a sharp breath.

"I don't even want to talk about it!"

She swept past him down the hill toward the horses. Hastily untying hers, she swung up into the saddle and trotted off down the path.

Alec stood stock-still for several moments, forelorn and bewildered. He could not have felt more the bumbling fool. This wasn't at all why he had suggested the little side-excursion to Marbrae. Why did he bring it up?

Now he wondered if he would ever have another chance.

Slowly he walked toward his horse, climbed into the saddle, and followed her down the mountain and toward Port Strathy.

38 / Decisions

Joanna rode into the Cuttahay farm still ahead of Alec but considerably cooled down from her outburst on Marbrae. She walked toward the house, and a look of surprise stirred her tired features when she was greeted by Olive Sinclair who sat inside with Letty and Nathaniel.

In answer to her questioning gaze, Olive was the first to speak.

"Oh, lass," she said, "I'm afraid it's not good news I'm bringing."

"Something's happened to Dorey!" said Joanna in alarm.

"No. He's still missing, to be sure. But no harm's come to him that anyone knows of."

Just then Alec walked through the door but said nothing.

"Olive rode oot," said Nathaniel, "t' tell us Sercombe's moved up the meetin' by a day—tomorrow at noon!"

"Oh no!" exclaimed Alec. " 'Tis not enough time! We only jist left Ogilvie tellin' him not t' come till the day after."

"We should have expected the scoun'rel t' do somethin' underhanded," said Nathaniel.

" 'Tis a miracle we heard about it at all," said Olive. "He tried to keep it from us, and that's for sure. You know I'm usually the first to hear of any bit of gossip that happens in the town. But this morning 'twas nary a soul entered my store. Then after lunch, Rose Creary comes in. She looked around for a while and picked up a few things. Then she comes up to the counter—she was real tight-lipped she was, all this time. But then just as she was about to leave, she blurts oot, 'Miss Sinclair, ye have as much right to know as anyone!' "

" 'Know what?' I asked.

" 'Aboot the meetin'. It's been changed t' tomorrow an' Mr. Sercombe said that if that girl from America was t' come she would try t' spoil everythin' fer the toon.'

" 'But why shouldn't I be told?' I asked—and a perfectly logical question it was, if you ask me.

" 'He said that if ye or the Cuttahays or the vet knew they would tell her—an' then she would make trouble fer all o' us. He was spreadin' the word aroun' the toon fer everyone t' come but t' keep quiet aboot it t' ye all. Weel, I dinna ken the girl mysel'. Though I did see her once or twice an' she seemed nice enough.'

" 'And why did you decide to go ahead and tell me, Rose?' I asked.

" ' 'Tis jist that, weel, if the lass has somethin' t' say it seems we ought t' have a chance t' hear it—that's what I'm thinkin'.' So some of our thanks should go to Rose," Olive concluded with a long sigh.

"Weel, there's one positive side t' yer account," said Alec. The others cast questioning glances his way. "The Crearys dinna appear t' hae gone completely over t' Sercombe's way o' thinkin' in this—an' that makes me think there jist might be others who'll listen t' Joanna."

" 'Tis true, lad," said Nathaniel. "But ye'll be forgettin'—'tis evidence that's wanted jist noo, not talk."

"And Mr. Ogilvie has it," said Joanna dejectedly. "And he's not coming back for two days."

"I'll have t' ride back an' fetch him," said Alec.

"Lad, ye must be exhausted," Nathaniel said.

"There's no choice," replied Alec. "I can rest a wee here first, an' then be off. Ogilvie an' that paper hae t' be at the meeting or else all is lost, whether he has time t' send his wires or not. But we'll do what we can no matter how many judges or lawyers we hae t' wake up between now an' then."

"I'll fix ye some bread an' broth," said Letty rising. "An' then make a bed fer ye."

"Maybe ye can get the motor car from Innes," suggested Nathaniel.

"O'er these roads, I'm afraid it wouldn't be as fast as usin' my horse an' takin' a short-cut or two," Alec replied. "If the meetin's at noon, I should be able t' get back in time. The rest o' ye go an' don't wait fer me if I'm not back. Stall Sercombe however ye can."

"But what aboot poor Dorey?" asked Letty.

"He's the only person who can verify who I am," said Joanna.

"I'll go fetch Walter with mornin's first light an' he an' I will go an' find him," said Nathaniel. "Somebody must o' seen him."

"In the meantime," said Letty, "ye must get some warm food in yer stomach, Alec, an' then lay yersel' down fer a rest, poor lad."

Alec laughed. "Ye forget, Letty, that young men like me are built rugged, like oor Scottish coast!"

"Na, maybe so. But I'd still have ye rested an' wi' food in ye before startin' oot."

"I concede t' yer motherin' instincts, Letty," replied Alec with another laugh. "I'll jist see t' my horse an' then ye can hae yer way with me."

Alec turned and left the house. Olive rose to help Letty with the bed and supper. Nathaniel poked at the fire and threw in another log. Trying to slip out unnoticed, Joanna followed Alec outside. He had removed the saddle and now stood by his horse rubbing him down and talking softly in his ear.

He heard the soft footfall of Joanna's approaching step but did not turn around.

"Alec," she said, "you will be back for the meeting, won't you?"

"The way I figure't," he replied with his back turned, "I hae t' be."

An awkward silence followed.

"Alec . . . I'm sorry."

"No need, mem."

"Yes . . . yes, there is. I shouldn't have snapped at you. Forgive me . . . please."

Alec turned and faced her. "Ye should know ye was already forgiven, even before ye asked," he said, hesitated a moment, then added, "It's jist sometimes hard fer a man like me not t' be a bit envious o' a man like that Channing o' yers, who—"

"Alec," Joanna interrupted, "believe me, you have nothing to be envious about—especially of him."

Alec did not reply but continued stroking his horse's back.

"Do you think there's time for Ogilvie to do anything?" Joanna asked, returning the conversation to the predicament at hand.

"We'll jist hae t' do oor best."

"Alec . . ." said Joanna, then hesitated and looked away.

"What is it?"

"I just don't know if, well . . . I don't think I could face the meeting and everything that might happen if—"

"If what?"

"—if you weren't there with me, Alec."

Alec turned toward her and looked into her eyes. "I'll be there," he said. "But . . . Joanna," he went on, and as he said her name his voice revealed a slight quiver, "ye be careful, do ye hear?"

He reached out cautiously and took her hand in his. "If fer some reason I should not make it back, ye watch yersel'."

"I will, Alec."

"I couldn't live wi' mysel' if somethin' was t' happen t' ye while I was away."

"Don't worry. Nothing will happen."

"Those men hae no scruples. They may try t' harm ye."

"You just hurry back as fast as you can. And, Alec . . . you be careful, too."

"I'll ride like the wind."

Near the point where Ramsey Head's rocky bulk shot into the northern Scottish sea sat a cluster of remote sea caves. Most remained under water except during extremely low tides. Two or three, however, managed to remain snug and dry no matter what the watermark. They provided frequent shelter for the many wild goats roaming the grassy heights of the Head when they came down the leeward side of the promontory during the fiercest of the wind's wintry blasts. But today the voice of other occupants kept the goats from drawing too close.

Two men crouched in the dark depths of the cave farthest to the east of Strathy. One reclined against the rock wall with a rifle resting across his knees. He was just bringing a flask of whiskey to his lips with shaky hand.

It was Tom Forbes.

"Consider yersel' lucky, yer lairdship," he said with a slurred voice, then took a swallow from his bottle. "It could hae gone worse fer ye if I hadna stepped in fer ye."

"Thank you, Tom," replied the other man with a tone of genuine gratitude. Dorey Duncan sat opposite his captor, pale and bedraggled, his hands and feet rather sloppily bound with a length of rotting hemp.

"None o' yer 'thank ye, Tom,' nonsense, yer lairdship," Tom shot back. "I know yer kind, as if I weren't even good enough fer ye t' git angry wi'."

Forbes took another long swallow from his flask.

"Weel, the shoe's on the other foot, noo. Ye ain't got nothin'—an' it'll be me as gits called yer lairdship—me who folks'll look up t'. That's why I told them not t' harm ye—I want a Duncan"—he spat the name out with revulsion—"t' see someone else struttin' aroun' their gran' estate!"

"I'm sorry you feel the way you do, and I can understand, Tom. But believe me—"

"Pah!" Tom spit at the ground. "An' ye're jist an innocent bairn, aren't ye?"

"I doubt I'm innocent of anything—though I don't know what your grievance is." Even as the words were out of his mouth Dorey wondered if this wasn't one more sin to lay to his account, a sin of omission, remaining silent far too long. Yes, he had seen Alastair's carelessness toward his tenants. But he had said nothing. What could he have done?

But finally—now that it appeared too late—Dorey was beginning to realize that he loved Stonewycke and Port Strathy and these people. Yet all his life he had never shown compassion to them, to people like Tom Forbes. Even the gardens had been tended for his own pleasure.

"Maybe ye was jist a crazy loon all these years," Forbes broke into Dorey's thoughts with a sneer. "But it doesna matter—it should hae been ye yersel' what hanged."

"What . . . I . . . I don't . . ." Dorey stammered. But he did not know what to say.

Lately things had been growing clearer to him, yet there was still such a fog at times—a terrible fog. It reminded him of—

But before he could lay hold of the half-formed image seeking to shape itself in his mind, Tom Forbes's voice cut through the air again.

"My daddy only did yer dirty work. I was jist a child, but I heard him tell my mither what happened—he was driven t' kill the laird Falkirk. But ye . . . ye . . ." Forbes's voice blabbered to silence, his alcohol-dimmed brain unable to choose between accusations. He lifted his flask once more to his lips. Dorey rubbed his hands across his face. "Oh, God," he moaned. "How could I have let his happen. . . ?"

It had been raining. Such a storm poured down from the heavens that it could cleanse the earth with the sheer force of its power. When Ian had stumbled from the stables at Stonewycke after James's violent outburst, he thought he would never return there again. But somehow he made his way back, vaguely sensing he must have the horse Maukin, for in his muddled thoughts he saw only one solution to his problems— he had to finish what he had begun at the inn earlier that evening. He had to find George Falkirk, the man who stood between him and his love.

Yet even as Ian led the chestnut mare from the stable he felt a reluctance in his step. He wanted desperately to see his Maggie, to feel her closeness, to hear her gentle voice. "Oh, Maggie . . ."

But he was afraid.

There was the fear of what James would do if he tried to come back. But there was something else as well—a nebulous ache in his heart, a fear he could not even name, that Maggie would not—could not— choose him over her father. And Ian Duncan—who had run away from his fears all his young life—could not face this above all fears. And so he crept from the estate, and when he was far enough away, he mounted the mare and galloped into the lash of the storm. All his fears and frustrations galvanized into one awful goal: Falkirk would pay for what he had done!

At Kairn Ian had the dubious fortune of discovering his adversary alone in the stable. Whatever he was up to saddling his golden stallion at that late hour, Ian could not guess. But it made things easier for him.

"Falkirk!" Ian shouted.

And when the handsome, arrogant face of the gentleman turned toward Ian, there might have been something of a smirk on it. For at that moment, Ian—drenched to the skin with pale face and wild eyes— did not appear an enemy to be taken seriously. Still, Falkirk had mis- judged Ian once that day, and had received a thorough thrashing as his reward. He would not be so foolish again.

"You have your nerve!" Falkirk shouted in return. "I've had it with the likes of you. If it's another fight you want, then let's get on with it." And with the words he charged Ian, knocking him to the straw- covered dirt floor of the stable.

The events of the evening had drained much of Ian's strength. He was not nearly the foe he had been in the Bluster 'N Blow earlier. But strength was not so necessary when anger and fear dominated his very soul. For some moments the two men grappled in the dirt until at last Ian thrust Falkirk's powerful form away from him.

Regaining their feet, they stood glowering at one another. Then Falkirk's eye strayed to a nearby table where lay a knife used for cutting leather. He grabbed it quickly and lunged toward Ian.

"I'll be in my rights to kill you!" Falkirk cried. "You're a maniac!"

"No!" Ian rejoined, dodging his thrust. "It is I who would be right—!"

The knife shot toward Ian once more. In vain he tried to grab Fal- kirk's wrist to deflect the blade, but he misjudged and hit the blade instead, slashing his hand across its palm. Blood gushed down Ian's arm and onto the floor.

Ian froze. Likewise shocked into momentary inactivity, Falkirk made no move toward him.

In that brief flicker of suspended time, suddenly Ian realized that one of them was going to kill the other. He had come thinking of killing. But in the blind rage which was driving him, actual killing had been far from real. All at once he knew it could *really* happen. Either he or Falkirk would die. It could end in no other way.

His mind suddenly filled with abhorrence at the thought.

But Ian was never to know whether he would then have turned away. For in the next instant Falkirk sprang to life and lunged at Ian with the bloodied knife. This time Ian caught Falkirk's arm and thrust him force- fully away. Falkirk stumbled backwards, tripped, and fell—crashing his head against the corner of the table where the knife had lain. The young lord's body sprawled out on the hard, packed dirt, a trickle of blood oozing down his temple. Slowly Ian approached, but Falkirk did not move again.

"I've killed him!" The words rasped soundlessly from Ian's lips. He waited only long enough to see that the proud figure still did not move, then he clutched his injured hand to his body and flew, in an agony of self-incriminating despair. The storm swallowed him up, and the first of many fogs settled over his brain. He would not know until almost fifty years later that George Falkirk had stirred once more that night, had risen to argue once more, only to be brought down again and for the last time by the hand of a greedy cohort of the hapless heir of Kairn.

Dorey looked down at his hand and rubbed the scar on his palm as if its old wound still lay gaping open and bleeding. For so many years he had fled from pain—from the pain of remembering. But even now as it finally flooded over him, he realized that his ability to feel the old pain again indicated the beginning of healing.

Suddenly he saw the events of that terrible night as if they had just happened. His hands now trembled as they had then when he fled the scene of the crime he feared he had committed. Yet pain was not all he could now recall, for there were also visions of sweet moments with Maggie; riding the spirited chestnut Maukin and the graceful black mare Raven, discovering the beauty of the land, and no less the beauty of Maggie Duncan herself. There had been pain—yes. But there had been wonderful times also. And perhaps Dorey regretted most that as his mind had obliterated the pain, it had also denied him the treasured memories, the memories that would have been a comfort to his old age. If only . . . if only . . .

"Oh, God . . ."

Ian Duncan had cursed God that day many years ago. Was it possible for Dorey to call upon Him now?

How could he?

For now he saw so plainly what he had done. He had heaped the blame for all that had happened upon God because . . . because he was too much a coward to place the blame where it rightly belonged—on himself. And if that was so, was not God merciful indeed to have protected him all these years from the agony of self-recrimination and from the constant threat of self-destruction which had assailed young Ian Duncan?

"But why, God? Why have you done this for me? Why have you

watched over me all this time until I was ready to see things as they really were?''

Then Joanna's words came into his mind. *If your sins have followed you, perhaps it is because God could not let go of you . . . because He loves you and wants you to find forgiveness.*

You never meant ill, did you, God?

All those years you were reaching out to me, protecting me, caring for me, waiting for me to open my eyes. Oh, how little I deserved it!

Dear God, can you ever forgive me for what I have done . . . for what I have done to you by accusing you for the result of my own sin?

''Oh, God . . . *please forgive me!*''

Yet even as he softly spoke the words, Dorey knew he was forgiven. At last he knew the cleansing balm he had kept at a distance for so long. For the enmity he had nurtured in his heart against God was finally sundered—broken like the chains of his guilt and the fog of his past. At long last he knew not only peace but a purity that comes only from utter emptiness and humility. In accepting God's forgiveness, he had himself forgiven God for imagined wrongs . . . and he had forgiven himself.

He was free!

Yet the present turmoils still surrounded him. Tom Forbes, clutching a half-empty flask of liquor, continued to gape at Dorey accusingly. He was completely unaware of the silent reawakening of Dorey's mind, and the rebirth of his spirit.

''Go ahead, sleep, old man,'' Tom scoffed. ''Git guid an' used t' the hard earth—it might be the only bed ye'll ken from noo on!'' He erupted into a roar of laughter which echoed through the rocky cave.

Dorey wondered how many others in Port Strathy shared Tom's bitter feelings against the Duncan family, supposedly their protectors. It was hardly any wonder that the townspeople were in favor of a sale of the land which would profit them and signal the departure of the Duncan name from the land forever. The change would not be grieved. Indeed, it would be welcomed.

If only Joanna had come sooner, thought Dorey.

If only . . .

What good did it do to bemoan past mistakes and things that might have been? Yet perhaps that would be his greatest heartbreak—knowing that at the bottom of it all, he had been the cause of the rent in the land. He had torn the family apart, had divided the once proud name of Stonewycke, and had driven the one person away who would have cared for the land and its people as a rightful landowner should.

Joanna might have cared the way Maggie did. But now it seemed it would be too late for her also.

''Make yersel' comfortable, crazy auld Dorey,'' said Tom at length.

" 'Tis boun' t' be a long night fer ye. I'm goin' t' get some wood fer the fire an' a crust o' bread fer ye. By noon tomorrow, it'll all be o'er an' ye'll be free again."

Tom rose and staggered out of the cave. Dorey tested the ropes that bound him but was unable to make them yield. Then he settled back into further thoughts of days gone by.

Dorey was free, it was true; a peace he had never known before surged through him. The prayer his own dear Maggie had prayed for him—thinking him already dead—that day so long ago on the American prairie had at last been answered. He had found his peace with God, as had Maggie, through the miracle of forgiveness. And in God's wisdom the miracle had come to him through the grandchild of their brief yet far-reaching love. They were three lives—Maggie, Ian, and Joanna, their granddaughter, the new Lady of Stonewycke—brought together in love, torn apart in pain, and brought together again. Yet all three were sealed together for eternity by the everlasting bonds of God's forgiveness. All that now remained in Dorey's heart as necessary to complete his repentance was his public vindication—to restore some of what he felt he had robbed Maggie of so long ago. Slowly the darkness of evening descended around Dorey, and the only sounds he heard were the lapping of waves on the cave's mouth and the shrill call of sea gulls in the lengthening shadows.

"I was sure he'd be back by now," said Joanna half to herself.

She continued to pace back and forth in the small cottage, glancing out the window every couple of minutes.

Notwithstanding her fatigue from the previous day, she had arisen before seven o'clock and her uneasiness had been growing steadily ever since. Of course Alec would have already been in Culden while she slept. By ten o'clock, she had begun anticipating his return in earnest. Her rational side reminded herself that Ogilvie would have to do in a few mere hours what should take several days; and that for him and Alec to reach Strathy by noon would be no small miracle in itself. But her emotional side started with every sound, and she scanned the road for the cloud of dust which would signal approaching horses.

But no horses came.

Olive had returned to open her store as usual. In town, children were playing and yelling in the street in anticipation of the great holiday. The mood was festive. The sounds of workmen hammering and sawing in the distance blended with the nearby shouts of energetic youngsters and the steadily increasing buzz of conversing townspeople beginning to gather in the shops and on the streets.

This was a long-awaited day!

By eleven o'clock, small clusters of people began making their way to the grassy meadow to the west of the harbor where a makeshift podium was nearing completion. Jason Channing sat comfortably in Palmer Sercombe's office and lifted a glass of cognac toward his friend, toasting their success.

But at the Cuttahay cottage Joanna could concentrate on nothing but the anticipated sound of a rider galloping toward them. Then her heart skipped and she ran to the door. The clop-clop of horse's hooves and the jingling of harness could be heard outside. She threw open the door.

At any other time she would have been delighted to see Olive's friendly countenance. But today, her face fell. Yet the normally austere woman was grinning broadly. She threw aside the reins and nearly bounded from the wagon.

"Joanna!" she exclaimed. "We've made a terrible mistake. This explains everything. Look!" She was waving a piece of paper.

Puzzled, Joanna stepped forward. A hundred ideas reeled through her mind, but none came near to guessing what had caused such excitement in the storekeeper.

"I told you that machine's been a plague," Olive said. "I'd tear it out myself, except for once it brought good news and we didn't even know it!"

"I don't understand."

"We've had telegrams go astray and get delayed in Glasgow before, but none this important. It's certainly not fair what it put you through—"

"Olive! Please, what are you talking about?"

"I'm sorry, lass. I just got so excited I got ahead of myself. Look for yourself. We should have received this telegram *first*!" She handed the paper to Joanna.

Joanna scanned the few lines of the telegram. She looked up at Olive, her brow wrinkled in bewilderment then she reread the wire. Perhaps she had had too many disillusionments lately to accept this message with the outright ecstasy that Olive had. Perhaps she was afraid to believe that such a wonderful thing could have happened. But her newfound faith had already taught her that God could do anything, that miracles do indeed happen. Whatever the case, she knew God was in control and that she need not fear, she need not even fear disappointment. He was there to support her in all things.

So for the third time she read the wire, scrutinizing it with both wisdom and hope:

JOANNA STOP HAVE WONDERFUL NEWS STOP MARGARET HAS WAKENED FROM COMA AND IS ON ROAD TO RECOVERY STOP SHE IS ENCOURAGED YOU HAVE GONE TO SCOTLAND STOP THIS NEWS HAS BEEN BEST HEALER OF ALL SAVE FOR THE GREAT HEALER STOP WILL KEEP YOU INFORMED OF PROGRESS STOP PRAYER IS THE MIGHTIEST MEDICINE STOP DR. BLAKELY.

According to the date on the wire, it had arrived in Scotland the day after Joanna stepped foot in Port Strathy. She looked at the date again and again. It had been sent *before* the one she had thought brought tidings of her grandmother's death. This explained why the other had lacked any personal note or words of comfort. Suddenly it was clear: the previous telegram—sent after this one—had merely been a progress report—her grandmother was well and home in the old house on Claymor Street.

As the news settled over Joanna and she was able to fully accept it for the miracle it was, a smile gradually stole over her face.

Olive gave her a hug; by that time Letty had come out and the three shared the joyous news together as they had also shared the grief.

"It must not have been too long after I left that she came out of the coma," Joanna said. "If only I had waited a few more days."

"Aye, lass, but if ye had waited," Letty remarked, "ye would not hae been here in time t' stop Mr. Sercombe."

Joanna nodded, but a shadow began to creep across her face. "I haven't stopped him yet," she said. "I'm beginning to wonder if I can."

"The Lord has done some mighty things," Olive started. "We can leave it in His hands without fear."

"Yes, I know that now," said Joanna. "But now more than ever, it means so much more. This is my grandmother's land. I can't lose it now when she is so close to finally having it after so long. And then there's Dorey . . ." her voice trailed away in a heavy sigh as she began to feel the heavy responsibility now upon her.

"Dinna worry aboot Dorey," Letty replied, her voice full of faith in her heart. "Nathaniel and Walter are lookin' fer him. He'll be found."

"Oh, he *has* to be," Joanna said. "He must be told that his Maggie is alive!"

At length Olive climbed back into her wagon; she had to finish up a few things at the store before the meeting, but she would meet them there, she said. Letty and Joanna went back into the house to continue the interminable waiting.

The time of the meeting drew nearer and there was still no sign of Alec.

At about eleven-thirty, Nathaniel came riding up on his plow horse. Walter, he explained, was still out looking for Dorey.

Despite her prayers for faith and strength, there still remained a gnawing anxiety within Joanna.

"Come now," said Nathaniel. "Dorey or no Dorey, we've got t' get t' toon fer the meetin'. Who can tell what we might be called on t' do there?"

"What about Alec?" Joanna framed the question reluctantly.

"We canna be waitin' fer him. If he isn't there, we must do what the Lord puts in oor path t' do. If Alec an' Ogilvie are na the means t' stop Sercombe, the Lord'll show us somethin' else. Now come, lass, ready yerself. I'll bring the wagon aroun' and we'll be off."

Thirty minutes later Nathaniel and Letty Cuttahay entered the outskirts of the town which had been home to them all their lives, bringing with them their "adopted" daughter from America. What the future held for this town, none of the three could tell. But they would know in less than an hour.

"Where can Walter be?" said Nathaniel. "As if it's not enough that Alec's not back yet. Walter's one o' the few allies we have."

"Dinna ye be too sure o' that," said Letty with the confidence that sprang from her deep faith. "I'm thinkin' we may find more people side wi' oor Joanna than we think, after they've heard her story."

"Perhaps Walter's not coming back means he's found Dorey," said Joanna hopefully.

"I'm hopin' ye may be right there, lass," Nathaniel replied. "But we'll not hae t' wait long fer an answer. Here comes Innes now!"

The two women looked up to see the factor driving up in Alastair's motor car. The engine sputtered to a stop and Innes climbed out with a look of desperation on his face.

"What news do ye bring, Walter?" asked Nathaniel, clearly distressed when he saw the look on Walter's face.

"None too good, I'm afraid," returned Innes. "I've searched the town high an' low . . . but no Dorey. I asked everyone I dared. No one's seen a thing."

"Weel," said Nathaniel thoughtfully, "the meetin's aboot t' begin, an' we're no good wantin' him."

"I'm goin' back t' try the hoose once more," said Walter, "an' I'll do my best t' be back in twenty or thirty minutes. It's oor last chance."

The automobile coughed and hissed away in the direction from which it had come.

"God go wi' ye, man!" shouted Nathaniel after him.

As Nathaniel led the team toward the meadow, it was obvious that nearly the whole town had already arrived and was waiting in readiness. Random noises of anticipation rippled through the crowd, then fell sharply as the wagon neared. Heads turned, many showing surprise at the sight of Joanna, then gradually they returned to their previous conversations as Nathaniel parked the wagon and secured the horses. They found their way to the rear of the crowd and sat down on the green grass.

Olive approached and took a seat next to Letty.

"Don't mind them," she said to Joanna, gesturing toward the crowd with her arm. "They're just a little surprised to see you, that's all. They'll get used to the idea of your presence in time."

A hastily built wooden dais stood at the head of the open area. It was covered with a huge canopy that flapped a monotonous cadence in the gentle sea breezes. In addition to the men, women, and children seated on the ground, some twenty or thirty men—fisherfolk and farmers and several shopkeepers—clustered about the platform, no doubt discussing the events soon to commence. Two or three out-of-towners in fine suits were also on hand to witness the event.

Joanna, Olive Sinclair, and the Cuttahays were soon swallowed up by the enlarging crowd. Joanna could not help noticing an occasional unfriendly glance her way. A few moments before 12 o'clock, Rose

Creary slipped silently into place next to Miss Sinclair but seemed to avoid Joanna's gaze.

"Rose," said Joanna, facing her squarely, "I hear I owe you a debt of thanks."

"Hoot, mem!" said Rose finally looking her way. "I did nothin' more than what should o' been done."

"It took perhaps more courage than you are aware of," said Joanna, "and I want you to know that I appreciate it."

"I'm honored t' be counted one o' yer people," said Rose. "An' I know Mr. Creary'll stan' by ye, too."

Rose beckoned her husband, who now joined the small group with their children in tow. Doug offered no word, but lifted his cap and smiled a bit of a nervous smile toward Joanna.

Any further conversation was interrupted by a stirring of activity in the front of the crowd. There were scattered shouts and applause as a handsome new automobile drove up and stopped directly in front of the platform. With a flourish Palmer Sercombe stepped out, flashed a broad grin, and waved to the assembly. Following him was Jason Channing and two other men in dark suits carrying briefcases and looking sufficiently important for their task. Joanna could see a distinct look of triumph in Sercombe's otherwise impassive countenance. She sighed, knowing his triumph might indeed be well-founded.

Oh, Alec, she thought, *why aren't you here?*

Climbing the steps of the podium behind the lawyer, Channing maintained a detached look of smug indifference.

"How could I have loved him?" Joanna wondered in disbelief.

Across the crowd his piercing eyes looked for hers. She refused to look away and set her jaw, her eyes hanging on to their grip with determination in silent combat. *I'm not beat yet, Jason Channing*, she thought. Yet even as she did so, her heart pulsed with a fear of the power he represented. She turned away at last, shot a quick glance over her shoulder, but no Alec was yet to be seen.

The vicar, William P. Donaldson, approached the podium, took a deep breath, and spoke with a deep and melodious voice.

"A most cordial afternoon, my good people," he began. "Let us open this auspicious occasion with a word of prayer."

He paused while the crowd spread out below him settled into silence like a bird settling its wings. He was a thickset man with round face, pink cheeks, and squinty eyes. Spectacles would have greatly improved his vision, but they remained safely tucked into his pocket only to show themselves in times of dire emergency.

"Oh, Lord God Almighty, we thank Thee for looking down upon Thy humble servants with pleasure, and we beseech Thee this day to bestow Thy blessings on the proceedings which are to follow. And, Lord God, we thank Thee for the kindness and generosity of the men who are making possible this step forward for Port Strathy and its people. Amen.''

Joanna struggled to keep her eyes closed, trying to focus her mind on the words of the vicar. When she opened them she saw Nathaniel was missing. Her eyes scanned the crowd and finally she spotted him at the edge of the meadow, near a clump of trees. Walter Innes stood with him and they appeared deep in conversation. But her attention was immediately diverted back to the dais when she heard the vicar say, "And now I give you our very own . . . Palmer Sercombe!"

Cheers and applause rose from the crowd.

The lawyer stood, walked to the podium, shook the vicar's hand, and turned toward the assembly as a smile formed on his lips.

"My dear people of Port Strathy," he began. Each word was precisely measured and carefully chosen. "This is indeed a momentous occasion for *our* town, one which will go down in history as the moment when prosperity began to shine her light upon us, and when each one of you here began to walk down her golden path—"

He was interrupted by further cheers.

"I am glad," he went on, "—indeed, I am honored, to have a small part in it. It is with sadness, however, that I recall it has come on the wings of sorrow. But you can be certain our dear Alastair Duncan is even now looking down on these proceedings with his approval . . .''

Joanna glanced about, wishing Nathaniel were beside her telling her what to do. She could discern nothing from looking in his direction, although his countenance seemed serious as he and Innes spoke.

". . . and now without further ado," Sercombe was saying, "I would like to introduce the man who is making all this possible, for you and for our town"—the lawyer waved his hand in his companion's direction—"Mr. Jason Channing! Please, Mr. Channing, would you offer a word to our people?"

"Thank you," said Channing, rising. "I certainly appreciate your kind reception and I look forward to many enchanting times in your fair town, for which I have such great expectations."

The cheers grew louder and louder.

Sercombe held up his hands, beckoning for quiet.

"Now, I see no reason to delay any further. Let us get on with the purpose of this gathering." The lawyer's words were met with the roaring assent of the crowd. "You have all been called here, not only to witness, but thereby to actually participate in a historic signing of legal documents . . .''

Joanna's heart pounded within her chest and she could feel the blood rushing from her extremities. Sercombe's words faded into a blur and she could hardly make out what he was saying. Several officials around the table behind the podium busied themselves in readiness.

She knew the dreaded moment had at last arrived. It was up to her, stranger though she was to most, to stop the proceedings. Terrified, she exhaled a long sigh and looked quickly about her one last time. The eyes of Letty, Olive and Rose were all upon her. She felt a pressure on her arm and reached over to return Olive's squeeze of encouragement.

One last glance at the Creary family sitting so close instantly brought into focus whom all this was for.

It was not for her!

It was for them, and all these people like them, who possessed precious little and were being given empty promises. It was all she needed to strengthen her resolve to the decision point.

Joanna licked her dry lips, tried to swallow, and wished desperately for a glass of water.

41 / Maggie's Legacy Fulfilled

Walter Innes had raced back up the hill to the great house. After another futile search of the grounds, he saddled the only remaining horse and began to scour the countryside, looking into every deserted shed and barn of the outlying parts of the estate. Again he returned to the house, hoping that perhaps Dorey might somehow have escaped and found his way home. But another quick look around told Walter that the house was still deserted.

Dejectedly he walked toward the stables, thinking—trying to remember something, anything which might provide a clue to Dorey's whereabouts.

Suddenly he remembered the day he had seen Tom Forbes rummaging around in there.

"What could've he been about?" mumbled the factor to himself, hurrying to the place where he had accosted Forbes in the middle of what appeared to be a search.

Ten minutes later, Walter Innes was back in the car tearing down the road toward the town meeting with renewed energy. Maybe they didn't know where Dorey was, but at least now they held one further bit of evidence of who was involved.

When he reached the meadow, he did not even wait for the vicar to finish his prayer before walking hastily toward Nathaniel. He fairly dragged the man away from his place in the crowd.

"Nathaniel," he said with urgency in his voice. "Ye was right all along—but 'tis a sorry pass!"

"What did ye find?"

Innes pulled a shiny object from the pocket of his trousers, looked hurriedly about him to make sure no other eyes were near, opened his hand to show Nathaniel, then after an instant closed his fingers over it once more and dropped it back into hiding from whence it had come.

"Do ye think it's Forbes's?" Nathaniel asked.

"He was lookin' in the stables that day fer somethin'. An' besides this, Flame Dance's harness is missin'—the one the laird was usin' the day o' his fall. I remember wonderin' if I should bury it wi' the poor horse, after—weel . . . ye know. But I decided not to, an' then laid it in a chest wi' the laird's other ridin' things. But now—it's gone."

"Not much we can say wi'oot the harness," said Nathaniel. "Would jist be their word again' oor's. An' Forbes would have any number o' reasons why his knife was in the stable."

"But if they—"

"I know. 'Tis a serious thing; they'll be havin' t' face the Lord, at least. But we mustn't make accusations wi'oot proof, ye know."

" 'Tis worse than I imagined them capable o' doing," said Walter in dismay.

"If we're t' do anythin' wi' it, somethin' will turn up oor way."

His words were cut short by a tremor radiating through the crowd. At first Nathaniel could not discern what had caused the people to stir. Then he saw Joanna making her way slowly forward toward the dais.

"By golly!" he exclaimed proudly, "the lass is goin' t' do it!

Joanna walked straight ahead, looking neither to the right nor left. At this moment, she had no desire to see the looks of disapproval and hostility on any of the faces which were now straining in her direction. What she would say she couldn't imagine. But the impulse inside her had compelled her to rise. Alec had said to stall them however possible.

Sercombe's mouth hung open in mid-sentence. Channing leaned forward in his chair, neither annoyed nor angry. He appeared almost eager for the inevitable confrontation.

"What may I ask . . . what is all this about?" asked Sercombe, struggling to maintain his cool composure.

"Mr. Sercombe," said Joanna. Her voice sounded small, and all at once she was aware of the utter silence of the crowd, every eye riveted on her.

"Mr. Sercombe," she repeated, gathering strength, "I . . . I cannot allow these proceedings to continue."

Rediscovering his momentarily lost sense of composure, and sensing the sympathies of the crowd behind him, Sercombe said, "What seems to be the problem, Miss Matheson?" His tone had shifted; now he attempted to patronize her, as if his best strategy was not to take her seriously.

"You know very well what the problem is." Joanna took a breath to still her pounding heart.

She had drawn the battle-line in the dirt now.

"I think maybe it's time the townsfolk here," she continued, "learned the whole story about this sale . . . and about why I'm here."

"They know all there is to know," he replied with a caustic edge to his tone. "Unfortunately, why you're here is a matter for speculation. Although I must say your greedy scheme to dash the only hope this town will ever have to rise above its poverty is—"

"There is nothing I want more for Port Strathy," interrupted Joanna with rising voice, "than prosperity! But the cost is too high, Mr. Sercombe, and when the price is paid there will be no prosperity at all, only heartache. Why don't you tell them of your own greedy scheme to—"

"Miss Matheson! You are out of order! If you do not return to your seat this moment, I'll have no choice but to have you bodily removed."

"Let the leddy talk, Sercombe!" yelled a voice from the back of the crowd. It was Doug Creary.

"Shut up, Creary!" hollered another. "She's none o' yer concern!"

"Please . . . please, my dear people," puffed the vicar, rising. "Peace, please. This can all be settled in an orderly fashion, I'm sure."

"Give her a chance t' have her say," came MacDuff's craggy voice.

"She is only trying to cause trouble for you all," said Sercombe.

"That's right," murmured numerous voices throughout the assembly. "We know how this sale will help the town! She's jist tryin' t' spoil it all!"

"Sit down, ye foreigner!"

"Go back where ye came from. We don't need the likes o' ye here!"

Losing her composure amid the shouts and catcalls, Joanna felt a rush of blood to her cheeks. She couldn't get flustered now!

"Sit doon, lady! We wants none o' yer troublemakin' here!"

Suddenly a deep, smooth voice rose over the tumult: "I'd like to hear what the lady has to say."

The words had come from behind Joanna. She swung around and saw the speaker to be Channing. His eyes glinted with merry confidence and the slight upturned corners of his mouth were the only hint that he viewed this challenge as a highstakes game. He nodded at her with an imperceptible motion of his cocked head and invited her to play the game.

"Thank you, Mr. Channing," said Joanna, coolly returning his nod. She then turned toward the quieted crowd and began, "I came to this town a stranger. But even before I set foot in Scotland, half my heart was here. For this very town is the home of my ancestors—people like Robert, Anson, Talmud Ramsey and Atlanta Duncan. And my grandmother, Margaret Duncan, told me—"

"Now we know yer game!" yelled a surly voice, as the rest of the crowd began to buzz as it registered its astonishment.

"So ye come to get yer clutches on the inheritance?" shouted one. "Weel, it won't work, lassie. That ploy's been tried too many times."

"Hey, I'm a Duncan too!" shouted another, who had already drunk more than was good for him. His jeers were accompanied by laughter which drowned out any hope Joanna might have had to continue.

Behind her she could feel the black eyes of Jason Channing reveling over her discomposure.

"I never even knew about the inheritance when I came," Joanna said more loudly, trying in vain to make herself heard. "I don't even care about it—"

"A likely story!" came a shout followed by an uproarious guffaw. "Did ye hear that . . . she never knew a thing about the inheritance? Ha . . . ha . . . ha!"

". . . but if the inheritance is rightfully mine," she continued, "I will lay claim to it in order to prevent these two men from carrying out their intended villany. Mr. Channing, you have been gracious enough to allow me to speak—I should like to return the favor. Perhaps you would like to tell these folk just what your plans for Port Strathy and the surrounding area involve."

The crowd quieted.

Channing stood. If her maneuver caught him the least bit off guard, he did not show it.

"Port Strathy shall remain untouched, unchanged—except for the better, and strengthened with a new harbor and various other improvements I have in mind for the homes and land. I intend to bring Port Strathy forward into the twentieth century. The people shall receive everything they expect, I assure you, and much more."

Once again there were cheers amid the spectators. This was what they had come for.

Joanna blanched. Dare she, in front of all these people, call him a liar to his face? And without proof?

"Miss Matheson," said Sercombe, at length coming to himself after being caught off guard by Channing's move, "unless you have something beyond these groundless statements regarding your own dubious ancestry, I think it best that you leave the proceedings of this assemblage in hands more capable than your own."

He turned toward Joanna as the final words left his lips, but the look on her face startled even him. Joanna had not even heard the lawyer's last little speech, for she was staring with wonder over the heads of the crowd toward the edge of the meadow. At first, those seated near the front only wondered what had suddenly come over this strange girl, but gradually heads began to turn to follow her stare.

Her trance at once broken, Joanna descended the steps from the platform, and began making her way through the crowd toward the object of her gaze.

A lone figure shuffled forward, as if his strength had all been used up long ago. But, though slow and tired, his step was far from feeble as straight on he came.

Joanna reached the old man, threw her arms around him. "Grandfather!" she said, "what have they done to you!" Tears filled her eyes.

At the word a general murmuring began near the front of the crowd, but it was soon stilled by the continuation of events before them.

"I'm fine, my dear," he said, but she could sense he was weak. Dorey continued toward the platform. Every eye was upon him.

A flustered Sercombe tried to regather the momentum but it was of no use. A great curiosity concerning this man who had so long been an anomaly among them kept every eye riveted on him as he advanced toward his goal.

"You must rest, Dorey dear," Joanna said. "I have something to tell you."

"No, Joanna, there is something I must do."

"It can wait. I must talk to you, Dorey. There is news of—"

"It has waited too long already, do you understand . . . too long."

She nodded. It was the only response she could give, for tears were streaming down her cheeks at the mere thought of what she had to tell him.

Nathaniel had risen from his place and approached to assist Dorey.

"Dorey," he said, "it was Tom Forbes that had ye?"

"Yes, poor soul—he had been wronged so terribly. He was all confused."

"Where is he?"

"Out in the caves at Ramsey Head—in a drunken stupor. Nathaniel, have mercy on him. There is hope even for the most wretched of us."

While Dorey mounted the dais, Nathaniel spoke a few words to Innes, who then made a hasty departure from the meadow for the shoreline to the east of town.

The silent townspeople readily observed the change in Dorey. For with all his disheveled appearance from two days in a cave, there was in him a certain grim lucidity. He appeared more than ever the laird he perhaps should have been.

The crowd spread apart before him. The heckling had ceased. For whatever reason—either his look of helplessness or the gentle spirit that seemed to have overtaken him—they were all now willing to listen with respect. Even Sercombe could find no words to swing the tide of events back in his direction.

With Joanna standing beside him, Dorey addressed his fellow villagers:

"I have lived among you these many years known only as Dorey—a name conferred upon me because I could not bear the sound of my true name. Palmer Sercombe and Alastair were among the very few who knew I was a Duncan. I could not face who I was or what I had done, and they showed mercy to me by allowing me the comfort of anonymity.

"But I must now face many things, even if I bear a name that may not be worthy of your respect. Indeed, in my own right I have lived beneath the station that was mine. I have seen how the roots of bitterness have grown deep through the years and no mere apology from me will suffice to heal your wounded hearts. You have been tenants and servants of a house and a family that has, in recent years, not done for you all it could have, or should have. For my own part in this, I am now truly sorrowful. Most of you knew me only as a sick old man residing under the care of the laird. In reality I was more a part of this family than you know. For just before her voyage to America, Alastair's older sister—the true heir to Stonewycke—Margaret Duncan and I were married. And this young woman who stands before you today is the daughter of the child we bore."

A renewed ripple of astonishment passed through the crowd.

"It was my intention to join my beloved Maggie in America, but then—events overtook me, and—" He paused, wiped his sweating brow, then attempted to continue.

But before he could speak, Joanna leaned toward him and whispered something no one else heard into his ear. In his intense joy, he closed his eyes and breathed: "Dear Lord . . . !" He could find no other words. For what could he say? The dream of a lifetime had been fulfilled.

His Maggie was alive! Could he believe his ears?

Yet there still remained the terrible fate of Maggie's dear land to deal with. He had walked out of the cave on Ramsey Head with a purpose, and with Joanna's whispered words it became even more imperative that he somehow continue.

He took a deep breath and with a new timbre of excitement, began again. "Today, however, is a day of new beginnings. Today, I ask you to listen and make a choice. This land is not yours—but in every way, each of you *is* the land. By your sweat and toil and tears the estate and land known as Stonewycke has become the sweet and fertile valley that it is. Can you now stand by and watch this valley we all love so dearly pass on to strangers bent on destroying it for their own gain so that you may have a few farthings today which will be quickly gone tomorrow? Can you allow this to happen when . . ." He paused and looked back to where Joanna sat. The radiance of her face told him it *had* to be true!

". . . *when there is still one alive*," he continued, "whose love for the land, though it has been from afar, is nevertheless more binding in that her devotion goes as deep as blood."

He stopped, looked at Joanna again, smiled, and then went on, gathering strength as he spoke.

"My good people, it is for this very love of the land that this legacy passed down from one generation to another to finally rest on the shoulders of the granddaughter of the true heiress of Stonewycke—Lady Margaret Duncan, who has entrusted it into the hands of this young woman now standing before you. She came here a stranger, but she saw immediately the most precious quality of this place—the folk like the Crearys, and MacDuffs and Cuttahays, and she was not afraid to take a stand against some very dangerous men. Not because she cares for her own gain, but because she sees the richness of the life you now enjoy, a life that is filled with simple peace and beauty. And neither she nor I want to see you lose—"

Dorey coughed and he wavered on his feet. Joanna moved quickly to his side, took his arm, and led him to the chair which had been vacated by the vicar. She had by now lost all interest in the meeting. She was beginning to realize that what was happening here today went beyond land ownership and inheritances. Lives had been miraculously healed, hearts had been made whole. God had been at work and He would not cease until that work was done.

She took Dorey's hand and for the moment it seemed enough to be near the man she had unknowingly come to Scotland to find.

But Palmer Sercombe was not touched by the display of emotion. He walked aloofly to the podium.

"Mr. Duncan," he said, "you have made some rather strong claims— I might even be induced to listen to them. But still . . . I see no evidence or proof. And thus, given that the *legal* right to conclude this business was given me by the late laird, it is now time to move ahead with—"

"Proof, ye say!" came a creaky voice from midway through the crowd. It was old Stevie Mackinaw who had broken his habit of reclusiveness to attend this historic meeting. "I hae ben i' this toon longer den efen Mr. Doorey Dooncan—an' anyone wi' eyes t' see't can see that the leddy up tere is the image o' Mawgret Dooncan."

Sercombe chuckled. "Now we have evidence from a lunatic and a senile old man!" he jeered. "Come now. I think we have heard enough."

With a flourish Sercombe produced a folded sheaf of papers from the breast pocket. "I have here the document which will finalize the transfer of the Duncan estate to Mr. Jason Channing," he said. "As you know, it provides for a cash settlement to every tenant family under the Duncan domain, money which you will all receive within the week."

He turned toward the table behind him, picked up a fountain pen which was prominently located on it, and affixed his signature to the paper.

"And now, Mr. Channing . . . if you will?"

Channing stood, and with only a fleeting look at Joanna where she still sat at Dorey's side, he took the pen and signed his name. Then he drew a check from his own pocket, handed it to Sercombe, and the two men shook hands to the sound of scattered applause and a few cheers from the townspeople.

Interrupting the momentary celebration, however, all heads began to turn toward the road from the south, where a new sound came thundering toward them.

As Joanna's heart sank within her, the galloping sound of an approaching horse arrested her attention.

Its hoofs slashed at the grass as it tore between the last of the trees and into the meadow. The gray gelding's flanks were foaming, but the rider continued to dig his heels unmercifully into its sides. He reined in the horse as it pranced sideways, drew near the gathering, jumped down, threw the reins aside, and hastened toward the platform.

"Alec!" said Joanna, springing up and running toward him.

"What is the meaning of this intrusion, MacNeil?" demanded Sercombe with a sneer.

"I've got information that may alter yer proceedin's a mite, Mr. Sercombe."

"Now I've seen everything," muttered Channing with a laugh. "What with castles in the background, I'm almost reminded of—"

"Ye better keep that mouth o' yers shut, Mr. Channing," snapped Alec in return, "an' think twice before ye open it unwisely again. I'm in no mood fer the likes o' yer comments."

"Another threat, country boy?" replied Channing.

Alec bristled but any would-be response was cut off by Sercombe.

"I'm afraid you're too late, MacNeil," said Sercombe. "This meeting is all but over. The papers are signed and the transactions are complete."

"I think we'll all be stayin' fer jist a wee bit longer," said Alec. "Mr. Gordon Ogilvie will be here in a moment. His horse is a bit slower than mine. But whatever ye may have done already, he has some interestin' things he'll be wantin' t' discuss wi' ye."

"Any discussions can be carried on with the new owner of the land," said Sercombe. Then turning to address the crowd, he said, "Thank you all for coming. This meeting is adjourned. You will be receiving notification of what will be coming to you within ten days."

"All o' ye stay where ye are!" shouted Alec. "An' that goes fer ye too, Mr. Sercombe," he added as an aside. Then he said again to the crowd in a loud, commanding voice, "These proceedin's aren't done wi' yet, an' ye all will be wantin' t' hear what remains t' be said!"

"MacNeil . . . if you don't—" Sercombe began, the wrath clearly visible on his face. But before he could complete the sentence a second horse broke clear into the meadow and Ogilvie rode up. He dismounted in front of the platform, puffing profusely and mopping great beads of sweat from his brow.

"My, my," he wheezed. "I do hope there won't be much more of this."

"What is the meaning of this interruption?" Sercombe snarled, his temper at last rising to the surface.

Ogilvie cleared his throat.

"Pardon the intrusion," he began, "but I had small choice. I daresay you will humor me a moment while I get some papers from my satchel."

"Ogilvie, you always were a buffoon and an idiot. I'll humor no one," said Sercombe. "We have all the legal counsel we need for the present. Now you can just turn around and go back the way you—"

"No need to become abusive, Mr. Sercombe. But with or without your permission . . ."

He paused and took out a single paper from the leather case he had been carrying.

". . . with or without your permission, I'm afraid you will have to heed this. I have here an injunction blocking the sale of the Duncan estate."

Sercombe snatched the paper from his hands, looked hastily at it, and tore it into several pieces.

"It's too late," he said with scorn. "The transaction is consummated."

"Hardly, sir," returned Ogilvie. "The sale was never binding in the first place."

"Bah! That's a lie!"

"It is impossible to sell what was never yours, Mr. Sercombe. You are an attorney. You know the laws of the land. Miss Matheson is the legal heir to the estate since she is the laird's closest living relative. I believe I am correct when I state that the terms of the laird's will specify that your Power of Appointment is to take a subordinate position with respect to the establishment of the proper heir. And certainly you cannot be ignorant of the steps required in such a case. But you never so much as attempted a proper search."

"This . . . this woman has no credentials!" Sercombe spat out the words. "She has given me no reason to believe her story, save for some ancient-looking deed which any charleton could steal or forge."

"That is the purpose of this injunction. I have sent inquiries to America. Miss Matheson's 'credentials' shall arrive forthwith. Until which time there shall be no sale or any transactions regarding the Duncan estate. But from what I have seen I will go on record as saying that

I believe Miss Matheson's claim is well-founded. And the two magistrates with whom I spoke this morning—none too pleased at being aroused so early, I must say—agreed with me that there is at least sufficient evidence to block what you have tried to do today. And now, Mr. Sercombe, I believe you will find this in order."

The crowd, straining to hear every word, reacted to the conversation between the two lawyers with a mingling of whispers, questions, and puzzled glances. They knew Alec, but most had never seen Ogilvie in their lives.

"Does this mean we don't git oor harbor?" yelled one.

"What aboot oor money?" called out another.

"My dear people," began Sercombe, still trying to patch together his scheme with his oily-smooth voice, "I can assure you this is little more than a well-orchestrated hoax. We will fight this woman and her cohorts—in the courts if need be. You will get what you so rightly deserve. I will not allow this greedy little strumpet to swindle you."

Alec stepped forward. "Ye're lucky I'm a man o' great restraint," he said through clenched teeth. "I'll let yer words go fer now, because Mr. Ogilvie has somethin' more t' say. But one more word o' that kind aboot Joanna Matheson, my friend, an' I'll not be responsible fer what'll follow. An' that's no threat; that's a solemn promise!"

"Just a bit of information I procured by wire from Aberdeen," Ogilvie said. "I have a friend on the License and Planning Council who was able to inform me that an American industrialist was recently granted a Writ of Variance which would enable him to build a dam on the River Lindow. By the time of completion in 1917, the entire Strathy valley would be a reservoir for the hydroelectric station of his design."

"Mr. Channing," said Joanna, standing again and breaking her long silence, "would you care to comment on your plans once more to the people?"

"Business is business," he replied icily.

Gradually the townspeople pieced together bits of conversation. Most were by now more than a little confused and a general buzz of anxious questions filled the air.

"The *whole* valley? . . . electricity . . . Mr. Sercombe, did ye know all aboot this? . . . what aboot the harbor?"

One by one they began to recall Dorey's words which reminded them how greatly they did love the land. Their strong Scottish hearts began speaking more loudly than their hopes of newfound prosperity.

As the tumult began to become disruptive, Nathaniel walked up with Tom Forbes firmly in tow. His drunken night in the dank and dirty cave told on his appearance.

"You drunken fool!" said Sercombe under his breath. "Don't say anything!"

But Tom scarcely heard. By now there was a crowd about Nathaniel who was attempting to lead Tom's staggering form up onto the platform where he could be heard.

"Tell them what ye told me, Tom," he said.

"He were dyin' onywa'—I jist helpt speed't along a wee. 'Twas merciful, it wa'." The slurred words tumbled unrestrained past his swollen tongue. "But killin's na fer me. I wouldn't kill 'at girl when he askt—nor ol' Dorey neither. We was all goin' t' get sompthin' oot o' it—'at's what he said. But the laird wa' dyin' . . . he wa' dyin' onywa', so 'twasn't the same. I'm no killer."

"How did ye do it, Tom?" asked Nathaniel.

"Jist took a litt'l slit o' the harness. He'd fa' evenshuly . . . didn't haf t' cut clean thru. But I can't fin' m' knife . . . haf ye seen m' knife, Nathaniel?"

"Who was ye workin' wi', Tom?" asked Nathaniel. "Who made ye cut the old laird's harness so he'd fall?"

"Why . . . Sercommy, who else? Ye know that, Nathaniel."

The crowd gasped and glanced around for the lawyer whose fortunes had shifted so abruptly.

But he was gone.

By the time Tom's drunken admission was completed, Sercombe was behind several trees making for his office as fast as his legs would carry him. No sense hanging around arguing with these fools any longer. Let them have their bloody land; it was worthless anyway. Let them have their wretched, smelly fish and their pale flowers. There were better things in life than this cursed place.

"He's gone!" Nathaniel exclaimed.

"He'll not git far," said Walter Innes. "I'll be after him."

"Don't trouble yourself," said Ogilvie. "Before Alec and I left Culden we instructed the magistrate to take the necessary measures if our suspicions proved correct. I believe someone is already on the way to see our friend, Mr. Sercombe."

As Joanna listened to these proceedings her mind seemed to whirl. Suddenly she felt detached, as if she were watching some nightmarish drama from an audience in a theater. How could any of this be real, arguing and swindling and kidnapping—and even murder? And yet here were these real people acting out this drama . . . and, regardless of how detached and horrified she felt, she was one of them. Then she remembered something she had till now forgotten:

". . . *if only the land had belonged to the people instead of our corrupt family. . .*"

Her grandmother's words, though they had been lost in the confusion of so much else. Now they seemed the most important of all. In Margaret Duncan's time the struggles over this rich land called Stonewycke had caused nothing but strife and pain and, who knew what the strifes in earlier centuries had been? They still had not ceased. And to that legacy of deception and greed could now be added murder. It had to stop. The words re-echoed in Joanna's mind—*It had to stop!*

Perhaps Sercombe was right. Perhaps it was time for a change. Joanna thought of the aging document she had found in Maggie's nursery.

But Channing's voice jarred her thoughts back to discord around her.

"I think it's time for me to take my leave," he said, standing.

Joanna turned and faced him squarely. "Just how much did you know about all this?" she asked.

"If I was involved in any of Sercombe's ruthless schemes, not to mention murder, do you think I would be hanging around? I'm as innocent as a newborn babe."

"I suppose we could never prove anything beyond the fact that you are a heartless opportunist."

"And you can't go to jail for that, baby." He stopped and shot Joanna a broad smile. "But I'm ready to write out another check, sweetheart . . . this time pay to the order of Joanna Matheson. Just say the word and we can share in all this, together!"

Joanna stared with piercing gaze into the black eyes which had once so swept her off her feet.

"Jason Channing, I renounce you to your face. Now, as you said, it is time for you to take your leave. Go, and never return to Port Strathy again!"

Channing's smile became ashen. He turned slowly, almost in disbelief that she had rejected his offer, and slunk away through the crowd.

"Now, Mr. Ogilvie," said Joanna, forming her resolve in words that had only until this moment been in her thoughts, "will you be so kind as to share with the good people of Port Strathy about the other document we discovered?"

"With pleasure, My Lady," returned Ogilvie. Then he turned toward the crowd, many of whom had settled back into their places, and began:

"Let me first congratulate both you, My Lady, and you good people of Port Strathy. I am confident you will find yourselves far more fortunate to have Lady Joanna heir to the Duncan estate than you could imagine. When Lady Joanna came to me with the deed to the land she had in her possession—given to her by her grandmother Margaret Duncan prior to her death—we were at first puzzled by a veiled reference to some other deed which had been drawn up generations ago by the laird at that time, Anson Ramsey. It was only yesterday when the 'Transfer Document' came to light, found in the house by Lady Joanna and Alec MacNeil. They brought it to me and I saw at once that it was a portentous discovery."

He paused to take a breath. Joanna seized the opportunity to finish for him.

"My grandmother, Margaret Duncan, is *not* dead, Mr. Ogilvie," she said. "We just learned the wonderful news today." Then turning to the crowd she went on.

"Thinking she was dying, my grandmother sent me to Port Strathy to make right the injustices that had been done to this land. When I came, I had no idea what I might be called upon to do. For a time I thought the only way to stop the destruction that would take place would be to claim the inheritance. But I realize now that it was not the *property* my grandmother was concerned about—it was *you*! I have seen that from the time she was a girl here. She was intensely concerned with the well-being of the tenants and fisherfolk of Stonewycke.

"She was not unlike her great-great-grandfather, Anson Ramsey. His love for Stonewycke also went far deeper than just mere acreage. He could see what Dorey said to us all just a short time ago—you folk *are* the land. It is you who have built it up, tilled it, worked it. Yet, you were always at the mercy of lairds and ladies who alternately abused or ignored you. Anson couldn't bear the thought of his sons, whose motives he didn't trust, misusing the land and its people. So he had a document drawn up which transferred the ownership of the vast majority of the Stonewycke lands to each of its individual tenants. Each person was to own outright his particular house and plot of land, the Ramsey family retaining the house on the hill with a surrounding area of 1,000 acres."

"Unfortunately," broke in Ogilvie again, "Anson's life was cut tragically short; he never had a chance to implement his desire, and the Transfer Document was lost. Somehow, we assume, it found its way into Atlanta Duncan's hands, and then yesterday, Miss Matheson found it where it had lain hidden all these years."

"I have struggled greatly," Joanna said, "over what should become of Stonewycke. I know now that I should do what should have been done a century ago. And I know that the true Lady of Stonewycke will give her affirmation to this. As soon as all the legalities are settled, the Duncan family will refile Anson's Transfer Document, and the land shall belong to you!"

A great cheer broke from the astounded crowd.

Joanna stood by, tears running unchecked down her cheeks, with a great smile of joy on her face. Slowly Dorey rose, walked to her side and placed his arm about her.

" 'Tis a wonderful thing you've done," he said. "After all these years, at last the strife will be ended. Maggie can come home in peace. How could we ever have known that our love for each other and the land would find its fulfillment through our own granddaughter."

"All I wanted when I came I have found, which is wealth enough. And that is you, my dear grandfather!"

"Ah, you know how to bring joy to an old man's heart!"

"As for the estate," said Joanna as loudly as she could above the commotion, "there can be only two persons who should rightfully have dominion over it and its adjoining lands. That is my grandfather, Mr. Theodore Ian Duncan, and his beloved wife, Margaret Duncan. He will be laird and she will be the Lady of the property—as soon as we can bring her here—for as long as they live."

Another roar went up from the townspeople who by this time had left their places and clustered toward the front to shake Dorey's bony hand and offer their best wishes to she who from that day forward was known simply as Lady Joanna. And as they came, all former hostilities aside, behind the two stood Nathaniel and Letty, Olive and Alec—each of whom beamed with pride at the Lady their lass had become. Off to one side, suddenly shyly reticent because of the great tears which had formed in his eyes, stood old Stevie Mackinaw who had known Maggie longer than anyone in the town. It would be many months before he would again sleep an entire night through in the anticipation of once again laying eyes upon his beloved Lady of Stonewycke.

Foam-tipped waves washed up around Joanna's bare feet.

The morning's sun shone bright against the vivid blue sky, and the cold water splashing freely about her ankles sent little shivers of refreshment up her spine.

In every way it was a perfect day.

Channing had set sail yesterday for London. Sercombe had not been seen since the meeting, but Mr. Ogilvie remained confident that he would be rounded up to face justice before the week's end. Tomorrow, Joanna would leave for America to bring her grandmother back home to Scotland. But for now she basked in a few moments of rest, feeling peaceful and free to enjoy the beauty about her.

Alec walked along the sandy beach at her side. How different this day was from the first time they met here! But he was thinking neither about the sunshine nor the beach nor the events of the past several days. His eyes, and his heart, were focused entirely on the young woman at his side.

"Ye look every bit the fishergirl, lass," he said smiling. "Only there never was one so bonny!"

"That's the nicest compliment I could ask for, Alec."

"Weel, ye are bonny. Any man would be proud—"

"I mean calling me a fishergirl," she said.

"How's that such an honor, My Leddy?"

"Don't you see, Alec! It's the farmers and fishermen and plain folk around here that make the land what it is. I want to be a part of that. When I think of my grandmother's life up on the hill—in the grim old house—all the subterfuge and mistrust and scheming. Give me the simple life under a homely roof with oatcakes and boiled potatoes!"

"But it's what's in their hearts that matters," he said. "Tom Forbes's simple life as a fisherman didn't help him."

"Yes," Joanna replied. "And I think Letty and Nathaniel would always be their humble selves even if they lived in a palace."

Alec stopped a moment. He picked up a stone and tossed it out into the lapping waves. There was something he had to say, and he hadn't realized until now how difficult it would be to say it.

At length he spoke, gazing not at Joanna, but at the sparkling green water.

"I suppose yer own home'll be callin' ye noo?"

"Oh, Alec! I could never go back there to live. This is my home now."

"Will ye go live at the big hoose, wi' yer grandmother an' Dorey?"

"I don't know. I don't want to lose the life Nathaniel and Letty have shown me. They've taught me so much about life's true values."

"Ah, but ye're a gran' leddy now."

"I don't want to leave the simplicity of life I've found here."

"But ye'll be happy wherever ye are. An' ye'll bring yer light even t' the big stone hoose on the hill."

"I think I would be happier in a cottage. Let my grandmother manage the house and the estate. For me . . . I want to live and love and raise my children under a humble Scottish peasant roof."

"Ye will one day be the heiress o' Stonewycke an' its title."

"Do you think that matters to me? That doesn't change who I am. I don't want people—people I love—to feel differently toward me now."

"But ye are a highborn lady."

"Oh, Alec, don't do this to me!"

"It's jist that I know my place, an' I'm feared o'—"

"But you also know me. Your station, or mine, makes no difference to me. I feel the same toward you. Please, Alec, feel the same toward me."

She turned, and added quietly, ". . . that is, if you do have feelings for me."

"Joanna," Alec stammered, "I . . . I couldn't presume t'—"

"Please, presume!" she pleaded.

"Are ye sayin'. . . ?"

"Yes. Haven't you known?"

Alec could not lift his eyes to meet hers. It seemed as if the whole sky was pressing down its silent weight upon him. Her words had raised a storm in his heart. Could she possibly mean what his throbbing soul had heard?

Almost trembling he spoke, although the voice that came was scarcely more than a whisper: "But . . . I'm nothin' but a poor vet . . . nothin' t' offer ye but a simple cottage."

"And love?" Joanna added.

"Ye . . . ye're not sayin' ye would consider marryin' one so far beneath ye?"

"I don't need to consider anything," Joanna replied. "I belong with you, Alec."

"Lass," he breathed with intense quiet, "I love ye."

He could say no more, although the pulsating joy in his heart seemed ready to explode. A quiet, contented joy filled Joanna's heart. For the first time in her life she knew she belonged. In the simple love of this strong man she had at last found her true home.

All at once Alec threw his hat into the sky, leapt into the air with his hands extended high above him, and shouted aloud—a yell of child-like animated delight.

Joanna walked close to his side and slipped her hand tenderly through his arm, laid her head against his shoulder, and silently they continued on down the strip of sand—together and in love on the little Scottish beach on a lovely summer's morning.

Epilogue: The Lady of Stonewycke————

It seemed the heather was especially vibrant this year.

Of course, the scraggly bush with its magenta flame could not have known how special this particular moment of this particular year would be. But it almost seemed to have prolonged its season just to give a returning child of Scotland an extra measure of intense joy and delight.

In nearly fifty years, Maggie Duncan had all but stopped thinking of her homeland. But she could never stop dreaming of it. If it was not the brilliant heather, then her dreams were filled with wild waves crashing against a jagged coastline, or the eerie breeze whistling across the surface of a lonesome and barren moor. True, the dreams had often turned into nightmares from which she would awaken drenched with perspiration. Yet in the end she had determined to put the past behind her and to give her new life the chance it deserved—the chance her daughter deserved also.

But always her homeland tugged at her in the depths of her being.

God had worked wondrously in Maggie's life. She had learned to forgive, and to accept His life within her as the mainstay of her existence. But He did not, nor would He perhaps want to erase the memories of her beloved land.

She did not speak much of it at first. The hurts were too deep. And later—by then it did not seem of much use. But when death had reached out and had nearly closed in upon her, she could not prevent her weakened mind from speaking of what still lay so near to her heart. Had God's hand not been upon her all her life? This accident could have been no mere chance.

Indeed, the eye of the Almighty had never lost sight of her heart's desire and only, as the years passed, was waiting for His perfect timing to fulfill the legacy He had begun in her heart so many years ago.

Today Maggie looked the very picture of that young Scottish lass who had climbed this very hill so many years ago. But this day's rendezvous was even more special. Her gray hair was pulled back into a neat bun, but the autumn breeze blew several errant strands about her face. Her step was slower and more cautious, especially one leg, than it had been in the old days. But the glow on her face was nonetheless evident.

It looks just the same, thought Maggie, *except perhaps that our two patient friends, Raven and Maukin, are missing.*

She smiled. *Imagine me upon that spirited black mare now!* The thought brought a laugh to her lips. She could not contain the merriment which threatened to burst her heart in very gladness; certainly mere age could not keep it back.

Such had not been the case as she had lain on that hospital bed in Denver, however. There was a moment she had nearly given up. God had been good to her. Perhaps too good. But she was tired. Her weary bones told her it was time to rest. She had fought the good fight. She had learned to depend on God, though it had required the most painful of circumstances to bring her to the point of relinquishing her self. But now it was time to go home . . . home to be with her beloved Ian at last.

Yet Maggie's spirit ran too deep to succumb easily to temporal yearnings. Even though the death which reached out for her was near and real, her truest self could not yield to its compelling lure. The God who had guided her through life stretched out His hand to bridge the gap in her personal strength.

She awoke one sunshiny morning, and her soul immediately told her that all this had not been for nothing. Some unknown sense of anticipation gradually stole over her, though she had no idea what to expect.

Then Joanna's telegram had come.

How could she even fathom the words which shouted out to her from the page?

Her Ian—alive! . . . still waiting for her after all these years!

The very thing she had dreamed of for nearly fifty years, the thing even her deep faith could not believe, was true!

How quickly the remaining days of recovery had passed after that. "Miraculous!" had been Dr. Blakely's conclusion. But it was no more a miracle than life itself, than the Creator of life bringing about His marvelous will. Two people of His choosing, brought together in His perfect time: it was worth any wait! By the time Joanna had arrived, Margaret was already back on her feet. Dr. Blakely's colleagues were confounded at her progress, but the doctor himself had learned long ago never to be surprised; he, too, served a higher Master.

When she had at last seen him in Aberdeen, Maggie realized all over again that any period of waiting, no matter how long, will, when it is over, seem but a passing moment in the memory. Suddenly it had not been years at all, but only days since they had parted. The waterfront of the gray city brought back ancient memories, mingled with the unpleasantness and sting of parting. Yet when her eyes first saw his face, all that melted away. She looked beyond the signs of the years—the white hair, the deep crows' feet, the stooped shoulders—and knew he had not changed.

But when he smiled, then she knew he *had* changed. There was a new look in his eyes, a look deeper than mere age could account for. She had not time to ponder upon it, however, for he gently took her in his arms, then bent over and kissed her tenderly on the forehead, a kiss warm and real.

"Ian!" she said, speaking the name to the one she had not once addressed since that day on this very dock when they had parted forty-seven years before. He struggled to speak her name, but could not. She looked up into his face, wet with tears, smiled the smile he had remembered so often in his dreams, and was content.

Maggie's thoughts returned from Aberdeen to the present. There was so much to remember again. Like when Joanna had shown her the key found in the back of the tapestry, she had looked at it dully for a moment. Then suddenly she recalled what she had thus far only revealed in her delirium—"it's in the nursery." She had forgotten having hidden the key that fateful night, and now took Joanna to the overgrown, walled garden, and, after some effort, had managed to fit the key into the rusted lock. But search as they might, the treasure she had dug up that stormy night was never to be found. There were *some* things she could not remember, it seemed. Either she had forgotten where they had buried it, or else Digory had later carried it off to forever free the family of the poison of the greed it was sure to create. Dying a poor man as he had, Maggie was certain the faithful servant had put the treasure someplace where it would never tempt the heart of man again. And after all, the treasure had never meant anything to her; unearthing it had only been a way to thwart Falkirk and her father. Inside, a part of her rejoiced that it was not be be found.

Now the only memory she need concern herself with was the love she and Ian had shared then, and could now share again. This climb up the hill bordering Strathy's fair valley was richer by far than any earthly treasure. But the slope had become steeper and she was a little out of breath. She was aware of her weak leg, but at least there was no pain. The doctor had agreed that the trip to Scotland would be the best thing for her, but had admonished her to "take it easy." She had not been strictly obedient in that, but how could she when the heather was in bloom and when this "muckle land" made her feel so young again!

Soon a figure came into sight at the top of the heather-covered hill. Tall and lean, with head held high, Ian Duncan bore himself with a dignity "auld Dorey" had never had the will or the courage to assume. All life had drastically changed for him that day in the damp cave on

Ramsey Head. At last he had ceased his flight from the One whose love had been pursuing him, and finally bowed in acknowledgment of the God who had never once forsaken him. Maggie's own prayer for him, resounding through the ages and across the miles, found its fulfillment at the hand of the master Potter who had fashioned them both—the One who had created them to love Him first, and who now willed that they spend the rest of their lives loving each other. And in that healing in the cave, Dorey was for the first time able to face himself, and was thus given the courage Ian Duncan had always been meant to have.

As Maggie drew closer to the object of her morning walk, he smiled and held out his hand. It brought to her mind the undefined change she had noticed at the moment of their first reunion in Aberdeen. His smile had lost its haunted, troubled quality. In his youth, though he had been an expert at masking it, there was always the vague impression that his smiles and laughter had been bought with a price.

All that was now gone. No shadows hovered about his smile. His face at last reflected the contentment the Creator intended—overspread with joy, not only having his Maggie by his side, but also in the peace, pure and undefiled, which dwelt in his heart.

She returned his smile, then laughed in unashamed delight.

She reached for his hand, and their fingers touched and intertwined. If they held each other tighter than necessary upon occasion, they could not be blamed; they had so many years to make up for. They had learned how precious was every moment in life; not a single second was to be looked upon lightly.

This morning was no less special than that first one in Aberdeen as the breeze now wafting over them did its best to bend the purple heads of the thick wild bushes. It was all so reminiscent of the days of their youth. Yet suddenly Maggie realized it was even better. They were now *one* as they might never have had a chance to be in their rebellious youth—one for the first time in the love of their common Lord.

"It is as if time has waited for us," Ian murmured into the wind.

"Yes," Maggie answered peacefully. "So little has changed . . . and yet so much."

"One thing has not changed," he said gazing into her eyes, "and will never change. And that is my love for you, my dear Maggie."

"Nor mine for you, my husband."

Together they turned and walked slowly down the hillside, with the morning sun at their backs and the sea of heather at their feet.

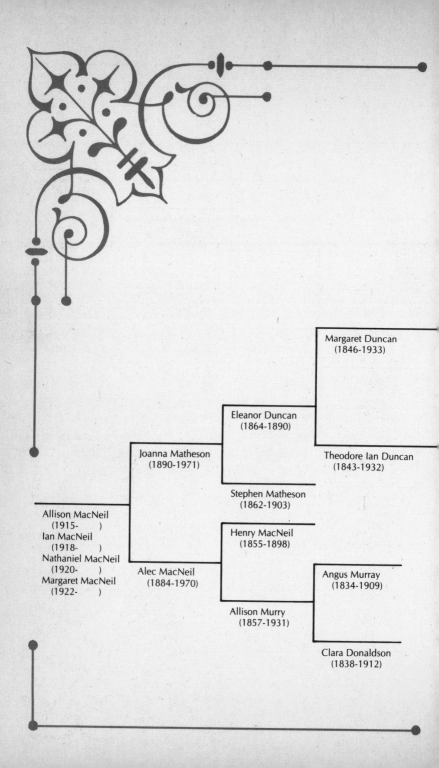

Margaret Duncan
(1846-1933)

Eleanor Duncan
(1864-1890)

Theodore Ian Duncan
(1843-1932)

Joanna Matheson
(1890-1971)

Stephen Matheson
(1862-1903)

Henry MacNeil
(1855-1898)

Allison MacNeil
(1915-   )
Ian MacNeil
(1918-   )
Nathaniel MacNeil
(1920-   )
Margaret MacNeil
(1922-   )

Angus Murray
(1834-1909)

Alec MacNeil
(1884-1970)

Allison Murry
(1857-1931)

Clara Donaldson
(1838-1912)

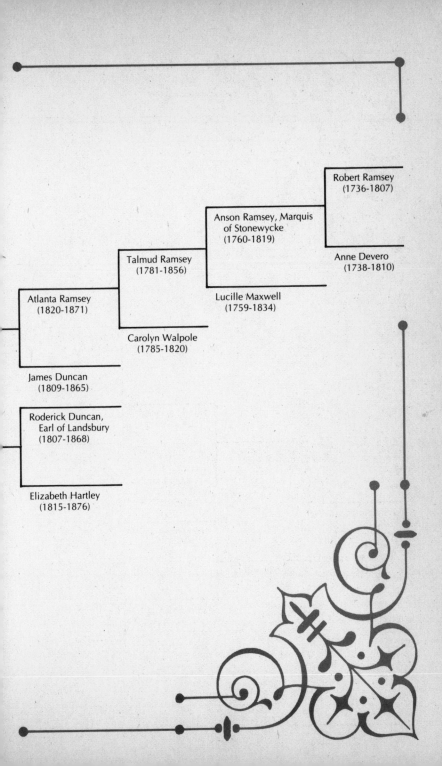

Robert Ramsey
(1736-1807)

Anson Ramsey, Marquis
of Stonewycke
(1760-1819)

Anne Devero
(1738-1810)

Talmud Ramsey
(1781-1856)

Lucille Maxwell
(1759-1834)

Atlanta Ramsey
(1820-1871)

Carolyn Walpole
(1785-1820)

James Duncan
(1809-1865)

Roderick Duncan,
Earl of Landsbury
(1807-1868)

Elizabeth Hartley
(1815-1876)